The Friendship Omnibus

Ruskin Bond is known for his signature simplistic and witty writing style. He is the author of several bestselling short stories, novellas, collections, essays and children's books; and has contributed a number of poems and articles to various magazines and anthologies. At the age of 23, he won the prestigious John Llewellyn Rhys Prize for his first novel, *The Room on the Roof*. He was also the recipient of the Padma Shri in 1999, Lifetime Achievement Award by the Delhi government in 2012 and the Padma Bhushan in 2014.

Born in 1934, Ruskin Bond grew up in Jamnagar, Shimla, New Delhi and Dehradun. Apart from three years in the United Kingdom, he has spent all his life in India and now lives in Landour, Mussoorie, with his adopted family.

RUSKIN BOND

The Friendship Omnibus

RUPA

Published by
Rupa Publications India Pvt. Ltd 2024
7/16, Ansari Road, Daryaganj
New Delhi 110002

Sales centres:
Bengaluru Chennai
Hyderabad Jaipur Kathmandu
Kolkata Mumbai Prayagraj

Copyright © Ruskin Bond 2024

All rights reserved.
This is a work of fiction. Names, characters, places and incidents are either the product of the author's imagination or are used fictitiously and any resemblance to any actual person, living or dead, events or locales is entirely coincidental.

No part of this publication may be reproduced, transmitted, or stored in a retrieval system, in any form or by any means, electronic, mechanical, photocopying, recording or otherwise, without the prior permission of the publisher.

P-ISBN: 978-93-6156-168-9
E-ISBN: 978-93-6156-236-5

First impression 2024

10 9 8 7 6 5 4 3 2 1

The moral right of the author has been asserted.

Printed in India

This book is sold subject to the condition that it shall not, by way of trade or otherwise, be lent, resold, hired out, or otherwise circulated, without the publisher's prior consent, in any form of binding or cover other than that in which it is published.

CONTENTS

Introduction   *vii*

1. Friends of My Youth — 1
2. The Fight — 15
3. Untouchable — 22
4. The Woman on Platform No. 8 — 27
5. The Playing Fields of Shimla — 33
6. 'Let's Go to the Pictures!' — 41
7. The Tunnel — 48
8. The Yellow Umbrella — 55
9. A Long Walk for Bina — 61
10. And Now We Are Twelve — 84
11. The Story of Madhu — 93
12. The Blue Umbrella — 98
13. The Big Race — 120
14. A Village in Garhwal — 125
15. Koki Plays the Game — 135
16. Romi and the Wildfire — 141
17. The Flute Player — 150
18. From Small Beginnings — 159
19. The Four Feathers — 172

20. Four Boys on a Glacier	177
21. Breakfast at Barog	182
22. Here Comes Mr Oliver	188
23. The Thief	194
24. Calypso Christmas	201
25. The Room of Many Colours	206
26. Most Beautiful	230
27. Sita and the River	238
28. The Last Truck Ride	280
29. Running Away	288
30. The Prospect of Flowers	305

INTRODUCTION

What can we write about friendship that has not been said yet? Well, nothing and everything. Each friendship is its own vibrant ecosystem filled with sunshine, rain and everything in between. The warmth of a friendship can find you when you least expect it, and when you most need it. This warmth can be momentary or last a lifetime, but its essence stays with you as you go through life. With some friends you get to celebrate every milestone, every win, and mourn every loss, while some others pass you by like a fresh breeze in the summer heat—fleeting yet essential.

The Friendship Omnibus is a celebration of and ode to friendships of all kinds. There are tales of unlikely friendships and connections that you may find when you least expect it, like 'The Woman on Platform No. 8' and 'Untouchable'. Others like 'The Fight' highlight how the seeds of a friendship can be planted even in seemingly hostile grounds. There are stories of childhood friendships like 'Playing Fields of Shimla' and 'Four Boys on a Glacier', and of those that blossomed despite age differences, like 'The Prospect of Flowers'. 'The Blue Umbrella' is a lesson in how kindness can create the perfect atmosphere for an endearing connection, and tales like 'Here Comes Mr Oliver' show how our most loyal companion need not always be human.

Both enduring friendships spanning decades and momentary but meaningful connections have their own place and value. A kind gesture from a stranger, a warm hug from an old friend, a sense of familiarity in a place, lively conversations about things old and new—all of these keep us alive, keep us human. I hope the stories here offer you laughter, remembrance, and most of all, I hope they can offer you companionship and warmth.

Ruskin Bond

FRIENDS OF MY YOUTH

1
SUDHEER

Friendship is all about doing things together. It may be climbing a mountain, fishing in a mountain stream, cycling along a country road, camping in a forest clearing, or simply travelling together and sharing the experiences that a new place can bring.

On at least two of these counts, Sudheer qualified as a friend, albeit a troublesome one, given to involving me in his adolescent escapades.

I met him in Dehra soon after my return from England. He turned up at my room saying he'd heard I was a writer and asking if I had any comics to lend him.

'I don't write comics,' I said; but there were some comics lying around, left over from my own boyhood collection so I gave these to the lanky youth who stood smiling in the doorway, and he thanked me and said he'd bring them back. From my window I saw him cycling off in the general direction of Dalanwala.

He turned up again a few days later and dumped a large pile of new-looking comics on my desk. 'Here are all the latest,' he announced. 'You can keep them for me. I'm not allowed to read comics at home.'

It was only weeks later that I learnt he was given to pilfering comics and magazines from the town's bookstores. In no time at all, I'd become a receiver of stolen goods!

My landlady had warned me against Sudheer and so had one or two others. He had acquired a certain notoriety for having been expelled from his school. He had been in charge of the library, and before a consignment of newly acquired books could be registered and library stamped, he had sold them back to the bookshop from which they had originally been purchased. Very enterprising but not to be countenanced in a very *pukka* public school. He was now studying in a municipal school too poor to afford a library.

Sudheer was an amoral scamp all right, but I found it difficult to avoid him, or to resist his undeniable and openly affectionate manner. He could make you laugh. And anyone who can do that is easily forgiven for a great many faults.

One day he produced a couple of white mice from his pockets and left them on my desk.

'You keep them for me,' he said. 'I'm not allowed to keep them at home.'

There were a great many things he was not allowed to keep at home. Anyway, the white mice were given a home in an old cupboard, where my landlady kept unwanted dishes, pots and pans, and they were quite happy there, being fed on bits of bread or *chapatti*, until one day I heard shrieks from the storeroom, and charging into it, found my dear stout landlady having hysterics as one of the white mice sought refuge under her blouse and the other ran frantically up and down her back.

Sudheer had to find another home for the white mice. It was that or finding another home for myself.

Most young men, boys and quite a few girls used bicycles. There was a cycle hire shop across the road, and Sudheer persuaded me to hire cycles for both of us. We cycled out of town, through tea gardens and mustard fields, and down a forest road until we discovered a small, shallow river where we bathed and wrestled on the sand. Although I was three or four years older than Sudheer, he was much the stronger, being about six feet tall and broad in the shoulders. His parents had come from Bhanu, a rough-and-ready district on the North West Frontier, as a result of the partition of the country. His father ran a small press situated behind the Sabzi Mandi and brought out a weekly newspaper called *The Frontier Times*.

We came to the stream quite often. It was Sudheer's way of playing truant from school without being detected in the bazaar or at the cinema. He was sixteen when I met him, and eighteen when we parted, but I can't recall that he ever showed any interest in his school work.

He took me to his home in the Karanpur bazaar, then a stronghold of the Bhanu community. The Karanpur boys were an aggressive lot and resented Sudheer's friendship with an *angrez*. To avoid a confrontation, I would use the back alleys and side streets to get to and from the house in which they lived. Sudheer had been overindulged by his mother, who protected him from his father's wrath. Both parents felt I might have an 'improving' influence on their son, and encouraged our friendship. His elder sister seemed more doubtful. She felt he was incorrigible, beyond redemption, and that I was not much better, and she was probably right.

The father invited me to his small press and asked me if I'd like to work with him. I agreed to help with the newspaper for a couple of hours every morning. This involved proofreading and editing news agency reports. Uninspiring work, but useful.

Meanwhile, Sudheer had got hold of a pet monkey, and he carried it about in the basket attached to the handlebar of his bicycle. He used it to ingratiate himself with the girls. 'How sweet! How pretty!' they would exclaim, and Sudheer would get the monkey to show them its tricks.

After some time, however, the monkey appeared to be infected by Sudheer's amorous nature, and would make obscene gestures that were not appreciated by his former admirers. On one occasion, the monkey made off with a girl's *dupatta*. A chase ensued, and the dupatta was retrieved, but the outcome of it all was that Sudheer was accosted by the girl's brothers and given a black eye and a bruised cheek. His father took the monkey away and returned it to the itinerant juggler who had sold it to the young man.

Sudheer soon developed an insatiable need for money. He wasn't getting anything at home, apart from what he pinched from his mother and sister, and his father urged me not to give the boy any money. After paying for my boarding and lodging I had very little to spare, but Sudheer seemed to sense when a money order or cheque arrived, and would hang around, spinning tall tales of great financial distress until, in order to be rid of him, I would give him five to ten rupees. (In those days, a magazine payment seldom exceeded fifty rupees.)

He was becoming something of a trial, constantly interrupting me in my work, and even picking up confectionery from my landlady's small shop and charging it to my account. I had stopped going for bicycle rides. He had wrecked one of the cycles and the shopkeeper held me responsible for repairs.

The sad thing was that Sudheer had no other friends. He did not go in for team games or for music or other creative pursuits which might have helped him to move around with people of his own age group. He was a loner with a propensity for mischief. Had he entered a bicycle race, he would have won easily. Forever eluding a variety of pursuers, he was extremely fast on his bike. But we did not have cycle races in Dehra.

And then, for a blessed two or three weeks, I saw nothing of my unpredictable friend.

I discovered later that he had taken a fancy to a young schoolteacher, about five years his senior, who lived in a hostel up at Rajpur. His cycle rides took him in that direction. As usual, his charm proved irresistible, and it wasn't long before the teacher and the acolyte were taking rides together down lonely forest roads. This was all right by me, of course, but it wasn't the norm with the middle-class matrons of small-town India, at least not in 1957. Hostel wardens, other students, and naturally Sudheer's parents, were all in a state of agitation. So I wasn't surprised when Sudheer turned up in my room to announce that he was on his way to Nahan to study at an Inter College there.

Nahan was a small hill town about sixty miles from Dehra. Sudheer was banished to the home of his *mama*, an uncle who was a sub-inspector in the local police force. He had promised to see that Sudheer stayed out of trouble.

Whether he succeeded or not, I could not tell, for a couple of months later I gave up my rooms in Dehra and left for Delhi. I lost touch with Sudheer's family, and it was only several years later, when I bumped into an old acquaintance, that I was given news of my erstwhile friend.

He had apparently done quite well for himself. Taking off for Calcutta, he had used his charm and his fluent English to land a job as an assistant on a tea estate. Here he had proved quite efficient, earning the approval of his manager and employers. But his roving eye soon got him into trouble. The women working in the tea gardens became prey to his amorous and amoral nature. Keeping one mistress was acceptable. Keeping several was asking for trouble. He was found dead early one morning with his throat cut.

2
THE ROYAL CAFE SET

Dehra was going through a slump in those days, and there wasn't much work for anyone—least of all for my neighbour Suresh Mathur, an income tax lawyer, who was broke for two reasons. To begin with, there was not much work going around, as those with taxable incomes were few and far between. Apart from that, when he did get work, he was slow and half-hearted about getting it done. This was because he seldom got up before eleven in the morning, and by the time he took a bus down from Rajpur and reached his own small office (next door to my rooms), or the income tax office a little further on, it was lunchtime and all the tax officials were out. Suresh would then repair to the Royal Cafe for a beer or two (often at my expense) and this would stretch into a gin and tonic, after which he would stagger up to his first-floor office and collapse on the sofa for an afternoon nap. He would wake up at six, after the income tax office had closed.

I occupied two rooms next to his office, and we were on friendly terms, sharing an enthusiasm for the humorous works of P.G. Wodehouse. I think he modelled himself on Bertie Wooster, for he would often turn up wearing mauve or yellow socks, or a pink shirt and a bright green tie—enough to make anyone in his company feel quite liverish. Unlike Bertie Wooster, he did not have a Jeeves to look after him and get him out of various scrapes. I tried not to be too friendly, as Suresh was in the habit of borrowing lavishly from all his friends, conveniently forgetting to return the amounts. I wasn't well off and could ill afford the company of a spendthrift friend. Sudheer was trouble enough.

Dehra, in those days, was full of people living on borrowed money or no money at all. Hence, the large number of disconnected telephone and electric lines. I did not have electricity myself, simply because the previous tenant had taken off, leaving me with outstandings of over a thousand rupees, then a princely sum. My monthly income seldom exceeded 500 rupees. No matter. There was plenty of kerosene available, and the oil lamp lent a romantic glow to my literary endeavours.

Looking back, I am amazed at the number of people who were quite broke. There was William Matheson, a Swiss journalist, whose remittances from Zurich never seemed to turn up; my landlady, whose husband had deserted her two years previously; Mr Madan, who dealt in second-hand cars that no one wanted; the owner of the corner restaurant, who sat in solitary splendour surrounded by empty tables; and the proprietor of the Ideal Book Depot, who was selling off his stock of unsold books and becoming a departmental store. We complain that few people buy or read books today, but I can assure you that there were even fewer customers in the fifties and sixties. Only doctors, dentists and the proprietors of English schools were making money.

Suresh spent whatever cash came his way, and borrowed more. He had an advantage over the rest of us—he owned an old bungalow, inherited from his father, up at Rajpur in the foothills, where he lived alone with an old manservant. And owning a property gave him some standing with his creditors. The grounds boasted of a mango and litchi orchard, and these he gave out on contract every year, so that his friends did not even get to enjoy some of his produce. The proceeds helped him to pay his office rent in town, with a little left over to give small amounts on account to the owner of the Royal Cafe.

If a lawyer could be hard up, what chance had a journalist? And yet, William Matheson had everything going for him from the start, when he came out to India as an assistant to Von Hesseltein, correspondent for some of the German papers. Von Hesseltein passed on some of the assignments to William, and for a time, all went well. William lived with Von Hesseltein and his family, and was also friendly with Suresh, often paying for the drinks at the Royal Cafe. Then William committed the folly (if not the sin) of having an affair with Von Hesseltein's wife. Von Hesseltein was not the understanding sort. He threw William out of the house and stopped giving him work.

William hired an old typewriter and set himself up as a correspondent in his own right, living and working from a room in the Doon Guest House. At first he was welcome there, having paid a three-month advance for room and board. He bombarded the Swiss and German papers with his articles, but there were very few takers. No one in Europe was really interested in India's five-year plans, or Corbusier's Chandigarh, or the Bhakra Nangal Dam. Book publishing in India was confined to textbooks, otherwise William might have published a vivid account of his experiences in the French Foreign Legion. After two or three rums at the Royal Cafe, he would regale us with tales of his exploits in the Legion, before and after the siege of Dien Bien Phu. Some of his stories had the ring of truth, others (particularly his sexual exploits) were obviously tall tales; but I was happy to pay for the beer or coffee in order to hear him spin them out.

Those were glorious days for an unknown freelance writer. I was realizing my dream of living by my pen, and I was doing it from a small town in North India, having turned my back on both London and New Delhi. I had no ambitions to be a great writer, or even a famous one, or even a rich one. All I wanted to do was *write*. And I wanted a few readers and the occasional cheque so I could carry on living my dream.

The cheques came along in their own desultory way—fifty rupees from the *Weekly*, or thirty-five from *The Statesman* or the same from *Sport and Pastime*, and so on—just enough to get by, and to be the envy of Suresh Mathur, William Matheson, and a few others, professional people who felt that I had no business earning more than they did. Suresh even declared that I should have been paying tax, and offered to represent me, his other clients having gone elsewhere.

And there was old Colonel Wilkie, living on a small pension in a corner room of the White House Hotel. His wife had left him some years before, presumably because of his drinking, but he claimed to have left her because of her obsession with moving the furniture—it seems she was always shifting things about, changing rooms, throwing out perfectly sound tables and chairs and replacing them with fancy stuff picked up here and there. If he took a liking to a particular easy chair and showed signs of settling down in it, it would disappear the next day to be replaced by something horribly ugly and uncomfortable.

'It was a form of mental torture,' said Colonel Wilkie, confiding in me over a glass of beer on the White House verandah. 'The sitting room was cluttered with all sorts of ornamental junk and flimsy side tables, so that I was constantly falling over the damn things. It was like a minefield! And the mines were never in the same place. You've noticed that I walk with a limp?'

'First World War?' I ventured. 'Wounded at Ypres? Or was it Flanders?'

'Nothing of the sort,' snorted the Colonel. 'I did get one or two flesh wounds but they were nothing as compared to the damage inflicted on me by those damned shifting tables and chairs. Fell over a coffee table and dislocated my shoulder. Then broke an ankle negotiating a stool that was in the wrong place. Bookshelf fell on me. Tripped on a rolled-up carpet. Hit by a curtain rod. Would you have put up with it?'

'No,' I had to admit.

'Had to leave her, of course. She went off to England. Send her an allowance. Half my pension! All spent on furniture!'

'It's a superstition of sorts, I suppose. Collecting things.'

The Colonel told me that the final straw was when his favourite spring bed had suddenly been replaced by a bed made up of hard wooden slats. It was sheer torture trying to sleep on it, and he had left his house and moved into the White House Hotel as a permanent guest.

Now he couldn't allow anyone to touch or tidy up anything in his room. There were beer stains on the tablecloth, cobwebs on his family pictures, dust on his books, empty medicine bottles on his dressing table, and mice nesting in his old, discarded boots. He had gone to the other extreme and wouldn't have anything changed or moved in his room.

I didn't see much of the room because we usually sat out on the verandah, waited upon by one of the hotel bearers, who came over with bottles of beer that I dutifully paid for, the Colonel having exhausted his credit. I suppose he was in his late sixties then. He never went anywhere, not even for a walk in the compound. He blamed this inactivity on his gout, but it was really inertia and an unwillingness to leave the precincts of the bar, where he could cadge the occasional drink from a sympathetic guest. I am that age now, and not half as active as I used to be, but there are people to live for and tales to tell, and I keep writing. It is important to keep writing.

Colonel Wilkie had given up on life. I suppose he could have gone off to England, but he would have been more miserable there, with no one to buy him a drink (since he wasn't likely to reciprocate) and the possibility of his wife turning up again to rearrange the furniture.

3
BIBIJI

My landlady was a remarkable woman, and this little memoir of Dehra in the 1950s would be incomplete without a sketch of hers.

She would often say, 'Ruskin, one day you must write my life story,' and I would promise to do so. And although she really deserves a book to herself, I shall try to do justice to her in these few pages.

She was, in fact, my Punjabi stepfather's first wife. Does that sound confusing? It was certainly complicated. And you might well ask, why on earth were you living with your stepfather's first wife instead of your stepfather and mother?

The answer is simple. I got on rather well with this rotund, well-built lady, and sympathized with her predicament. She had been married at a young age to my stepfather, who was something of a playboy, and who ran the photographic saloon he had received as part of her dowry. When he left her for my mother, he sold the saloon and gave his first wife part of the premises. In order to sustain herself and two small children, she started a small provision store and thus became Dehra's first lady shopkeeper.

I had just started freelancing from Dehra and was not keen on joining my mother and stepfather in Delhi. When 'Bibiji'—as I called her—offered me a portion of her flat on very reasonable terms, I accepted without hesitation and was to spend the next two years above her little shop on Rajpur Road. Almost fifty years later, the flat is still there, but it is now an ice cream parlour! Poetic justice, perhaps.

Bibiji sold the usual provisions. Occasionally, I lent a helping hand and soon learnt the names of the various lentils arrayed before us—*moong, malka, masoor, arhar, channa, rajma*, etc. She bought her rice, flour and other items wholesale from the *mandi*, and sometimes I would accompany her on an early morning march to the mandi (about two miles distant) where we would load a handcart with her purchases. She was immensely strong and could lift sacks of wheat or rice that left me gasping. I can't say I blame my rather skinny stepfather for staying out of her reach.

She had a helper, a Bihari youth, who would trundle the cart back to the shop and help with the loading and unloading. Before opening the shop (at around 8 a.m.) she would make our breakfast—*parathas* with my favourite *shalgam* pickle, and in winter, a delicious *kanji* made from the juice of red carrots. When the shop opened, I would go upstairs to do my writing while she conducted the day's business.

Sometimes she would ask me to help her with her accounts, or in making out a bill, for she was barely literate. But she was an astute shopkeeper; she knew instinctively who was good for credit and who was strictly *nakad* (cash). She would also warn me against friends who borrowed money without any intention of returning it; warnings that I failed to heed. Friends in perpetual need there were aplenty—Sudheer, William, Suresh and a couple of others—and I am amazed that I didn't have to borrow, too, considering the uncertain nature of my income. Those little cheques and money orders from magazines did not always arrive in time. But sooner or later something *did* turn up. I was very lucky.

■

Bibiji had a friend, a neighbour, Mrs Singh, an attractive woman in her thirties who smoked a hookah and regaled us with tales of ghosts and *chudails* from her village near Agra. We did not see much of her husband who was an excise inspector. He was busy making money.

Bibiji and Mrs Singh were almost inseparable, which was quite understandable in view of the fact that both had absentee husbands. They were really happy together. During the day Mrs Singh would sit in the shop, observing the customers. And afterwards she would entertain us with clever imitations of the more odd or eccentric among them. At night, after the shop was closed, Bibiji and her friend would make themselves comfortable on the same cot (creaking beneath their combined weights), wrap themselves in a *razai* or blanket and invite me to sit on the next *charpai* and listen to their yarns or tell them a few of my own. Mrs Singh had a small son, not very bright, who was continually eating laddoos, jalebis, *barfis* and other sweets. Quite appropriately, he was called Laddoo. And I believe he grew into one.

Bibiji's son and daughter were then at a residential school. They came home occasionally. So did Mr Singh, with more sweets for his son. He did not appear to find anything unusual in his wife's intimate relationship with Bibiji. His mind was obviously on other things.

Bibiji and Mrs Singh both made plans to get me married. When I protested, saying I was only twenty-three, they said I was old enough. Bibiji had an eye on an Anglo-Indian schoolteacher who sometimes came to the shop, but Mrs Singh turned her down, saying she had very spindly legs. Instead, she suggested the daughter of the local padre, a glamorous-looking, dusky beauty, but Bibiji vetoed the proposal, saying the young lady used too much make-up and already displayed too much fat around the waistline. Both agreed that I should marry a plain-looking girl who could cook, use a sewing machine and speak a little English.

'And be strong in the legs,' I added, much to Mrs Singh's approval.

They did not know it, but I was enamoured of Kamla, a girl from the hills, who lived with her parents in quarters behind the flat. She was always giving me mischievous glances with her dark, beautiful, expressive eyes. And whenever I passed her on the landing, we exchanged pleasantries and friendly banter; it was as though we had known each other for a long time. But she was already betrothed, and that too to a much older man, a widower, who owned some land outside the town. Kamla's family was poor, her father was in debt, and it was to be a marriage of convenience. There was nothing much I could do about it—landless and without prospects—but after the marriage had taken place and she had left for her new home, I befriended her younger brother and through him sent her my good wishes from time to time. She is just a distant memory now, but a bright one, like a forget-me-not blooming on a bare rock. Would I have married her, had I been able to? She was simple, unlettered; but I might have taken the chance.

Those two years on Rajpur Road were an eventful time, what with the visitations of Sudheer, the company of William and Suresh, the participation in Bibiji's little shop, the evanescent friendship with Kamla. I did a lot of writing and even sold a few stories here and there; but the returns were modest, barely adequate. Everyone was urging me to try my luck in Delhi. And so I bid goodbye to sleepy little Dehra (as it then was) and took a bus to the capital. I did no better there as a writer, but I found a job of sorts and that kept me going for a couple of years.

But to return to Bibiji, I cannot just leave her in limbo. She continued to run her shop for several years, and it was only failing health that forced her to close it. She sold the business and went to live with her married daughter in New Delhi. I saw her from time to time. In spite of high blood pressure, diabetes and eventually blindness, she lived on into her eighties. She was always glad to see me, and never gave up trying to find a suitable bride for me.

The last time I saw her, shortly before she died, she said, 'Ruskin, there is this widow—lady who lives down the road and comes over sometimes. She has two children but they are grown up. She feels lonely in her big house. If you like, I'll talk to her. It's time you settled down. And she's only sixty.'

'Thanks, Bibiji,' I said, holding both ears. 'But I think I'll settle down in my next life.'

THE FIGHT

Ranji had been less than a month in Rajpur when he discovered the pool in the forest. It was the height of summer, and his school had not yet opened and, having as yet made no friends in this semi-hill station, he wandered about a good deal by himself into the hills and forests that stretched away interminably on all sides of the town. It was hot, very hot, at that time of year, and Ranji walked about in his vest and shorts, his brown feet white with the chalky dust that flew up from the ground. The earth was parched, the grass brown, the trees listless, hardly stirring, waiting for a cool wind or a refreshing shower of rain.

It was on such a day—a hot, tired day—that Ranji found the pool in the forest. The water had a gentle translucency and you could see the smooth round pebbles at the bottom of the pool. A small stream emerged from a cluster of rocks to feed the pool. During the monsoon, this stream would be a gushing torrent, cascading down from the hills, but during the summer it was barely a trickle. The rocks, however, held the water in the pool, and it did not dry up like the pools in the plains.

When Ranji saw the pool, he did not hesitate to get into it. He had often gone swimming, alone or with friends, when he had lived with his parents in a thirsty town in the middle of the Rajputana desert. There, he had known only sticky, muddy pools, where buffaloes wallowed and women washed clothes.

He had never seen a pool like this—so clean and cold and inviting. He threw off all his clothes, as he had done when he went swimming in the plains, and leapt into the water. His limbs were supple, free of any fat, and his dark body glistened in patches of sunlit water.

The next day he came again to quench his body in the cool waters of the forest pool. He was there for almost an hour, sliding in and out of the limpid green water, or lying stretched out on the smooth yellow rocks in the shade of broad-leaved sal trees. It was while he lay thus, naked on a rock, that he noticed another boy standing a little distance away, staring at him in a rather hostile manner. The other boy was a little older than Ranji, taller, thick-set, with a broad nose and thick, red lips. He had only just noticed Ranji, and he stood at the edge of the pool, wearing a pair of bathing shorts, waiting for Ranji to explain himself.

When Ranji did not say anything, the other called out, 'What are you doing here, mister?'

Ranji, who was prepared to be friendly, was taken aback at the hostility of the other's tone.

'I am swimming,' he replied. 'Why don't you join me?'

'I always swim alone,' said the other. 'This is my pool, I did not invite you here. And why are you not wearing any clothes?'

'It is not your business if I do not wear clothes. I have nothing to be ashamed of.'

'You skinny fellow, put on your clothes.'

'Fat fool, take yours off.'

This was too much for the stranger to tolerate. He strode up to Ranji, who still sat on the rock and, planting his broad feet firmly on the sand, said (as though this would settle the matter once and for all), 'Don't you know I am a Punjabi? I do not take replies from villagers like you!'

'So you like to fight with villagers?' said Ranji. 'Well, I am not a villager. I am a Rajput!'

'I am a Punjabi!'

'I am a Rajput!'

They had reached an impasse. One had said he was a Punjabi, the other had proclaimed himself a Rajput. There was little else that could be said.

'You understand that I am a Punjabi?' said the stranger, feeling that perhaps this information had not penetrated Ranji's head.

'I have heard you say it three times,' replied Ranji.

'Then why are you not running away?'

'I am waiting for *you* to run away!'

'I will have to beat you,' said the stranger, assuming a violent attitude, showing Ranji the palm of his hand.

'I am waiting to see you do it,' said Ranji.

'You will see me do it,' said the other boy.

Ranji waited. The other boy made a strange, hissing sound. They stared each other in the eye for almost a minute. Then the Punjabi boy slapped Ranji across the face with all the force he could muster. Ranji staggered, feeling quite dizzy. There were thick, red finger marks on his cheek.

'There you are!' exclaimed his assailant. 'Will you be off now?'

For answer, Ranji swung his arm up and pushed a hard, bony fist into the other's face.

And then they were at each other's throats, swaying on the rock, tumbling on to the sand, rolling over and over, their legs and arms locked in a desperate, violent struggle. Gasping and cursing, clawing and slapping, they rolled right into the shallows of the pool.

Even in the water the fight continued as, spluttering and covered with mud, they groped for each other's head and throat. But after five minutes of frenzied, unscientific struggle, neither boy had emerged victorious. Their bodies heaving with exhaustion, they stood back from each other, making tremendous efforts to speak.

'Now…now do you realize…I am a Punjabi?' gasped the stranger.

'Do you know I am a Rajput?' said Ranji with difficulty.

They gave a moment's consideration to each other's answers, and in that moment of silence there was only their heavy breathing and the rapid beating of their hearts.

'Then you will not leave the pool?' said the Punjabi boy.

'I will not leave it,' said Ranji.

'Then we shall have to continue the fight,' said the other.

'All right,' said Ranji.

But neither boy moved, neither took the initiative.

The Punjabi boy had an inspiration.

'We will continue the fight tomorrow,' he said. 'If you dare to come here again tomorrow, we will continue this fight and I will not show you mercy as I have done today.'

'I will come tomorrow,' said Ranji. 'I will be ready for you.'

They turned from each other then and, going to their respective rocks, put on their clothes and left the forest by different routes.

When Ranji got home, he found it difficult to explain the cuts and bruises that showed on his face, legs and arms. It was difficult to conceal the fact that he had been in an unusually violent fight, and his mother insisted on his staying at home for the rest of the day. That evening, though, he slipped out of the house and went to the bazaar, where he found comfort and solace in a bottle of vividly coloured lemonade and a banana leaf full of hot, sweet jalebis. He had just finished the lemonade when he saw his adversary coming down the road. His first impulse was to turn away and look elsewhere, his second to throw the lemonade bottle at his enemy. But he did neither of these things. Instead, he stood his ground and scowled at his passing adversary. And the Punjabi boy said nothing either, but scowled back with equal ferocity.

The next day was as hot as the previous one. Ranji felt weak and lazy and not at all eager for a fight. His body was stiff and sore after the previous day's encounter. But he could not refuse the challenge. Not to turn up at the pool would be an acknowledgement of defeat. From the way he felt just then, he knew he would be beaten in another fight. But he could not acquiesce in his own defeat. He must defy his enemy to the last, or outwit him, for only then could he gain his respect. If he surrendered now, he would be beaten for all time; but to fight and be beaten today left him free to fight and be beaten again. As long as he fought, he had a right to the pool in the forest.

He was half hoping that the Punjabi boy would have forgotten the challenge, but these hopes were dashed when he saw his opponent sitting, stripped to the waist, on a rock on the other side of the pool. The Punjabi boy was rubbing oil on his body, massaging it into his broad thighs. He saw Ranji beneath the sal trees, and called a challenge across the waters of the pool.

'Come over on this side and fight!' he shouted.

But Ranji was not going to submit to any conditions laid down by his opponent.

'Come *this* side and fight!' he shouted back with equal vigour.

'Swim across and fight me here!' called the other. 'Or perhaps you cannot swim the length of this pool?'

But Ranji could have swum the length of the pool a dozen times without tiring, and here he would show the Punjabi boy his superiority. So, slipping out of his vest and shorts, he dived straight into the water, cutting through it like a knife, and surfaced with hardly a splash. The Punjabi boy's mouth hung open in amazement.

'You can dive!' he exclaimed.

'It is easy,' said Ranji, treading water, waiting for a further challenge. 'Can't you dive?'

'No,' said the other. 'I jump straight in. But if you will tell me how, I will make a dive.'

'It is easy,' said Ranji. 'Stand on the rock, stretch your arms out and allow your head to displace your feet.'

The Punjabi boy stood up, stiff and straight, stretched out his arms, and threw himself into the water. He landed flat on his belly, with a crash that sent the birds screaming out of the trees.

Ranji dissolved into laughter.

'Are you trying to empty the pool?' he asked, as the Punjabi boy came to the surface, spouting water like a small whale.

'Wasn't it good?' asked the boy, evidently proud of his feat.

'Not very good,' said Ranji. 'You should have more practice. See, I will do it again.'

And pulling himself up on a rock, he executed another perfect dive. The other boy waited for him to come up, but, swimming underwater, Ranji circled him and came upon him from behind.

'How did you do that?' asked the astonished youth.

'Can't you swim underwater?' asked Ranji.

'No, but I will try it.'

The Punjabi boy made a tremendous effort to plunge to the bottom of the pool and indeed he thought he had gone right down, though his bottom, like a duck's, remained above the surface.

Ranji, however, did not discourage him.

'It was not bad,' he said. 'But you need a lot of practice.'

'Will you teach me?' asked his enemy.

'If you like, I will teach you.'

'You must teach me. If you do not teach me, I will beat you. Will you come here every day and teach me?'

'If you like,' said Ranji. They had pulled themselves out of the water, and were sitting side by side on a smooth grey rock.

'My name is Suraj,' said the Punjabi boy. 'What is yours?'

'It is Ranji.'

'I am strong, am I not?' asked Suraj, bending his arm so that a ball of muscle stood up stretching the white of his flesh.

'You are strong,' said Ranji. 'You are a real *pahelwan*.'

'One day I will be the world's champion wrestler,' said Suraj, slapping his thighs, which shook with the impact of his hand. He looked critically at Ranji's hard, thin body.

'You are quite strong yourself,' he conceded. 'But you are too bony. I know you people do not eat enough. You must come and have your food with me.

'I drink one *seer* of milk every day. We have got our own cow! Be my friend, and I will make you a pahelwan like me! I know—if you teach me to dive and swim underwater, I will make you a pahelwan! That is fair, isn't it?'

'That is fair!' said Ranji, though he doubted if he was getting the better of the exchange.

Suraj put his arm around the younger boy and said, 'We are friends now, yes?'

They looked at each other with honest, unflinching eyes, and in that moment love and understanding were born.

'We are friends,' said Ranji.

The birds had settled again on their branches, and the pool was quiet and limpid in the shade of the sal trees.

'It is our pool,' said Suraj. 'Nobody else can come here without our permission. Who would dare?'

'Who would dare?' said Ranji, smiling with the knowledge that he had won the day.

UNTOUCHABLE

The sweeper boy splashed water over the *khus* matting that hung in the doorway and for a while the air was cooled.

I sat on the edge of my bed, staring out of the open window, brooding upon the dusty road shimmering in the noonday heat. A car passed and the dust rose in billowing clouds.

Across the road lived the people who were supposed to look after me while my father lay in hospital with malaria. I was supposed to stay with them, sleep with them. But except for meals, I kept away. I did not like them and they did not like me.

For a week, longer probably, I was going to live alone in the red-brick bungalow on the outskirts of the town, on the fringe of the jungle. At night the sweeper boy would keep guard, sleeping in the kitchen. Apart from him, I had no company; only the neighbours' children, and I did not like them and they did not like me.

Their mother said, 'Don't play with the sweeper boy, he is unclean. Don't touch him. Remember, he is a servant. You must come and play with my boys.'

Well, I did not intend playing with the sweeper boy; but neither did I intend playing with her children. I was going to sit on my bed all week and wait for my father to come home.

Sweeper boy... All day he pattered up and down between the house and the water tank, with the bucket clanging against his knees.

Back and forth, with a wide, friendly smile.

I frowned at him.

He was about my age, ten. He had short-cropped hair, very white teeth, and muddy feet, hands and face. All he wore was an old pair of khaki shorts; the rest of his body was bare, burnt a deep brown.

At every trip to the water tank he bathed, and returned dripping and glistening from head to toe.

I dripped with sweat.

It was supposedly below my station to bathe at the tank, where the gardener, water-carrier, cooks, *ayahs*, sweepers and their children all collected. I was the son of a '*sahib*' and convention ruled that I did not play with servant children.

But I was just as determined not to play with the other sahibs' children, for I did not like them and they did not like me.

I watched the flies buzzing against the windowpane, the lizards scuttling across the rafters, the wind scattering petals of scorched, long-dead flowers.

The sweeper boy smiled and saluted in play. I avoided his eyes and said, 'Go away.'

He went into the kitchen.

I rose and crossed the room, and lifted my sun helmet off the hatstand.

A centipede ran down the wall, across the floor.

I screamed and jumped on the bed, shouting for help.

The sweeper boy darted in. He saw me on the bed, the centipede on the floor, and picking a large book off the shelf, slammed it down on the repulsive insect.

I remained standing on my bed, trembling with fear and revulsion.

He laughed at me, showing his teeth, and I blushed and said, 'Get out!'

I would not, could not, touch or approach the hat or hatstand.

I sat on the bed and longed for my father to come home.

A mosquito passed close by me and sang in my ear. Half-heartedly, I clutched at it and missed; and it disappeared behind the dressing table.

That mosquito, I reasoned, gave the malaria to my father. And now it was trying to give it to me!

The next-door lady walked through the compound and smiled thinly from outside the window. I glared back at her.

The sweeper boy passed with the bucket and grinned. I turned away.

In bed at night, with the lights on, I tried reading. But even books could not quell my anxiety.

The sweeper boy moved about the house, bolting doors, fastening windows. He asked me if I had any orders.

I shook my head.

He skipped across to the electric switch, turned off the light, and slipped into his quarters. Outside, inside, all was dark; only one shaft of light squeezed in through a crack in the sweeper boy's door, and then that too went out.

I began to wish I had stayed with the neighbours. The darkness worried me—silent and close—silent, as if in suspense.

Once a bat flew flat against the window, falling to the ground outside; once an owl hooted. Sometimes a dog barked. And I tautened, as a jackal howled hideously in the jungle behind the bungalow. But nothing could break the overall stillness, the night's silence...

Only a dry puff of wind...

It rustled in the trees, and put me in mind of a snake slithering over dry leaves and twigs. I remembered a tale I had been told not long ago, of a sleeping boy who had been bitten by a cobra.

I would not, could not, sleep. I longed for my father...

The shutters rattled, the doors creaked. It was a night for ghosts.

Ghosts!

God, why did I have to think of them?

My God! There, standing by the bathroom door...

My father! My father dead from the malaria and come to see me!

I threw myself at the switch. The room lit up. I sank down on the bed in complete exhaustion, the sweat soaking my nightclothes.

It was not my father I had seen. It was his dressing gown hanging on the bathroom door. It had not been taken with him to the hospital.

I turned off the light.

The hush outside seemed deeper, nearer. I remembered the centipede, the bat, thought of the cobra and the sleeping boy; pulled the sheet tight over my head. If I could see nothing, well then, nothing could see me.

A thunderclap shattered the brooding stillness.

A streak of lightning forked across the sky, so close that even through the sheet I saw a tree and the opposite house silhouetted against the flashing canvas of gold.

I dived deeper beneath the bedclothes, gathered the pillow about my ears.

But at the next thunderclap, louder this time, louder than I had ever heard, I leapt from my bed. I could not stand it. I fled, blundering into the sweeper boy's room.

The boy sat on the bare floor.

'What is happening?' he asked.

The lightning flashed, and his teeth and eyes flashed with it. Then he was a blur in the darkness.

'I am afraid,' I said.

I moved towards him and my hand touched a cold shoulder.

'Stay here,' he said. 'I too am afraid.'

I sat down, my back against the wall; beside the untouchable, the outcaste…and the thunder and lightning ceased, and the rain came down, swishing and drumming on the corrugated roof.

'The rainy season has started,' observed the sweeper boy, turning to me. His smile played with the darkness, and then he laughed. And I laughed too, but feebly.

But I was happy and safe. The scent of the wet earth blew in through the skylight and the rain fell harder.

THE WOMAN ON PLATFORM NO. 8

It was my second year at boarding school, and I was sitting on Platform No. 8 at Ambala station, waiting for the northern-bound train. I think I was about twelve at the time. My parents considered me old enough to travel alone, and I had arrived by bus at Ambala early in the evening; now there was a wait till midnight before my train arrived. Most of the time I had been pacing up and down the platform, browsing through the bookstall, or feeding broken biscuits to stray dogs. Trains came and went, the platform would be quiet for a while and then, when a train arrived, it would be an inferno of heaving, shouting, agitated human bodies. As the carriage doors opened, a tide of people would sweep down upon the nervous little ticket collector at the gate, and every time this happened I would be caught in the rush and swept outside the station. Now tired of this game and of ambling about the platform, I sat down on my suitcase and gazed dismally across the railway tracks.

Trolleys rolled past me, and I was conscious of the cries of the various vendors—the men who sold curd and lemon, the sweetmeat seller, the newspaper boy—but I had lost interest in all that was going on along the busy platform, and continued to stare across the railway tracks, feeling bored and a little lonely.

'Are you all alone, my son?' asked a soft voice close behind me.

I looked up and saw a woman standing near me. She was leaning over, and I saw a pale face and dark, kind eyes. She wore no jewels, and was dressed very simply in a white sari.

'Yes, I am going to school,' I said, and stood up respectfully. She seemed poor, but there was a dignity about her that commanded respect.

'I have been watching you for some time,' she said. 'Didn't your parents come to see you off?'

'I don't live here,' I said. 'I had to change trains. Anyway, I can travel alone.'

'I am sure you can,' she said, and I liked her for saying that, and I also liked her for the simplicity of her dress, and for her deep, soft voice and the serenity of her face.

'Tell me, what is your name?' she asked.

'Arun,' I said.

'And how long do you have to wait for your train?'

'About an hour, I think. It comes at twelve o'clock.'

'Then come with me and have something to eat.'

I was going to refuse, out of shyness and suspicion, but she took me by the hand, and then I felt it would be silly to pull my hand away. She told a coolie to look after my suitcase, and then she led me away down the platform. Her hand was gentle, and she held mine neither too firmly nor too lightly. I looked up at her again. She was not young. And she was not old. She must have been over thirty, but had she been fifty, I think she would have looked much the same.

She took me into the station dining room, ordered tea and samosas and jalebis, and at once I began to thaw and take a new interest in this kind woman. The strange encounter had little effect on my appetite. I was a hungry schoolboy, and I ate as much as I could in as polite a manner as possible. She took obvious pleasure in watching me eat, and I think it was the food that strengthened the bond between us and cemented our friendship, for under the influence of the tea and sweets I began to talk quite freely and told her about my school, my friends, my likes and dislikes. She questioned me quietly from time to time, but preferred listening; she drew me out very well, and I had soon forgotten that we were strangers. But she did not ask me about my family or where I lived, and I did not ask her where she lived. I accepted her for what she had been to me—a quiet, kind and gentle woman who gave sweets to a lonely boy on a railway platform...

After about half an hour, we left the dining room and began walking back along the platform. An engine was shunting up and down beside Platform No. 8, and as it approached, a boy leapt off the platform and ran across the rails, taking a short cut to the next platform. He was at a safe distance from the engine, but as he leapt across the rails, the woman clutched my arm. Her fingers dug into my flesh, and I winced with pain. I caught her fingers and looked up at her, and I saw a spasm of pain and fear and sadness pass across her face. She watched the boy as he climbed the platform, and it was not until he had disappeared in the crowd that she relaxed her hold on my arm. She smiled at me reassuringly and took my hand again, but her fingers trembled against mine.

'He was all right,' I said, feeling that it was she who needed reassurance.

She smiled gratefully at me and pressed my hand. We walked together in silence until we reached the place where I had left my suitcase. One of my schoolfellows, Satish, a boy of about my age, had turned up with his mother.

'Hello, Arun!' he called. 'The train's coming in late, as usual. Did you know we have a new headmaster this year?'

We shook hands, and then he turned to his mother and said, 'This is Arun, Mother. He is one of my friends, and the best bowler in the class.'

'I am glad to know that,' said his mother, a large imposing

woman who wore spectacles. She looked at the woman who held my hand and said, 'And I suppose you're Arun's mother?'

I opened my mouth to make some explanation, but before I could say anything the woman replied, 'Yes, I am Arun's mother.'

I was unable to speak a word. I looked quickly up at the woman, but she did not appear to be at all embarrassed, and was smiling at Satish's mother.

Satish's mother said, 'It's such a nuisance having to wait for the train right in the middle of the night. But one can't let the child wait here alone. Anything can happen to a boy at a big station like this—there are so many suspicious characters hanging about. These days one has to be very careful of strangers.'

'Arun can travel alone, though,' said the woman beside me, and somehow I felt grateful to her for saying that. I had already forgiven her for lying; and besides, I had taken an instinctive dislike to Satish's mother.

'Well, be very careful, Arun,' said Satish's mother looking sternly at me through her spectacles. 'Be very careful when your mother is not with you. And never talk to strangers!'

I looked from Satish's mother to the woman who had given me tea and sweets, and back at Satish's mother.

'I like strangers,' I said.

Satish's mother definitely staggered a little, as obviously she was not used to being contradicted by small boys.

'There you are, you see! If you don't watch over them all the time, they'll walk straight into trouble. Always listen to what your mother tells you,' she said, wagging a fat little finger at me. 'And never, never talk to strangers.'

I glared resentfully at her, and moved closer to the woman who had befriended me. Satish was standing behind his mother, grinning at me, and delighting in my clash with his mother. Apparently he was on my side.

The station bell clanged, and the people who had till now been squatting resignedly on the platform began bustling about.

'Here it comes!' shouted Satish, as the engine whistle shrieked and the front lights played over the rails.

The train moved slowly into the station, the engine hissing and sending out waves of steam. As it came to a stop, Satish jumped on the footboard of a lighted compartment and shouted, 'Come on, Arun, this one's empty!' and I picked up my suitcase and made a dash for the open door.

We placed ourselves at the open windows, and the two women stood outside on the platform, talking up to us. Satish's mother did most of the talking.

'Now don't jump on and off moving trains, as you did just now,' she said. 'And don't stick your heads out of the windows, and don't eat any rubbish on the way.' She allowed me to share the benefit of her advice, as she probably didn't think my 'mother' a very capable person. She handed Satish a bag of fruit, a cricket bat and a big box of chocolates, and told him to share the food with me. Then she stood back from the window to watch how my 'mother' behaved.

I was smarting under the patronizing tone of Satish's mother, who obviously thought mine a very poor family; and I did not intend giving the other woman away. I let her take my hand in hers, but I could think of nothing to say. I was conscious of Satish's mother staring at us with hard, beady eyes, and I found myself hating her with a firm, unreasoning hate. The guard walked up the platform, blowing his whistle for the train to leave. I looked straight into the eyes of the woman who held my hand, and she smiled in a gentle, understanding way. I leaned out of the window then, and put my lips to her cheek and kissed her.

The carriage jolted forward, and she drew her hand away.

'Goodbye, Mother!' said Satish, as the train began to slowly move out of the station. Satish and his mother waved to each other.

'Goodbye,' I said to the other woman, 'goodbye—Mother…' I didn't wave or shout, but sat still in front of the window, gazing at the woman on the platform. Satish's mother was talking to her, but she didn't appear to be listening; she was looking at me, as the train took me away. She stood there on the busy platform, a pale sweet woman in white, and I watched her until she was lost in the milling crowd.

THE PLAYING FIELDS OF SHIMLA

It had been a lonely winter for a twelve-year-old boy.

I hadn't really got over my father's untimely death two years previously; nor had I as yet reconciled myself to my mother's marriage to the Punjabi gentleman who dealt in second-hand cars. The three-month winter break over, I was almost happy to return to my boarding school in Shimla—that elegant hill station once celebrated by Kipling and soon to lose its status as the summer capital of the Raj in India.

It wasn't as though I had many friends at school. I had always been a bit of a loner, shy and reserved, looking out only for my father's rare visits—on his brief leaves from RAF duties—and to my sharing his tent or air force hutment outside Delhi or Karachi. Those unsettled but happy days would not come again. I needed a friend but it was not easy to find one among a horde of rowdy, pea-shooting fourth formers, who carved their names on desks and stuck chewing gum on the class teacher's chair. Had I grown up with other children, I might have developed a taste for schoolboy anarchy; but, in sharing my father's loneliness after his separation from my mother, I had turned into a premature adult. The mixed nature of my reading—Dickens, Richmal Crompton, Tagore and *Champion* and *Film Fun* comics—probably reflected the confused state of my life. A book reader was rare even in those pre-electronic times. On rainy days most boys played cards or Monopoly, or listened to Artie Shaw on the wind-up gramophone in the common room.

After a month in the fourth form I began to notice a new boy, Omar, and then only because he was a quiet, almost taciturn person who took no part in the form's feverish attempts to imitate the Marx Brothers at the circus. He showed no resentment at the prevailing anarchy, nor did he make a move to participate in it. Once, he caught me looking at him, and he smiled ruefully, tolerantly. Did I sense another adult in the class? Someone who was a little older than his years?

Even before we began talking to each other, Omar and I developed an understanding of sorts, and we'd nod almost respectfully to each other when we met in the classroom corridors or the environs of the dining hall or dormitory. We were not in the same house. The house system practised its own form of apartheid, whereby a member of, say, Curzon House was not expected to fraternize with someone belonging to Rivaz or Lefroy! Those public schools certainly knew how to clamp you into compartments. However, these barriers vanished when Omar and I found ourselves selected for the School Colts' hockey team—Omar as a fullback, I as goalkeeper. I think a defensive position suited me by nature. In all modesty I have to say that I made a good goalkeeper, both at hockey and football. And fifty years on, I am still keeping goal. Then I did it between goalposts, now I do it off the field—protecting a family, protecting my independence as a writer...

The taciturn Omar now spoke to me occasionally, and we combined well on the field of play. A good understanding is needed between goalkeeper and fullback. We were on the same wavelength. I anticipated his moves, he was familiar with mine. Years later, when I read Conrad's *The Secret Sharer*, I thought of Omar.

It wasn't until we were away from the confines of school, classroom and dining hall that our friendship flourished. The hockey team travelled to Sanawar on the next mountain range, where we were to play a couple of matches against our old rivals, the Lawrence Royal Military School. This had been my father's old school, but I did not know that in his time it had also been a military orphanage. Grandfather, who had been a private foot soldier—of the likes of Kipling's Mulvaney, Otheris and Learoyd—had joined the Scottish Rifles after leaving home at the age of seventeen. He had died while his children were still very young, but my father's more rounded education had enabled him to become an officer.

Omar and I were thrown together a good deal during the visit to Sanawar, and in our more leisurely moments, strolling undisturbed around a school where we were guests and not pupils, we exchanged life histories and other confidences. Omar, too, had lost his father—had I sensed that before?—shot in some tribal encounter on the Frontier, for he hailed from the lawless lands beyond Peshawar. A wealthy uncle was seeing to Omar's education. The RAF was now seeing to mine.

We wandered into the school chapel, and there I found my father's name—A.A. Bond—on the school's roll of honour board: old boys who had lost their lives while serving during the two World Wars.

'What did his initials stand for?' asked Omar.

'Aubrey Alexander.'

'Unusual name, like yours. Why did your parents call you Ruskin?'

'I am not sure. I think my father liked the works of John Ruskin, who wrote on serious subjects like art and architecture. I don't think anyone reads him now. They'll read me, though!' I had already started writing my first book. It was called *Nine Months* (the length of the school term, not a pregnancy), and it described some of the happenings at school and lampooned a few of our teachers. I had filled three slim exercise books with this premature literary project, and I allowed Omar to go through them. He must have been my first reader and critic. 'They're very interesting,' he said, 'but you'll get into trouble if someone finds them. Especially Mr Oliver.' And he read out an offending verse—

Oily, Oily, Oily, with his balls on a trolley,
And his arse all painted green!

I have to admit it wasn't great literature. I was better at hockey and football. I made some spectacular saves, and we won our matches against Sanawar. When we returned to Shimla, we were school heroes for a couple of days and lost some of our reticence; we were even a little more forthcoming with other boys. And then Mr Fisher, my housemaster, discovered my literary opus, *Nine Months,* under my mattress, and took it away and read it (as he told me later) from cover to cover. Corporal punishment then being in vogue, I was given six of the best with a springy malacca cane, and my manuscript was torn up and deposited in Fisher's waste-paper basket. All I had to show for my efforts were some purple welts on my bottom. These were proudly displayed to all who were interested, and I was a hero for another two days.

'Will you go away too when the British leave India?' Omar asked me one day.

'I don't think so,' I said. 'My stepfather is Indian.'

'Everyone is saying that our leaders and the British are going to divide the country. Shimla will be in India, Peshawar in Pakistan!'

'Oh, it won't happen,' I said glibly. 'How can they cut up such a big country?' But even as we chatted about the possibility, Nehru and Jinnah and Mountbatten and all those who mattered were preparing their instruments for major surgery.

Before their decision impinged on our lives and everyone else's, we found a little freedom of our own—in an underground tunnel that we discovered below the third flat.

It was really part of an old, disused drainage system, and when Omar and I began exploring it, we had no idea just how far it extended. After crawling along on our bellies for some twenty feet, we found ourselves in complete darkness. Omar had brought along a small pencil torch, and with its help we continued writhing forward (moving backwards would have been quite impossible) until we saw a glimmer of light at the end of the tunnel. Dusty, musty, very scruffy, we emerged at last on to a grassy knoll, a little way outside the school boundary.

It's always a great thrill to escape beyond the boundaries that adults have devised. Here we were in an unknown territory. To travel without passports—that would be the ultimate freedom!

But more passports were on their way, and more boundaries.

Lord Mountbatten, viceroy and governor-general-to-be, came for our Founder's Day and gave away the prizes. I had won a prize for something or the other, and mounted the rostrum to receive my book from this towering, handsome man in his pinstripe suit. Bishop Cotton's was then the premier school of India, often referred to as the 'Eton of the East'. Viceroys and governors had graced its functions. Many of its boys had gone on to eminence in the civil services and armed forces. There was one 'old boy' about whom they maintained a stolid silence—General Dyer, who had ordered the massacre at Amritsar and destroyed the trust that had been building up between Britain and India.

Now Mountbatten spoke of the momentous events that were happening all around us—the War had just come to an end, the United Nations held out the promise of a world living in peace and harmony, and India, an equal partner with Britain, would be among the great nations...

A few weeks later, Bengal and Punjab provinces were bisected. Riots flared up across northern India, and there was a great exodus of people crossing the newly drawn frontiers of Pakistan and India. Homes were destroyed, thousands lost their lives.

The common-room radio and the occasional newspaper kept us abreast of events, but in our tunnel, Omar and I felt immune from all that was happening, worlds away from all the pillage, murder and revenge. And outside the tunnel, on the pine knoll below the school, there was fresh untrodden grass, sprinkled with clover and daisies, the only sounds the hammering of a woodpecker, the distant insistent call of the Himalayan barbet. Who could touch us there?

'And when all the wars are done,' I said, 'a butterfly will still be beautiful.'

'Did you read that somewhere?'

'No, it just came into my head.'

'Already you're a writer.'

'No, I want to play hockey for India or football for Arsenal. Only winning teams!'

'You can't win forever. Better to be a writer.'

When the monsoon rains arrived, the tunnel was flooded, the drain choked with rubble. We were allowed out to the cinema to see Lawrence Olivier's *Hamlet,* a film that did nothing to raise our spirits on a wet and gloomy afternoon—but it was our last picture that year, because communal riots suddenly broke out in Shimla's Lower Bazaar, an area that was still much as Kipling had described it—'a man who knows his way there can defy all the police of India's summer capital'—and we were confined to school indefinitely.

One morning after chapel, the headmaster announced that

the Muslim boys—those who had their homes in what was now Pakistan—would have to be evacuated, sent to their homes across the border with an armed convoy.

The tunnel no longer provided an escape for us. The bazaar was out of bounds. The flooded playing field was deserted. Omar and I sat on a damp wooden bench and talked about the future in vaguely hopeful terms; but we didn't solve any problems. Mountbatten and Nehru and Jinnah were doing all the solving.

It was soon time for Omar to leave—he along with some fifty other boys from Lahore, Pindi and Peshawar. The rest of us—Hindus, Christians, Parsis—helped them load their luggage into the waiting trucks. A couple of boys broke down and wept. So did our departing school captain, a Pathan who had been known for his stoic and unemotional demeanour. Omar waved cheerfully to me and I waved back. We had vowed to meet again some day.

The convoy got through safely enough. There was only one casualty—the school cook, who had strayed into an off-limits area in the foothill town of Kalka and been set upon by a mob. He wasn't seen again.

Towards the end of the school year, just as we were all getting ready to leave for the school holidays, I received a letter from Omar. He told me something about his new school and how he missed my company and our games and our tunnel to freedom. I replied and gave him my home address, but I did not hear from him again. The land, though divided, was still a big one, and we were very small.

Some seventeen or eighteen years later I did get news of Omar, but in an entirely different context. India and Pakistan were at war and in a bombing raid over Ambala, not far from Shimla, a Pakistani plane was shot down. Its crew died in the crash. One of them, I learnt later, was Omar.

Did he, I wonder, get a glimpse of the playing fields we knew so well as boys?

Perhaps memories of his schooldays flooded back as he flew over the foothills. Perhaps he remembered the tunnel through which we were able to make our little escape to freedom.

But there are no tunnels in the sky.

'LET'S GO TO THE PICTURES!'

My love affair with the cinema began when I was five and ended when I was about fifty. Not because I wanted it to, but because all my favourite cinema halls were closing down—being turned into shopping malls or garages or just disappearing altogether.

There was something magical about sitting in a darkened cinema hall, the audience silent, completely focussed on the drama unfolding on the big screen. You could escape to a different world—run away to Dover with David Copperfield, sail away to a treasure island with Long John Silver, dance the light fantastic with Fred Astaire or Gene Kelly, sing with Saigal or Deanna Durbin or Nelson Eddy, fall in love with Madhubala or Elizabeth Taylor. And until the lights came on at the end of the show you were in their world, far removed from the troubles of one's own childhood or the struggles of early manhood.

Watching films on TV cannot be the same. People come and go, the power comes and goes, other viewers keep switching the channels, food is continually being served or consumed, family squabbles are ever present, and there is no escape from those dreaded commercials that are repeated every ten or fifteen minutes, or even between overs if you happen to be watching cricket.

No longer do we hear that evocative suggestion: 'Let's go to the pictures!'

Living in Mussoorie where there are no longer any functioning cinemas, the invitation is heard no more. I'm afraid there isn't half as much excitement in the words 'Let's put on the TV!'

For one thing, going to the pictures meant going out—on foot, or on a bicycle, or in the family car. When I lived on the outskirts of Mussoorie it took me almost an hour to climb the hill into town to see a film at one of our tiny halls—but walk I did, in hot sun or drenching rain or icy wind, because going to the pictures was an event in itself, a break from more mundane activities, quite often a social occasion. You would meet friends from other parts of the town, and after the show you would join them in a cafe for a cup of tea and the latest gossip. A stroll along the Mall and a visit to the local bookshop would bring the evening to a satisfying end. A long walk home under the stars, a drink before dinner, something to listen to on the radio... 'And then to bed,' as Mr Pepys would have said.

Not that everything went smoothly in our small-town cinemas. In Shimla, Mussoorie and other hill stations, the roofs were of corrugated tin sheets, and when there was heavy rain or a hailstorm it would be impossible to hear the soundtrack. You had then to imagine that you were back in the silent film era.

Mussoorie's oldest cinema, the Picture Palace, did in fact open early in the silent era. This was in 1912, the year electricity came to the town. Later, its basement floor was also turned into a cinema, the Jubilee, which probably made it India's first multiplex hall. Sadly, both closed down about five years ago, along with the Rialto, the Majestic and the Capitol (below Halman's Hotel).

In Shimla, we had the Ritz, the Regal and the Rivoli. This was when I was a schoolboy at Bishop Cotton's. How we used to look forward to our summer and autumn breaks. We would be allowed into town during these holidays, and we lost no time in tramping up to the Ridge to take in the latest films. Sometimes we'd arrive wet or perspiring, but the changeable weather did not prevent us from enjoying the film. One-and-a-half hours escape from the routine and discipline of boarding school life. Fast foods had yet to be invented, but roasted peanuts or *bhuttas* would keep us going. They were cheap too. The cinema ticket was just over a rupee. If you had five rupees in your pocket you could enjoy a pleasant few hours in the town.

It was during the winter holidays—three months of time on my hands—that I really caught up with the films of the day.

New Delhi, the winter of 1943. Second World War was still in progress. The halls were flooded with British and American movies. My father would return from Air Headquarters, where he'd been working on cyphers all day. 'Let's go to the pictures,' he'd say, and we'd be off to the Regal or Rivoli or Odeon or Plaza, only a short walk from our rooms on Atul Grove Road.

Comedies were my favourites. Laurel and Hardy, Abbot and Costello, George Formby, Harold Lloyd, the Marx Brothers... And sometimes we'd venture further afield, to the old Ritz at Kashmere Gate, to see Sabu in *The Thief of Baghdad* or *Cobra Woman*. These *Arabian Nights*-type entertainments were popular in the old city.

The Statesman, the premier newspaper of that era, ran ads for all the films in town, and I'd cut them out and stick them in a scrapbook. I could rattle off the cast of all the pictures I'd seen, and today, sixty years later, I can still name all the actors (and sometimes the director) of almost every 1940s film.

My father died when I was ten and I went to live with my mother and stepfather in Dehradun. Dehra too, was well served with cinemas, but I was a lonely picturegoer. I had no friends or companions in those years, and I would trudge off on my own to the Orient or Odeon or Hollywood, to indulge in a few hours of escapism. Books were there, of course, providing another and better form of escape, but books had to be read in the home, and sometimes I wanted to get away from the house and pursue a solitary other-life in the anonymous privacy of a darkened cinema hall.

It has gone now, the little Odeon cinema opposite the old Parade Ground in Dehra. Many of my age, and younger, will remember it with affection, for it was probably the most popular meeting place for English cinema buffs in the '40s and '50s. You could get a good idea of the popularity of a film by looking at the number of bicycles ranged outside. Dehra was a bicycle town. The scooter hadn't been invented, and cars were few. I belonged to a minority of walkers. I have walked all over the towns and cities I have lived in—Dehradun, New and Old Delhi, London, St Helier (in Jersey) and our hill stations. Those walks often ended at the cinema!

The Odeon was a twenty-minute walk from the Old Survey Road, where we lived at the time, and after the evening show I would walk home across the deserted parade ground, the starry night adding to my dreams of a starry world, where tap dancers, singing cowboys, swashbuckling swordsmen and glamorous women in *sarongs* reigned supreme in the firmament. I wasn't just a daydreamer; I was a star-dreamer.

During the intervals (five-minute breaks between the shorts and the main feature), the projectionist or his assistant would play a couple of gramophone records for the benefit of the audience. Unfortunately, the management had only two or three records, and the audience would grow restless listening to the same tunes at every show. I must have been compelled to listen to 'Don't Fence Me In' about a hundred times, and felt thoroughly fenced in.

At home, I had a good collection of gramophone records, passed on to me by relatives and neighbours who were leaving

India around the time of Independence. I decided it would be a good idea to give some of them to the cinema's management so that we could be provided with a little more variety during the intervals. I made a selection of about twenty records—mostly dance music of the period—and presented them to the manager, Mr Suri.

Mr Suri was delighted. And to show me his gratitude, he presented me with a Free Pass which permitted me to see all the pictures I liked without having to buy a ticket! Any day, any show, for as long as Mr Suri was the manager! Could any ardent picturegoer have asked for more?

This unexpected bonanza lasted for almost two years with the result that during my school holidays I saw a film every second day. Two days was the average run for most films. Except *Gone With the Wind*, which ran for a week, to my great chagrin. I found it so boring that I left in the middle.

Usually I did enjoy films based on famous or familiar books. Dickens was a natural for the screen. *David Copperfield, Oliver Twist, Great Expectations, Nicholas Nickleby, A Tale of Two Cities, Pickwick Papers, A Christmas Carol* all made successful films, true to the originals. Daphne du Maurier's novels also transferred well to the screen. As did Somerset Maugham's works: *Of Human Bondage, The Razor's Edge, The Letter, Rain* and several others.

Occasionally I brought the management a change of records. Mr Suri was not a very communicative man, but I think he liked me (he knew something about my circumstances) and with a smile and a wave of the hand he would indicate that the freedom of the hall was mine.

Eventually, school finished, I was packed off to England, where my picture-going days went into a slight decline. No Free Passes any more. But on Jersey island, where I lived and worked for a year, I found an out-of-the-way cinema which specialized in showing old comedies, and here I caught up with many British film comedians such as Tommy Trinder, Sidney Howard, Max Miller, Will Hay, Old Mother Riley (a man in reality) and Gracie Fields. These artistes had been but names to me, as their films had never come to India. I was thrilled to be able to discover and enjoy their considerable talents. You would be hard put to find their films today; they have seldom been revived.

In London for two years I had an office job and most of my spare time was spent in writing (and rewriting) my first novel. All the same, I took to the streets and discovered the Everyman cinema in Hampstead, which showed old classics, including the films of Jean Renoir and Orson Welles. And the Academy in Leicester Square, which showed the best films from the continent. I also discovered a couple of seedy little cinemas in the East End, which appropriately showed the early gangster films of James Cagney and Humphrey Bogart.

I also saw the first Indian film to get a regular screening in London. It was called *Aan,* and was the usual extravagant mix of music and melodrama. But it ran for two or three weeks. Homesick Indians (which included me) flocked to see it. One of its stars was Nadira, who specialized in playing the scheming sultry villainess. A few years ago she came out of retirement to take the part of Miss Mackenzie in a TV serial based on some of my short stories set in Mussoorie. A sympathetic role for a change. And she played it to perfection.

It was four years before I saw Dehra again. Mr Suri had gone elsewhere. The little cinema had closed down and was about to be demolished, to make way for a hotel and a block of shops.

We must move on, of course. There's no point in hankering after distant pleasures and lost picture palaces. But there's no harm in indulging in a little nostalgia. What is nostalgia, after all, but an attempt to preserve that which was good in the past?

And last year I was reminded of that golden era of the silver screen. I was rummaging around in a *kabari* shop in one of Dehradun's bazaars where I came across a pile of old 78 RPM records, all looking a little the worse for wear. And on a couple of them I found my name scratched on the labels. 'Pennies from Heaven' was the title of one of the songs. It had certainly saved me a few rupees. That and the goodwill of Mr Suri, the Odeon's manager, all those years ago.

I bought the records. Can't play them now. No wind-up gramophone! But I am a sentimental fellow and I keep them among my souvenirs as a reminder of the days when I walked home alone across the silent, moonlit parade ground, after the evening show was over.

THE TUNNEL

It was almost noon, and the jungle was very still, very silent. Heat waves shimmered along the railway embankment where it cut a path through the tall evergreen trees. The railway lines were two straight black serpents disappearing into the tunnel in the hillside.

Suraj stood near the cutting, waiting for the mid-day train. It wasn't a station, and he wasn't catching a train. He was waiting so that he could watch the steam-engine come roaring out of the tunnel.

He had cycled out of the town and taken the jungle path until he had come to a small village. He had left the cycle there, and walked over a low, scrub-covered hill and down to the tunnel exit.

Now he looked up. He had heard, in the distance, the shrill whistle of the engine. He couldn't see anything because the train was approaching from the other side of the hill; but presently a sound, like distant thunder, issued from the tunnel, and he knew the train was coming through.

A second or two later, the steam-engine shot out of the tunnel, snorting and puffing like some green, black and gold dragon, some beautiful monster out of Suraj's dreams. Showering sparks left and right, it roared a challenge to the jungle.

Instinctively, Suraj stepped back a few paces. And then the train had gone, leaving only a plume of smoke to drift lazily over tall shisham trees.

The jungle was still again. No one moved. Suraj turned from his contemplation of the drifting smoke and began walking along the embankment, towards the tunnel.

The tunnel grew darker as he walked further into it. When he had gone about twenty yards, it became pitch black. Suraj had to turn and look back at the opening to reassure himself that there was still daylight outside. Ahead of him, the tunnel's other opening was just a small round circle of light.

The tunnel was still full of smoke from the train, but it would be several hours before another train came through. Till then, it belonged to the jungle again.

Suraj didn't stop, because there was nothing to do in the tunnel and nothing to see. He had simply wanted to walk through, so that he would know what the inside of a tunnel was really like. The walls were damp and sticky. A bat flew past. A lizard scuttled between the lines.

Coming straight from the darkness into the light, Suraj was dazzled by the sudden glare. He put a hand up to shade his eyes and looked up at the tree-covered hillside. He thought he saw something moving between the trees.

It was just a flash of orange and gold, and a long swishing tail. It was there between the trees for a second or two, and then it was gone.

About fifty feet from the entrance to the tunnel stood the watchman's hut. Marigolds grew in front of the hut, and at the back there was a small vegetable patch. It was the watchman's duty to inspect the tunnel and keep it clear of obstacles. Every day, before the train came through, he would walk the length of the tunnel. If all was well, he would return to his hut and take a nap. If something was wrong, he would walk back up the line and wave a red flag and the engine-driver would slow down. At night, the watchman lit an oil lamp and made a similar inspection of the tunnel. Of course, he could not stop the train if there was a porcupine on the line. But if there was any danger to the train, he'd go back up the line and wave his lamp to the approaching engine. If all was well, he'd hang his lamp at the door of the hut and go to sleep.

He was just settling down on his cot for an afternoon nap when he saw the boy emerge from the tunnel. He waited until Suraj was only a few feet away and then said: 'Welcome, welcome, I don't often have visitors. Sit down for a while, and tell me why you were inspecting my tunnel.'

'Is it your tunnel?' asked Suraj.

'It is,' said the watchman. 'It is truly my tunnel, since no one else will have anything to do with it. I have only lent it to the government.'

Suraj sat down on the edge of the cot.

'I wanted to see the train come through,' he said. 'And then, when it had gone, I thought I'd walk through the tunnel.'

'And what did you find in it?'

'Nothing. It was very dark. But when I came out, I thought I saw an animal—up on the hill—but I'm not sure, it moved away very quickly.'

'It was a leopard you saw,' said the watchman. 'My leopard.'

'Do you own a leopard too?'

'I do.'

'And do you lend it to the government?'

'I do not.'

'Is it dangerous?'

'No, it's a leopard that minds its own business. It comes to this range for a few days every month.'

'Have you been here a long time?' asked Suraj.

'Many years. My name is Sunder Singh.'

'My name's Suraj.'

'There's one train during the day. And another during the night. Have you seen the night mail come through the tunnel?'

'No. At what time does it come?'

'About nine o'clock, if it isn't late. You could come and sit here with me, if you like. And after it has gone, I'll take you home.'

'I shall ask my parents,' said Suraj. 'Will it be safe?'

'Of course. It's safer in the jungle than in the town. Nothing happens to me out here, but last month when I went into the town, I was almost run over by a bus.'

Sunder Singh yawned and stretched himself out on the cot. 'And now I'm going to take a nap, my friend. It is too hot to be up and about in the afternoon.'

'Everyone goes to sleep in the afternoon,' complained Suraj. 'My father lies down as soon as he's had his lunch.'

'Well, the animals also rest in the heat of the day. It is only the tribe of boys who cannot, or will not, rest.'

Sunder Singh placed a large banana-leaf over his face to keep away the flies, and was soon snoring gently. Suraj stood up, looking up and down the railway tracks. Then he began walking back to the village.

The following evening, towards dusk, as the flying foxes swooped silently out of the trees, Suraj made his way to the watchman's hut.

It had been a long hot day, but now the earth was cooling, and a light breeze was moving through the trees. It carried with it a scent of mango blossoms, the promise of rain.

Sunder Singh was waiting for Suraj. He had watered his small garden, and the flowers looked cool and fresh. A kettle was boiling on a small oil-stove.

'I'm making tea,' he said. 'There's nothing like a glass of hot tea while waiting for a train.'

They drank their tea, listening to the sharp notes of the tailorbird and the noisy chatter of the seven-sisters. As the brief twilight faded, most of the birds fell silent. Sunder Singh lit his oil-lamp and said it was time for him to inspect the tunnel. He moved off towards the tunnel, while Suraj sat on the cot, sipping his tea. In the dark, the trees seemed to move closer to him. And the night life of the forest was conveyed on the breeze—the sharp call of a barking-deer, the cry of a fox, the quaint tonk-tonk of a nightjar. There were some sounds that Suraj couldn't recognize—sounds that came from the trees, creakings and whisperings, as though the trees were coming alive, stretching their limbs in the dark, shifting a little, reflexing their fingers.

Sunder Singh stood inside the tunnel, trimming his lamp. The night sounds were familiar to him and he did not give them much thought; but something else—a padded footfall, a rustle of dry leaves—made him stand alert for a few seconds, peering into the darkness. Then, humming softly to himself, he returned to where Suraj was waiting. Another ten minutes remained for the night mail to arrive.

As Sunder Singh sat down on the cot beside Suraj, a new sound reached both of them quite distinctly—a rhythmic sawing sound, as if someone was cutting through the branch of a tree.

'What's that?' whispered Suraj.

'It's the leopard,' said Sunder Singh.

'I think it's in the tunnel.'

'The train will soon be here,' reminded Suraj.

'Yes, my friend. And if we don't drive the leopard out of the tunnel, it will be run over and killed. I can't let that happen.'

'But won't it attack us if we try to drive it out?' asked Suraj, beginning to share the watchman's concern.

'Not this leopard. It knows me well. We have seen each other many times. It has a weakness for goats and stray dogs, but it won't harm us. Even so, I'll take my axe with me. You stay here, Suraj.'

'No, I'm going with you. It'll be better than sitting here alone in the dark!'

'All right, but stay close behind me. And remember, there's nothing to fear.'

Raising his lamp high, Sunder Singh advanced into the tunnel, shouting at the top of his voice to try and scare away the animal. Suraj followed close behind, but he found he was unable to do any shouting. His throat was quite dry.

They had gone just about twenty paces into the tunnel when the light from the lamp fell upon the leopard. It was crouching between the tracks, only fifteen feet away from them. It was not a very big leopard, but it looked lithe and sinewy. Baring its teeth and snarling, it went down on its belly, tail twitching.

Suraj and Sunder Singh both shouted together. Their voices rang through the tunnel. And the leopard, uncertain as to how many terrifying humans were there in the tunnel with him, turned swiftly and disappeared into the darkness.

To make sure that it had gone, Sunder Singh and Suraj walked the length of the tunnel. When they returned to the entrance, the rails were beginning to hum. They knew the train was coming.

Suraj put his hand to the rails and felt its tremor. He heard the distant rumble of the train. And then the engine came round the bend, hissing at them, scattering sparks into the darkness, defying the jungle as it roared through the steep sides of the cutting. It charged straight at the tunnel, and into it, thundering past Suraj like the beautiful dragon of his dreams.

And when it had gone, the silence returned and the forest

seemed to breathe, to live again. Only the rails still trembled with the passing of the train.

And they trembled to the passing of the same train, almost a week later, when Suraj and his father were both travelling in it.

Suraj's father was scribbling in a notebook, doing his accounts. Suraj sat at an open window staring out at the darkness. His father was going to Delhi on a business trip and had decided to take the boy along. 'I don't know where he gets to, most of the time,' he'd complained. 'I think it's time he learnt something about my business.'

The night mail rushed through the forest with its hundreds of passengers. Tiny flickering lights came and went, as they passed small villages on the fringe of the jungle.

Suraj heard the rumble as the train passed over a small bridge. It was too dark to see the hut near the cutting, but he knew they must be approaching the tunnel. He strained his eyes looking out into the night; and then, just as the engine let out a shrill whistle, Suraj saw the lamp.

He couldn't see Sunder Singh, but he saw the lamp, and he knew that his friend was out there.

The train went into the tunnel and out again. It left the jungle behind and thundered across the endless plains; and Suraj stared out at the darkness, thinking of the lonely cutting in the forest, and the watchman with the lamp who would always remain a firefly for those travelling thousands, as he lit up the darkness for steam-engines and leopards.

THE YELLOW UMBRELLA

The postman knocks, or used to, in the old days when I lived in Maplewood Lodge, down in the forest on the outskirts of Mussoorie. Now the courier services have taken over, and the postman is something of a rarity, but back in the '60s and '70s, I would always be looking out for him because he brought me cheques from publishers and magazines, and in those days, it was the only mode of payment apart from the occasional money order. I was making a living entirely from my writing, and those 'cheques in the mail' were essential for my survival.

Prakash was my postman for two or three years. His daily beat brought him from the post office on the Mall to the school on the ridge above my cottage, a walk of about two and a half miles. He was nearing sixty, on the verge of retirement, and the long walk would tire him out.

I had been in the cottage just three or four days when he came trudging down the forest path with a couple of letters for me. I was at my desk on the verandah when I heard a stentorian voice calling: 'Postman, postman!'

I got up from my desk. He looked at my typewriter.

'This is your work, your office?' he asked.

'Yes, I am a writer,' I said.

'No, you are a typer,' he said.

'You mean a typist? I do my writing on this typewriter.' (In those days I used to type my stories.)

'So you are a typer-writer,' he insisted.

And from that day on he always addressed me as Mr Typer-writer.

Well, I didn't mind as long as I got my letters. And he was very regular, turning up every day (except holidays) around noon, calling out, 'Postman! Letters for Mr Typer-writer!' He had some difficulty pronouncing my real name.

He would usually find me at my desk or in the tiny garden where I was trying to grow snapdragons and petunias. On hot days he would ask me for a glass of water, and after he had quenched his thirst he would sit on the low garden wall for five or ten minutes and bring me up to date on what was happening in the town. A movie was being made on the Mall, and there was much excitement because the beautiful Hema Malini was in town. Or something more mundane such as a leopard having been seen on the Camel's Back Road, or a beauty contest underway at the Savoy. I seldom went into town, so Prakash the postman was my local newspaper.

The months passed quietly, the seasons changed, my work progressed. Those all-important cheques arrived from time to time, so did the winter rains and a fall of snow. Prakash had a rough voice but he wasn't very strong, and in his old, frayed overcoat he was beginning to look older than his years. Instead of a glass of water, I would give him a glass of hot sweet tea, and he would perk up and plod back up the hill to his quarters in the town. He was married but his wife lived in their village on the next range. She had to look after his old mother and a cow and a couple of goats.

'I will retire soon,' he told me, 'and then I will get another cow and maybe a mule to bring our milk and vegetables to Mussoorie. Big business!'

When summer came again he abandoned his overcoat and started wearing a cap to shield him from the sun. When the monsoon arrived, he started carrying an umbrella. It was shabby and torn, and did not give him much protection. And the rains were heavy that year.

'Won't the post office give you a decent umbrella?' I asked.

'They gave me this one five years ago,' he said. 'Now they don't have a budget for umbrellas.'

'Well, I'll get you one,' I said. 'I'm going into town tomorrow, and I'll get you a good umbrella.'

'That's very kind of you,' said Prakash. 'I would like a blue umbrella.'

'Why blue?'

He told me that he had often seen a little village girl, Binya, coming from or going to school, and she had a pretty blue umbrella. He wanted one just like it!

'Well, I'll see what I can find,' I said. And I walked into town, looking for a blue umbrella.

But the umbrella shops had all run out of blue umbrellas. Suddenly, they had become very popular.

I didn't think Prakash would care for an ordinary black umbrella. So I settled for a bright yellow umbrella, and the following day, when he arrived with his old umbrella blown inside out by a strong wind, I presented him with the yellow umbrella.

'Yellow is the colour of the sun,' I said. 'It will keep you sunny and cheerful!'

He accepted it graciously and carried it about wherever he went, even when the rains were over. You could tell when he was coming because of that blob of bright yellow moving about on the hillside.

Then one day, in the middle of October, someone else arrived with my post.

He was a young man, neatly dressed, very polite. 'Your letters, sir, I'm the new postman.'

It was quite a shock.

'What happened to Prakash?' I asked anxiously. 'I hope he isn't sick.'

'He's fine, sir. He took his retirement pension and went back to his village.'

'Oh, I see.'

I was a little disappointed that he hadn't told me he was going, but he was probably in a hurry to buy that cow. The new postman was fine, and I did not expect to see Prakash again.

It was late October. I'd been working hard, and I felt like getting away from the typewriter, even if it was only for a couple of days. I was a good walker and had done some trekking over the years. I decided to take a long walk to Dhanaulti, where there was an old forest rest house set amidst deodars and horse-chestnuts.

In those days there was no motor road to Dhanaulti, just a footpath used by pilgrims on their arduous trek to Gangotri. Dhanaulti was about twenty miles from my cottage, and I expected to be there by evening if I walked at a steady pace. My friend and helper, Pran Singh, made some sandwiches for me and filled a water-bottle with lemon juice; these went into my haversack (the modern backpack had yet to be invented) and I set off cheerfully, hoping to enjoy the sparkling autumn air and the wonderful views from the winding path to Dhanaulti.

I'd covered about five miles, past the village of Suakholi, when I found the path blocked by a herd of goats, and in order to avoid them I left the narrow path and scrambled up the slope of the hill, made slippery by fallen pine needles. On my way down I slipped and fell, twisting my ankle. I wasn't badly hurt, but the ankle was painful, and I continued limping along, wishing I'd brought along a stout walking-stick.

Still, I struggled on, as I was now about half way to Dhanaulti, and when I saw some wayside huts about half a mile distant, I decided I'd rest in the village and then decide whether to go or not.

As I approached, I noticed a large yellow blob outside one of the shacks. It was a yellow umbrella! And beneath it, sheltering from the sun was Prakash, my old postman.

As soon as he saw me, he got up, exclaiming: 'Typer-writer sir! What are you doing here?'

'Just taking a walk. Is this your village?'

'Yes, my fields are just below. But you have hurt yourself, come and sit down. Better still, come inside and rest.'

His small tile-roofed dwelling was first off the road. It was two-storied, the ground floor being reserved for his cows. Yes, there were now two of them.

He took me upstairs and made me comfortable on an old cane chair. He called for his wife and asked her to make us some tea. She was a round, plump, jolly woman who was delighted to have an unexpected visitor. The tea was followed by hot *pakoras* and walnuts from their own walnut tree.

'You have sprained your ankle,' said Prakash. 'See, it is quite swollen. You should not walk any further. Better to stay the night.'

But I knew that Prakash would not have a spare cot or even a spare mattress, so I said, 'I'll manage, it's not too bad.'

Just then a pack of mules arrived, on its way to Mussoorie; the mules were loaded with sacks of beans and radishes. The mule-driver was singing the latest Hindi hit song.

'Hey, Melaram!' shouted Prakash. 'Do you have space on one of your mules?'

'For a friend of yours there will be space,' answered the mule-driver.

'Then deliver my friend the Typer-writer to the first doctor you find in Mussoorie.'

'At your command,' said Melaram. 'It shall be done.' He brought over one of his mules, transferred its load to another mule, and made a saddle of sorts out of empty gunny-bags. They were straggled on to the patient animal, and I was helped on to it by the two men, while Prakash's wife looked on with unconcealed amusement.

It was the first time I had taken a ride on a mule, and I hoped there would not be another. Two hours of riding a mule can give you a very sore bottom.

'Come again, Typer-writer sir,' said Prakash, and we trotted off, the mule-driver in the lead, followed by my mount and several others. I looked back to see Prakash waving to me, holding up the yellow umbrella, which had turned to burnished gold in the setting sun.

There's an old saying, 'One good turn deserves another.' A bit of a cliché but true. There's such a thing as law of compensation, a sort of Karma, that works best in this life. Kindness begets kindness, and never mind the sore bottom.

A LONG WALK FOR BINA

I

A leopard, lithe and sinewy, drank at the mountain stream, and then lay down on the grass to bask in the late February sunshine. Its tail twitched occasionally and the animal appeared to be sleeping. At the sound of distant voices it raised its head to listen, then stood up and leapt lightly over the boulders in the stream, disappearing among the trees on the opposite bank.

A minute or two later, three children came walking down the forest path. They were a girl and two boys, and they were singing in their local dialect an old song they had learnt from their grandparents.

Five more miles to go!
We climb through rain and snow.
A river to cross...
A mountain to pass...
Now we've four more miles to go!

Their school satchels looked new, their clothes had been washed and pressed. Their loud and cheerful singing startled a spotted forktail. The bird left its favourite rock in the stream and flew down the dark ravine.

'Well, we have only three more miles to go,' said the bigger boy, Prakash, who had been this way hundreds of times. 'But first we have to cross the stream.'

He was a sturdy twelve-year-old with eyes like black currants and a mop of bushy hair that refused to settle down on his head. The girl and her small brother were taking this path for the first time.

'I'm feeling tired, Bina,' said the little boy.

Bina smiled at him, and Prakash said, 'Don't worry, Sonu, you'll get used to the walk. There's plenty of time.' He glanced at the old watch he'd been given by his grandfather. It needed constant winding. 'We can rest here for five or six minutes.'

They sat down on a smooth boulder and watched the clear water of the shallow stream tumbling downhill. Bina examined the old watch on Prakash's wrist. The glass was badly scratched and she could barely make out the figures on the dial. 'Are you sure it still gives the right time?' she asked.

'Well, it loses five minutes every day, so I put it ten minutes ahead at night. That means by morning it's quite accurate! Even our teacher, Mr Mani, asks me for the time. If he doesn't ask, I tell him! The clock in our classroom keeps stopping.'

They removed their shoes and let the cold mountain water run over their feet. Bina was the same age as Prakash. She had pink cheeks, soft brown eyes, and hair that was just beginning to lose its natural curls. Hers was a gentle face, but a determined little chin showed that she could be a strong person. Sonu, her younger brother, was ten. He was a thin boy who had been sickly as a child but was now beginning to fill out. Although he did not look very athletic, he could run like the wind.

◆

Bina had been going to school in her own village of Koli, on the other side of the mountain. But it had been a primary school, finishing at Class 5. Now, in order to study in Class 6, she would have to walk several miles every day to Nauti, where there was a high school going up to Class 8. It had been decided that Sonu would also shift to the new school, to give Bina company. Prakash, their neighbour in Koli, was already a pupil at the Nauti school. His mischievous nature, which sometimes got him into trouble, had resulted in his having to repeat a year.

But this didn't seem to bother him. 'What's the hurry?' he had told his indignant parents. 'You're not sending me to a foreign land when I finish school. And our cows aren't running away, are they?'

'You would prefer to look after the cows, wouldn't you?' asked Bina, as they got up to continue their walk.

'Oh, school's all right. Wait till you see old Mr Mani. He always gets our names mixed up, as well as the subjects he's supposed to be teaching. At our last lesson, instead of maths, he gave us a geography lesson!'

'More fun than maths,' said Bina.

'Yes, but there's a new teacher this year. She's very young they say, just out of college. I wonder what she'll be like.'

Bina walked faster and Sonu had some trouble keeping up with them. She was excited about the new school and the prospect of different surroundings. She had seldom been outside her own village, with its small school and single ration shop. The day's routine never varied—helping her mother in the fields, or with household tasks like fetching water from the spring or cutting grass and fodder for the cattle. Her father, who was a soldier, was away for nine months in the year and Sonu was still too small for the heavier tasks.

As they neared Nauti Village, they were joined by other children coming from different directions. Even where there were no major roads, the mountains were full of little lanes and shortcuts. Like a game of snakes and ladders, these narrow paths zigzagged around the hills and villages, cutting through fields and crossing narrow ravines until they came together to form a fairly busy road along which mules, cattle and goats joined the throng.

Nauti was a fairly large village, and from here a broader but dustier road started for Tehri. There was a small bus, several trucks and (for part of the way) a road roller. The road hadn't been completed because the heavy diesel roller couldn't take the steep climb to Nauti. It stood on the roadside halfway up the road from Tehri.

Prakash knew almost everyone in the area, and exchanged greetings and gossip with other children as well as with muleteers, bus drivers, milkmen and labourers working on the road. He loved telling everyone the time, even if they weren't interested.

'It's nine o'clock,' he would announce, glancing at his wrist. 'Isn't your bus leaving today?'

'Off with you!' the bus driver would respond, 'I'll leave when I'm ready.'

As the children approached Nauti, the small flat school buildings came into view on the outskirts of the village, fringed by a line of long-leaved pines. A small crowd had assembled on the one playing field. Something unusual seemed to have happened. Prakash ran forward to see what it was all about. Bina and Sonu stood aside, waiting in a patch of sunlight near the boundary wall.

Prakash soon came running back to them. He was bubbling over with excitement.

'It's Mr Mani!' he gasped. 'He's disappeared! People are saying a leopard must have carried him off!'

II

Mr Mani wasn't really old. He was about fifty-five and was expected to retire soon. But for the children, most adults over forty seemed ancient! And Mr Mani had always been a bit absent-minded, even as a young man.

He had gone out for his early morning walk, saying he'd be back by eight o'clock, in time to have his breakfast and be ready for class. He wasn't married, but his sister and her husband stayed with him. When it was past nine o'clock his sister presumed he'd stopped at a neighbour's house for breakfast (he loved tucking into other people's breakfast) and that he had gone on to school from there. But when the school bell rang at ten o'clock, and everyone but Mr Mani was present, questions were asked and guesses were made.

No one had seen him return from his walk and enquiries made in the village showed that he had not stopped at anyone's house. For Mr Mani to disappear was puzzling; for him to disappear without his breakfast was extraordinary.

Then a milkman returning from the next village said he had seen a leopard sitting on a rock on the outskirts of the pine forest. There had been talk of a cattle-killer in the valley, of leopards and other animals being displaced by the construction of a dam. But as yet no one had heard of a leopard attacking a man. Could Mr Mani have been its first victim? Someone found a strip of red cloth entangled in a blackberry bush and went running through the village showing it to everyone. Mr Mani had been known to wear red pyjamas. Surely he had been seized and eaten! But where were his remains? And why had he been in his pyjamas?

Meanwhile Bina and Sonu and the rest of the children had followed their teachers into the school playground. Feeling a little lost, Bina looked around for Prakash. She found herself facing a dark, slender young woman wearing spectacles, who must have been in her early twenties—just a little too old to be another student. She had a kind, expressive face and she seemed a little concerned by all that had been happening.

Bina noticed that she had lovely hands; it was obvious that the new teacher hadn't milked cows or worked in the fields!

'You must be new here,' said the teacher, smiling at Bina. 'And is this your little brother?'

'Yes, we've come from Koli Village. We were at school there.'

'It's a long walk from Koli. You didn't see any leopards, did you? Well, I'm new too. Are you in the sixth class?'

'Sonu is in the third. I'm in the sixth.'

'Then I'm your new teacher. My name is Tania Ramola. Come along, let's see if we can settle down in our classroom.'

◆

Mr Mani turned up at twelve o'clock, wondering what all the fuss was about. No, he snapped, he had not been attacked by a leopard; and yes, he had lost his pyjamas and would someone kindly return them to him?

'How did you lose your pyjamas, sir?' asked Prakash.

'They were blown off the washing line!' snapped Mr Mani.

After much questioning, Mr Mani admitted that he had gone further than he had intended, and that he had lost his way coming back. He had been a bit upset because the new teacher, a slip of a girl, had been given charge of the sixth, while he was still with the fifth, along with that troublesome boy Prakash, who kept on reminding him of the time! The Headmaster had explained that as Mr Mani was due to retire at the end of the year, the school did not wish to burden him with a senior class. But Mr Mani looked upon the whole thing as a plot to get rid of him. He glowered at Miss Ramola whenever he passed her. And when she smiled at him, he looked the other way!

Mr Mani had been getting even more absent-minded of late—putting on his shoes without his socks, wearing his homespun waistcoat inside out, mixing up people's names and, of course, eating other people's lunches and dinners. His sister had made a mutton broth for the postmaster, who was down with 'flu', and had asked Mr Mani to take it over in a thermos. When the postmaster opened the thermos, he found only a few drops of broth at the bottom—Mr Mani had drunk the rest somewhere along the way.

When sometimes Mr Mani spoke of his coming retirement, it was to describe his plans for the small field he owned just behind the house. Right now, it was full of potatoes, which did not require much looking after; but he had plans for growing dahlias, roses, French beans, and other fruits and flowers.

The next time he visited Tehri, he promised himself, he would buy some dahlia bulbs and rose cuttings. The monsoon season would be a good time to put them down. And meanwhile, his potatoes were still flourishing.

III

Bina enjoyed her first day at the new school. She felt at ease with Miss Ramola, as did most of the boys and girls in her class. Tania Ramola had been to distant towns such as Delhi and Lucknow—places they had only heard about—and it was said that she had a brother who was a pilot and flew planes all over the world. Perhaps he'd fly over Nauti some day!

Most of the children had of course seen planes flying overhead, but none of them had seen a ship, and only a few had been on a train. Tehri mountain was far from the railway and hundreds of miles from the sea. But they all knew about the big dam that was being built at Tehri, just forty miles away.

Bina, Sonu and Prakash had company for part of the way home, but gradually the other children went off in different directions. Once they had crossed the stream, they were on their own again.

It was a steep climb all the way back to their village. Prakash had a supply of peanuts that he shared with Bina and Sonu, and at a small spring they quenched their thirst.

When they were less than a mile from home, they met a postman who had finished his round of the villages in the area and was now returning to Nauti.

'Don't waste time along the way,' he told them. 'Try to get home before dark.'

'What's the hurry?' asked Prakash, glancing at his watch. 'It's only five o'clock.'

'There's a leopard around. I saw it this morning, not far from the stream. No one is sure how it got here. So don't take any chances. Get home early.'

'So, there really is a leopard,' said Sonu.

They took his advice and walked faster, and Sonu forgot to complain about his aching feet.

They were home well before sunset.

There was a smell of cooking in the air and they were hungry.

'Cabbage and roti,' said Prakash gloomily. 'But I could eat anything today.'

He stopped outside his small slate-roofed house, and Bina and Sonu waved goodbye and carried on across a couple of ploughed fields until they reached their small stone house.

'Stuffed tomatoes,' said Sonu, sniffing just outside the front door.

'And lemon pickle,' said Bina, who had helped cut, sun and salt the lemons a month previously.

Their mother was lighting the kitchen stove. They greeted her with great hugs and demands for an immediate dinner. She was a good cook who could make even the simplest of dishes taste delicious. Her favourite saying was, 'Home-made bread is better than roast meat abroad,' and Bina and Sonu had to agree.

Electricity had yet to reach their village, and they took their meal by the light of a kerosene lamp. After the meal, Sonu settled down to do a little homework, while Bina stepped outside to look at the stars.

Across the fields, someone was playing a flute. 'It must be Prakash,' thought Bina. 'He always breaks off on the high notes.' But the flute music was simple and appealing, and she began singing softly to herself in the dark.

IV

Mr Mani was having trouble with the porcupines. They had been getting into his garden at night and digging up and eating his potatoes. From his bedroom window—left open now that the mild April weather had arrived—he could listen to them enjoying the vegetables he had worked hard to grow. *Scrunch, scrunch! katar, katar,* as their sharp teeth sliced through the largest and juiciest of potatoes. For Mr Mani it was as though they were biting through his own flesh. And the sound of them digging industriously as they rooted up those healthy, leafy plants made him tremble with rage and indignation. The unfairness of it all!

Yes, Mr Mani hated porcupines. He prayed for their destruction, their removal from the face of the earth. But, as his friends were quick to point out, 'The creator made porcupines too,' and in any case you could never see the creatures or catch them, they were completely nocturnal.

Mr Mani got out of bed every night, torch in one hand, a stout stick in the other but, as soon as he stepped into the garden, the crunching and digging stopped and he was greeted by the most infuriating of silences. He would grope around in the dark, swinging wildly with the stick, but not a single porcupine was to be seen or heard. As soon as he was back in bed, the sounds would start all over again—*scrunch, scrunch, katar, katar...*

Mr Mani came to his class tired and dishevelled, with rings under his eyes and a permanent frown on his face. It took some time for his pupils to discover the reason for his misery, but when they did, they felt sorry for their teacher and took to discussing ways and means of saving his potatoes from the porcupines.

It was Prakash who came up with the idea of a moat or water ditch. 'Porcupines don't like water,' he said knowledgeably.

'How do you know?' asked one of his friends.

'Throw water on one and see how it runs! They don't like getting their quills wet.'

There was no one who could disprove Prakash's theory, and the class fell in with the idea of building a moat, especially as it meant getting most of the day off.

'Anything to make Mr Mani happy,' said the Headmaster, and the rest of the school watched with envy as the pupils of Class 5, armed with spades and shovels collected from all parts of the village, took up their positions around Mr Mani's potato field and began digging a ditch.

By evening the moat was ready, but it was still dry and the porcupines got in again that night and had a great feast.

'At this rate,' said Mr Mani gloomily, 'there won't be any potatoes left to save.'

But the next day, Prakash and the other boys and girls managed to divert the water from a stream that flowed past the village. They had the satisfaction of watching it flow gently into the ditch. Everyone went home in a good mood. By nightfall, the ditch had overflowed, the potato field was flooded, and Mr Mani found himself trapped inside his house. But Prakash and his friends had won the day. The porcupines stayed away that night!

◆

A month had passed, and wild violets, daisies and buttercups now sprinkled the hill slopes and, on her way to school, Bina gathered enough to make a little posy. The bunch of flowers fitted easily into an old ink well. Miss Ramola was delighted to find this little display in the middle of her desk.

'Who put these here?' she asked in surprise.

Bina kept quiet, and the rest of the class smiled secretively. After that, they took turns bringing flowers for the classroom.

On her long walks to school and home again, Bina became aware that April was the month of new leaves. The oak leaves were bright green above and silver beneath, and when they rippled in the breeze they were clouds of silvery green. The path was strewn with old leaves, dry and crackly. Sonu loved kicking them around.

Clouds of white butterflies floated across the stream. Sonu was chasing a butterfly when he stumbled over something dark and repulsive. He went sprawling on the grass. When he got to his feet, he looked down at the remains of a small animal.

'Bina! Prakash! Come quickly!' he shouted.

It was part of a sheep, killed some days earlier by a much larger animal.

'Only a leopard could have done this,' said Prakash.

'Let's get away, then,' said Sonu. 'It might still be around!'

'No, there's nothing left to eat. The leopard will be hunting elsewhere by now. Perhaps it's moved on to the next valley.'

'Still, I'm frightened,' said Sonu. 'There may be more leopards!'

Bina took him by the hand. 'Leopards don't attack humans!' she said.

'They will, if they get a taste for people!' insisted Prakash.

'Well, this one hasn't attacked any people as yet,' said Bina, although she couldn't be sure. Hadn't there been rumours of a leopard attacking some workers near the dam? But she did not want Sonu to feel afraid, so she did not mention the story. All she said was, 'It has probably come here because of all the activity near the dam.'

All the same, they hurried home. And for a few days, whenever they reached the stream, they crossed over very quickly, unwilling to linger too long at that lovely spot.

V

A few days later, a school party was on its way to Tehri to see the new dam that was being built.

Miss Ramola had arranged to take her class, and Mr Mani, not wishing to be left out, insisted on taking his class as well. That meant there were about fifty boys and girls taking part in the outing. The little bus could only take thirty. A friendly truck driver agreed to take some children if they were prepared to sit on sacks of potatoes. And Prakash persuaded the owner of the diesel roller to turn it around and head it back to Tehri—with him and a couple of friends up on the driving seat.

Prakash's small group set off at sunrise, as they had to walk some distance in order to reach the stranded road roller. The bus left at 9.00 a.m. with Miss Ramola and her class, and Mr Mani and some of his pupils. The truck was to follow later.

It was Bina's first visit to a large town, and her first bus ride.

The sharp curves along the winding, downhill road made several children feel sick. The bus driver seemed to be in a tearing hurry. He took them along at a rolling, rollicking speed that made Bina feel quite giddy. She rested her head on her arms and refused to look out of the window. Hairpin bends and cliff edges, pine forests and snow-capped peaks, all swept past her, but she felt too ill to want to look at anything. It was just as well—those sudden drops, hundreds of feet to the valley below, were quite frightening. Bina began to wish that she hadn't come—or that she had joined Prakash on the road roller instead!

Miss Ramola and Mr Mani didn't seem to notice the lurching and groaning of the old bus. They had made this journey many times. They were busy arguing about the advantages and disadvantages of large dams—an argument that was to continue on and off for much of the day.

Meanwhile, Prakash and his friends had reached the roller. The driver hadn't turned up, but they managed to reverse it and get it going in the direction of Tehri. They were soon overtaken by both bus and truck but kept moving along at a steady chug. Prakash spotted Bina at the window of the bus and waved cheerfully. She responded feebly.

Bina felt better when the road levelled out near Tehri. As they crossed an old bridge over the wide river, they were startled by a loud bang that made the bus shudder. A cloud of dust rose above the town.

'They're blasting the mountain,' said Miss Ramola.

'End of a mountain,' said Mr Mani, mournfully.

While they were drinking cups of tea at the bus stop, waiting for the potato truck and the road roller, Miss Ramola and Mr Mani continued their argument about the dam. Miss Ramola maintained that it would bring electric power and water for irrigation to large areas of the country, including the surrounding area. Mr Mani declared that it was a menace, as it was situated in an earthquake zone. There would be a terrible disaster if the dam burst! Bina found it all very confusing. And what about the animals in the area, she wondered, what would happen to them?

The argument was becoming quite heated when the potato truck arrived. There was no sign of the road roller, so it was decided that Mr Mani should wait for Prakash and his friends while Miss Ramola's group went ahead.

◆

Some eight or nine miles before Tehri, the road roller had broken down, and Prakash and his friends were forced to walk. They had not gone far, however, when a mule train came along—five or six mules that had been delivering sacks of grain in Nauti. A boy rode on the first mule, but the others had no loads.

'Can you give us a ride to Tehri?' called Prakash.

'Make yourselves comfortable,' said the boy.

There were no saddles, only gunny sacks strapped on to the mules with rope. They had a rough but jolly ride down to the Tehri bus stop. None of them had ever ridden mules; but they had saved at least an hour on the road.

Looking around the bus stop for the rest of the party, they could find no one from their school. And Mr Mani, who should have been waiting for them, had vanished.

VI

Tania Ramola and her group had taken the steep road to the hill above Tehri. Half an hour's climbing brought them to a little plateau which overlooked the town, the river and the dam site.

The earthworks for the dam were only just coming up, but a wide tunnel had been bored through the mountain to divert the river into another channel. Down below, the old town was still spread out across the valley and from a distance it looked quite charming and picturesque.

'Will the whole town be swallowed up by the waters of the dam?' asked Bina.

'Yes, all of it,' said Miss Ramola. 'The clock tower and the old palace. The long bazaar, and the temples, the schools and the jail, and hundreds of houses, for many miles up the valley. All those people will have to go—thousands of them! Of course they'll be resettled elsewhere.'

'But the town's been here for hundreds of years,' said Bina. 'They were quite happy without the dam, weren't they?'

'I suppose they were. But the dam isn't just for them—it's for the millions who live further downstream, across the plains.'

'And it doesn't matter what happens to this place?'

'The local people will be given new homes somewhere else.' Miss Ramola found herself on the defensive and decided to change the subject. 'Everyone must be hungry. It's time we had our lunch.'

Bina kept quiet. She didn't think the local people would want to go away. And it was a good thing, she mused, that there was only a small stream and not a big river running past her village. To be uprooted like this—a town and hundreds of villages—and put down somewhere on the hot, dusty plains—seemed to her unbearable.

'Well, I'm glad I don't live in Tehri,' she said.

She did not know it, but all the animals and most of the birds had already left the area. The leopard had been among them.

♦

They walked through the colourful, crowded bazaar, where fruit sellers did business beside silversmiths, and pavement vendors sold everything from umbrellas to glass bangles. Sparrows attacked sacks of grain, monkeys made off with bananas, and stray cows and dogs rummaged in refuse bins, but nobody took any notice. Music blared from radios. Buses blew their horns. Sonu bought a whistle to add to the general din, but Miss Ramola told him to put it away. Bina had kept five rupees aside, and now she used it to buy a cotton headscarf for her mother.

As they were about to enter a small restaurant for a meal, they were joined by Prakash and his companions; but of Mr Mani there was still no sign.

'He must have met one of his relatives,' said Prakash. 'He has relatives everywhere.'

After a simple meal of rice and lentils, they walked the length of the bazaar without finding Mr Mani. At last, when they were about to give up the search, they saw him emerge from a by-lane, a large sack slung over his shoulder.

'Sir, where have you been?' asked Prakash. 'We have been looking for you everywhere.'

On Mr Mani's face was a look of triumph.

'Help me with this bag,' he said breathlessly.

'You've bought more potatoes, sir,' said Prakash.

'Not potatoes, boy. Dahlia bulbs!'

VII

It was dark by the time they were all back in Nauti. Mr Mani had refused to be separated from his sack of dahlia bulbs, and had been forced to sit in the back of the truck with Prakash and most of the boys.

Bina did not feel so ill on the return journey. Going uphill was definitely better than going downhill! But by the time the bus reached Nauti it was too late for most of the children to walk back to the more distant villages. The boys were put up in different homes, while the girls were given beds in the school verandah.

The night was warm and still. Large moths fluttered around the single bulb that lit the verandah. Counting moths, Sonu soon fell asleep. But Bina stayed awake for some time, listening to the sounds of the night. A nightjar went tonk-tonk in the bushes, and somewhere in the forest an owl hooted softly. The sharp call of a barking deer travelled up the valley from the direction of the stream. Jackals kept howling. It seemed that there were more of them than ever before.

Bina was not the only one to hear the barking deer. The leopard, stretched full length on a rocky ledge, heard it too. The leopard raised its head and then got up slowly. The deer was its natural prey. But there weren't many left, and that was why the leopard, robbed of its forest by the dam, had taken to attacking dogs and cattle near the villages.

As the cry of the barking deer sounded nearer, the leopard left its lookout point and moved swiftly through the shadows towards the stream.

VIII

In early June, the hills were dry and dusty, and forest fires broke out, destroying shrubs and trees, killing birds and small animals. The resin in the pines made these trees burn more fiercely, and the wind would take sparks from the trees and carry them into the dry grass and leaves, so that new fires would spring up before the old ones had died out. Fortunately, Bina's village was not in the pine belt; the fires did not reach it. But Nauti was surrounded by a fire that raged for three days, and the children had to stay away from school.

And then, towards the end of June, the monsoon rains arrived and there was an end to the forest fires. The monsoon lasts three months and the lower Himalayas would be drenched in rain, mist and cloud for the next three months.

The first rain arrived while Bina, Prakash and Sonu were returning home from school. Those first few drops on the dusty path made them cry out with excitement. Then the rain grew heavier and a wonderful aroma rose from the earth.

'The best smell in the world!' exclaimed Bina.

Everything suddenly came to life. The grass, the crops, the trees, the birds. Even the leaves of the trees glistened and looked new.

That first wet weekend, Bina and Sonu helped their mother plant beans, maize and cucumbers. Sometimes, when the rain was very heavy, they had to run indoors. Otherwise they worked in the rain, the soft mud clinging to their bare legs.

Prakash now owned a dog, a black dog with one ear up and one ear down. The dog ran around getting in everyone's way, barking at cows, goats, hens and humans, without frightening any of them. Prakash said it was a very clever dog, but no one else seemed to think so. Prakash also said it would protect the village from the leopard, but others said the dog would be the first to be taken—he'd run straight into the jaws of Mr Spots!

In Nauti, Tania Ramola was trying to find a dry spot in the quarters she'd been given. It was an old building and the roof was leaking in several places. Mugs and buckets were scattered about the floor in order to catch the drips.

Mr Mani had dug up all his potatoes and presented them to the friends and neighbours who had given him lunches and dinners. He was having the time of his life, planting dahlia bulbs all over his garden.

'I'll have a field of many-coloured dahlias!' he announced. 'Just wait till the end of August!'

'Watch out for those porcupines,' warned his sister. 'They eat dahlia bulbs too!'

Mr Mani made an inspection tour of his moat, no longer in flood, and found everything in good order. Prakash had done his job well.

◆

Now, when the children crossed the stream, they found that the water level had risen by about a foot. Small cascades had turned into waterfalls. Ferns had sprung up on the banks. Frogs chanted.

Prakash and his dog dashed across the stream. Bina and Sonu followed more cautiously. The current was much stronger now and the water was almost up to their knees. Once they had crossed the stream, they hurried along the path, anxious not to be caught in a sudden downpour.

By the time they reached school, each of them had two or three leeches clinging to their legs. They had to use salt to remove them. The leeches were the most troublesome part of the rainy season. Even the leopard did not like them. It could not lie in the long grass without getting leeches on its paws and face.

One day, when Bina, Prakash and Sonu were about to cross the stream they heard a low rumble, which grew louder every second. Looking up at the opposite hill, they saw several trees shudder, tilt outwards and begin to fall. Earth and rocks bulged out from the mountain, then came crashing down into the ravine.

'Landslide!' shouted Sonu.

'It's carried away the path,' said Bina. 'Don't go any further.'

There was a tremendous roar as more rocks, trees and bushes fell away and crashed down the hillside.

Prakash's dog, who had gone ahead, came running back, tail between his legs.

They remained rooted to the spot until the rocks had stopped falling and the dust had settled. Birds circled the area, calling wildly. A frightened barking deer ran past them.

'We can't go to school now,' said Prakash. 'There's no way around.'

They turned and trudged home through the gathering mist.

In Koli, Prakash's parents had heard the roar of the landslide. They were setting out in search of the children when they saw them emerge from the mist, waving cheerfully.

IX

They had to miss school for another three days, and Bina was afraid they might not be able to take their final exams. Although Prakash was not really troubled at the thought of missing exams, he did not like feeling helpless just because their path had been swept away. So he explored the hillside until he found a goat-track going around the mountain. It joined up with another path near Nauti. This made their walk longer by a mile, but Bina did not mind. It was much cooler now that the rains were in full swing.

The only trouble with the new route was that it passed close to the leopard's lair. The animal had made this area its own since being forced to leave the dam area.

One day Prakash's dog ran ahead of them barking furiously. Then he ran back whimpering.

'He's always running away from something,' observed Sonu. But a minute later he understood the reason for the dog's fear.

They rounded a bend and Sonu saw the leopard standing in their way. They were struck dumb—too terrified to run. It was a strong, sinewy creature. A low growl rose from its throat. It seemed ready to spring.

They stood perfectly still, afraid to move or say a word. And the leopard must have been equally surprised. It stared at them for a few seconds, then bounded across the path and into the oak forest.

Sonu was shaking. Bina could hear her heart hammering.

Prakash could only stammer: 'Did you see the way he sprang? Wasn't he beautiful?'

He forgot to look at his watch for the rest of the day.

A few days later, Sonu stopped and pointed to a large outcrop of rock on the next hill.

The leopard stood far above them, outlined against the sky. It looked strong, majestic. Standing beside it were two young cubs.

'Look at those little ones!' exclaimed Sonu.

'So it's a female, not a male,' said Prakash.

'That's why she was killing so often,' said Bina. 'She had to feed her cubs too.'

They remained still for several minutes, gazing up at the leopard and her cubs. The leopard family took no notice of them.

'She knows we are here,' said Prakash, 'but she doesn't care. She knows we won't harm them.'

'We are cubs too!' said Sonu.

'Yes,' said Bina. 'And there's still plenty of space for all of us. Even when the dam is ready there will still be room for leopards and humans.'

X

The school exams were over. The rains were nearly over too. The landslide had been cleared, and Bina, Prakash and Sonu were once again crossing the stream.

There was a chill in the air, for it was the end of September.

Prakash had learnt to play the flute quite well, and he played on the way to school and then again on the way home. As a result he did not look at his watch so often. One morning they found a small crowd in front of Mr Mani's house.

'What could have happened?' wondered Bina. 'I hope he hasn't got lost again.'

'Maybe he's sick,' said Sonu.

'Maybe it's the porcupines,' said Prakash.

But it was none of these things.

Mr Mani's first dahlia was in bloom, and half the village had turned up to look at it! It was a huge red double dahlia, so heavy that it had to be supported with sticks. No one had ever seen such a magnificent flower!

Mr Mani was a happy man. And his mood only improved over the coming week, as more and more dahlias flowered—crimson, yellow, purple, mauve, white—button dahlias, pom-pom dahlias, spotted dahlias, striped dahlias... Mr Mani had them all! A dahlia even turned up on Tania Ramola's desk—he got along quite well with her now—and another brightened up the Headmaster's study.

A week later, on their way home—it was almost the last day of the school term—Bina, Prakash and Sonu talked about what they might do when they grew up.

'I think I'll become a teacher,' said Bina. 'I'll teach children about animals and birds, and trees and flowers.'

'Better than maths!' said Prakash.

'I'll be a pilot,' said Sonu. 'I want to fly a plane like Miss Ramola's brother.'

'And what about you, Prakash?' asked Bina.

Prakash just smiled and said, 'Maybe I'll be a flute player,' and he put the flute to his lips and played a sweet melody.

'Well, the world needs flute players too,' said Bina, as they fell into step beside him.

The leopard had been stalking a barking deer. She paused when she heard the flute and the voices of the children. Her own young ones were growing quickly, but the girl and the two boys did not look much older.

They had started singing their favourite song again.

Five more miles to go!
We climb through rain and snow,
A river to cross...
A mountain to pass...
Now we've four more miles to go!

The leopard waited until they had passed, before returning to the trail of the barking deer.

AND NOW WE ARE TWELVE

People often ask me why I've chosen to live in Mussoorie for so long—almost forty years without any significant breaks.

'I forgot to go away,' I tell them, but of course, that isn't the real reason.

The people here are friendly, but then people are friendly in a great many other places. The hills, the valleys are beautiful; but they are just as beautiful in Kulu or Kumaon.

'This is where the family has grown up and where we all live,' I say, and those who don't know me are puzzled because the general impression of the writer is of a reclusive old bachelor.

Unmarried I may be, but single I am not. Not since Prem came to live and work with me in 1970. A year later, he was married. Then his children came along and stole my heart; and when they grew up, their children came along and stole my wits. So now I'm an enchanted bachelor, head of a family of twelve. Sometimes I go out to bat, sometimes to bowl, but generally I prefer to be twelfth man, carrying out the drinks!

In the old days, when I was a solitary writer living on baked beans, the prospect of my suffering from obesity was very remote. Now there is a little more of author than there used to be, and the other day five-year-old Gautam patted me on my tummy (or balcony, as I prefer to call it) and remarked: 'Dada, you should join the WWF.'

'I'm already a member,' I said. 'I joined the World Wildlife Fund years ago.'

'Not that,' he said. 'I mean the World Wrestling Federation.'

If I have a tummy today, it's thanks to Gautam's grandfather and now his mother who, over the years, has made sure that I am well-fed and well-proportioned.

Forty years ago, when I was a lean young man, people would look at me and say, 'Poor chap, he's definitely undernourished. What on earth made him take up writing as a profession?' Now they look at me and say, 'You wouldn't think he was a writer, would you? Too well nourished!'

It was a cold, wet and windy March evening when Prem came back from the village with his wife and first-born child, then just four months old. In those days, they had to walk to the house from the bus stand; it was a half-hour walk in the cold rain, and the baby was all wrapped up when they entered the front room. Finally, I got a glimpse of him, and he of me, and it was friendship at first sight. Little Rakesh (as he was to be called) grabbed me by the nose and held on. He did not have much of a nose to grab, but he had a dimpled chin and I played with it until he smiled.

The little chap spent a good deal of his time with me during those first two years of his in Maplewood—learning to crawl, to toddle and then to walk unsteadily about the little sitting room. I would carry him into the garden, and later, up the steep gravel path to the main road. Rakesh enjoyed these little excursions, and so did I, because in pointing out trees, flowers, birds, butterflies, beetles, grasshoppers, et al., I was giving myself a chance to observe them better instead of just taking them for granted.

In particular, there was a pair of squirrels that lived in the big oak tree outside the cottage. Squirrels are rare in Mussoorie though common enough down in the valley. This couple must have come up for the summer. They became quite friendly, and although they never got around to taking food from our hands, they were soon entering the house quite freely. The sitting room window opened directly on to the oak tree whose various denizens—ranging from stag beetles to small birds and even an acrobatic bat—took to darting in and out of the cottage at various times of the day or night.

Life at Maplewood was quite idyllic, and when Rakesh's baby brother, Suresh, came into the world, it seemed we were all set for a long period of domestic bliss; but at such times tragedy is often lurking just around the corner. Suresh was just over a year old when he contracted tetanus. Doctors and hospitals were of no avail. He suffered—as any child would from this terrible affliction—and left this world before he had a chance of getting to know it. His parents were broken-hearted. And I feared for Rakesh, for he wasn't a very healthy boy, and two of his cousins in the village had already succumbed to tuberculosis.

It was to be a difficult year for me. A criminal charge was brought against me for a slightly risque story I'd written for a Bombay magazine. I had to face trial in Bombay and this involved three journeys there over a period of a year and a half, before an irate but perceptive judge found the charges baseless and gave me an honourable acquittal.

It's the only time I've been involved with the law and I sincerely hope it is the last. Most cases drag on interminably, and the main beneficiaries are the lawyers. My trial would have been much longer had not the prosecutor died of a heart attack in the middle of the proceedings. His successor did not pursue it with the same vigour. His heart was not in it. The whole issue had started with a complaint by a local politician, and when he lost interest so did the prosecution. Nevertheless the trial, once begun, had to be seen through. The defence (organized by the concerned magazine) marshalled its witnesses (which included Nissim Ezekiel and the Marathi playwright Vijay Tendulkar). I made a short speech which couldn't have been very memorable as I have forgotten it! And everyone, including the judge, was bored with the whole business. After that, I steered clear of controversy publications. I have never set out to shock the world. Telling a meaningful story was all that really mattered. And that is still the case.

I was looking forward to continuing our idyllic existence in Maplewood, but it was not to be. The powers-that-be, in the shape of the Public Works Department (PWD), had decided to build a 'strategic' road just below the cottage and without any warning to us, all the trees in the vicinity were felled (including the friendly old oak) and the hillside was rocked by explosives and bludgeoned by bulldozers. I decided it was time to move. Prem and Chandra (Rakesh's mother) wanted to move too; not because of the road, but because they associated the house with the death of little Suresh, whose presence seemed to haunt every room, every corner of the cottage. His little cries of pain and suffering still echoed through the still hours of the night.

I rented rooms at the top of Landour, a good thousand feet higher up the mountain. Rakesh was now old enough to go to school, and every morning I would walk with him down to the little convent school near the clock tower. Prem would go to fetch him in the afternoon. The walk took us about half an hour, and on the way Rakesh would ask for a story and I would have to rack my brains in order to invent one. I am not the most inventive of writers, and fantastical plots are beyond me. My forte is observation, recollection and reflection. Small boys prefer action. So I invented a leopard who suffered from acute indigestion because he'd eaten one human too many and a belt buckle was causing an obstruction.

This went down quite well until Rakesh asked me how the leopard got around the problem of the victim's clothes.

'The secret,' I said, 'is to pounce on them when their trousers are off!'

Not the stuff of which great picture books are made, but then, I've never attempted to write stories for beginners. Red Riding Hood's granny-eating wolf always scared me as a small boy, and yet parents have always found it acceptable for toddlers. Possibly they feel grannies are expendable.

Mukesh was born around this time and Savitri (Dolly) a couple of years later. When Dolly grew older, she was annoyed at having been named Savitri (my choice), which is now considered very old fashioned; so we settled for Dolly. I can understand a child's dissatisfaction with given names.

My first name was Owen, which in Welsh means 'brave'. As I am not in the least brave, I have preferred not to use it. One given name and one surname should be enough.

When my granny said, 'But you should try to be brave, otherwise how will you survive in this cruel world?' I replied: 'Don't worry, I can run very fast.'

Not that I've ever had to do much running, except when I was pursued by a lissome Australian lady who thought I'd make a good obedient husband. It wasn't so much the lady I was running from, but the prospect of spending the rest of my life in some remote cattle station in the Australian outback. Anyone who has tried to drag me away from India has always met with stout resistance.

Up on the heights of Landour lived a motley crowd. My immediate neighbours included a Frenchwoman who played the sitar (very badly) all through the night; a Spanish lady with two husbands, one of whom practised acupuncture—rather ineffectively as far as he was concerned, for he seemed to be dying of some mysterious debilitating disease. The other came and went rather mysteriously, and finally ended up in Tihar

Jail, having been apprehended at Delhi airport carrying a large amount of contraband hashish.

Apart from these and a few other colourful characters, the area was inhabited by some very respectable people, retired brigadiers, air marshals and rear admirals, almost all of whom were busy writing their memoirs. I had to read or listen to extracts from their literary efforts. This was slow torture. A few years before, I had done a stint of editing for a magazine called *Imprint*. It had involved going through hundreds of badly written manuscripts, and in some cases (friends of the owner!) rewriting some of them for publication. One of life's joys had been to throw up that particular job, and now here I was, besieged by all the top brass of the Army, Navy and Air Force, each one determined that I should read, inwardly digest, improve, and if possible find a publisher for their outpourings. Thank goodness they were all retired. I could not be shot or court-martialled. But at least two of them set their wives upon me, and these intrepid ladies would turn up around noon with my 'homework'—typescripts to read and edit! There was no escape. My own writing was of no consequence to them. I told them that I was taking sitar lessons, but they disapproved, saying I was more suited to the tabla.

When Prem discovered a set of vacant rooms further down the Landour slope, close to the school and bazaar, I rented them without hesitation. This was Ivy Cottage. Come up and see me sometimes, but leave your manuscripts behind.

When we came to Ivy Cottage in 1980, we were six, Dolly having just been born. Now, twenty-four years later, we are twelve. I think that's a reasonable expansion. The increase has been brought about by Rakesh's marriage twelve years ago, and Mukesh's marriage two years ago. Both precipitated themselves into marriage when they were barely twenty, and both were lucky. Beena and Binita, who happen to be real sisters, have brightened and enlivened our lives with their happy, positive natures and the wonderful children they have brought into the world. More about them later.

Ivy Cottage has, on the whole, been kind to us, and particularly kind to me. Some houses like their occupants, others don't. Maplewood, set in the shadow of the hill, lacked a natural cheerfulness; there was a settled gloom about the place. The house at the top of Landour was too exposed to the elements to have any sort of character. The wind moaning in the deodars may have inspired the sitar player but it did nothing for my writing. I produced very little up there.

On the other hand, Ivy Cottage—especially my little room facing the sunrise—has been conducive to creative work. Novellas, poems, essays, children's stories, anthologies, have all come tumbling on to whatever sheets of paper happen to be nearest me. As I write by hand, I have only to grab for the nearest pad, loose sheet, page-proof or envelope whenever the muse takes hold of me; which is surprisingly often.

I came here when I was nearing fifty. Now I'm seventy, and instead of drying up, as some writers do in their later years, I find myself writing with as much ease and assurance as when I was twenty. And I enjoy writing. It's not a burdensome task. I may not have anything of earth-shattering significance to convey to the world, but in conveying my sentiments to you, dear readers, and in telling you something about my relationship with people and the natural world, I hope to bring a little pleasure and sunshine into your life.

Life isn't a bed of roses, not for any of us, and I have never had the comforts or luxuries that wealth can provide. But here I am, doing my own thing, in my own time and my own way. What more can I ask of life? Give me a big cash prize and I'd still be here. I happen to like the view from my window. And I like to have Gautam coming up to me, patting me on the tummy, and telling me that I'll make a good goalkeeper one day.

It's a Sunday morning, as I come to the conclusion of this chapter. There's bedlam in the house. Siddharth's football keeps smashing against the front door. Shrishti is practising her dance routine in the back verandah. Gautam has cut his finger and is trying his best to bandage it with Sellotape. He is, of course, the youngest of Rakesh's three musketeers, and probably the most independent-minded. Siddharth, now ten, is restless, never quite able to expend all his energy. 'Does not pay enough attention,' says his teacher. It must be hard for anyone to pay attention in a class of sixty! How does the poor teacher pay attention?

If you, dear reader, have any ambitions to be a writer, you must first rid yourself of any notion that perfect peace and quiet is the first requirement. There is no such thing as perfect peace and quiet except perhaps in a monastery or a cave in the mountains. And what would you write about, living in a cave? One should be able to write in a train, a bus, a bullock cart, in good weather or bad, on a park bench or in the middle of a noisy classroom.

Of course, the best place is the sun-drenched desk right next to my bed. It isn't always sunny here, but on a good day like this, it's ideal. The children are getting ready for school, dogs are barking in the street, and down near the water tap there's an altercation between two women with empty buckets, the tap having dried up. But these are all background noises and will subside in due course. They are not directed at me.

Hello! Here's Atish, Mukesh's little ten-month old infant, crawling over the rug, curious to know why I'm sitting on the edge of my bed scribbling away, when I should be playing with him. So I shall play with him for five minutes and then come back to this page. Giving him my time is important. After all, I won't be around when he grows up.

Half an hour later. Atish soon tired of playing with me, but meanwhile Gautam had absconded with my pen. When I asked him to return it, he asked, 'Why don't you get a computer? Then we can play games on it.'

'My pen is faster than any computer,' I tell him, 'I wrote three pages this morning without getting out of bed. And yesterday I wrote two pages sitting under Billoo's chestnut tree.'

'Until a chestnut fell on your head,' says Gautam, 'Did it hurt?'

'Only a little,' I said, putting on a brave front.

He had saved the chestnut and now he showed it to me. The smooth brown horse-chestnut shone in the sunlight.

'Let's stick it in the ground,' I said. 'Then in the spring a chestnut tree will come up.'

So we went outside and planted the chestnut on a plot of wasteland. Hopefully a small tree will burst through the earth at about the time this little book is published.

THE STORY OF MADHU

I met little Madhu several years ago, when I lived alone in an obscure town near the Himalayan foothills. I was in my late twenties then, and my outlook on life was still quite romantic; the cynicism that was to come with the thirties had not yet set in.

I preferred the solitude of the small district town to the kind of social life I might have found in the cities; and in my books, my writing and the surrounding hills, there was enough for my pleasure and occupation.

On summer mornings I would often sit beneath an old mango tree, with a notebook or a sketch pad on my knees. The house which I had rented (for a very nominal sum) stood on the outskirts of the town; and a large tank and a few poor houses could be seen from the garden wall. A narrow public pathway passed under the low wall.

One morning, while I sat beneath the mango tree, I saw a young girl of about nine, wearing torn clothes, darting about on the pathway and along the high banks of the tank.

Sometimes she stopped to look at me; and, when I showed that I noticed her, she felt encouraged and gave me a shy, fleeting smile. The next day I discovered her leaning over the garden wall, following my actions as I paced up and down on the grass.

In a few days an acquaintance had been formed. I began to take the girl's presence for granted, and even to look for her; and she, in turn, would linger about on the pathway until she saw me come out of the house.

One day, as she passed the gate, I called her to me. 'What is your name?' I asked. 'And where do you live?'

'Madhu,' she said, brushing back her long untidy black hair and smiling at me from large black eyes. She pointed across the road: 'I live with my grandmother.'

'Is she very old?' I asked.

Madhu nodded confidingly and whispered: 'A hundred years…'

'We will never be that old,' I said. She was very slight and frail, like a flower growing in a rock, vulnerable to wind and rain.

I discovered later that the old lady was not her grandmother but a childless woman who had found the baby girl on the banks of the tank. Madhu's real parentage was unknown; but the wizened old woman had, out of compassion, brought up the child as her own.

My gate once entered, Madhu included the garden in her circle of activities. She was there every morning, chasing butterflies, stalking squirrels and mynahs, her voice brimming with laughter, her slight figure flitting about between the trees.

Sometimes, but not often, I gave her a toy or a new dress; and one day she put aside her shyness and brought me a present of a nosegay, made up of marigolds and wild blue cotton flowers.

'For you,' she said, and put the flowers in my lap.

'They are very beautiful,' I said, picking out the brightest marigold and putting it in her hair. 'But they are not as beautiful as you.'

Over a year passed before I began to take more than a mildly patronizing interest in Madhu.

It occurred to me after some time that she should be taught to read and write, and I asked a local teacher to give her lessons in the garden for an hour every day. She clapped her hands with pleasure at the prospect of what was to be for her a fascinating new game.

In a few weeks Madhu was surprising us with her capacity for absorbing knowledge. She always came to me to repeat the lessons of the day, and pestered me with questions on a variety of subjects. How big was the world? And were the stars really like our world? Or were they the sons and daughters of the Sun and the Moon?

My interest in Madhu deepened, and my life, so empty till then, became imbued with a new purpose. As she sat on the grass beside me, reading aloud, or listening to me with a look of complete trust and belief, all the love that had been lying dormant in me during my years of self-exile surfaced in a sudden surge of tenderness.

Three years glided away imperceptibly, and at the age of thirteen Madhu was on the verge of blossoming into a woman. I began to feel a certain responsibility towards her.

It was dangerous, I knew, to allow a child so pretty to live almost alone and unprotected, and to run unrestrained about the grounds. And in a censorious society she would be made to suffer if she spent too much time in my company.

She could see no need for any separation; but I decided to send her to a mission school in the next district, where I could visit her from time to time.

'But why?' said Madhu. 'I can learn more from you, and from the teacher who comes. I am so happy here.'

'You will meet other girls and make many friends,' I told her. 'I will come to see you. And, when you come home, we will be even happier. It is good that you should go.'

It was the middle of June, a hot and oppressive month in the Siwaliks. Madhu had expressed her readiness to go to school, and when, one evening, I did not see her as usual in the garden, I thought nothing of it; but the next day I was informed that she had fever and could not leave the house.

Illness was something Madhu had not known before, and for this reason I felt afraid. I hurried down the path which led to the old woman's cottage. It seemed strange that I had never once entered it during my long friendship with Madhu.

It was a humble mud hut, the ceiling just high enough to enable me to stand upright, the room dark but clean. Madhu was lying on a string cot exhausted by fever, her eyes closed, her long hair unkempt, one small hand hanging over the side.

It struck me then how little, during all this time, I had thought of her physical comforts. There was no chair; I knelt down, and took her hand in mine. I knew, from the fierce heat of her body, that she was seriously ill.

She recognized my touch, and a smile passed across her face before she opened her eyes. She held on to my hand, then laid it across her cheek.

I looked round the little room in which she had grown up. It had scarcely an article of furniture apart from two string cots, on one of which the old woman sat and watched us, her white, wizened head nodding like a puppet's.

In a corner lay Madhu's little treasures. I recognized among them the presents which during the past four years I had given her. She had kept everything. On her dark arm she still wore a small piece of ribbon which I had playfully tied there about a year ago. She had given her heart, even before she was conscious of possessing one, to a stranger unworthy of the gift.

As the evening drew on, a gust of wind blew open the door of the dark room, and a gleam of sunshine streamed in, lighting up a portion of the wall. It was the time when every evening she would join me under the mango tree. She had been quiet for almost an hour, and now a slight pressure of her hand drew my eyes back to her face.

'What will we do now?' she said. 'When will you send me to school?'

'Not for a long time. First you must get well and strong. That is all that matters.' She didn't seem to hear me. I think she knew she was dying, but she did not resent its happening.

'Who will read to you under the tree?' she went on. 'Who will look after you?' she asked, with the solicitude of a grown woman.

'You will, Madhu. You are grown up now. There will be no one else to look after me.'

The old woman was standing at my shoulder. A hundred years—and little Madhu was slipping away. The woman took Madhu's hand from mine, and laid it gently down. I sat by the cot a little longer, and then I rose to go, all the loneliness in the world pressing upon my heart.

THE BLUE UMBRELLA

I

'Neelu! Neelu!' cried Binya.

She scrambled barefoot over the rocks, ran over the short summer grass, up and over the brow of the hill, all the time calling 'Neelu, Neelu!' Neelu—Blue—was the name of the blue-grey cow. The other cow, which was white, was called Gori, meaning Fair One. They were fond of wandering off on their own, down to the stream or into the pine forest, and sometimes they came back by themselves and sometimes they stayed away—almost deliberately, it seemed to Binya.

If the cows didn't come home at the right time, Binya would be sent to fetch them. Sometimes her brother, Bijju, went with her, but these days he was busy preparing for his exams and didn't have time to help with the cows.

Binya liked being on her own, and sometimes she allowed the cows to lead her into some distant valley, and then they would all be late coming home. The cows preferred having Binya with them because she let them wander. Bijju pulled them by their tails if they went too far.

Binya belonged to the mountains, to this part of the Himalaya known as Garhwal. Dark forests and lonely hilltops held no terrors for her. It was only when she was in the market town, jostled by the crowds in the bazaar, that she felt rather nervous and lost. The town, five miles from the village, was also a pleasure resort for tourists from all over India.

Binya was probably ten. She may have been nine or even eleven, she couldn't be sure because no one in the village kept birthdays; but her mother told her she'd been born during a winter when the snow had come up to the windows, and that was just over ten years ago, wasn't it? Two years later, her father had died, but his passing had made no difference to their way of life. They had three tiny terraced fields on the side of the mountain, and they grew potatoes, onions, ginger, beans, mustard and maize—not enough to sell in the town, but enough to live on.

Like most mountain girls, Binya was quite sturdy, fair of skin, with pink cheeks and dark eyes, and her black hair tied in a pigtail. She wore pretty glass bangles on her wrists, and a necklace of glass beads. From the necklace hung a leopard's claw. It was a lucky charm, and Binya always wore it. Bijju had one, too, only his was attached to a string.

Binya's full name was Binyadevi, and Bijju's real name was Vijay, but everyone called them Binya and Bijju. Binya was two years younger than her brother.

She had stopped calling for Neelu; she had heard the cowbells tinkling, and knew the cows hadn't gone far. Singing to herself, she walked over fallen pine needles into the forest glade on the spur of the hill. She heard voices, laughter, the clatter of plates and cups, and stepping through the trees, she came upon a party of picnickers.

They were holidaymakers from the plains. The women were dressed in bright saris, the men wore light summer shirts and the children had pretty new clothes. Binya, standing in the shadows between the trees, went unnoticed; for some time she watched the picnickers, admiring their clothes, listening to their unfamiliar accents and gazing rather hungrily at the sight of all their food. And then her gaze came to rest on a bright blue umbrella, a frilly thing for women, which lay open on the grass beside its owner.

Now Binya had seen umbrellas before, and her mother had a big black umbrella which nobody used anymore because the field rats had eaten holes in it, but this was the first time Binya had seen such a small, dainty, colourful umbrella and she fell in love with it. The umbrella was like a flower, a great blue flower that had sprung up on the dry brown hillside.

She moved forward a few paces so that she could see the umbrella better. As she came out of the shadows into the sunlight, the picnickers saw her.

'Hello, look who's here!' exclaimed the older of the two women. 'A little village girl!'

'Isn't she pretty?' remarked the other. 'But how torn and dirty her clothes are!'

It did not seem to bother them that Binya could hear and understand everything they said about her.

'They're very poor in the hills,' said one of the men.

'Then let's give her something to eat.' And the older woman beckoned to Binya to come closer.

Hesitantly, nervously, Binya approached the group.

Normally she would have turned and fled, but the attraction was the pretty blue umbrella. It had cast a spell over her, drawing her forward almost against her will.

'What's that on her neck?' asked the younger woman.

'A necklace of sorts.'

'It's a pendant—see, there's a claw hanging from it!'

'It's a tiger's claw,' said the man beside her. (He had never seen a tiger's claw.) 'A lucky charm. These people wear them to keep away evil spirits.' He looked to Binya for confirmation, but Binya said nothing.

'Oh, I want one too!' said the woman, who was obviously his wife.

'You can't get them in shops.'

'Buy hers, then. Give her two or three rupees, she's sure to need the money.'

The man, looking slightly embarrassed but anxious to please his young wife, produced a two-rupee note and offered it to Binya, indicating that he wanted the pendant in exchange. Binya put her hand to the necklace, half afraid that the excited woman would snatch it away from her. Solemnly, she shook her head.

The man then showed her a five-rupee note, but again Binya shook her head.

'How silly she is!' exclaimed the young woman.

'It may not be hers to sell,' said the man. 'But I'll try again. How much do you want—what can we give you?' And he waved his hand towards the picnic things scattered about on the grass.

Without any hesitation Binya pointed to the umbrella.

'My umbrella!' exclaimed the young woman. 'She wants my umbrella. What cheek!'

'Well, you want her pendant, don't you?'

'That's different.'

'Is it?'

The man and his wife were beginning to quarrel with each other.

'I'll ask her to go away,' said the older woman.

'We're making such fools of ourselves.'

'But I want the pendant!' cried the other, petulantly.

And then, on an impulse, she picked up the umbrella and held it out to Binya.

'Here, take the umbrella!'

Binya removed her necklace and held it out to the young woman, who immediately placed it around her own neck. Then Binya took the umbrella and held it up. It did not look so small in her hands; in fact, it was just the right size.

She had forgotten about the picnickers, who were busy examining the pendant. She turned the blue umbrella this way and that, looked through the bright blue silk at the pulsating sun, and then, still keeping it open, turned and disappeared into the forest glade.

II

Binya seldom closed the blue umbrella. Even when she had it in the house, she left it lying open in a corner of the room. Sometimes, Bijju snapped it shut, complaining that it got in the way. She would open it again a little later. It wasn't beautiful when it was closed.

Whenever Binya went out—whether it was to graze the cows, or fetch water from the spring, or carry milk to the little tea shop on the Tehri road—she took the umbrella with her. That patch of sky blue silk could always be seen on the hillside.

Old Ram Bharosa (Ram the Trustworthy) kept the tea shop on the Tehri road. It was a dusty, un-metalled road. Once a day, the Tehri bus stopped near his shop and passengers got down to sip hot tea or drink a glass of curd. He kept a few bottles of Coca-Cola too, but as there was no ice, the bottles got hot in the sun and so were seldom opened. He also kept sweets and toffees, and when Binya or Bijju had a few coins to spare, they would spend them at the shop. It was only a mile from the village.

Ram Bharosa was astonished to see Binya's blue umbrella.

'What have you there, Binya?' he asked.

Binya gave the umbrella a twirl and smiled at Ram Bharosa. She was always ready with her smile, and would willingly have lent it to anyone who was feeling unhappy.

'That's a lady's umbrella,' said Ram Bharosa. 'That's only for memsahibs. Where did you get it?'

'Someone gave it to me—for my necklace.'

'You exchanged it for your lucky claw!'

Binya nodded.

'But what do you need it for? The sun isn't hot enough, and it isn't meant for the rain. It's just a pretty thing for rich ladies to play with!'

Binya nodded and smiled again. Ram Bharosa was quite right; it was just a beautiful plaything. And that was exactly why she had fallen in love with it.

'I have an idea,' said the shopkeeper. 'It's no use to you, that umbrella. Why not sell it to me? I'll give you five rupees for it.'

'It's worth fifteen,' said Binya.

'Well, then, I'll give you ten.'

Binya laughed and shook her head.

'Twelve rupees?' said Ram Bharosa, but without much hope.

Binya placed a five-paise coin on the counter.

'I came for a toffee,' she said.

Ram Bharosa pulled at his drooping whiskers, gave Binya a wry look and placed a toffee in the palm of her hand. He watched Binya as she walked away along the dusty road. The blue umbrella held him fascinated, and he stared after it until it was out of sight.

The villagers used this road to go to the market town. Some used the bus, a few rode on mules and most people walked. Today, everyone on the road turned their heads to stare at the girl with the bright blue umbrella.

Binya sat down under the shade of a pine tree. The umbrella, still open, lay beside her. She cradled her head in her arms, and presently she dozed off. It was that kind of day, sleepily warm and summery.

And while she slept, a wind sprang up.

It came quietly, swishing gently through the trees, humming

softly. Then it was joined by other random gusts, bustling over the tops of the mountains. The trees shook their heads and came to life. The wind fanned Binya's cheeks. The umbrella stirred on the grass.

The wind grew stronger, picking up dead leaves and sending them spinning and swirling through the air. It got into the umbrella and began to drag it over the grass. Suddenly it lifted the umbrella and carried it about six feet from the sleeping girl. The sound woke Binya.

She was on her feet immediately, and then she was leaping down the steep slope. But just as she was within reach of the umbrella, the wind picked it up again and carried it further downhill.

Binya set off in pursuit. The wind was in a wicked, playful mood. It would leave the umbrella alone for a few moments but as soon as Binya came near, it would pick up the umbrella again and send it bouncing, floating, dancing away from her.

The hill grew steeper. Binya knew that after twenty yards it would fall away in a precipice. She ran faster. And the wind ran with her, ahead of her, and the blue umbrella stayed up with the wind.

A fresh gust picked it up and carried it to the very edge of the cliff. There it balanced for a few seconds, before toppling over, out of sight.

Binya ran to the edge of the cliff. Going down on her hands and knees, she peered down the cliff face. About a hundred feet below, a small stream rushed between great boulders. Hardly anything grew on the cliff face—just a few stunted bushes, and, halfway down, a wild cherry tree growing crookedly out of the rocks and hanging across the chasm. The umbrella had stuck in the cherry tree.

Binya didn't hesitate. She may have been timid with

strangers, but she was at home on a hillside. She stuck her bare leg over the edge of the cliff and began climbing down. She kept her face to the hillside, feeling her way with her feet, only changing her handhold when she knew her feet were secure. Sometimes she held on to the thorny bilberry bushes, but she did not trust the other plants, which came away very easily.

Loose stones rattled down the cliff. Once on their way, the stones did not stop until they reached the bottom of the hill; and they took other stones with them, so that there was soon a cascade of stones, and Binya had to be very careful not to start a landslide.

As agile as a mountain goat, she did not take more than five minutes to reach the crooked cherry tree. But the most difficult task remained—she had to crawl along the trunk of the tree, which stood out at right angles from the cliff. Only by doing this could she reach the trapped umbrella.

Binya felt no fear when climbing trees. She was proud of the fact that she could climb them as well as Bijju. Gripping the rough cherry bark with her toes, and using her knees as leverage, she crawled along the trunk of the projecting tree until she was almost within reach of the umbrella. She noticed with dismay that the blue cloth was torn in a couple of places.

She looked down, and it was only then that she felt afraid. She was right over the chasm, balanced precariously about eighty feet above the boulder-strewn stream. Looking down, she felt quite dizzy. Her hands shook, and the tree shook too. If she slipped now, there was only one direction in which she could fall—down, down, into the depths of that dark and shadowy ravine.

There was only one thing to do; concentrate on the patch of blue just a couple of feet away from her. She did not look down or up, but straight ahead, and willing herself forward, she managed to reach the umbrella.

She could not crawl back with it in her hands. So, after dislodging it from the forked branch in which it had stuck, she let it fall, still open, into the ravine below.

Cushioned by the wind, the umbrella floated serenely downwards, landing in a thicket of nettles.

Binya crawled back along the trunk of the cherry tree. Twenty minutes later, she emerged from the nettle clump, her precious umbrella held aloft. She had nettle stings all over her legs, but she was hardly aware of the smarting. She was as immune to nettles as Bijju was to bees.

III

About four years previously, Bijju had knocked a hive out of an oak tree, and had been badly stung on the face and legs. It had been a painful experience. But now, if a bee stung him, he felt nothing at all—he had been immunized for life!

He was on his way home from school. It was two o'clock and he hadn't eaten since six in the morning. Fortunately, the kingora bushes—the bilberries—were in fruit, and already Bijju's lips were stained purple with the juice of the wild, sour fruit.

He didn't have any money to spend at Ram Bharosa's shop, but he stopped there anyway to look at the sweets in their glass jars.

'And what will you have today?' asked Ram Bharosa.

'No money,' said Bijju.

'You can pay me later.'

Bijju shook his head. Some of his friends had taken sweets on credit, and at the end of the month they had found they'd eaten more sweets than they could possibly pay for! As a result, they'd had to hand over to Ram Bharosa some of their most treasured possessions—such as a curved knife for cutting grass or a small hand-axe or a jar for pickles or a pair of earrings—and these had become the shopkeeper's possessions and were kept by him or sold in his shop.

Ram Bharosa had set his heart on having Binya's blue umbrella, and so naturally he was anxious to give credit to either of the children, but so far neither had fallen into the trap.

Bijju moved on, his mouth full of kingora berries. Halfway home, he saw Binya with the cows. It was late evening, and the sun had gone down, but Binya still had the umbrella open. The two small rents had been stitched up by her mother.

Bijju gave his sister a handful of berries. She handed him the umbrella while she ate the berries.

'You can have the umbrella until we get home,' she said. It was her way of rewarding Bijju for bringing her the wild fruit.

Calling 'Neelu! Gori!' Binya and Bijju set out for home, followed at some distance by the cows.

It was dark before they reached the village, but Bijju still had the umbrella open.

◆

Most of the people in the village were a little envious of Binya's blue umbrella. No one else had ever possessed one like it. The schoolmaster's wife thought it was quite wrong for a poor cultivator's daughter to have such a fine umbrella while she, a second-class BA, had to make do with an ordinary black one. Her husband offered to have their old umbrella dyed blue; she gave him a scornful look, and loved him a little less than before. The pujari, who looked after the temple, announced that he would buy a multi-coloured umbrella the next time he was in the town. A few days later, he returned looking annoyed and grumbling that they weren't available except in Delhi. Most people consoled themselves by saying that Binya's pretty umbrella wouldn't keep out the rain, if it rained heavily;

that it would shrivel in the sun, if the sun was fierce; that it would collapse in the wind, if the wind was strong; that it would attract lightning, if lightning fell near it; and that it would prove unlucky, if there was any ill luck going about. Secretly, everyone admired it.

Unlike the adults, the children didn't have to pretend. They were full of praise for the umbrella. It was so light, so pretty, so bright a blue! And it was just the right size for Binya. They knew that if they said nice things about the umbrella, Binya would smile and give it to them to hold for a little while—just a very little while!

Soon it was the time of the monsoon. Big black clouds kept piling up, and thunder rolled over the hills.

Binya sat on the hillside all afternoon, waiting for the rain. As soon as the first big drop of rain came down, she raised the umbrella over her head. More drops, big ones, came pattering down. She could see them through the umbrella silk, as they broke against the cloth.

And then there was a cloudburst, and it was like standing under a waterfall. The umbrella wasn't really a rain umbrella, but it held up bravely. Only Binya's feet got wet. Rods of rain fell around her in a curtain of shivered glass.

Everywhere on the hillside people were scurrying for shelter. Some made for a charcoal burner's hut, others for a mule-shed, or Ram Bharosa's shop. Binya was the only one who didn't run. This was what she'd been waiting for—rain on her umbrella—and she wasn't in a hurry to go home. She didn't mind getting her feet wet. The cows didn't mind getting wet either.

Presently, she found Bijju sheltering in a cave. He would have enjoyed getting wet, but he had his schoolbooks with him and he couldn't afford to let them get spoilt. When he saw Binya, he came out of the cave and shared the umbrella. He was a head taller than his sister, so he had to hold the umbrella for her, while she held his books.

The cows had been left far behind.

'Neelu, Neelu!' called Binya.

'Gori!' called Bijju.

When their mother saw them sauntering home through the driving rain, she called out: 'Binya! Bijju! Hurry up, and bring the cows in! What are you doing out there in the rain?'

'Just testing the umbrella,' said Bijju.

IV

The rains set in, and the sun only made brief appearances. The hills turned a lush green. Ferns sprang up on walls and tree trunks. Giant lilies reared up like leopards from the tall grass. A white mist coiled and uncoiled as it floated up from the valley. It was a beautiful season, except for the leeches.

Every day, Binya came home with a couple of leeches fastened to the flesh of her bare legs. They fell off by themselves just as soon as they'd had their thimbleful of blood, but you didn't know they were on you until they fell off, and then, later, the skin became very sore and itchy. Some of the older people still believed that to be bled by leeches was a remedy for various ailments. Whenever Ram Bharosa had a headache, he applied a leech to his throbbing temple.

Three days of incessant rain had flooded out a number of small animals who lived in holes in the ground. Binya's mother suddenly found the roof full of field rats. She had to drive them out; they ate too much of her stored-up wheat flour and rice. Bijju liked lifting up large rocks to disturb the scorpions who were sleeping beneath. And snakes came out to bask in the sun.

Binya had just crossed the small stream at the bottom of the hill when she saw something gliding out of the bushes and coming towards her. It was a long black snake. A clatter of loose stones frightened it. Seeing the girl in its way, it rose up, hissing, prepared to strike. The forked tongue darted out, the venomous head lunged at Binya.

Binya's umbrella was open as usual. She thrust it forward, between herself and the snake, and the snake's hard snout thudded twice against the strong silk of the umbrella. The reptile then turned and slithered away over the wet rocks, disappearing into a clump of ferns.

Binya forgot about the cows and ran all the way home to tell her mother how she had been saved by the umbrella. Bijju had to put away his books and go out to fetch the cows. He carried a stout stick, in case he met with any snakes.

◆

First the summer sun, and now the endless rain, meant that the umbrella was beginning to fade a little. From a bright blue it had changed to a light blue. But it was still a pretty thing, and tougher than it looked, and Ram Bharosa still desired it. He did not want to sell it; he wanted to *own* it. He was probably the richest man in the area—so why shouldn't he have a blue umbrella? Not a day passed without his getting a glimpse of Binya and the umbrella; and the more he saw the umbrella, the more he wanted it.

The schools closed during the monsoon, but this didn't mean that Bijju could sit at home doing nothing. Neelu and Gori were providing more milk than was required at home, so Binya's mother was able to sell a kilo of milk every day: half a kilo to the schoolmaster, and half a kilo (at reduced rate) to the temple pujari. Bijju had to deliver the milk every morning.

Ram Bharosa had asked Bijju to work in his shop during the holidays, but Bijju didn't have time—he had to help his mother with the ploughing and the transplanting of the rice seedlings. So Ram Bharosa employed a boy from the next village, a boy called Rajaram. He did all the washing-up, and ran various errands. He went to the same school as Bijju, but the two boys were not friends.

One day, as Binya passed the shop, twirling her blue umbrella, Rajaram noticed that his employer gave a deep sigh and began muttering to himself.

'What's the matter, Babuji?' asked the boy.

'Oh, nothing,' said Ram Bharosa. 'It's just a sickness that has come upon me. And it's all due to that girl Binya and her wretched umbrella.'

'Why, what has she done to you?'

'Refused to sell me her umbrella! There's pride for you. And I offered her ten rupees.'

'Perhaps, if you gave her twelve…'

'But it isn't new any longer. It isn't worth eight rupees now. All the same, I'd like to have it.'

'You wouldn't make a profit on it,' said Rajaram.

'It's not the profit I'm after, wretch! It's the thing itself. It's the beauty of it!'

'And what would you do with it, Babuji? You don't visit anyone—you're seldom out of your shop. Of what use would it be to you?'

'Of what use is a poppy in a cornfield? Of what use is a rainbow? Of what use are you, numbskull? Wretch! I, too, have a soul. I want the umbrella, because—because I want its beauty to be mine!'

Rajaram put the kettle on to boil, began dusting the counter, all the time muttering: 'I'm as useful as an umbrella,' and then, after a short period of intense thought, said: 'What will you give me, Babuji, if I get the umbrella for you?'

'What do you mean?' asked the old man.

'You know what I mean. What will you give me?'

'You mean to steal it, don't you, you wretch? What a delightful child you are! I'm glad you're not my son or my enemy. But look, everyone will know it has been stolen, and then how will I be able to show off with it?'

'You will have to gaze upon it in secret,' said Rajaram with a chuckle. 'Or take it into Tehri, and have it coloured red! That's your problem. But tell me, Babuji, do you want it badly enough to pay me three rupees for stealing it without being seen?'

Ram Bharosa gave the boy a long, sad look. 'You're a sharp boy,' he said. 'You'll come to a bad end. I'll give you two rupees.'

'Three,' said the boy.

'Two,' said the old man.

'You don't really want it, I can see that,' said the boy.

'Wretch!' said the old man. 'Evil one! Darkener of my doorstep! Fetch me the umbrella, and I'll give you three rupees.'

V

Binya was in the forest glade where she had first seen the umbrella. No one came there for picnics during the monsoon. The grass was always wet and the pine needles were slippery underfoot. The tall trees shut out the light, and poisonous-looking mushrooms, orange and purple, sprang up everywhere. But it was a good place for porcupines, who seemed to like the mushrooms, and Binya was searching for porcupine quills.

The hill people didn't think much of porcupine quills, but far away in southern India, the quills were valued as charms and sold at a rupee each. So Ram Bharosa paid a tenth of a rupee for each quill brought to him, and he in turn sold the quills at a profit to a trader from the plains.

Binya had already found five quills, and she knew there

would be more in the long grass. For once, she had put her umbrella down. She had to put it aside if she was to search the ground thoroughly.

It was Rajaram's chance.

He'd been following Binya for some time, concealing himself behind trees and rocks, creeping closer whenever she became absorbed in her search. He was anxious that she should not see him and be able to recognize him later.

He waited until Binya had wandered some distance from the umbrella. Then, running forward at a crouch, he seized the open umbrella and dashed off with it.

But Rajaram had very big feet. Binya heard his heavy footsteps and turned just in time to see him as he disappeared between the trees. She cried out, dropped the porcupine quills, and gave chase.

Binya was swift and sure-footed, but Rajaram had a long stride. All the same, he made the mistake of running downhill. A long-legged person is much faster going uphill than down. Binya reached the edge of the forest glade in time to see the thief scrambling down the path to the stream. He had closed the umbrella so that it would not hinder his flight.

Binya was beginning to gain on the boy. He kept to the path, while she simply slid and leapt down the steep hillside. Near the bottom of the hill the path began to straighten out, and it was here that the long-legged boy began to forge ahead again.

Bijju was coming home from another direction. He had a bundle of sticks which he'd collected for the kitchen fire. As he reached the path, he saw Binya rushing down the hill as though all the mountain spirits in Garhwal were after her.

'What's wrong?' he called. 'Why are you running?'

Binya paused only to point at the fleeing Rajaram.

'My umbrella!' she cried. 'He has stolen it!'

Bijju dropped his bundle of sticks, and ran after his sister. When he reached her side, he said, 'I'll soon catch him!' and went sprinting away over the lush green grass. He was fresh, and he was soon well ahead of Binya and gaining on the thief.

Rajaram was crossing the shallow stream when Bijju caught up with him. Rajaram was the taller boy, but Bijju was much stronger. He flung himself at the thief, caught him by the legs, and brought him down in the water. Rajaram got to his feet and tried to drag himself away, but Bijju still had him by a leg. Rajaram overbalanced and came down with a great splash. He had let the umbrella fall. It began to float away on the current. Just then Binya arrived, flushed and breathless, and went dashing into the stream after the umbrella.

Meanwhile, a tremendous fight was taking place. Locked in fierce combat, the two boys swayed together on a rock, tumbled on to the sand, rolled over and over the pebbled bank until they were again thrashing about in the shallows of the stream. The magpies, bulbuls and other birds were disturbed, and flew away with cries of alarm.

Covered with mud, gasping and spluttering, the boys groped for each other in the water. After five minutes of frenzied struggle, Bijju emerged victorious.

Rajaram lay flat on his back on the sand, exhausted, while Bijju sat astride him, pinning him down with his arms and legs.

'Let me get up!' gasped Rajaram. 'Let me go—I don't want your useless umbrella!'

'Then why did you take it?' demanded Bijju. 'Come on—tell me why!'

'It was that skinflint Ram Bharosa,' said Rajaram.

'He told me to get it for him. He said if I didn't fetch it, I'd lose my job.'

By early October, the rains were coming to an end. The leeches disappeared. The ferns turned yellow, and the sunlight on the green hills was mellow and golden, like the limes on the small tree in front of Binya's home. Bijju's days were happy ones as he came home from school, munching on roasted corn. Binya's umbrella had turned a pale milky blue, and was patched in several places, but it was still the prettiest umbrella in the village, and she still carried it with her wherever she went.

The cold, cruel winter wasn't far off, but somehow October seems longer than other months, because it is a kind month: the grass is good to be upon, the breeze is warm and gentle and pine-scented. That October, everyone seemed contented—everyone, that is, except Ram Bharosa.

The old man had by now given up all hope of ever possessing Binya's umbrella. He wished he had never set eyes on it. Because of the umbrella, he had suffered the tortures of greed, the despair of loneliness. Because of the umbrella, people had stopped coming to his shop!

Ever since it had become known that Ram Bharosa had tried to have the umbrella stolen, the village people had turned against him. They stopped trusting the old man; instead of buying their soap and tea and matches from his shop, they preferred to walk an extra mile to the shops near the Tehri bus stand. Who would have dealings with a man who had sold his soul for an umbrella? The children taunted him, twisted his name around. From 'Ram the Trustworthy' he became 'Trusty Umbrella Thief'.

The old man sat alone in his empty shop, listening to the eternal hissing of his kettle and wondering if anyone would ever again step in for a glass of tea. Ram Bharosa had lost his own appetite, and ate and drank very little. There was no money coming in. He had his savings in a bank in Tehri, but it was a terrible thing to have to dip into them! To save money, he had dismissed the blundering Rajaram. So he was left without any company. The roof leaked and the wind got in through the corrugated tin sheets, but Ram Bharosa didn't care.

Bijju and Binya passed his shop almost every day. Bijju went by with a loud but tuneless whistle. He was one of the world's whistlers; cares rested lightly on his shoulders. But, strangely enough, Binya crept quietly past the shop, looking the other way, almost as though she was in some way responsible for the misery of Ram Bharosa.

She kept reasoning with herself, telling herself that the umbrella was her very own, and that she couldn't help it if others were jealous of it. But had she loved the umbrella too much? Had it mattered more to her than people mattered? She couldn't help feeling that, in a small way, she was the cause of the sad look on Ram Bharosa's face ('His face is a yard long,' said Bijju) and the ruinous condition of his shop. It was all due to his own greed, no doubt, but she didn't want him to feel too bad about what he'd done, because it made her feel bad about herself; and so she closed the umbrella whenever she came near the shop, opening it again only when she was out of sight.

One day towards the end of October, when she had ten paise in her pocket, she entered the shop and asked the old man for a toffee.

She was Ram Bharosa's first customer in almost two weeks. He looked suspiciously at the girl. Had she come to taunt him, to flaunt the umbrella in his face? She had placed her coin on the counter. Perhaps it was a bad coin. Ram Bharosa picked it up and bit it; he held it up to the light; he rang it on the ground. It was a good coin. He gave Binya the toffee.

Binya had already left the shop when Ram Bharosa saw the closed umbrella lying on his counter. There it was, the blue umbrella he had always wanted, within his grasp at last! He had only to hide it at the back of his shop, and no one would know that he had it, no one could prove that Binya had left it behind.

He stretched out his trembling, bony hand, and took the umbrella by the handle. He pressed it open. He stood beneath it, in the dark shadows of his shop, where no sun or rain could ever touch it.

'But I'm never in the sun or in the rain,' he said aloud. 'Of what use is an umbrella to me?'

And he hurried outside and ran after Binya.

'Binya, Binya!' he shouted. 'Binya, you've left your umbrella behind!'

He wasn't used to running, but he caught up with her and held out the umbrella, saying, 'You forgot it—the umbrella!'

In that moment it belonged to both of them.

But Binya didn't take the umbrella. She shook her head and said, 'You keep it. I don't need it anymore.'

'But it's such a pretty umbrella!' protested Ram Bharosa. 'It's the best umbrella in the village.'

'I know,' said Binya. 'But an umbrella isn't everything.'

And she left the old man holding the umbrella, and went tripping down the road, and there was nothing between her and the bright blue sky.

VI

Well, now that Ram Bharosa has the blue umbrella—a gift from Binya, as he tells everyone—he is sometimes persuaded to go out into the sun or the rain, and as a result he looks much healthier. Sometimes he uses the umbrella to chase away pigs or goats. It is always left open outside the shop, and anyone who wants to borrow it may do so; and so in a way it has become everyone's umbrella. It is faded and patchy, but it is still the best umbrella in the village.

People are visiting Ram Bharosa's shop again. Whenever Bijju or Binya stop for a cup of tea, he gives them a little extra milk or sugar. They like their tea sweet and milky.

A few nights ago, a bear visited Ram Bharosa's shop. There had been snow on the higher ranges of the Himalaya, and the bear had been finding it difficult to obtain food; so it had come lower down, to see what it could pick up near the village. That night it scrambled on to the tin roof of Ram Bharosa's shop, and made off with a huge pumpkin which had been ripening on the roof. But in climbing off the roof, the bear had lost a claw.

Next morning Ram Bharosa found the claw just outside the door of his shop. He picked it up and put it in his pocket. A bear's claw was a lucky find.

A day later, when he went into the market town, he took the claw with him, and left it with a silversmith, giving the craftsman certain instructions. The silversmith made a locket for the claw, then he gave it a thin silver chain. When Ram Bharosa came again, he paid the silversmith ten rupees for his work.

The days were growing shorter, and Binya had to be home a little earlier every evening. There was a hungry leopard at large, and she couldn't leave the cows out after dark.

She was hurrying past Ram Bharosa's shop when the old man called out to her.

'Binya, spare a minute! I want to show you something.'

Binya stepped into the shop.

'What do you think of it?' asked Ram Bharosa, showing her the silver pendant with the claw.

'It's so beautiful,' said Binya, just touching the claw and the silver chain.

'It's a bear's claw,' said Ram Bharosa. 'That's even luckier than a leopard's claw. Would you like to have it?'

'I have no money,' said Binya.

'That doesn't matter. You gave me the umbrella, I give you the claw! Come, let's see what it looks like on you.'

He placed the pendant on Binya, and indeed it looked very beautiful on her.

Ram Bharosa says he will never forget the smile she gave him when she left the shop.

She was halfway home when she realized she had left the cows behind.

'Neelu, Neelu!' she called. 'Oh, Gori!'

There was a faint tinkle of bells as the cows came slowly down the mountain path.

In the distance she could hear her mother and Bijju calling for her.

She began to sing. They heard her singing, and knew she was safe and near.

She walked home through the darkening glade, singing of the stars, and the trees stood still and listened to her, and the mountains were glad.

THE BIG RACE

Dawn crept quietly over the sleeping town. Only a cock was aware of it, and crowed. Koki heard a soft tapping on the windowpane, and immediately sat up in bed. She was ten years old. Her hair fell about her shoulders in a disorderly fashion and there were slight shadows under her dark eyes, but she was wide awake and listening. The tapping was repeated.

Koki got out of bed and tiptoed across to the window and unlatched it. Ranji was standing outside, looking somewhat disgruntled.

'Come on,' he said. 'It's nearly time.'

Koki put her finger to her lips, for she did not want her parents and grandmother to wake up.

'You go and tell Bhim,' she whispered. 'I'll meet you at the *maidan*.'

Ranji hurried off in the direction of Bhim's house, and Koki turned from the window and went to the dressing table. She combed her hair carelessly and tied it roughly with a ribbon. She was excited and in a hurry, and had slept in her dress, which was very crushed. Now, she was ready to leave.

Very quietly, she pulled open a dressing table drawer, and brought out a cardboard box in which were punctured little holes. She opened the lid of the box to see if Rajkumari was all right.

Rajkumari, a dumpy rhino beetle, was asleep on the core of an apple. Koki did not disturb her. She closed the box and barefoot crept out of the house through the back door.

As soon as she was outside, Koki broke into a run. She did not stop running until she reached the maidan.

On the maidan, the slanting rays of the early morning sun were just beginning to make emeralds of the dewdrops. Later in the day the grass would dry and be prickly to the feet, but now it was cool and soft. A group of boys had gathered at one corner of the maidan, talking excitedly, and among them were Ranji and Bhim, a lanky, bespectacled boy of fourteen. Koki was the only girl among them.

Bhim's beetle was the favourite for the race. It was a large bamboo beetle, with a slim body and long, slender legs, rather like its master's. It was called 2001. Ranji's beetle was a stone carrier with what looked like a very long pair of whiskers. It was appropriately named Moocha. Koki's beetle was not half as big as the other two. Though she did not know how to tell its sex, she was sure it was a female and had called it Rajkumari.

There were only three entries. Strictly speaking, betting wasn't allowed, but the boys made a few quiet bets among themselves. The prize was a giant insect (there was some disagreement as to whether it was a beetle or an outsize cockroach), which was meant to enable the winner to breed larger racing beetles.

There was some confusion when Ranji's Moocha escaped from his box and took a preliminary canter over the grass; but he was soon caught and returned to his enclosure. Moocha appeared to be in good form, in fact he would be tough competition for Bhim's 2001.

The course was about two metres long, the tracks fifteen centimetres wide. The tracks were fenced with strips of cardboard so that the contestants did not get in each other's way or leave the course altogether. They were held at the starting post by another piece of cardboard, which would be placed behind them as soon as the race began—just to make sure that no one backed out.

A little Sikh boy in a yellow pyjama-suit was acting as starter, and he kept blowing his whistle for order and attention. When the onlookers saw that the race was about to begin, they fell silent. The little Sikh boy then announced the rules of the race—the contestants were not to be touched during the race, or blown at from behind, or enticed forward with bits of food. They could, however, be cheered on as loudly as anyone wished.

Moocha and 2001 were already at the starting post, but Koki was giving Rajkumari a few words of advice. Rajkumari seemed reluctant to leave her apple core and needed to be taken forcibly to the starting post.

There was further delay when Moocha and 2001 got their horns and whiskers entangled. They had to be separated and calmed down before being placed in their respective tracks. The race was about to start.

Koki knelt on the grass, very quiet and serious, looking from Rajkumari to the finishing line and back again. Ranji was biting his fingernails. Bhim's glasses had clouded over, and he had to keep taking them off and wiping them on his shirt. There was a hush amongst the dozen or so spectators.

'Pee-ee-eeep!' The little Sikh boy blew his whistle.

They were off!

Or rather, Moocha and 2001 were off. Rajkumari was still at the starting post, wondering what had happened to her apple core.

Everyone was cheering madly, and Ranji was jumping up and down, and Bhim's glasses had been knocked off. Moocha was going at a spanking rate. 2001 wasn't taking a great deal of interest in the proceedings, but he was moving and anything could happen in a race like this.

Koki was on the verge of tears. All the coaching she had given Rajkumari seemed to be of no avail. Her beetle was still looking bewildered and hurt.

'Stop sulking,' said Koki. 'I won't keep you if you don't try.'

Then Moocha stopped suddenly, less than a metre from the finishing line. He seemed to be having trouble with his whiskers, and kept twitching them this way and that. 2001 was catching up slowly but surely, and both Ranji and Bhim were shouting themselves hoarse. Nobody paid any attention to Rajkumari, who was considered to be out of the race; but Koki was using all her willpower to get her racer going.

As 2001 approached Moocha, he seemed to sense his rival's trouble and stopped to find out what was the matter. They could not see each other over the cardboard fence, but otherwise appeared to be communicating very well. Ranji and Bhim were becoming quite frantic in their efforts to rally their faltering steeds, and the cheering on all sides was deafening.

Rajkumari, goaded with rage and frustration at having been deprived of her apple core, now took it into her head to make a bid for liberty and new pastures, and rushed forward in great style.

Koki shouted with joy, but the others did not notice the new challenge until Rajkumari had drawn level with her conferring rivals. There was a gasp from the crowd as Rajkumari strode across the finishing line in record time.

Everyone cheered the gallant outsider. Ranji and Bhim very sportingly shook Koki's hand, congratulating her on Rajkumari's victory. The little Sikh boy in the yellow pyjama-suit blew his whistle for silence and presented Koki with her prize.

Koki gazed in rapture at the new beetle—or was it a cockroach? She stroked its back with her thumb. The insect didn't seem to mind. Then, lest Rajkumari should feel jealous, Koki closed the prize box and, picking up her victorious beetle, returned her to the apple core.

The crowd began to break up. Ranji decided that he would trim Moocha's whiskers before the next race, and Bhim thought 2001 was in need of a special diet.

'Just wait till next Sunday,' said Ranji. 'Then watch my Moocha leave the rest of you standing!'

Bhim said nothing. He looked very thoughtful. There were some new training methods which he was going to try out for next time.

Koki walked home, a cardboard box under each arm. Her thoughts were busy with the future. She would breed beetles (or would they be cockroaches?) until she had a stable of about twenty. Her racers would win every event, both here and in the next town. They might make her famous. Beetle racing would become a national sport!

Meanwhile, she was happy, and Rajkumari was happy on the apple core, and the new insect was just being an insect and did not know and did not care about anything except how to get out of that wretched box.

A VILLAGE IN GARHWAL

I wake to what sounds like the din of a factory buzzer, but is in fact the music of a single vociferous cicada in the lime tree near my window.

Through the open window, I focus on a pattern of small, glossy lime leaves; then through them I see the mountains, the Himalayas, striding away into an immensity of sky.

'In a thousand ages of the gods I could not tell thee of the glories of Himachal'—so confessed a Sanskrit poet at the dawn of Indian history and he came closer than anyone else to capturing the spell of the Himalayas. The sea has had Conrad and Stevenson and Masefield, but the mountains continue to defy the written word. We have climbed their highest peaks and crossed their most difficult passes, but still they keep their secrets and their reserve; they remain remote, mysterious, spirit-haunted.

No wonder then, that the people who live on the mountain slopes in the mist-filled valleys of Garhwal have long since learnt humility, patience and a quiet resignation. Deep in the crouching mist lie their villages; while climbing the mountain slopes are forests of rhododendron, spruce and deodar, soughing in the wind from the ice-bound passes. Pale women plough, they laugh at the thunder as their men go down to the plains for work; for little grows on the beautiful mountains in the north wind.

When I think of Manjari village in Garhwal, I see a small river, a tributary of the Ganga, rushing along the bottom of a steep, rocky valley. On the banks of the river and on the terraced hills above, there are small fields of corn, barley, mustard, potatoes and onions. A few fruit trees grow near the village. Some hillsides are rugged and bare, just masses of quartz or granite. On hills exposed to wind, only grass and small shrubs are able to obtain a foothold.

This landscape is typical of Garhwal, one of India's most northerly regions with its massive snow ranges bordering on Tibet. Although thinly populated, it does not provide much of a living for its people. Most Garhwali cultivators are poor, some are very poor. 'You have beautiful scenery,' I observed after crossing the first range of hills.

'Yes,' said my friend, 'but we cannot eat the scenery.'

And yet, these are cheerful people, sturdy and with wonderful powers of endurance. Somehow they manage to wrest a precarious living from the unhelpful, calcinated soil. I am their guest for a few days.

My friend Gajadhar has brought me to his home, to his village above the little Nayar River. We took a train into the foothills and then we took a bus and finally, made dizzy by the hairpin bends devised in the last century by a brilliantly diabolical road engineer, we alighted at the small hill station of Lansdowne, chief recruiting centre for the Garhwal Regiment.

Lansdowne is just over six thousand feet high. From there we walked, covering twenty-five miles between sunrise and sunset, until we came to Manjari village, clinging to the terraced slopes of a very proud, very permanent mountain.

And this is my fourth morning in the village.

Other mornings I was woken by the throaty chuckles of the red-billed blue magpies as they glided between oak trees and medlars; but today the cicada has drowned all birdsong. It is a little out of season for cicadas but perhaps this sudden warm spell in late September has deceived him into thinking it is mating season again.

Early though it is, I am the last to get up. Gajadhar is exercising in the courtyard, going through an odd combination of Swedish exercises and yoga. He has a fine physique with the sturdy legs that most Garhwalis possess. I am sure he will realize his ambition of joining the Indian army as a cadet. His younger brother, Chakradhar, who is slim and fair with high cheekbones, is milking the family's buffalo. Normally, he would be on his long walk to school, five miles distant; but this is a holiday, so he can stay at home and help with the household chores.

His mother is lighting a fire. She is a handsome woman, even though her ears, weighed down by heavy silver earrings, have lost their natural shape. Garhwali women usually invest their savings in silver ornaments. And at the time of marriage, it is the boy's parents who make a gift of land to the parents of an attractive girl; a dowry system in reverse. There are fewer women than men in the hills and their good looks and sturdy physique give them considerable status among the menfolk.

Chakradhar's father is a corporal in the Indian army and is away for most of the year.

When Gajadhar marries, his wife will stay in the village to help his mother and younger brother look after the fields, house, goats and buffalo. Gajadhar will see her only when he comes home on leave. He prefers it that way; he does not think a simple hill girl should be exposed to the sophisticated temptations of the plains.

The village is far above the river and most of the fields depend on rainfall. But water must be fetched for cooking, washing and drinking. And so, after a breakfast of hot, sweet milk and thick *chapattis* stuffed with minced radish, the brothers and I set off down the rough track to the river.

The sun has climbed the mountains, but it has yet to reach the narrow valley. We bathe in the river. Gajadhar and Chakradhar dive off a massive rock; but I wade in circumspectly, unfamiliar with the river's depths and currents. The water, a milky blue, has come from the melting snows; it is very cold. I bathe quickly and then dash for a strip of sand where a little sunshine has split down the mountainside in warm, golden pools of light. At the same time, the song of the whistling thrush emerges like a dark secret from the wooded shadows.

A little later, buckets filled, we toil up the steep mountain. We must go by a better path this time if we are not to come tumbling down with our buckets of water. As we climb, we are mocked by a barbet which sits high up in a spruce calling feverishly in its monotonous mournful way.

'We call it the *mewli* bird,' says Gajadhar. 'There is a story about it. People say that the souls of men who have suffered injuries in the law courts of the plains and who have died of their disappointments, transmigrate into the mewli birds. That is why the birds are always crying *un-nee-ow, un-nee-ow,* which means "injustice, injustice".'

The path leads us past a primary school, a small temple and a single shop in which it is possible to buy salt, soap and a few other necessities. It is also the post office. And today it is serving as a lock-up.

The villagers have apprehended a local thief, who specializes in stealing jewellery from women while they are working in the fields. He is awaiting escort to the Lansdowne Police Station, and the shopkeeper-cum-postmaster-cum-constable brings him out for us to inspect. He is a mild-looking fellow, clearly shy of the small crowd that has gathered round him. I wonder how he manages to deprive the strong hill-women of their jewellery; it could not be by force! In any case, crimes of violence are rare in Garhwal; and robbery too, is uncommon for the simple reason that there is very little to rob.

The thief is rather glad of my presence, as it distracts attention from him. Strangers seldom come to Manjari. The crowd leaves him, turns to me, eager to catch a glimpse of the stranger in its midst. The children exclaim, point at me with delight, chatter among themselves. I might be a visitor from another planet instead of just an itinerant writer from the plains.

The postman has yet to arrive. The mail is brought in relays from Lansdowne. The Manjari postman, who has to cover eight miles and delivers letters at several small villages on his route, should arrive around noon. He also serves as a newspaper, bringing the villagers news of the outside world. Over the years, he has acquired a reputation for being highly inventive, sometimes creating his own news, so much so that when he told the villagers that men had landed on the moon, no one believed him. There are still a few sceptics.

Gajadhar has been walking out of the village every day, anxious to meet the postman. He is expecting a letter giving the results of his army entrance examination. If he is successful he will be called for an interview. And then, if he is accepted, he will be trained as an officer-cadet. After two years he will become a second lieutenant. His father, after twelve years in the army, is still only a corporal. But his father never went to school. There were no schools in the hills during his father's youth.

The Manjari school is only up to Class 5 and it has about forty pupils. If these children (most of them boys) want to study any further, then, like Chakradhar, they must walk the five miles to the high school in the next big village.

'Don't you get tired walking ten miles every day?' I ask Chakradhar.

'I am used to it,' he says. 'I like walking.'

I know that he only has two meals a day—one at seven in the morning when he leaves home, and the other at six or seven in the evening when he returns from school—and I ask him if he does not get hungry on the way.

'There is always the wild fruit,' he replies.

It appears that he is an expert on wild fruit: the purple berries of the thorny bilberry bushes ripening in May and June; wild strawberries like drops of blood on the dark green monsoon grass; small sour cherries and tough medlars in the winter months. Chakradhar's strong teeth and probing tongue extract whatever tang or sweetness lies hidden in them. And in March, there are the rhododendron flowers. His mother makes them into jam. But Chakradhar likes them as they are: he places the petals on his tongue and chews till the sweet juice trickles down his throat.

He has never been ill.

'But what happens when someone is ill?' I ask, knowing that in Manjari there are no medicines, no dispensary or hospital.

'He goes to bed until he is better,' says Gajadhar. 'We have a few home remedies. But if someone is very sick, we carry the person to the hospital at Lansdowne.' He pauses as though wondering how much he should say, then shrugs and says: 'Last year my uncle was very ill. He had a terrible pain in his stomach. For two days he cried out with the pain. So we made a litter and started out for Lansdowne. We had already carried him fifteen miles when he died. And then we had to carry him back again.'

Some of the villages have dispensaries managed by compounders but the remoter areas of Garhwal are completely without medical aid. To the outsider, life in the Garhwal hills may seem idyllic and the people simple. But the Garhwali is far from being simple and his life is one long struggle, especially if he happens to be living in a high-altitude village snowbound for four months in the year, with cultivation coming to a standstill and people having to manage with the food gathered and stored during the summer months.

Fortunately, the clear mountain air and the simple diet keep the Garhwalis free from most diseases, and help them recover from the more common ailments. The greatest dangers come from unexpected disasters, such as an accident with an axe or scythe, or an attack by a wild animal. A few years back, several Manjari children and old women were killed by a man-eating leopard. The leopard was finally killed by the villagers who hunted it down with spears and axes. But the leopard that sometimes prowls round the village at night looking for a stray dog or goat slinks away at the approach of a human.

I do not see the leopard, but at night I am woken by a rumbling and thumping on the roof. I wake Gajadhar and ask him what is happening.

'It is only a bear,' he says.

'Is it trying to get in?'

'No, it's been in the cornfield and now it's after the pumpkins on the roof.'

A little later, when we look out of the small window, we see a black bear making off like a thief in the night, a large pumpkin held securely to his chest.

At the approach of winter when snow covers the higher mountains, the brown and black Himalayan bears descend to lower altitudes in search of food. Because they are short-sighted and suspicious of anything that moves, they can be dangerous; but, like most wild animals, they will avoid men if they can and are aggressive only when accompanied by their cubs.

Gajadhar advises me to run downhill if chased by a bear. He says that bears find it easier to run uphill than downhill.

I am not interested in being chased by a bear, but the following night, Gajadhar and I stay up to try and prevent the bear from depleting his cornfield. We take up our position on a highway promontory of rock, which gives us a clear view of the moonlit field.

A little after midnight, the bear comes down to the edge of the field but he is suspicious and has probably smelt us. He is, however, hungry; and so, after standing up as high as possible on his hind legs and peering about to see if the field is empty, he comes cautiously out of the forest and makes his way towards the corn.

When about halfway, his attention is suddenly attracted by some Buddhist prayer-flags which have been strung up recently between two small trees by a band of wandering Tibetans. On spotting the flags, the bear gives a little grunt of disapproval and begins to move back into the forest; but the fluttering of the little flags is a puzzle that he feels he must make out (for a bear is one of the most inquisitive animals); so after a few backward steps, he again stops and watches them.

Not satisfied with this, he stands on his hind legs looking at the flags, first at one side and then at the other. Then seeing that they do not attack him and do not appear dangerous, he makes his way right up to the flags taking only two or three steps at a time and having a good look before each advance. Eventually, he moves confidently up to the flags and pulls them all down. Then, after careful examination of the flags, he moves into the field of corn.

But Gajadhar has decided that he is not going to lose any more corn, so he starts shouting, and the rest of the village wakes up and people come out of their houses beating drums and empty kerosene tins.

Deprived of his dinner, the bear makes off in a bad temper.

He runs downhill and at a good speed too; and I am glad that I am not in his path just then. Uphill or downhill, an angry bear is best given a very wide berth.

For Gajadhar, impatient to know the result of his army entrance examination, the following day is a trial of his patience.

First, we hear that there has been a landslide and that the postman cannot reach us. Then, we hear that although there has been a landslide, the postman has already passed the spot in safety. Another alarming rumour has it that the postman disappeared with the landslide. This is soon denied. The postman is safe. It was only the mailbag that disappeared.

And then, at two in the afternoon, the postman turns up. He tells us that there was indeed a landslide but that it took place on someone else's route. Apparently, a mischievous urchin who passed him on the way was responsible for all the rumours. But we suspect the postman of having something to do with them.

Gajadhar has passed his examination and will leave with me in the morning. We have to be up early in order to reach Lansdowne before dark. But Gajadhar's mother insists on celebrating her son's success by feasting her friends and neighbours. There is a partridge (a present from a neighbour who had decided that Gajadhar will make a fine husband for his daughter) and two chickens: rich fare for folk whose normal diet consists mostly of lentils, potatoes and onions.

After dinner, there are songs and Gajadhar's mother sings of the homesickness of those who are separated from their loved ones and their home in the hills. It is an old Garhwali folk song:

Oh, mountain-swift, you are from my father's home;
Speak, oh speak, in the courtyard of my parents,
My mother will hear you; She will send my brother to fetch me.
A grain of rice alone in the cooking pot cries,

'I wish I could get out!'
Likewise I wonder: 'Will I ever reach my father's house?'

The hookah is passed round and stories are told. Tales of ghosts and demons mingle with legends of ancient kings and heroes. It is almost midnight by the time the last guest has gone. Chakradhar approaches me as I am about to retire for the night.

'Will you come again?' he asks.

'Yes, I'll come again,' I reply. 'If not next year, then the year after. How many years are left before you finish school?'

'Four.'

'Four years. If you walk ten miles a day for four years, how many miles will that make?'

'Four thousand and six hundred miles,' says Chakradhar after a moment's thought, 'but we have two months' holiday each year. That means I'll walk about twelve thousand miles in four years.'

The moon has not yet risen. Lanterns swing in the dark.

The lanterns flit silently over the hillside and go out one by one. This Garhwali day, which is just like any other day in the hills, slips quietly into the silence of the mountains.

I stretch myself out on my cot. Outside the small window the sky is brilliant with stars. As I close my eyes, someone brushes against the lime tree, brushing its leaves; and the fresh fragrance of limes comes to me on the night air, making the moment memorable for all time.

KOKI PLAYS THE GAME

'There's a cricket match on Saturday, isn't there?' asked Koki.
'That's right,' said Ranji. 'We're playing the Public School team.'

'I might come and watch,' said Koki.

'As you like. It won't be much of a game. We'll beat them easily.'

Ranji's own cricket team was quite different from his school team. It consisted of boys big and small, long and short, from various walks of life. Even Koki, a girl, was allowed honorary membership, and had sometimes been 'twelfth man'—an extra. She knew the game well, and often bowled to Ranji in the mornings when he wanted batting practice. Only a couple of the teammates could afford to go to private schools like Ranji's; most of them went to the local government school, and two or three had stopped going to school altogether.

There was Bhartu, who delivered newspapers in the mornings; the brothers Mukesh and Rakesh, whose father kept a sweet shop; and a tailor's son, Amir Ali. There was Billy Jones, an Anglo-Indian boy; 'Lumboo', the Tall One; Sitaram, the washerman's son and several others. And there was also Bhim, who couldn't play at all, but who made a good umpire (when his glasses weren't steamed over) and who accompanied the team wherever it went.

This Saturday they were playing on their 'home' ground, a patch of wasteland behind a new cinema called the Apsara ('Heavenly Dancer').

The Public School boys had all arrived first, which was only natural since they lived together in the same boarding school. The members of Ranji's team came from different directions, so it was some time before they had all assembled. Even then, they were two short. But Ranji won the toss and decided to bat, hoping that the missing team members would arrive in time to take their turn at the wicket.

'If Mukesh and Rakesh aren't here in time, we won't have them in the team,' said Ranji sternly.

'Don't sack them,' said Lumboo. 'They always bring us sweets and snacks from their father's shop. We need them in the team even if they don't score any runs.'

'Well, if they turn up *without* refreshments, they'll be sacked,' said Ranji, always ready to be fair.

The two umpires had gone out to set up the stumps—Bhim, on behalf of Ranji's team, and a teacher from the Public School.

'I don't like the look of that teacher,' said Amir Ali.

'Well, we won't take any risks.'

Billy Jones and Lumboo always opened the batting. Lumboo's height helped him to deal with the fast-rising ball. He took the first ball.

The Public School's opening bowler was speedy but inaccurate. This was because he was trying to bowl too fast. His first ball went for a wide, which gave Ranji's team its first run. The second ball wasn't quite so wide, but it was still about a foot from the leg stump. Lumboo took a swipe at it and missed. The third ball pitched halfway down the wicket and kept low. It struck Lumboo on the pads.

'How's that!' shouted the bowler, wicketkeeper and slip-fielders in unison.

The Public School's umpire did not hesitate. Up went his finger. Lumboo was given out leg-before-wicket. Lumboo stood aghast. He looked down at where his feet were placed, then back at his stumps.

'I'm not in front of the wicket,' he complained to no one in particular.

'The umpire's word is law,' said the wicketkeeper.

Lumboo slowly walked back to where his teammates reclined against a pile of bricks.

'I wasn't out!' he protested.

'Never mind,' said Ranji, whose turn it was to bat. 'You'll get your chance when you come on to bowl.'

He walked to the wicket with a confident air, his bat resting on his shoulder. He took guard carefully and, tapping his bat on the ground, faced the bowler. He received a straight ball, fast, and met it on the half-volley, driving it straight back past the bowler. It sped to the boundary, amidst delighted cries from Ranji's teammates. Four runs.

The next ball was short, just outside the off stump. Ranji stepped back and square-cut it past point. Another four. There were more cheers, and this time Ranji distinctly heard a girl's voice shouting: 'Good shot, Ranji!'

He looked back to where his teammates were gathered. There was no girl among them. He turned and looked toward the opposite boundary, and there, under the giant cinema hoarding, stood Koki. She waved to him.

Ranji did not wave back. He felt acutely self-conscious. Settling down to face the bowler again, he was aware of two things at once—of the bowler making faces and charging up to bowl, and of Koki standing on the boundary and waiting for him to hit another four.

This loss of concentration caused him to misjudge the next ball. Instead of playing forward, he played back.

The ball took the edge of his bat and flew straight into the wicketkeeper's gloves.

'How's that!' shouted all the fielders, appealing for a catch.

Ranji did not wait for the umpire—in this case, Bhim, to give him out. He knew he'd touched the ball. Scowling, he walked back to his team. It was all Koki's fault!

Now, there was a good partnership between Sitaram and Bhartu. Sitaram, who helped his father with the town's washing on Sundays, was in the habit of laying out clothes on a flat stone and pounding them with a stout stick—the method followed by most washermen.

He dealt with the cricket ball in much the same way—clouting it hard, and sending it to various points of the compass. He hit up 25 valuable runs before he was out, caught off a big hit. Bhartu pushed and prodded, merely keeping one end going, until he too was out to an LBW decision. Billy Jones had gone the same way, taking the ball on his pads. No one was happy with the LBW decisions.

'We must have neutral umpires,' said Amir Ali.

'But who wants to be an umpire?' said Ranji. 'We won't find anyone. We'll have to use our own team members—or let the other side provide *both* umpires!'

'Not after today,' said Lumboo.

Meanwhile, Mukesh and Rakesh had arrived, carrying paper bags full of samosas and jalebis. As a result, everyone cheered up. Wickets fell almost as rapidly as the snacks and sweets were consumed. Mukesh and Rakesh, who were the last men in, held out for several overs until Rakesh was given out—LBW! Ranji's team was all out for 87 runs—not really a match-winning score, except on a tricky wicket.

It was the Public School team's turn to bat. One of their opening batsmen was bowled by Lumboo for naught. The other batsman was twice rapped on the pads by balls from Ranji, but his loud appeals for LBW were turned down—by the Public School's umpire, naturally! Muttering to himself, Ranji hurled down a thunderbolt of a ball. It rose sharply and struck the batsman on the hand. Howling with pain, he dropped his bat and wrung his hand. Then he showed everyone a swollen finger and decided to 'retire hurt'.

'There's more than one way of getting them out,' muttered Ranji, as he passed the umpire.

The next two batsmen were good players, not as nervous as the openers. One of them got what might have been a faint tickle to an out-swinger from Lumboo, but he was given the benefit of the doubt by Bhim—who, as umpires went, was as impartial as a star. He showed no favours to his own team, no matter what the other umpire did. It just isn't fair, thought Ranji.

The number three and four batsmen put on 40 runs between them, and by mid-afternoon Ranji's players were feeling tired and hungry. Then three quick wickets fell to Sitaram's spinners. Three wickets remained, and 20 runs were needed by the Public School for victory.

This was when Bhartu, running to take a catch, collided with chubby Mukesh. Both of them went sprawling on the grass, and when they got up the ball was found lodged in the back of Mukesh's pants. How it got there no one could tell, but after much discussion the umpires had to agree that it qualified as a catch and the batsman was given out. But Bhartu had to leave the ground with a bleeding nose.

Ranji looked around for a replacement. There was no one in sight except Koki.

'Come and field,' said Ranji brusquely.

Koki needed no persuading. She slipped off her sandals

and dashed barefoot on to the field, taking up Bhartu's position near the boundary.

The tail-end batsmen were now swinging at the ball in a desperate attempt to hit the remaining runs. A hard-hit drive sped past Koki and went for four runs. Ranji gave her a hard look. Then the two batsmen got into a muddle while trying to take a quick run, and one of them was run out.

The last man came in. The Public School was 8 runs behind. But a couple of boundaries would take care of that.

The batsmen ran two. And then one of them, over-confident and sure of victory, swung out at a slow, tempting ball from Sitaram, and the ball flew towards Koki in a long, curving arc.

Koki had to run a few yards to her left. Then she leapt like a gazelle and took the ball in both hands. Ranji's team had won, and Koki had made the winning catch.

It was her last appearance as 'twelfth man'. From that day onwards she was a regular member of the team.

ROMI AND THE WILDFIRE

1

As Romi was about to mount his bicycle, he saw smoke rising from behind the distant line of trees.

'It looks like a forest fire,' said Prem, his friend and classmate.

'It's well to the east,' said Romi. 'Nowhere near the road.'

'There's a strong wind,' said Prem, looking at the dry leaves swirling across the road.

It was the middle of May, and it hadn't rained in the Terai for several weeks. The grass was brown, the leaves of the trees covered with dust. Even though it was getting on to six o'clock in the evening, the boys' shirts were damp with sweat.

'It will be getting dark soon,' said Prem. 'You'd better spend the night at my house.'

'No, I said I'd be home tonight. My father isn't keeping well. The doctor has given me some tablets for him.'

'You'd better hurry, then. That fire seems to be spreading.'

'Oh, it's far off. It will take me only forty minutes to ride through the forest. Bye, Prem—see you tomorrow!'

Romi mounted his bicycle and pedalled off down the main road of the village, scattering stray hens, stray dogs and stray villagers.

'Hey, look where you're going!' shouted an angry villager, leaping out of the way of the oncoming bicycle. 'Do you think you own the road?'

'Of course I own it,' called Romi cheerfully, and cycled on.

His own village lay about seven miles distant, on the other side of the forest; but there was only a primary school in his village, and Romi was now in High School. His father, who was a fairly wealthy sugarcane farmer, had only recently bought him the bicycle. Romi didn't care too much for school and felt there weren't enough holidays; but he enjoyed the long rides, and he got on well with his classmates.

He might have stayed the night with Prem had it not been for the tablets which the *Vaid*—the village doctor—had given him for his father.

Romi's father was having back trouble, and the medicine had been specially prepared from local herbs.

Having been given such a fine bicycle, Romi felt that the least he could do in return was to get those tablets to his father as early as possible.

He put his head down and rode swiftly out of the village. Ahead of him, the smoke rose from the burning forest and the sky glowed red.

2

He had soon left the village far behind. There was a slight climb, and Romi had to push harder on the pedals to get over the rise. Once over the top, the road went winding down to the edge of the sub-tropical forest.

This was the part Romi enjoyed most. He relaxed, stopped pedalling, and allowed the bicycle to glide gently down the slope. Soon the wind was rushing past him, blowing his hair about his face and making his shirt billow out behind. He burst into song.

A dog from the village ran beside him, barking furiously. Romi shouted at the dog, encouraging him in the race.

Then the road straightened out, and Romi began pedalling again. The dog, seeing the forest ahead, turned back to the village. It was afraid of the forest.

The smoke was thicker now, and Romi caught the smell of burning timber. But ahead of him, the road was clear. He rode on.

It was a rough, dusty road, cut straight through the forest. Tall trees grew on either side, cutting off the last of the daylight. But the spreading glow of the fire on the right lit up the road, and giant tree-shadows danced before the boy on the bicycle.

Usually the road was deserted. This evening it was alive with wild creatures fleeing from the forest fire.

The first animal that Romi saw was a hare, leaping across the road in front of him. It was followed by several more hares. Then a band of monkeys streamed across, chattering excitedly.

They'll be safe on the other side, thought Romi. *The fire won't cross the road.*

But it was coming closer. And realizing this, Romi pedalled harder. In half-an-hour he should be out of the forest.

Suddenly, from the side of the road, several pheasants rose in the air, and with a *whoosh*, flew low across the path, just in front of the oncoming bicycle. Taken by surprise, Romi fell off. When he picked himself up and began brushing his clothes, he saw that his knee was bleeding. It wasn't a deep cut, but he allowed it to bleed a little, took out his handkerchief and bandaged his knee. Then he mounted the bicycle again.

He rode a bit slower now, because birds and animals kept coming out of the bushes.

Not only pheasants but smaller birds, too, were streaming across the road—parrots, jungle crows, owls, magpies—and the air was filled with their cries.

Everyone's on the move, thought Romi. *It must be a really big fire.*

He could see the flames now, reaching out from behind the trees on his right, and he could hear the crackling as the dry leaves caught fire. The air was hot on his face. Leaves, still alight or turning to cinders, floated past.

A herd of deer crossed the road, and Romi had to stop until they had passed. Then he mounted again and rode on; but now, for the first time, he was feeling afraid.

3

From ahead came a faint clanging sound. It wasn't an animal sound, Romi was sure of that. A fire-engine? There were no fire-engines within fifty miles.

The clanging came nearer, and Romi discovered that the noise came from a small boy who was running along the forest path, two milk-cans clattering at his side.

'Teju!' called Romi, recognizing the boy from a neighbouring village. 'What are you doing out here?'

'Trying to get home, of course,' said Teju, panting along beside the bicycle.

'Jump on,' said Romi, stopping for him.

Teju was only eight or nine—a couple of years younger than Romi. He had come to deliver milk to some road-workers, but the workers had left at the first signs of the fire, and Teju was hurrying home with his cans still full of milk.

He got up on the cross-bar of the bicycle, and Romi moved on again. He was quite used to carrying friends on the crossbar.

'Keep beating your milk-cans,' said Romi. 'Like that, the animals will know we are coming. My bell doesn't make enough noise. I'm going to get a horn for my cycle!'

'I never knew there were so many animals in the jungle,' said Teju. 'I saw a python in the middle of the road. It stretched right across!'

'What did you do?'

'Just kept running and jumped right over it!'

Teju continued to chatter but Romi's thoughts were on the fire, which was much closer now. Flames shot up from the dry grass and ran up the trunks of trees and along the branches. Smoke billowed out above the forest.

Romi's eyes were smarting and his hair and eyebrows felt scorched. He was feeling tired but he couldn't stop now, he had to get beyond the range of the fire. Another ten or fifteen minutes of steady riding would get them to the small wooden bridge that spanned the little river separating the forest from the sugarcane fields.

Once across the river, they would be safe. The fire could not touch them on the other side because the forest ended at the river's edge. But could they get to the river in time?

4

Clang, clang, clang, went Teju's milk-cans. But the sound of the fire grew louder too.

A tall silk-cotton tree, its branches leaning across the road, had caught fire. They were almost beneath it when there was a crash and a burning branch fell to the ground a few yards in front of them.

The boys had to get off the bicycle and leave the road, forcing their way through a tangle of thorny bushes on the left, dragging and pushing at the bicycle and only returning to the road some distance ahead of the burning tree.

'We won't get out in time,' said Teju, back on the cross-bar but feeling disheartened.

'Yes, we will,' said Romi, pedalling with all his might. 'The fire hasn't crossed the road as yet.'

Even as he spoke, he saw a small flame leap up from the

grass on the left. It wouldn't be long before more sparks and burning leaves were blown across the road to kindle the grass on the other side.

'Oh, look!' exclaimed Romi, bringing the bicycle to a sudden stop.

'What's wrong now?' asked Teju, rubbing his sore eyes. And then, through the smoke, he saw what was stopping them.

An elephant was standing in the middle of the road.

Teju slipped off the cross-bar, his cans rolling on the ground, bursting open and spilling their contents.

The elephant was about forty feet away. It moved about restlessly, its big ears flapping as it turned its head from side to side, wondering which way to go.

From far to the left, where the forest was still untouched, a herd of elephants moved towards the river. The leader of the herd raised his trunk and trumpeted a call. Hearing it, the elephant on the road raised its own trunk and trumpeted a reply. Then it shambled off into the forest, in the direction of the herd, leaving the way clear.

'Come, Teju, jump on!' urged Romi. 'We can't stay here much longer!'

5

Teju forgot about his milk-cans and pulled himself up on the cross-bar. Romi ran forward with the bicycle, to gain speed, and mounted swiftly. He kept as far as possible to the left of the road, trying to ignore the flames, the crackling, the smoke and the scorching heat.

It seemed that all the animals who could get away, had done so. The exodus across the road had stopped.

'We won't stop again,' said Romi, gritting his teeth. 'Not even for an elephant!'

'We're nearly there!' said Teju. He was perking up again.

A jackal, overcome by the heat and smoke, lay in the middle of the path, either dead or unconscious. Romi did not stop. He swerved round the animal. Then he put all his strength into one final effort.

He covered the last hundred yards at top speed, and then they were out of the forest, free-wheeling down the sloping road to the river.

'Look!' shouted Teju. 'The bridge is on fire!'

Burning embers had floated down on to the small wooden bridge, and the dry, ancient timber had quickly caught fire. It was now burning fiercely.

Romi did not hesitate. He left the road, riding the bicycle over sand and pebbles. Then with a rush they went down the river-bank and into the water.

The next thing they knew, they were splashing around, trying to find each other in the darkness.

'Help!' cried Teju. 'I'm drowning!'

6

'Don't be silly,' said Romi. 'The water isn't deep—it's only up to the knees. Come here and grab hold of me.'

Teju splashed across and grabbed Romi by the belt.

'The water's so cold,' he said, his teeth chattering.

'Do you want to go back and warm yourself?' asked Romi. 'Some people are never satisfied. Come on, help me get the bicycle up. It's down here, just where we are standing.'

Together they managed to heave the bicycle out of the water and stand it upright.

'Now sit on it,' said Romi. 'I'll push you across.'

'We'll be swept away,' said Teju.

'No, we won't. There's not much water in the river at this

time of the year. But the current is quite strong in the middle, so sit still. All right?'

'All right,' said Teju nervously.

Romi began guiding the bicycle across the river, one hand on the seat and one hand on the handlebar. The river was shallow and sluggish in midsummer; even so, it was quite swift in the middle. But having got safely out of the burning forest, Romi was in no mood to let a little river defeat him.

He kicked off his shoes, knowing they would be lost; and then gripping the smooth stones of the river-bed with his toes, he concentrated on keeping his balance and getting the bicycle and Teju through the middle of the stream. The water here came up to his waist, and the current would have been too strong for Teju. But when they reached the shallows, Teju got down and helped Romi push the bicycle.

They reached the opposite bank, and sank down on the grass.

'We can rest now,' said Romi. 'But not all night—I've got some medicine to give to my father.' He felt in his pockets and found that the tablets in their envelope, had turned into a soggy mess. 'Oh well, he had to take them with water anyway,' he said.

They watched the fire as it continued to spread through the forest. It had crossed the road down which they had come. The sky was a bright red, and the river reflected the colour of the sky.

Several elephants had found their way down to the river. They were cooling off by spraying water on each other with their trunks. Further downstream there were deer and other animals.

Romi and Teju looked at each other in the glow from the fire. They hadn't known each other very well before. But now they felt they had been friends for years.

'What are you thinking about?' asked Teju.

'I'm thinking,' said Romi, 'that even if the fire is out in a day or two, it will be a long time before the bridge is repaired. So it will be a nice long holiday from school!'

'But you can walk across the river,' said Teju. 'You just did it.'

'Impossible,' said Romi. 'It's much too swift.'

THE FLUTE PLAYER

Down the main road passed big yellow buses, cars, pony-drawn tongas, motorcycles and bullock carts. This steady flow of traffic seemed, somehow, to form a barrier between the city on one side of the Trunk Road, and the distant sleepy villages on the other. It seemed to cut India in half—the India Kamla knew slightly, and the India she had never seen.

Kamla's grandmother lived on the outskirts of the city of Jaipur, and just across the road from the house there were fields and villages stretching away for hundreds of miles. But Kamla had never been across the main road. This separated the busy city from the flat green plains stretching endlessly towards the horizon.

Kamla was used to city life. In England, it was London and Manchester. In India, it was Delhi and Jaipur. Rainy Manchester was, of course, different in many ways from sun-drenched Jaipur, and Indian cities had stronger smells and more vibrant colours than their English counterparts. Nevertheless, they had much in common: busy people always on the move, money constantly changing hands, buses to catch, schools to attend, parties to go to, TV to watch. Kamla had seen very little of the English countryside, even less of India outside the cities.

Her parents lived in Manchester where her father was a doctor in a large hospital. She went to school in England. But this year, during the summer holidays, she had come to India to stay with her grandmother. Apart from a maidservant and a grizzled old nightwatchman, Grandmother lived quite alone in a small house on the outskirts of Jaipur. During the winter months, Jaipur's climate was cool and bracing but in the summer, a fierce sun poured down upon the city from a cloudless sky.

None of the other city children ventured across the main road into the fields of millet, wheat and cotton, but Kamla was determined to visit the fields before she returned to England. From the flat roof of the house she could see them stretching away for miles, the ripening wheat swaying in the hot wind. Finally, when there were only two days left before she went to Delhi to board a plane for London, she made up her mind and crossed the main road.

She did this in the afternoon, when Grandmother was asleep and the servants were in the bazaar. She slipped out of the back door and her slippers kicked up the dust as she ran down the path to the main road. A bus roared past and more dust rose from the road and swirled about her. Kamla ran through the dust, past the jacaranda trees that lined the road, and into the fields.

Suddenly, the world became an enormous place, bigger and more varied than it had seemed from the air, also mysterious and exciting—and just a little frightening.

The sea of wheat stretched away till it merged with the hot blinding blue of the sky. Far to her left were a few trees and the low white huts of a village. To her right lay hollow pits of red dust and a blackened chimney where bricks used to be made. In front, some distance away, Kamla could see a camel moving round a well, drawing up water for the fields. She set out in the direction of the camel.

Her grandmother had told her not to wander off on her own in the city; but this wasn't the city, and as far as she knew, camels did not attack people.

It took her a long time to get to the camel. It was about

half a mile away, though it seemed much nearer. And when Kamla reached it, she was surprised to find that there was no one else in sight. The camel was turning the wheel by itself, moving round and round the well, while the water kept gushing up in little trays to run down the channels into the fields. The camel took no notice of Kamla, did not look at her even once, just carried on about its business.

There must be someone here, thought Kamla, walking towards a mango tree that grew a few yards away. Ripe mangoes dangled like globules of gold from its branches. Under the tree, fast asleep, was a boy.

All he wore was a pair of dirty white shorts. His body had been burnt dark by the sun; his hair was tousled, his feet chalky with dust. In the palm of his outstretched hand was a flute. He was a thin boy, with long bony legs, but Kamla felt that he was strong too, for his body was hard and wiry.

Kamla came nearer to the sleeping boy, peering at him with some curiosity, for she had not seen a village boy before. Her shadow fell across his face. The coming of the shadow woke the boy. He opened his eyes and stared at Kamla. When she did not say anything, he sat up, his head a little to one side, his hands clasping his knees, and stared at her.

'Who are you?' he asked a little gruffly. He was not used to waking up and finding strange girls staring at him.

'I'm Kamla. I've come from England, but I'm really from India. I mean I've come home to India, but I'm really from England.' This was getting to be rather confusing, so she countered with an abrupt, 'Who are you?'

'I'm the strongest boy in the village,' said the boy, deciding to assert himself without any more ado. 'My name is Romi. I can wrestle and swim and climb any tree.'

'And do you sleep a lot?' asked Kamla innocently.

Romi scratched his head and grinned.

'I must look after the camel,' he said. 'It is no use staying awake for the camel. It keeps going round the well until it is tired, and then it stops. When it has rested, it starts going round again. It can carry on like that all day. But it eats a lot.'

Mention of the camel's food reminded Romi that he was hungry. He was growing fast these days and was nearly always hungry. There were some mangoes lying beside him, and he offered one to Kamla. They were silent for a few minutes. You cannot suck mangoes and talk at the same time. After they had finished, they washed their hands in the water from one of the trays.

'There are parrots in the tree,' said Kamla, noticing three or four green parrots conducting a noisy meeting in the topmost branches. They reminded her a bit of a pop group she had seen and heard at home.

'They spoil most of the mangoes,' said Romi.

He flung a stone at them, missed, but they took off with squawks of protest, flashes of green and gold wheeling in the sunshine.

'Where do you swim?' asked Kamla. 'Down in the well?'

'Of course not. I'm not a frog. There is a canal not far from here. Come, I will show you!'

As they crossed the fields, a pair of blue jays flew out of a bush, rockets of bright blue that dipped and swerved, rising and falling as they chased each other.

Remembering a story that Grandmother had told her, Kamla said, 'They are sacred birds, aren't they? Because of their blue throats.' She told him the story of the God Shiva having a blue throat because he had swallowed a poison that would have destroyed the world; he had kept the poison in his throat and would not let it go further. 'And so his throat is blue, like the blue jay's.'

Romi liked this story. His respect for Kamla greatly increased. But he was not to be outdone, and when a small grey squirrel dashed across the path he told her that squirrels, too, were sacred. Krishna, the god who had been born into a farmer's family like Romi's, had been fond of squirrels and would take them in his arms and stroke them.

'That is why squirrels have four dark lines down their backs,' said Romi. 'Krishna was very dark, as dark as I am, and the stripes are the marks of his fingers.'

'Can you catch a squirrel?' asked Kamla.

'No, they are too quick. But I caught a snake once. I caught it by its tail and dropped it in the old well. That well is full of snakes. Whenever we catch one, instead of killing it, we drop it in the well! They can't get out.'

Kamla shuddered at the thought of all those snakes swimming and wriggling about at the bottom of the deep well. She wasn't sure that she wanted to return to the well with him. But she forgot about the snakes when they reached the canal.

It was a small canal, about ten metres wide, and only waist-deep in the middle, but it was very muddy at the bottom. She had never seen such a muddy stream in her life.

'Would you like to get in?' asked Romi.

'No,' said Kamla. 'You get in.'

Romi was only too ready to show off his tricks in the water. His toes took a firm hold on the grassy bank, the muscles of his calves tensed and he dived into the water with a loud splash, landing rather awkwardly on his belly. It was a poor dive, but Kamla was impressed.

Romi swam across to the opposite bank and then back again. When he climbed out of the water, he was covered with mud. It made him look quite fierce.

'Come on in,' he invited. 'It's not deep.'

'It's dirty,' said Kamla, but felt tempted all the same.

'It's only mud,' said Romi. 'There's nothing wrong with mud. Camels like mud. Buffaloes love mud.'

'I'm not a camel—or a buffalo.'

'All right. You don't have to go right in, just walk along the sides of the channel.'

After a moment's hesitation, Kamla slipped her feet out of her slippers and crept cautiously down the slope till her feet were in the water. She went no further, but even so, some of the muddy water splashed on to her clean white skirt. What would she tell Grandmother? Her feet sank into the soft mud and she gave a little squeal as the water reached her knees. It was with some difficulty that she got each foot out of the sticky mud.

Romi took her by the hand, and they went stumbling along the side of the channel while little fish swam in and out of their legs, and a heron, one foot raised, waited until they had passed before snapping a fish out of the water. The little fish glistened in the sun before it disappeared down the heron's throat.

Romi gave a sudden exclamation and came to a stop. Kamla held on to him for support.

'What is it?' she asked, a little nervously.

'It's a tortoise,' said Romi. 'Can you see it?'

He pointed to the bank of the canal, and there, lying quite still, was a small tortoise. Romi scrambled up the bank and, before Kamla could stop him, had picked up the tortoise. As soon as he touched it, the animal's head and legs disappeared into its shell. Romi turned it over, but from behind the breastplate only the head and a spiky tail were visible.

'Look!' exclaimed Kamla, pointing to the ground where the tortoise had been lying. 'What's in that hole?'

They peered into the hole. It was about half a metre deep,

and at the bottom were five or six white eggs, a little smaller than a hen's eggs.

'Put it back,' said Kamla. 'It was sitting on its eggs.'

Romi shrugged and dropped the tortoise back on its hole. It peeped out from behind its shell, saw the children were still present, and retreated into its shell again.

'I must go,' said Kamla. 'It's getting late. Granny will wonder where I have gone.'

They walked back to the mango tree, and washed their hands and feet in the cool clear water from the well; but only after Romi had assured Kamla that there weren't any snakes in the well—he had been talking about an old disused well on the far side of the village. Kamla told Romi she would take him to her house one day, but it would have to be next year, or perhaps the year after, when she came to India again.

'Is it very far, where you are going?' asked Romi.

'Yes, England is across the seas. I have to go back to my parents. And my school is there, too. But I will take the plane from Delhi. Have you ever been to Delhi?'

'I have not been further than Jaipur,' said Romi. 'What is England like? Are there canals to swim in?'

'You can swim in the sea. Lots of people go swimming in the sea. But it's too cold most of the year. Where I live, there are shops and cinemas and places where you can eat anything you like. And people from all over the world come to live there. You can see red faces, brown faces, black faces, white faces!'

'I saw a red face once,' said Romi. 'He came to the village to take pictures. He took one of me sitting on the camel. He said he would send me the picture, but it never came.'

Kamla noticed the flute lying on the grass. 'Is it your flute?' she asked.

'Yes,' said Romi. 'It is an old flute. But the old ones are

best. I found it lying in a field last year. Perhaps it was God Krishna's! He was always playing the flute.'

'And who taught you to play it?'

'Nobody. I learnt by myself. Shall I play it for you?'

Kamla nodded, and they sat down on the grass, leaning against the trunk of the mango tree, and Romi put the flute to his lips and began to play.

It was a slow, sweet tune, a little sad, a little happy, and the notes were taken up by the breeze and carried across the fields. There was no one to hear the music except the birds and the camel and Kamla. Whether the camel liked it or not, we shall never know; it just kept going round and round the well, drawing up water for the fields. And whether the birds liked it or not, we cannot say, although it is true that they were all suddenly silent when Romi began to play. But Kamla was charmed by the music, and she watched Romi while he played, and the boy smiled at her with his eyes and ran his fingers along the flute. When he stopped playing, everything was still, everything silent, except for the soft wind sighing in the wheat and the gurgle of water coming up from the well.

Kamla stood up to leave.

'When will you come again?' asked Romi.

'I will try to come next year,' said Kamla.

'That is a long time. By then you will be quite old. You may not want to come.'

'I will come,' said Kamla.

'Promise?'

'Promise.'

Romi put the flute in her hands and said, 'You keep it. I can get another one.'

'But I don't know how to play it,' said Kamla.

'It will play by itself,' said Romi.

She took the flute and put it to her lips and blew on it, producing a squeaky little note that startled a lone parrot out of the mango tree. Romi laughed, and while he was laughing, Kamla turned and ran down the path through the fields. And when she had gone some distance, she turned and waved to Romi with the flute. He stood near the well and waved back at her.

Cupping his hands to his mouth, he shouted across the fields, 'Don't forget to come next year!'

And Kamla called back, 'I won't forget.'

But her voice was faint, and the breeze blew the words away and Romi did not hear them.

Was England home? wondered Kamla. Or was this Indian city home? Or was her true home in that other India, across the busy Trunk Road? Perhaps she would find out one day.

Romi watched her until she was just a speck in the distance, and then he turned and shouted at the camel, telling it to move faster. But the camel did not even glance at him; it just carried on as before, as India has carried on for thousands of years, round and round and round the well, while the water gurgled and splashed over the smooth stones.

FROM SMALL BEGINNINGS

And the last puff of the day-wind brought from the unseen villages, the scent of damp wood-smoke, hot cakes, dripping undergrowth, and rotting pine cones. That is the true smell of the Himalayas, and if once it creeps into the blood of a man, that man will at the last, forgetting all else, return to the hills to die.

—Rudyard Kipling

On the first clear September day, towards the end of the rains, I visited the pine knoll, my place of peace and power.

It was months since I'd last been there. Trips to the plains, a crisis in my affairs, involvements with other people and their troubles, and an entire monsoon had come between me and the grassy, pine-topped slope facing the Hill of Fairies (Pari Tibba to the locals). Now I tramped through late monsoon foliage—tall ferns, bushes festooned with flowering convolvulus—crossed the stream by way of its little bridge of stones and climbed the steep hill to the pine slope.

When the trees saw me, they made as if to turn in my direction. A puff of wind came across the valley from the distant snows. A long-tailed blue magpie took alarm and flew noisily out of an oak tree. The cicadas were suddenly silent. But the trees remembered me. They bowed gently in the breeze and beckoned me nearer, welcoming me home. Three pines, a straggling oak and a wild cherry. I went among them and acknowledged their welcome with a touch of my hand against their trunks—the cherry's smooth and polished; the pine's patterned and whorled; the oak's rough, gnarled, full of experience. He'd been there longest, and the wind had bent his upper branches and twisted a few, so that he looked shaggy and undistinguished. But like the philosopher who is careless about his dress and appearance, the oak has secrets, a hidden wisdom. He has learnt the art of survival!

While the oak and the pines are older than me and have been here many years, the cherry tree is exactly seven years old. I know because I planted it.

One day I had this cherry seed in my hand, and on an impulse I thrust it into the soft earth, and then went away and forgot all about it. A few months later I found a tiny cherry tree in the long grass. I did not expect it to survive. But the following year it was two feet tall. And then some goats ate its leaves, and a grass cutter's scythe injured the stem, and I was sure it would wither away. But it renewed itself, sprang up even faster, and within three years it was a healthy, growing tree, about five feet tall.

I left the hills for two years—forced by circumstances to make a living in Delhi—but this time I did not forget the cherry tree. I thought about it fairly often, sent telepathic messages of encouragement in its direction. And when, a couple of years ago, I returned in the autumn, my heart did a somersault when I found my tree sprinkled with pale pink blossom. (The Himalayan cherry flowers in November.) And later, when the fruit was ripe, the tree was visited by finches, tits, bulbuls and other small birds, all come to feast on the sour, red cherries.

Last summer I spent a night on the pine knoll, sleeping on

the grass beneath the cherry tree. I lay awake for hours, listening to the chatter of the stream and the occasional tonk-tonk of a nightjar, and watching through the branches overhead, the stars turning in the sky; I felt the power of the sky and earth, and the power of a small cherry seed...

And so when the rains are over, this is where I come, that I might feel the peace and power of this place. It's a big world and momentous events are taking place all the time. But this is where I have seen it happen.

This is where I will write my stories. I can see everything from here—my cottage across the valley; behind and above me, the town and the bazaar straddling the ridge; to the left, the high mountains and the twisting road to the source of the great river; below me, the little stream and the path to the village; ahead, the Hill of Fairies, the fields beyond; the wide valley below, and then another range of hills and then the distant plains. I can even see Prem Singh in the garden, putting the mattresses out in the sun.

From here he is just a speck on the far hill, but I know it is Prem by the way he stands. A man may have a hundred disguises, but in the end it is his posture that gives him away. Like my grandfather, who was a master of disguise and successfully roamed the bazaars as fruit vendor or basket maker; but we could always recognize him because of his pronounced slouch.

Prem Singh doesn't slouch, but he has this habit of looking up at the sky (regardless of whether it's cloudy or clear), and at the moment he's looking at the sky.

Eight years with Prem! He was just a sixteen-year-old boy when I first saw him, and now he has a wife and child.

I had been in the cottage for just over a year... He stood on the landing outside the kitchen door. A tall boy, dark, with good teeth and brown, deep-set eyes; dressed smartly in white drill—his only change of clothes. Looking for a job. I liked the look of him, but—

'I already have someone working for me,' I said.

'Yes, sir. He is my uncle.'

In the hills, everyone is a brother or an uncle.

'You don't want me to dismiss your uncle?'

'No, sir. But he says you can find a job for me.'

'I'll try. I'll make inquiries. Have you just come from your village?'

'Yes. Yesterday I walked ten miles to Pauri. There I got a bus.'

'Sit down. Your uncle will make some tea.'

He sat down on the steps, removed his white keds, wriggled his toes. His feet were both long and broad, large feet, but not ugly. He was unusually clean for a hill boy. And taller than most.

'Do you smoke?' I asked.

'No, sir.'

'It is true,' said his uncle, 'he does not smoke. All my nephews smoke, but this one, he is a little peculiar, he does not smoke—neither beedi nor hookah.'

'Do you drink?'

'It makes me vomit.'

'Do you take bhang?'

'No, sahib.'

'You have no vices. It's unnatural.'

'He is unnatural, sahib,' said his uncle.

'Does he chase girls?'

'They chase him, sahib.'

'So he left the village and came looking for a job.' I looked at him. He grinned, then looked away, began rubbing his feet.

'Your name is?'

'Prem Singh.'

'All right, Prem, I will try to do something for you.'

I did not see him for a couple of weeks. I forgot about finding him a job. But when I met him again, on the road to the bazaar, he told me that he had got a temporary job in the Survey, looking after the surveyor's tents.

'Next week we will be going to Rajasthan,' he said.

'It will be very hot. Have you been in the desert before?'

'No, sir.'

'It is not like the hills. And it is far from home.'

'I know. But I have no choice in the matter. I have to collect some money in order to get married.'

In his region there was a bride price, usually of two thousand rupees.

'Do you have to get married so soon?'

'I have only one brother and he is still very young. My mother is not well. She needs a daughter-in-law to help her in the fields and with the cows and in the house. We are a small family, so the work is greater.'

Every family has its few terraced fields, narrow and stony, usually perched on a hillside above a stream or river. They grow rice, barley, maize, potatoes—just enough to live on. Even if their produce is sufficient for marketing, the absence of roads makes it difficult to get the produce to the market towns. There is no money to be earned in the villages, and money is needed for clothes, soap, medicines, and for recovering the family jewellery from the moneylenders. So the young men leave their villages to find work, and to find work they must go to the plains. The lucky ones get into the army. Others enter domestic service or take jobs in garages, hotels, wayside tea shops, schools...

In Mussoorie the main attraction is the large number of schools, which employ cooks and bearers. But the schools were full when Prem arrived. He'd been to the recruiting centre at Roorkee, hoping to get into the army; but they found a deformity in his right foot, the result of a bone broken when a landslip carried him away one dark monsoon night; he was lucky, he said, that it was only his foot and not his head that had been broken.

He came to the house to inform his uncle about the job and to say goodbye. I thought: another nice person I probably won't see again; another ship passing in the night, the friendly twinkle of its lights soon vanishing in the darkness. I said 'come again', held his smile with mine so that I could remember him better, and returned to my study and my typewriter. The typewriter is the repository of a writer's loneliness. It stares unsympathetically back at him every day, doing its best to be discouraging. Maybe I'll go back to the old-fashioned quill pen and marble inkstand; then I can feel like a real writer, Balzac or Dickens, scratching away into the endless reaches of the night... Of course, the days and nights are seemingly shorter than they need to be! They must be, otherwise why do we hurry so much and achieve so little, by the standards of the past...

Prem goes, disappears into the vast faceless cities of the plains, and a year slips by, or rather I do, and then here he is again, thinner and darker and still smiling and still looking for a job. I should have known that hill men don't disappear altogether. The spirit-haunted rocks don't let their people wander too far, lest they lose them forever.

I was able to get him a job in the school. The Headmaster's wife needed a cook. I wasn't sure if Prem could cook very well but I sent him along and they said they'd give him a trial. Three days later the Headmaster's wife met me on the road and started gushing all over me. She was the type who gushes.

'We're so grateful to you! Thank you for sending me that lovely boy. He's so polite. And he cooks very well. A little too hot for my husband, but otherwise delicious—just delicious! He's a real treasure—a lovely boy.' And she gave me an arch look—the famous look which she used to captivate all the good-looking young prefects who became prefects, it was said, only if she approved of them.

I wasn't sure that she didn't want something more than a cook, and I only hoped that Prem would give every satisfaction.

He looked cheerful enough when he came to see me on his off-day.

'How are you getting on?' I asked.

'Lovely,' he said, using his mistress's favourite expression.

'What do you mean—lovely? Do they like your work?'

'The memsahib likes it. She strokes me on the cheek whenever she enters the kitchen. The sahib says nothing. He takes medicine after every meal.'

'Did he always take medicine—or only now that you're doing the cooking?'

'I am not sure. I think he has always been sick.'

He was sleeping in the Headmaster's verandah and getting sixty rupees a month. A cook in Delhi got a hundred and sixty. And a cook in Paris or New York got ten times as much. I did not say as much to Prem. He might ask me to get him a job in New York. And that would be the last I saw of him! He, as a cook, might well get a job making curries off Broadway; I, as a writer, wouldn't get to first base. And only my Uncle Ken knew the secret of how to make a living without actually doing any work. But then, of course, he had four sisters. And each of them was married to a fairly prosperous husband. So Uncle Ken divided his year among them. Three months with Aunt Ruby in Nainital. Three months with Aunt Susie in Kashmir. Three months with my mother (not quite so affluent) in Jamnagar. And three months in the Vet Hospital in Bareilly, where Aunt Mabel ran the hospital for her veterinary husband. In this way, he never overstayed his welcome. A sister can look after a brother for just three months at a time and no more. Uncle Ken had it worked out to perfection.

But I had no sisters and I couldn't live forever on the royalties of a single novel. So I had to write others. So I came to the hills.

The hill men go to the plains to make a living. I had to come to the hills to try and make mine.

'Prem,' I said, 'why don't you work for me?'

'And what about my uncle?'

'He seems ready to desert me any day. His grandfather is ill, he says, and he wants to go home.'

'His grandfather died last year.'

'That's what I mean—he's getting restless. And I don't mind if he goes. These days he seems to be suffering from a form of sleeping sickness. I have to get up first and make his tea...'

Sitting here under the cherry tree, whose leaves are just beginning to turn yellow, I rest my chin on my knees and gaze across the valley to where Prem moves about in the garden. Looking back over the seven years he has been with me, I recall some of the nicest things about him. They come to me in no particular order—just pieces of cinema—coloured slides slipping across the screen of memory...

Prem rocking his infant son to sleep—crooning to him, passing his large hand gently over the child's curly head—Prem following me down to the police station when I was arrested (on a warrant from Bombay, charging me with writing an allegedly obscene short story!), and waiting outside until I reappeared; his smile, when I found him in Delhi, his large, irrepressible laughter, most in evidence when he was seeing an old Laurel and Hardy movie.

Of course, there were times when he could be infuriating, stubborn, deliberately pig-headed, sending me little notes of resignation—but I never found it difficult to overlook these little acts of self-indulgence. He had brought much love and laughter into my life, and what more could a lonely man ask for?

It was his stubborn streak that limited the length of his stay in the Headmaster's household. Mr Good was tolerant enough. But Mrs Good was one of those women who, when they are pleased with you go out of their way to help, pamper and flatter; and who when they are displeased, become vindictive, going out of their way to harm or destroy. Mrs Good sought power—over her husband, her dog, her favourite pupils, her servant... She had absolute power over the husband and the dog, partial power over her slightly bewildered pupils; and none at all over Prem, who missed the subtleties of her designs upon his soul. He did not respond to her mothering, or to the way in which she tweaked him on the cheeks, brushed against him in the kitchen and made admiring remarks about his looks and physique. Memsahibs, he knew, were not for him. So he kept a stony face and went diligently about his duties. And she felt slighted, put in her place. Her liking turned to dislike. Instead of admiring remarks, she began making disparaging remarks about his looks, his clothes, his manners. She found fault with his cooking. No longer was it 'lovely'. She even accused him of taking away the dog's meat and giving it to a poor family living on the hillside—no more heinous crime could be imagined! Mr Good threatened him with dismissal. So Prem became stubborn. The following day he withheld the dog's food altogether; threw it down the *khud* where it was seized upon by innumerable strays, and went off to the pictures.

It was the end of his job. 'I'll have to go home now,' he told me. 'I won't get another job in this area. The mem will see to that.'

'Stay a few days,' I said.

'I have only enough money with which to get home.'

'Keep it for going home. You can stay with me for a few days, while you look around. Your uncle won't mind sharing his food with you.'

His uncle did mind. He did not like the idea of working for his nephew as well; it seemed to him no part of his duties. And he was apprehensive that Prem might get his job.

So Prem stayed no longer than a week.

Here on the knoll the grass is just beginning to turn October yellow. The first clouds approaching winter cover the sky. The trees are very still. The birds are silent. Only a cricket keeps singing on the oak tree. Perhaps there will be a storm before evening. A storm like that in which Prem arrived at the cottage with his wife and child—but that's jumping too far ahead...

After he had returned to his village, it was several months before I saw him again. His uncle told me he had taken a job in Delhi. There was an address. It did not seem complete, but I resolved that when I was next in Delhi I would try to see him.

The opportunity came in May, as the hot winds of summer blew across the plains. It was the time of year when people who can afford it, try to get away to the hills. I dislike New Delhi at the best of times, and I hate it in summer. People compete with each other in being bad-tempered and mean. But I had to go down—I don't remember why, but it must have seemed very necessary at the time—and I took the opportunity to try and see Prem.

Nothing went right for me. Of course the address was all wrong, and I wandered about in a remote, dusty, treeless colony called Vasant Vihar (Spring Garden) for over two hours, asking all the domestic servants I came across if they could put me in touch with Prem Singh of Village Koli, Pauri Garhwal. There were innumerable Prem Singhs, but apparently none who belonged to Village Koli. I returned to my hotel and took two days to recover from heatstroke before returning to Mussoorie, thanking God for mountains!

And then the uncle gave me notice. He'd found a better paid job in Dehra Dun and was anxious to be off. I didn't try to stop him.

For the next six months I lived in the cottage without any help. I did not find this difficult. I was used to living alone. It wasn't service that I needed but companionship. In the cottage it was very quiet. The ghosts of long-dead residents were sympathetic but unobtrusive. The song of the whistling thrush was beautiful, but I knew he was not singing for me. Up the valley came the sound of a flute, but I never saw the flute player. My affinity was with the little red fox who roamed the hillside below the cottage. I met him one night and wrote these lines:

> *As I walked home last night*
> *I saw a lone fox dancing*
> *In the cold moonlight.*
> *I stood and watched—then*
> *Took the low road, knowing*
> *The night was his by right.*
> *Sometimes, when words ring true,*
> *I'm like a lone fox dancing*
> *In the morning dew.*

During the rains, watching the dripping trees and the mist climbing the valley, I wrote a great deal of poetry. Loneliness is of value to poets. But poetry didn't bring me much money, and funds were low. And then, just as I was wondering if I would have to give up my freedom and take a job again, a publisher bought the paperback rights of one of my children's stories, and I was free to live and write as I pleased—for another three months!

That was in November. To celebrate, I took a long walk

through the Landour Bazaar and up the Tehri road. It was a good day for walking; and it was dark by the time I returned to the outskirts of the town. Someone stood waiting for me on the road above the cottage. I hurried past him.

If I am not for myself,
Who will be for me?
And if I am not for others,
What am I?
And if not now, when?

I startled myself with the memory of these words of Hillel, the ancient Hebrew sage. I walked back to the shadows where the youth stood, and saw that it was Prem.

'Prem!' I said. 'Why are you sitting out here, in the cold? Why did you not go to the house?'

'I went, sir, but there was a lock on the door. I thought you had gone away.'

'And you were going to remain here, on the road?'

'Only for tonight. I would have gone down to Dehra in the morning.'

'Come, let's go home. I have been waiting for you. I looked for you in Delhi, but could not find the place where you were working.'

'I have left them now.'

'And your uncle has left me. So will you work for me now?'

'For as long as you wish.'

'For as long as the gods wish.'

We did not go straight home, but returned to the bazaar and took our meal in the Sindhi Sweet Shop; hot *puri*s and strong sweet tea.

We walked home together in the bright moonlight. I felt sorry for the little fox dancing alone.

That was twenty years ago, and Prem and his wife and three children are still with me. But we live in a different house now, on another hill.

THE FOUR FEATHERS

Our school dormitory was a very long room with about thirty beds, fifteen on either side of the room. This was good for pillow fights. Class V would take on Class VI (the two senior classes in our Prep school) and there would be plenty of space for leaping, struggling small boys, pillows flying, feathers flying, until there was a cry of 'Here comes Fishy!' or 'Here comes Olly!' and either Mr Fisher, the headmaster, or Mr Oliver, the senior master, would come striding in, cane in hand, to put an end to the general mayhem. Pillow fights were allowed, up to a point; nobody got hurt. But parents sometimes complained if, at the end of the term, a boy came home with a pillow devoid of cotton-wool or feathers.

In that last year at Prep school in Shimla, there were four of us who were close friends—Bimal, whose home was in Bombay; Riaz, who came from Lahore; Bran, who hailed from Vellore; and your narrator, who lived wherever his father (then in the Air Force) was posted.

We called ourselves the 'Four Feathers', the feathers signifying that we were companions in adventure, comrades-in-arms and knights of the round table. Bimal adopted a peacock's feather as his emblem—he was always a bit showy. Riaz chose a falcon's feather—although we couldn't find one. Bran and I were at first offered crow's or *murghi* feathers, but we protested vigorously and threatened a walkout. Finally, I settled for a parrot's feather (taken from Mrs Fisher's pet parrot), and Bran found a woodpecker's, which suited him, as he was always knocking things about.

Bimal was all thin legs and arms, so light and frisky that at times he seemed to be walking on air. We called him 'Bambi', after the delicate little deer in the Disney film. Riaz, on the other hand, was a sturdy boy, good at games though not very studious; but always good-natured, always smiling.

Bran was a dark, good-looking boy from the South; he was just a little spoilt—hated being given out in a cricket match and would refuse to leave the crease—but he was affectionate and a loyal friend. I was the 'scribe'—good at inventing stories in order to get out of scrapes—but hopeless at sums, my highest marks being 22 out of 100.

On Sunday afternoons, when there were no classes or organized games, we were allowed to roam about on the hillside below the school. The Four Feathers would laze about on the short summer grass, sharing the occasional food parcel from home, reading comics (sometimes a book) and making plans for the long winter holidays. My father, who collected everything from stamps to seashells to butterflies, had given me a butterfly net and urged me to try and catch a rare species which, he said, was found only near Chotta Shimla. He described it as a large purple butterfly with yellow and black borders on its wings. A Purple Emperor, I think it was called. As I wasn't very good at identifying butterflies, I would chase anything that happened to flit across the school grounds, usually ending up with Common Red Admirals, Clouded Yellows or Cabbage Whites. But that Purple Emperor—that rare specimen being sought by collectors the world over—proved elusive. I would have to seek my fortune in some other line of endeavour.

One day, scrambling about among the rocks and thorny bushes below the school, I almost fell over a small bundle lying in the shade of a young spruce tree. On taking a closer look,

I discovered that the bundle was really a baby wrapped up in a tattered old blanket.

'Feathers, feathers!' I called. 'Come here and look. A baby's been left here!'

The Feathers joined me and we all stared down at the infant, who was fast asleep.

'Who would leave a baby on the hillside?' asked Bimal of no one in particular.

'Someone who doesn't want it,' said Bran.

'And hoped some good people would come along and keep it,' said Riaz.

'A panther might have come along instead,' I said. 'Can't leave it here.'

'Well, we'll just have to adopt it,' said Bimal.

'We can't adopt a baby,' said Bran.

'Why not?'

'We have to be married.'

'We don't.'

'Not us, you dope. The grown-ups who adopt babies.'

'Well, we can't just leave it here for grows-ups to come along,' I said.

'We don't even know if it's a boy or a girl,' said Riaz.

'Makes no difference. A baby's a baby. Let's take it back to school.'

'And keep it in the dormitory?'

'Of course not. Who's going to feed it? Babies need milk. We'll hand it over to Mrs Fisher. She doesn't have a baby.'

'Maybe she doesn't want one. Look, it's beginning to cry. Let's hurry!'

Riaz picked up the wide-awake and crying baby and gave it to Bimal who gave it to Bran who gave it to me. The Four Feathers marched up the hill to school with a very noisy baby.

'Now it's done potty in the blanket,' I complained. 'And some of it's on my shirt.'

'Never mind,' said Bimal. 'It's for a good cause. You're a Boy Scout, remember? You're supposed to help people in distress.'

The headmaster and his wife were in their drawing room, enjoying their afternoon tea and cakes. We trudged in, and Bimal announced, 'We've got something for Mrs Fisher.'

Mrs Fisher took one look at the bundle in my arms and let out a shriek. 'What have you brought here, Bond?'

'A baby, ma'am. I think it's a girl. Do you want to adopt it?'

Mrs Fisher threw up her arms in consternation, and turned to her husband. 'What are we to do, Frank? These boys are impossible. They've picked up someone's child!'

'We'll have to inform the police,' said Mr Fisher, reaching for the telephone. 'We can't have lost babies in the school.'

Just then there was a commotion outside, and a wild-eyed woman, her clothes dishevelled, entered at the front door accompanied by several menfolk from one of the villages. She ran towards us, crying out, 'My baby, my baby! *Mera bachcha*! You've stolen my baby!'

'We found it on the hillside,' I stammered.

'That's right,' said Bran. 'Finder's keepers!'

'Quiet, Adams,' said Mr Fisher, holding up his hand for order and addressing the villagers in a friendly manner.

'These boys found the baby alone on the hillside and brought it here before…before…'

'Before the hyenas got it,' I put in.

'Quite right, Bond. And why did you leave your child alone?' he asked the woman.

'I put her down for five minutes so that I could climb the plum tree and collect the plums. When I came down, the baby had gone! But I could hear it crying up on the hill. I called the menfolk and we come looking for it.'

'Well, here's your baby,' I said, thrusting it into her arms. By then I was glad to be rid of it! 'Look after it properly in the future.'

'Kidnapper!' she screamed at me.

Mr Fisher succeeded in mollifying the villagers. 'These boys are good Scouts,' he told them. 'It's their business to help people.'

'Scout law number 3, Sir,' I added. 'To be useful and helpful.'

And then the Headmaster turned the tables on the villagers. 'By the way, those plum trees belong to the school. So do the peaches and apricots. Now I know why they've been disappearing so fast!'

The villagers, a little chastened, went their way. Mr Fisher reached for his cane. From the way he fondled it, I knew he was itching to use it on our bottoms.

'No, Frank,' said Mrs Fisher, intervening on our behalf. 'It was really very sweet of them to look after that baby. And look at Bond—he's got baby-goo all over his clothes.'

'So he has. Go and take a bath, all of you. And what are you grinning about, Bond?'

'Scout law number 8, Sir. A Scout smiles and whistles under all difficulties.'

And so ended the first adventure of the Four Feathers.

FOUR BOYS ON A GLACIER

On a day that promised rain we bundled ourselves into the bus that was to take us to Kapkote (where people lost their caps and coats, punned Anil), the starting point of our Himalayan trek. I was seventeen at the time, and Anil and Somi were sixteen. Each of us carried a haversack, and we had also brought along a good-sized bedding-roll which, apart from blankets, contained bags of rice and flour, thoughtfully provided by Anil's mother. We had no idea how we would carry the bedding-roll once we started walking, but we didn't worry too much about details.

We were soon in the hills of Kumaon, on a winding road that took us up and up, until we saw the valley and our small town spread out beneath us, the river a silver ribbon across the plain. We took a sharp bend, the valley disappeared, and the mountains towered above us.

At Kapkote, we had refreshments and the shopkeeper told us we could spend the night in one of his rooms. The surroundings were pleasant, the hills wooded with deodars, the lower slopes planted with fresh green paddy. At night, there was a wind moaning in the trees and it found its way through the cracks in the windows and eventually through our blankets.

Next morning, we washed our faces at a small stream near the shop and filled our water bottles for the day's march. A boy from the nearby village approached us, and asked where we were going.

'To the glacier,' said Somi.

'I'll come with you,' said the boy. 'I know the way.'

'You're too small,' said Anil. 'We need someone who can carry our bedding-roll.'

'I'm small but I'm strong,' said the boy, who certainly looked sturdy. He had pink cheeks and a well-knit body.

'See!' he said, and, picking up a rock the size of a football, he heaved it across the stream.

'I think he can come with us,' I said.

And then, we were walking—at first above the little Sarayu River, then climbing higher along the rough mule track, always within sound of the water, which we glimpsed now and then, swift, green and bubbling.

We were at the forest rest house by six in the evening, after covering fifteen miles. Anil found the watchman asleep in a patch of fading sunlight and roused him. The watchman, who hadn't been bothered by visitors for weeks, grumbled at our intrusion but opened a room for us. He also produced some potatoes from his store, and these were roasted for dinner.

Just as we were about to get into our beds we heard a thud on the corrugated tin roof, and then the sound of someone—or something—scrambling about on the roof. Anil, Somi and I were alarmed; but Bisnu, who was already under the blankets, merely yawned, and turned over on his side.

'It's only a bear,' he said. 'Didn't you see the pumpkins on the roof? Bears love pumpkins.'

For half an hour we had to listen to the bear as it clambered about on the roof, feasting on the watchman's ripe pumpkins. At last, there was silence. Anil and I crawled out of our blankets and went to the window. And through the frosted glass we saw a black Himalayan bear ambling across the slope in front of the house.

Our next rest house lay in a narrow valley, on the banks of the rushing Pindar River, which twisted its way through the mountains. We walked on, past terraced fields and small stone houses, until there were no more fields or houses, only forest and sun and silence.

It was different from the silence of a room or an empty street. And then, the silence broke into sound—the sound of the river.

Far down in the valley, the Pindar tumbled over itself in its impatience to reach the plains. We began to run; slipped and stumbled, but continued running.

The rest house stood on a ledge just above the river, and the sound of the water rushing down the mountain-defile could be heard at all times. The sound of the birds, which we had grown used to, was drowned by the sound of the water, but the birds themselves could be seen, many-coloured, standing out splendidly against the dark green forest foliage—the red-crowned jay, the paradise flycatcher, the purple whistling thrush and others we could not recognize.

Higher up the mountain, above some terraced land where oats and barley were grown, stood a small cluster of huts. This, we were told by the watchman, was the last village on the way to the glacier. It was, in fact, one of the last villages in India because if we crossed the difficult passes beyond the glacier, we would find ourselves in Tibet.

Anil asked the watchman about the abominable snowman. The Nepalese believe in the existence of the snowman, and our watchman was Nepalese.

'Yes, I have seen the *yeti*,' he told us. 'A great shaggy, flat-footed creature. In the winter, when it snows heavily, he passes the bungalow at night. I have seen his tracks the next morning.'

'Does he come this way in the summer?' asked Somi, anxiously.

'No,' said the watchman. 'But sometimes I have seen the *lidini*. You have to be careful of her.'

'And who is the lidini?' asked Anil.

'She is the snow-woman, and far more dangerous. She has the same height as the yeti—about seven feet when her back is straight—and her hair is much longer. Also, she has very long teeth. Her feet face inwards, but she can run very fast, especially downhill. If you see a lidini, and she chases you, always run in an uphill direction. She tires quickly because of her crooked feet. But when running downhill she has no trouble at all, and you want to be very fast to escape her!'

'Well, we are quite fast,' said Anil with a nervous laugh. 'But its just a fairy-story, I don't believe a word of it.'

The watchman was most offended, and refused to tell us anything more about snowmen and snow-women. But he helped Bisnu make a fire, and presented us with a black, sticky sweet, which we ate with relish.

It was a fine, sunny morning when we set out to cover the last seven miles to the glacier. We had expected a stiff climb, but the rest house was eleven thousand feet above sea-level, and the rest of the climb was fairly gradual.

Suddenly, abruptly, there were no more trees. As the bungalow dropped out of sight, the trees and bushes gave way to short grass and little pink and blue alpine flowers. The snow peaks were close now, ringing us in on every side. We passed white waterfalls, cascading hundreds of feet down precipitous rock faces, thundering into the little river. A great white eagle hovered over us.

The hill fell away, and there, confronting us, was a great white field of snow and ice, cradled between two shining peaks.

We were speechless for several minutes. Then we proceeded cautiously on to the snow, supporting each other on the slippery surface. We could not go far because we were quite unequipped for any high-altitude climbing. But it was a satisfying feeling to know that we were the only young men from our town who had walked so far and so high.

The sun was reflected sharply from the snow and we felt surprisingly warm. It was delicious to feel the sun crawling over our bodies, sinking deep into our bones. Meanwhile, almost imperceptibly, clouds had covered some of the peaks, and white mist drifted down the mountain slopes. It was time to return: we would barely make it to the bungalow before it grew dark.

We took our time returning to Kapkote; stopped by the Sarayu River; bathed with the village boys we had seen on the way up; collected strawberries and ferns and wild flowers; and finally said goodbye to Bisnu.

Anil wanted to take Bisnu along with us, but the boy's parents refused to let him go, saying that he was too young for the life of a city.

'Never mind,' said Somi. 'We'll go on another trek next year, and we'll take you with us Bisnu.'

This promise pleased Bisnu, and he saw us off at the bus stop, shouldering our bedding-roll to the end. Then he climbed a pine tree to have a better view of us leaving. We saw him waving to us from the tree as the bus went round the bend from Kapkote, and then the hills were left behind and the plains stretched out below.

BREAKFAST AT BAROG

It's well over seventy years that I actually breakfasted at Barog, that little railway station on the Kalka–Shimla line, but last night I dreamt of it—dreamt of the station, the dining room, the hillside and the long dark Barog tunnel—which meant that it had been present in my subconscious all these years, and was now striving to come to the fore and revive a few poignant memories.

Should I go there again? The station is still there, and so is the tunnel. I'm told that the area has been built up over the years, so that it is now almost a mini hill station. That wouldn't surprise me. Our villages have become towns, our towns have become cities and in a few years' time our country will be one vast megacity with a few parks here and there to remind us that this was once a green planet.

I don't remember any dwellings around Barog, just that one little station and its one little restaurant with a cook and a waiter and its one little stationmaster. No, such a small station couldn't have had someone as important as a stationmaster. Someone quite junior must have been in charge.

Never mind. It was the breakfast that was important. And that I was with my father and on my way to Shimla and a boarding school. The boarding school was the least desirable part of the journey. It was almost two years since I had been in a school and I was perfectly happy to continue living in an ideal world where schools need not exist. The breakup of my parents' marriage had resulted in my being withdrawn from a convent school in Mussoorie and taken over by my father who was on active service with the RAF. It was 1942 and the Second World War was at its peak. Against all regulations he kept me with him, but to do this he had to rent a flat in New Delhi. Most of the day he was at work and I would have the flat to myself, surrounded by books, gramophone records and stamp albums. Evenings I would help him with his stamp collection, for he was an avid collector. On weekends, he would take me to see Delhi's historic monuments; there was no dearth of them. From the stamps I learnt geography, from the monuments history, from the books literature. I learnt more in two years at home than I did in a year at school.

But finally he was transferred—first Colombo, then Karachi, then Calcutta—and it was no longer possible for me to share his quarters. I was admitted to Bishop Cotton's in Shimla.

We took the railcar from Kalka. It glided over the rails without any of the huffing and puffing of the steam engine that dragged the little narrow gauge train up the steep mountain. I would be travelling in that train in the years to come, but on this, my first to Shimla, I was given the luxury of the railcar.

It glided into the Barog station punctually at 10.00 a.m., in time for breakfast.

The Barog breakfast was already well known and I did full justice to it. I skipped the cornflakes and concentrated on the scrambled eggs and buttered toasts. There was bacon too, and honey and marmalade.

'Tuck in, Ruskin,' said my father. 'School breakfasts won't be half as good.'

He didn't eat much himself. There was a lot on his mind in those days, apart from his work. There was his estranged wife, my mother; my invalid sister, now with his mother in

Calcutta; his frequent transfers; his own frequent attacks of malaria; and our future in India, once the War was over—for India's independence was just around the corner.

'When do we get to Shimla?' I asked, quite happy to remain in Barog forever.

'In a little over an hour. But first we go through the longest of all the tunnels on this line. It will take about five minutes. Time for you to make a wish.'

The railcar plunged into the tunnel and we were enveloped in the darkness of the mountain. I held my father's hand. A couple of soldiers sitting behind us broke into a song from an earlier war.

*'Pack up your troubles in your old kitbag,
And smile, smile, smile!'*

A glimmer of daylight appeared at the end of the tunnel and then we were out in the sunshine and the pine-scented air.

'Did you make your wish?' asked my father.

I nodded, 'I wished that my mother would come back.'

He was silent for a few moments. 'Do you miss her a lot?'

'I don't miss her,' I said firmly. 'I'm always happy with you. But you miss her all the time. I don't like to see you so sad.'

'I've often asked her to come back,' he said. 'But it's up to her. She wants a different kind of life.'

And that was true. She was still very young—in her late twenties—and she enjoyed parties and dances and a busy social life. My father was in his forties. He liked staying at home, listening to classical music. When he took a holiday, he went in search of rare butterflies. My mother was a butterfly too—pretty, merry, fluttering here and there—but most unwilling to be displayed in a butterfly museum.

I suppose, for most of us, big or small, life is just a succession of making mistakes and we spend most of our time trying to rectify them. Marriage was a mistake for both my parents. And I was a product of that mistake!

In the time he had, my father did his best for me. And how proud I was of him when he accompanied me down to my new school! He was wearing his dark blue RAF uniform with its flying officer's stripes, and uniforms, especially officers' uniforms, made a great impression among schoolboys in those wartime days. I was received with respect and curiosity. Word went around that my father was a fighter pilot and that he'd shot down dozens of Japanese planes! He was another Biggles, that fictional aviator. Nothing could have been further from reality. My father did not fly at all. He worked for a unit called Codes and Cyphers, helping to create new codes or breaking down enemy codes. It was important work and secret work but there was no glamour about it.

Not that I was averse to the glamour of being Biggles Junior. In my previous school, I'd been something of an outsider and the Irish nuns hadn't cared much for a quiet, sensitive boy. Here I was made to feel I belonged and in no time at all I made a number of friends. It was already halfway through the school year but I had no difficulty in catching up with my classmates.

This was 'prep' school—junior school—and certainly more fun than senior school, still a couple of years away, would ever be… Still, I was always looking forward to the winter break, when I would be with my father again, for at least three months. And there he was, waiting at the Old Delhi railway station as my train drew alongside the platform. He was still in Delhi, at Air Headquarters, and I made the most of my time with him. Connaught Place was close by, and two or three evenings every week, we would go to the cinema. There were four to choose from—the Regal, the Rivoli, the Odeon and the Plaza—all very new and smart and showing the latest films from Hollywood. I became a regular film buff. The bookshops were there too, and the record shops and Wenger's with its confectionery and the Milk Bar with its milkshakes and Kwality with its ice creams. It was hard to believe that there was a world war going on in Europe and Asia and North Africa and the Pacific; or that the Quit India Movement was at its height and that my father and I might have to leave the country in the near future. He spoke about it sometimes and of the possibility of my going to a school in England. We did not talk about my mother, but I noticed that he still kept a photograph of her in his desk drawer.

It was back to school in March, when the rhododendrons were in bloom. This time I went up with the school party, in the small train with its steam engine chugging slowly up the steep inclines. The journey took all day. We did stop briefly at Barog, but we were not allowed to get down from the train; one or two boys were certain to be left behind. I looked longingly at the little restaurant on the far side of the platform; but it was already teatime. Breakfast was for the railcar!

The school year rolled on. My father was transferred to Karachi and then to Calcutta. He had grown up in Calcutta and knew the city well. He wrote to me every week and in his last letter he told me what I could look forward to during the winter holidays—the New Market with its bookshops, the botanical gardens with its ancient banyan tree, the zoo, the riverfront, the great maidan where hundreds of people would be taking in the evening air... I was hoping he would come up to see me during the autumn break, but instead I had news of another kind.

It must be difficult for a young schoolmaster, as yet untouched by tragedy, to tell a ten-year-old that he has just lost his father. Mr Murtough was given this onerous duty. And he did his best, mumbling something ridiculous about God needing my father more than I did and so on...

My friends were more natural in expressing this sympathy—giving me their sweets or chocolates, offering to play games with me, talking to me in the middle of the night when they discovered I wasn't asleep... For the future did look bleak. I wasn't sure where I would be going next—my Calcutta granny or my Dehra granny, or my mother and stepfather... I did receive a letter from my mother, telling me that my father had died of the malaria that had plagued him for years; but it was an unemotional letter and it did little to bring me comfort.

But I did go to her when school closed for the winter and I was to spend the next few years in my stepfather's home. But that's another story.

I continued my school in Shimla, and every year in March, the small train would take me and my schoolmates up the mountain, through numerous tunnels and winding gradients, forests of pine and deodar, and we always stopped at Barog, before the biggest tunnel of all. But I never made another wish when passing through that tunnel.

That was over seventy years ago.

Is the railcar still running on that line? And do they still serve breakfast at Barog?

They say you should see Venice before you die. Or better still, Varanasi. But I'll settle for that little station among the pines. And if my father is standing on the platform, waiting for me, ready to take me by the hand, I'll be a small boy again and that railcar will take us to a different destination altogether.

HERE COMES MR OLIVER

Apart from being our Scoutmaster, Mr Oliver taught us maths, a subject in which I had some difficulty obtaining pass marks. Sometimes I scraped through; usually I got something like twenty or thirty out of a hundred.

'Failed again, Bond,' Mr Oliver would say. 'What will you do when you grow up?'

'Become a scoutmaster, sir.'

'Scoutmasters don't get paid. It's an honorary job. You could become a cook. That would suit you.' He hadn't forgotten our Scout camp, when I had been the camp's cook.

If Mr Oliver was in a good mood, he'd give me grace marks, passing me by a mark or two. He wasn't a hard man, but he seldom smiled. He was very dark, thin, stooped (from a distance he looked like a question mark) and balding. He was about forty, still a bachelor, and it was said that he had been unlucky in love—that the girl he was going to marry jilted him at the last moment, running away with a sailor while Mr Oliver waited at the church, ready for the wedding ceremony. No wonder he always had such a sorrowful look.

Mr Oliver did have one inseparable companion: a dachshund, a snappy little 'sausage' of a dog, who looked upon the human race, and especially small boys, with a certain disdain and frequent hostility. We called him Hitler. (This was 1945, and the dictator was at the end of his tether.) He was impervious to overtures of friendship, and if you tried to pat or stroke him he would do his best to bite your fingers or your shin or ankle. However, he was devoted to Mr Oliver and followed him everywhere except into the classroom; this our Headmaster would not allow. You remember that old nursery rhyme:

*Mary had a little lamb,
Its fleece was white as snow,
And everywhere that Mary went
The lamb was sure to go.*

Well, we made up our own version of the rhyme, and I must confess to having had a hand in its composition. It went like this:

*Olly had a little dog,
It was never out of sight,
And everyone that Olly met
The dog was sure to bite!*

It followed him about the school grounds. It followed him when he took a walk through the pines to the Brockhuist tennis courts. It followed him into town and home again. Mr Oliver had no other friend, no other companion. The dog slept at the foot of Mr Oliver's bed. It did not sit at the breakfast table, but it had buttered toast for breakfast, and soup and crackers for dinner. Mr Oliver had to take his lunch in the dining hall with the staff and boys, but he had an arrangement with one of the bearers whereby a plate of dal, rice and *chapatti*s made its way to Mr Oliver's quarters and his well-fed pet.

And then tragedy struck.

Mr Oliver and Hitler were returning to school after an evening walk through the pines. It was dusk, and the light was fading fast. Out of the shadows of the trees emerged a lean and hungry panther. It pounced on the hapless dog, flung it across the road, seized it between its powerful jaws, and made off with its victim into the darkness of the forest.

Mr Oliver was untouched but frozen into immobility for at least a minute. Then he began calling for help. Some bystanders, who had witnessed the incident, began shouting too. Mr Oliver ran into the forest, but there was no sign of dog or panther.

Mr Oliver appeared to be a broken man. He went about his duties with a poker face, but we could all tell that he was grieving for his lost companion, for in the classroom he was listless and indifferent to whether or not we followed his calculations on the blackboard. In times of personal loss, the Highest Common Factor made no sense.

Mr Oliver was no longer seen going on his evening walk. He stayed in his room, playing cards with himself. He played with his food, pushing most of it aside. There were no chapattis to send home.

'Olly needs another pet,' said Bimal, wise in the ways of adults.

'Or a wife,' said Tata, who thought along those lines.

'He's too old. He must be over forty.'

'A pet is best,' I said. 'What about a parrot?'

'You can't take a parrot for a walk,' said Bimal. 'Olly wants someone to walk beside him.'

'A cat maybe.'

'Hitler hated cats. A cat would be an insult to Hitler's memory.'

'Then he needs another dachshund. But there aren't any around here.'

'Any dog will do. We'll ask Chimpu to get us a pup.'

Chimpu ran the tuck shop. He lived in the Chotta Shimla bazaar, and occasionally we would ask him to bring us tops or marbles, or comics or other little things that we couldn't get in school. Five of us Boy Scouts contributed a rupee each, which we gave to Chimpu and asked him to get us a pup. 'A good breed,' we told him, 'not a mongrel.'

The next evening Chimpu turned up with a pup that seemed to be a combination of at least five different breeds, all good ones no doubt. One ear lay flat, the other stood upright. It was spotted like a Dalmatian, but it had the legs of a spaniel and the tail of a Pomeranian. It was floppy and playful, and the tail wagged a lot, which was more than Hitler's ever did.

'It's quite pretty,' said Tata. 'Must be a female.'

'He may not want a female,' said Bimal.

'Let's give it a try,' I said.

During our play hour, before the bell rang for supper, we left the pup on the steps outside Mr Oliver's front door. Then we knocked, and sped into the hibiscus bush that lined the pathway.

Mr Oliver opened the door. He looked down at the pup with an expressionless face. The pup began to paw at Mr Oliver's shoes, loosening one of his laces in the process.

'Away with you!' muttered Mr Oliver. 'Buzz off!' And he pushed the pup away, gently but firmly, and closed the door.

We went through the same procedure again, but the result was much the same. We now had a playful pup on our hands, and Chimpu had gone home for the night. We would have to conceal it in the dormitory.

At first we hid it in Bimal's locker, but it began to yelp and struggled to get out. Tata took it into the shower room, but it wouldn't stay there either. It began running around the dormitory, playing with socks, shoes, slippers and anything else it could get hold of.

'Watch out!' hissed one of the boys. 'Here comes Fisher!'

Mrs Fisher, the Headmaster's wife, was on her nightly rounds, checking to make sure we were all in bed and not up to some natural mischief. I grabbed the pup and hid it under my blanket. It was quiet there, happy to nibble at my toes. When Mrs Fisher had gone, I let the pup loose again, and for the rest of the night it had the freedom of the dormitory.

At the crack of dawn, before first light, Bimal and I sped out of the dormitory in our pyjamas, taking the pup with us. We banged hard on Mr Oliver's door, and kept knocking until we heard footsteps approaching. As soon as the door was slowly opened, we pushed the pup inside and ran for our lives.

Mr Oliver came to class as usual, but there was no pup with him. Three or four days passed, and still no sign of the pup! Had he passed it on to someone else, or simply let it wander off on its own?

'Here comes Olly!' called Bimal, from our vantage point near the school bell.

Mr Oliver was setting out for his evening walk. He was carrying a strong walnut-wood walking stick—to keep panthers at bay, no doubt. He looked neither left nor right, and if he noticed us watching him, Mr Oliver gave no sign. But then, scurrying behind him was the pup! The creature of many good breeds was accompanying Mr Oliver on his walk. It had been well brushed and was wearing a bright red collar. Like Mr Oliver, it took no notice of us. It walked along beside its new master.

Mr Oliver and the little pup were soon inseparable companions, and my friends and I were quite pleased with ourselves. Mr Oliver gave absolutely no indication that he knew where the pup had come from, but when the end-of-term exams were over, and Bimal and I were sure that we had failed our maths papers, we were surprised to find that we had passed after all—with grace marks!

'Good old Olly!' said Bimal. 'So he knew all the time.' Tata, of course, did not need grace marks—he was a wizard at maths—but Bimal and I decided we would thank Mr Oliver for his kindness.

'Nothing to thank me for,' said Mr Oliver gruffly, but with a twist at the corners of his mouth, which was the nearest he came to a smile. 'I've seen enough of you two in junior school. It's high time you went up to the senior school—and God help you there!'

THE THIEF

I was still a thief when I met Arun, and though I was only fifteen I was an experienced and fairly successful hand.

Arun was watching the wrestlers when I approached him. He was about twenty, a tall, lean fellow, and he looked kind and simple enough for my purpose. I hadn't had much luck of late and thought I might be able to get into this young person's confidence. He seemed quite fascinated by the wrestling. Two well-oiled men slid about in the soft mud, grunting and slapping their thighs. When I drew Arun into conversation he didn't seem to realize I was a stranger.

'You look like a wrestler yourself,' I said.

'So do you,' he replied, which put me out of my stride for a moment because at the time I was rather thin and bony and not very impressive physically.

'Yes,' I said. 'I wrestle sometimes.'

'What's your name?'

'Deepak,' I lied.

Deepak was about my fifth name. I had earlier called myself Ranbir, Sudhir, Trilok and Surinder.

After this preliminary exchange Arun confined himself to comments on the match, and I didn't have much to say. After a while he walked away from the crowd of spectators. I followed him.

'Hello,' he said. 'Enjoying yourself?'

I gave him my most appealing smile. 'I want to work for you,' I said.

He didn't stop walking. 'And what makes you think I want someone to work for me?'

'Well,' I said, 'I've been wandering about all day looking for the best person to work for. When I saw you I knew that no one else had a chance.'

'You flatter me,' he said.

'That's all right.'

'But you can't work for me.'

'Why not?'

'Because I can't pay you.'

I thought that over for a minute. Perhaps I had misjudged my man.

'Can you feed me?' I asked.

'Can you cook?' he countered.

'I can cook,' I lied.

'If you can cook,' he said, 'I'll feed you.'

He took me to his room and told me I could sleep in the verandah. But I was nearly back on the street that night. The meal I cooked must have been pretty awful because Arun gave it to the neighbour's cat and told me to be off. But I just hung around smiling in my most appealing way and then he couldn't help laughing. He sat down on the bed and laughed for a full five minutes and later patted me on the head and said, never mind, he'd teach me to cook in the morning.

Not only did he teach me to cook but he taught me to write my name and his and said he would soon teach me to write whole sentences, and add money on paper when you didn't have any in your pocket!

It was quite pleasant working for Arun. I made the tea in the morning and later went out shopping. I would take my time buying the day's supplies and make a profit of about twenty-five paise a day. I would tell Arun that rice was fifty-six paise a pound (it generally was), but I would get it at fifty paise a pound. I think he knew I made a little this way but he didn't mind. He wasn't giving me a regular wage.

I was really grateful to Arun for teaching me to write. I knew that once I could write like an educated man there would be no limit to what I could achieve. It might even be an incentive to be honest.

Arun made money by fits and starts. He would be borrowing one week, lending the next. He would keep worrying about his next cheque but as soon as it arrived he would go out and celebrate lavishly.

One evening he came home with a wad of notes and at night I saw him tuck the bundles under his mattress at the head of the bed.

I had been working for Arun for nearly a fortnight and, apart from the shopping hadn't done much to exploit him. I had every opportunity for doing so. I had a key to the front door which meant I had access to the room whenever Arun was out. He was the most trusting person I had ever met. And that was why I couldn't make up my mind to rob him.

It's easy to rob a greedy man because he deserves to be robbed. It's easy to rob a rich man because he can afford to be robbed. But it's difficult to rob a poor man, even one who really doesn't care if he's robbed. A rich man or a greedy man or a careful man wouldn't keep his money under a pillow or mattress. He'd lock it up in a safe place. Arun had put his money where it would be child's play for me to remove it without his knowledge.

It's time I did some real work, I told myself. I'm getting out of practice... If I don't take the money, he'll only waste it on his friends... He doesn't even pay me...

Arun was asleep. Moonlight came in from the verandah and

fell across the bed. I sat up on the floor, my blanket wrapped round me, considering the situation. There was quite a lot of money in that wad and if I took it I would have to leave town—I might make the 10.30 p.m. express to Amritsar...

Slipping out of the blanket, I crept on all fours through the door and up to the bed and peeped at Arun. He was sleeping peacefully with a soft and easy breathing. His face was clear and unlined. Even I had more markings on my face, though mine were mostly scars.

My hand took on an identity of its own as it slid around under the mattress, the fingers searching for the notes. They found them and I drew them out without a crackle.

Arun sighed in his sleep and turned on his side, towards me. My free hand was resting on the bed and his hair touched my fingers.

I was frightened when his hair touched my fingers, and crawled quickly and quietly out of the room.

When I was in the street I began to run. I ran down the bazaar road to the station. The shops were all closed but a few lights were on in the upper windows. I had the notes at my waist, held there by the string of my pyjamas. I felt I had to stop and count the notes though I knew it might make me late for the train. It was already 10.20 p.m. by the clock tower. I slowed down to a walk and my fingers flicked through the notes. There were about a hundred rupees in fives. A good haul. I could live like a prince for a month or two.

When I reached the station I did not stop at the ticket office (I had never bought a ticket in my life) but dashed straight on to the platform. The Amritsar Express was just moving out. It was moving slowly enough for me to be able to jump on the footboard of one of the carriages but I hesitated for some urgent, unexplainable reason.

I hesitated long enough for the train to leave without me.

When it had gone and the noise and busy confusion of the platform had subsided, I found myself standing alone on the deserted platform. The knowledge that I had a hundred stolen rupees in my pyjamas only increased my feeling of isolation and loneliness. I had no idea where to spend the night. I had never kept any friends because sometimes friends can be one's undoing. I didn't want to make myself conspicuous by staying at a hotel. And the only person I knew really well in town was the person I had robbed!

Leaving the station, I walked slowly through the bazaar keeping to dark, deserted alleys. I kept thinking of Arun. He would still be asleep, blissfully unaware of his loss.

I have made a study of men's faces when they have lost something of material value. The greedy man shows panic, the rich man shows anger, the poor man shows fear. But I knew that neither panic nor anger nor fear would show on Arun's face when he discovered the theft; only a terrible sadness not for the loss of the money but for my having betrayed his trust.

I found myself on the maidan and sat down on a bench with my feet tucked up under my haunches. The night was a little cold and I regretted not having brought Arun's blanket along. A light drizzle added to my discomfort. Soon it was raining heavily. My shirt and pyjamas stuck to my skin and a cold wind brought the rain whipping across my face. I told myself that sleeping on a bench was something I should have been used to by now but the verandah had softened me.

I walked back to the bazaar and sat down on the steps of a closed shop. A few vagrants lay beside me, rolled up tight in thin blankets. The clock showed midnight. I felt for the notes. They were still with me but had lost their crispness and were damp with rainwater.

Arun's money. In the morning he would probably have given me a rupee to go to the pictures but now I had it all. No more cooking his meals, running to the bazaar or learning to write whole sentences. Whole sentences...

They were something I had forgotten in the excitement of a hundred rupees. Whole sentences, I knew, could one day bring me more than a hundred rupees. It was a simple matter to steal (and sometimes just as simple to be caught) but to be a really big man, a wise and successful man, that was something. I should go back to Arun, I told myself, if only to learn how to write.

Perhaps it was also concern for Arun that drew me back. A sense of sympathy is one of my weaknesses, and through hesitation over a theft I had often been caught. A successful thief must be pitiless. I was fond of Arun. My affection for him, my sense of sympathy, but most of all my desire to write whole sentences, drew me back to the room.

I hurried back to the room extremely nervous, for it is easier to steal something than to return it undetected. If I was caught beside the bed now, with the money in my hand or with my hand under the mattress, there could be only one explanation: that I was actually stealing. If Arun woke up I would be lost.

I opened the door clumsily and stood in the doorway in clouded moonlight. Gradually my eyes became accustomed to the darkness of the room. Arun was still asleep. I went on all fours again and crept noiselessly to the head of the bed. My hand came up with the notes. I felt his breath on my fingers. I was fascinated by his tranquil features and easy breathing and remained motionless for a minute. Then my hand explored the mattress, found the edge, and slipped under it the notes.

I awoke late next morning to find that Arun had already made the tea. I found it difficult to face him in the harsh light of day. His hand was stretched out towards me. There was a five-rupee note between his fingers. My heart sank.

'I made some money yesterday,' he said. 'Now you'll get paid regularly.' My spirit rose as rapidly as it had fallen. I congratulated myself on having returned the money.

But when I took the note, I realized that he knew everything. The note was still wet from last night's rain.

'Today I'll teach you to write a little more than your name,' he said.

He knew but neither his lips nor his eyes said anything about their knowing.

I smiled at Arun in my most appealing way. And the smile came by itself, without my knowing it.

CALYPSO CHRISTMAS

My first Christmas in London had been a lonely one. My small bed-sitting-room near Swiss Cottage had been cold and austere, and my landlady had disapproved of any sort of revelry. Moreover, I hadn't the money for the theatre or a good restaurant. That first English Christmas was spent sitting in front of a lukewarm gas-fire, eating beans on toast, and drinking cheap sherry. My one consolation was the row of Christmas cards on the mantelpiece—most of them from friends in India.

But the following year I was making more money and living in a bigger, brighter, homelier room. The new landlady approved of my bringing friends—even girls—to the house, and had even made me a plum pudding so that I could entertain my guests. My friends in London included a number of Indian and Commonwealth students, and through them I met George, a friendly, sensitive person from Trinidad.

George was not a student. He was over thirty. Like thousands of other West Indians, he had come to England because he had been told that jobs were plentiful, that there was a free health scheme and national insurance, and that he could earn anything from ten to twenty pounds a week—far more than he could make in Trinidad or Jamaica. But, while it was true that jobs were to be had in England, it was also true that sections of local labour resented outsiders filling these posts. There were also those, belonging chiefly to the lower middle-classes, who were prone to various prejudices, and though these people were a minority, they were still capable of making themselves felt and heard.

In any case, London is a lonely place, especially for the stranger. And for the happy-go-lucky West Indian, accustomed to sunshine, colour and music, London must be quite baffling.

As though to match the grey-green fogs of winter, Londoners wore sombre colours, greys and browns. The West Indians couldn't understand this. Surely, they reasoned, during a grey season the colours worn should be vivid reds and greens—colours that would defy the curling fog and uncomfortable rain? But Londoners frowned on these gay splashes of colour; to them it all seemed an expression of some sort of barbarism. And then again Londoners had a horror of any sort of loud noise, and a blaring radio could (quite justifiably) bring in scores of protests from neighbouring houses. The West Indians, on the other hand, liked letting off steam; they liked holding parties in their rooms at which there was much singing and shouting. They had always believed that England was their mother country, and so, despite rain, fog, sleet and snow, they were determined to live as they had lived back home in Trinidad. And it is to their credit, and even to the credit of indigenous Londoners, that this is what they succeeded in doing.

George worked for British Railways. He was a ticket collector at one of the underground stations. He liked his work, and received about ten pounds a week for collecting tickets. A large, stout man, with huge hands and feet, he always had a gentle, kindly expression on his mobile face. Among other accomplishments he could play the piano, and as there was an old, rather dilapidated piano in my room, he would often come over in the evenings to run his fat, heavy fingers over the keys, playing tunes that ranged from hymns to jazz pieces. I thought he would be a nice person to spend Christmas with, so I asked him to come and share the pudding my landlady had made, and a bottle of sherry I had procured.

Little did I realize that an invitation to George would be interpreted as an invitation to all of George's friends and relations—in fact, anyone who had known him in Trinidad—but this was the way he looked at it, and at eight o'clock on Christmas Eve, while a chilly wind blew dead leaves down from Hampstead Heath, I saw a veritable army of West Indians marching down Belsize Avenue, with George in the lead.

Bewildered, I opened my door to them; and in streamed George, George's cousins, George's nephews and George's friends. They were all smiling and they all shook hands with me, making complimentary remarks about my room ('Man, that's some piano!', 'Hey, look at that crazy picture!', 'This rocking chair gives me fever!') and took no time at all to feel and make themselves at home. Everyone had brought something along for the party. George had brought several bottles of beer. Eric, a flashy, coffee-coloured youth, had brought cigarettes and more beer. Marian, a buxom woman of thirty-five, who called me 'darling' as soon as we met, and kissed me on the cheeks saying she adored pink cheeks, had brought bacon and eggs. Her daughter Lucy, who was sixteen and in the full bloom of youth, had brought a gramophone, while the little nephews carried the records. Other friends and familiars had also brought beer; and one enterprising fellow produced a bottle of Jamaican rum.

Then everything began to happen at once.

Lucy put a record on the gramophone, and the strains of 'Basin Street Blues' filled the room. At the same time, George sat down at the piano to hammer out an accompaniment to the record. His huge hands crushed down on the keys as though he were chopping up hunks of meat. Marian had lit the gas-fire and was busy frying bacon and eggs. Eric was opening beer bottles. In the midst of the noise and confusion I heard a knock on the door—a very timid, hesitant sort of knock—and opening it, found my landlady standing on the threshold.

'Oh, Mr Bond, the neighbours—' she began, and glancing into the room was rendered speechless.

'It's only tonight,' I said. 'They'll all go home after an hour. Remember, it's Christmas!'

She nodded mutely and hurried away down the corridor, pursued by something called 'Be Bop A-Lula'. I closed the door and drew all the curtains in an effort to stifle the noise; but everyone was stamping about on the floorboards, and I hoped fervently that the downstairs people had gone to the theatre. George had started playing calypso music, and Eric and Lucy were strutting and stomping in the middle of the room, while the two nephews were improvising on their own. Before I knew what was happening, Marian had taken me in her strong arms and was teaching me to do the calypso. The song playing, I think, was 'Banana Boat Song'.

Instead of the party lasting an hour, it lasted three hours. We ate innumerable fried eggs and finished off all the beer. I took turns dancing with Marian, Lucy and the nephews. There was a peculiar expression they used when excited. 'Fire!' they shouted. I never knew what was supposed to be on fire, or what the exclamation implied, but I too shouted 'Fire!' and somehow it seemed a very sensible thing to shout.

Perhaps their hearts were on fire, I don't know; but for all their excitability and flashiness and brashness they were lovable and sincere friends, and today, when I look back on my two years in London, that Christmas party is the brightest, most vivid memory of all, and the faces of George and Marian, Lucy and Eric, are the faces I remember best.

At midnight someone turned out the light. I was dancing with Lucy at the time, and in the dark she threw her arms around me and kissed me full on the lips. It was the first time I had been kissed by a girl, and when I think about it, I am glad that it was Lucy who kissed me.

When they left, they went in a bunch, just as they had come. I stood at the gate and watched them saunter down the dark, empty street. The buses and tubes had stopped running at midnight, and George and his friends would have to walk all the way back to their rooms at Highgate and Golders Green.

After they had gone, the street was suddenly empty and silent, and my own footsteps were the only sounds I could hear. The cold came clutching at me, and I turned up my collar. I looked up at the windows of my house, and at the windows of all the other houses in the street. They were all in darkness. It seemed to me that we were the only ones who had really celebrated Christmas.

THE ROOM OF MANY COLOURS

Last week I wrote a story, and all the time I was writing it I thought it was a good story; but when it was finished and I had read it through, I found that there was something missing, that it didn't ring true. So I tore it up. I wrote a poem, about an old man sleeping in the sun, and this was true, but it was finished quickly, and once again I was left with the problem of what to write next. And I remembered my father, who taught me to write; and I thought, why not write about my father, and about the trees we planted, and about the people I knew while growing up and about what happened on the way to growing up…

And so, like Alice, I must begin at the beginning. In the beginning there was this red insect, just like a velvet button, which I found on the front lawn of the bungalow. The grass was still wet with overnight rain.

I placed the insect on the palm of my hand and took it into the house to show my father.

'Look, Dad,' I said, 'I haven't seen an insect like this before. Where has it come from?'

'Where did you find it?' he asked.

'On the grass.'

'It must have come down from the sky,' he said. 'It must have come down with the rain.'

Later he told me how the insect really happened but I preferred his first explanation. It was more fun to have it dropping from the sky.

I was seven at the time, and my father was thirty-seven, but, right from the beginning, he made me feel that I was old enough to talk to him about everything—insects, people, trees, steam engines, King George, comics, crocodiles, the Mahatma, the Viceroy, America, Mozambique and Timbuctoo. We took long walks together, explored old ruins, chased butterflies and waved to passing trains.

My mother had gone away when I was four, and I had very dim memories of her. Most other children had their mothers with them, and I found it a bit strange that mine couldn't stay. Whenever I asked my father why she'd gone, he'd say, 'You'll understand when you grow up.' And if I asked him *where* she had gone, he'd look troubled and say, 'I really don't know.' This was the only question of mine to which he didn't have an answer.

But I was quite happy living alone with my father; I had never known any other kind of life.

We were sitting on an old wall, looking out to sea at a couple of Arab dhows and a tram steamer, when my father said, 'Would you like to go to sea one day?'

'Where does the sea go?' I asked.

'It goes everywhere.'

'Does it go to the end of the world?'

'It goes right round the world. It's a round world.'

'It can't be.'

'It is. But it's so big, you can't see the roundness. When a fly sits on a watermelon, it can't see right round the melon, can it? The melon must seem quite flat to the fly. Well, in comparison to the world, we're much, much smaller than the tiniest of insects.'

'Have you been around the world?' I asked.

'No, only as far as England. That's where your grandfather was born.'

'And my grandmother?'

'She came to India from Norway when she was quite small. Norway is a cold land, with mountains and snow, and the sea cutting deep into the land. I was there as a boy. It's very beautiful, and the people are good and work hard.'

'I'd like to go there.'

'You will, one day. When you are older, I'll take you to Norway.'

'Is it better than England?'

'It's quite different.'

'Is it better than India?'

'It's quite different.'

'Is India like England?'

'No, it's different.'

'Well, what does "different" mean?'

'It means things are not the same. It means people are different. It means the weather is different. It means trees and birds and insects are different.'

'Are English crocodiles different from Indian crocodiles?'

'They don't have crocodiles in England.'

'Oh, then it must be different.'

'It would be a dull world if it was the same everywhere,' said my father.

He never lost patience with my endless questioning. If he wanted a rest, he would take out his pipe and spend a long time lighting it. If this took very long I'd find something else to do. But sometimes I'd wait patiently until the pipe was drawing, and then return to the attack.

'Will we always be in India?' I asked.

'No, we'll have to go away one day. You see, it's hard to explain, but it isn't really our country.'

'Ayah says it belongs to the king of England, and the jewels in his crown were taken from India, and that when the Indians get their jewels back the king will lose India! But first they have to get the crown from the king, but this is very difficult, she says, because the crown is always on his head. He even sleeps wearing his crown!'

Ayah was my nanny. She loved me deeply, and was always filling my head with strange and wonderful stories.

My father did not comment on Ayah's views. All he said was, 'We'll have to go away some day.'

'How long have we been here?' I asked.

'Two hundred years.'

'No, I mean us.'

'Well, you were born in India, so that's seven years for you.'

'Then can't I stay here?'

'Do you want to?'

'I want to go across the sea. But can we take Ayah with us?'

'I don't know, son. Let's walk along the beach.'

We lived in an old palace beside a lake. The palace looked like a ruin from the outside, but the rooms were cool and comfortable. We lived in one wing, and my father organized a small school in another wing. His pupils were the children of the raja and the raja's relatives. My father had started life in India as a tea planter, but he had been trained as a teacher and the idea of starting a school in a small state facing the Arabian Sea had appealed to him. The pay wasn't much, but we had a palace to live in, the latest 1938 model Hillman to drive about in and a number of servants. In those days, of course, everyone had servants (although the servants did not have any!). Ayah was our own; but the cook, the bearer, the gardener and the *bhisti* were all provided by the state.

Sometimes I sat in the schoolroom with the other children (who were all much bigger than me), sometimes I remained in the house with Ayah, sometimes I followed the gardener, Dukhi, about the spacious garden.

Dukhi means 'sad', and though I never could discover if the gardener had anything to feel sad about, the name certainly suited him. He had grown to resemble the drooping weeds that he was always digging up with a tiny spade. I seldom saw him standing up. He always sat on the ground with his knees well up to his chin, and attacked the weeds from this position. He could spend all day on his haunches, moving about the garden simply by shuffling his feet along the grass.

I tried to imitate his posture, sitting down on my heels and putting my knees into my armpits, but I could never hold the position for more than five minutes.

Time had no meaning in a large garden, and Dukhi never hurried. Life, for him, was not a matter of one year succeeding another, but of five seasons—winter, spring, hot weather, monsoon and autumn—arriving and departing. His seedbeds always had to be in readiness for the coming season, and he did not look any further than the next monsoon. It was impossible to tell his age. He may have been thirty-six or eighty-six. He was either very young for his years or very old for them.

Dukhi loved bright colours, especially reds and yellows. He liked strongly scented flowers, like jasmine and honeysuckle. He couldn't understand my father's preference for the more delicately perfumed petunias and sweetpeas. But I shared Dukhi's fondness for the common bright orange marigold, which is offered in temples and is used to make garlands and nosegays. When the garden was bare of all colour, the marigold would still be there, gay and flashy, challenging the sun.

Dukhi was very fond of making nosegays, and I liked to watch him at work. A sunflower formed the centrepiece. It was surrounded by roses, marigolds and oleander, fringed with green leaves and bound together with silver thread. The perfume was overpowering. The nosegays were presented to me or my father on special occasions, that is, on a birthday or to guests of my father's who were considered important.

One day I found Dukhi making a nosegay, and said, 'No one is coming today, Dukhi. It isn't even a birthday.'

'It is a birthday, Chota Sahib,' he said. 'Chota Sahib' was the title he had given me. It wasn't much of a title compared to Raja Sahib, Diwan Sahib or Burra Sahib, but it was nice to have a title at the age of seven.

'Oh,' I said. 'And is there a party, too?'

'No party.'

'What's the use of a birthday without a party? What's the use of a birthday without presents?'

'This person doesn't like presents—just flowers.'

'Who is it?' I asked, full of curiosity.

'If you want to find out, you can take these flowers to her. She lives right at the top of that far side of the palace. There are twenty-two steps to climb. Remember that, Chota Sahib, you take twenty-three steps and you will go over the edge and into the lake!'

I started climbing the stairs.

It was a spiral staircase of wrought iron, and it went round and round and up and up, and it made me quite dizzy and tired.

At the top I found myself on a small balcony, which looked out over the lake and another palace, at the crowded city and the distant harbour. I heard a voice, a rather high, musical voice, saying (in English), 'Are you a ghost?' I turned to see who had spoken but found the balcony empty. The voice had come from a dark room.

I turned to the stairway, ready to flee, but the voice said, 'Oh, don't go, there's nothing to be frightened of!'

And so I stood still, peering cautiously into the darkness of the room.

'First, tell me—are you a ghost?'

'I'm a boy,' I said.

'And I'm a girl. We can be friends. I can't come out there, so you had better come in. Come along, I'm not a ghost either—not yet, anyway!'

As there was nothing very frightening about the voice, I stepped into the room. It was dark inside, and coming in from the glare, it took me some time to make out the tiny, elderly lady seated on a cushioned gilt chair. She wore a red sari, lots of coloured bangles on her wrists and golden earrings. Her hair was streaked with white, but her skin was still quite smooth and unlined, and she had large and very beautiful eyes.

'You must be Master Bond!' she said. 'Do you know who I am?'

'You're a lady with a birthday,' I said, 'but that's all I know. Dukhi didn't tell me any more.'

'If you promise to keep it a secret, I'll tell you who I am. You see, everyone thinks I'm mad. Do you think so too?'

'I don't know.'

'Well, you must tell me if you think so,' she said with a chuckle. Her laugh was the sort of sound made by the gecko, a little wall lizard, coming from deep down in the throat. 'I have a feeling you are a truthful boy. Do you find it very difficult to tell the truth?'

'Sometimes.'

'Sometimes. Of course, there are times when I tell lies—lots of little lies—because they're such fun! But would you call me a liar? I wouldn't, if I were you, but would *you*?'

'Are you a liar?'

'I'm asking you! If I were to tell you that I was a queen—that I *am* a queen—would you believe me?'

I thought deeply about this, and then said, 'I'll try to believe you.'

'Oh, but you *must* believe me. I'm a real queen, I'm a rani! Look, I've got diamonds to prove it!' And she held out her hands and there was a ring on each finger, the stones glowing and glittering in the dim light. 'Diamonds, rubies, pearls and emeralds! Only a queen can have these!' She was most anxious that I should believe her.

'You must be a queen,' I said.

'Right!' she snapped. 'In that case, would you mind calling me "Your Highness"?'

'Your Highness,' I said.

She smiled. It was a slow, beautiful smile. Her whole face lit up.

'I could love you,' she said. 'But better still, I'll give you something to eat. Do you like chocolates?'

'Yes, Your Highness.'

'Well,' she said, taking a box from the table beside her, 'these have come all the way from England. Take two. Only two, mind, otherwise the box will finish before Thursday, and I don't want that to happen because I won't get any more till Saturday. That's when Captain MacWhirr's ship gets in, the *SS Lucy*, loaded with boxes and boxes of chocolates!'

'All for you?' I asked in considerable awe.

'Yes, of course. They have to last at least three months. I get them from England. I get only the best chocolates. I like them with pink crunchy fillings, don't you?'

'Oh, yes!' I exclaimed, full of envy.

'Never mind,' she said, 'I may give you one, now and then—

if you're very nice to me! Here you are, help yourself...' She pushed the chocolate box towards me.

I took a silver-wrapped chocolate, and then just as I was thinking of taking a second, she quickly took the box away.

'No more!' she said. 'They have to last till Saturday.'

'But I took only *one*,' I said with some indignation.

'Did you?' She gave me a sharp look, decided I was telling the truth, and said graciously, 'Well, in that case you can have another.'

Watching the rani carefully, in case she snatched the box away again, I selected a second chocolate, this one with a green wrapper. I don't remember what kind of day it was outside, but I remember the bright green of the chocolate wrapper.

I thought it would be rude to eat the chocolates in front of a queen, so I put them in my pocket and said, 'I'd better go now. Ayah will be looking for me.'

'And when will you be coming to see me again?'

'I don't know,' I said.

'There's something I want you to do for me,' she said, placing one finger on my shoulder and giving me a conspiratorial look. 'Will you do it?'

'What is it, Your Highness?'

'What is it? Why do you ask? A real prince never asks where or why or whatever, he simply does what the princess asks of him. When I was a princess—before I became a queen, that is—I asked a prince to swim across the lake and fetch me a lily growing on the other bank.'

'And did he get it for you?'

'He drowned halfway across. Let that be a lesson to you. Never agree to do something without knowing what it is.'

'But I thought you said...'

'Never mind what I said. It's what I say that matters!'

'Oh, all right,' I said, fidgeting to be gone. 'What is it you want me to do?'

'Nothing.' Her tiny rosebud lips pouted and she stared sullenly at a picture on the wall. Now that my eyes had grown used to the dim light in the room, I noticed that the walls were hung with portraits of stout rajas and ranis, turbaned and bedecked in fine clothes. There were also portraits of Queen Victoria and King George V of England. And, in the centre of all this distinguished company, a large picture of Mickey Mouse.

'I'll do it if it isn't too dangerous,' I said.

'Then listen.' She took my hand and drew me towards her—what a tiny hand she had!—and whispered, 'I want a *red* rose from the palace garden. But be careful! Don't let Dukhi the gardener catch you. He'll know it's for me. He knows I love roses. And he hates me! I'll tell you why, one day. But if he catches you, he'll do something terrible.'

'To me?'

'No, to himself. That's much worse, isn't it? He'll tie himself into knots, or lie naked on a bed of thorns, or go on a long fast with nothing to eat but fruit, sweets and chicken! So you will be careful, won't you?'

'Oh, but he doesn't hate you,' I cried in protest, remembering the flowers he'd sent for her, and looking around I found that I'd been sitting on them. 'Look, he sent these flowers for your birthday!'

'Well, if he sent them for my birthday, you can take them back,' she snapped. 'But if he sent them for *me*...' and she suddenly softened and looked coy, 'then I might keep them. Thank you, my dear, it was a very sweet thought.' And she leaned forward as though to kiss me.

'It's late, I must go!' I said in alarm and, turning on my heels, ran out of the room and down the spiral staircase.

Father hadn't started lunch, or rather tiffin, as we called it then. He usually waited for me if I was late. I don't suppose he enjoyed eating alone.

For tiffin we usually had rice, mutton curry (koftas or meat balls, with plenty of gravy, was my favourite curry), fried dal and a hot lime or mango pickle. For supper, we had English food—a soup, roast pork and fried potatoes, a rich gravy made by my father and a custard or caramel pudding. My father enjoyed cooking, but it was only in the morning that he found time for it. Breakfast was his own creation. He cooked eggs in a variety of interesting ways, and favoured some Italian recipes which he had collected during a trip to Europe, long before I was born.

In deference to the feelings of our Hindu friends, we did not eat beef, but, apart from mutton and chicken, there was a plentiful supply of other meats—partridge, venison, lobster and even porcupine!

'And where have you been?' asked my father, helping himself to rice as soon as he saw me come in.

'To the top of the old palace,' I said.

'Did you meet anyone there?'

'Yes, I met a tiny lady who told me she was a rani. She gave me chocolates.'

'As a rule, she doesn't like visitors.'

'Oh, she didn't mind me. But is she really a queen?'

'Well, she's the daughter of a maharaja. That makes her a princess. She never married. There's a story that she fell in love with a commoner, one of the palace servants, and wanted to marry him, but of course they wouldn't allow that. She became very melancholic, and started living all by herself in the old palace. They give her everything she needs, but she doesn't go out or have visitors. Everyone says she's mad.'

'How do they know?' I asked.

'Because she's different from other people, I suppose.'

'Is that being mad?'

'No. Not really, I suppose madness is not seeing things as others see them.'

'Is that very bad?'

'No,' said Father, who for once was finding it very difficult to explain something to me. 'But people who are like that—people whose minds are so different that they don't think, step by step, as we do, whose thoughts jump all over the place—such people are very difficult to live with…'

'Step by step,' I repeated. 'Step by step…'

'You aren't eating,' said my father. 'Hurry up, and you can come with me to school today.'

I always looked forward to attending my father's classes. He did not take me to the schoolroom very often, because he wanted school to be a treat, to begin with, and then later the routine wouldn't be so unwelcome.

Sitting there with older children, understanding only half of what they were learning, I felt important and part grown-up. And of course I did learn to read and write, although I first learnt to read upside-down, by means of standing in front of the others' desks and peering across at their books. Later, when I went to school, I had some difficulty in learning to read the right way up; and even today I sometimes read upside-down, for the sake of variety. I don't mean that I read standing on my head, simply that I held the book upside-down.

I had at my command a number of rhymes and jingles, the most interesting of these being 'Solomon Grundy'.

Solomon Grundy,
Born on a Monday,
Christened on Tuesday,

> *Married on Wednesday,*
> *Took ill on Thursday,*
> *Worse on Friday,*
> *Died on Saturday,*
> *Buried on Sunday:*
> *This is the end of*
> *Solomon Grundy.*

Was that all that life amounted to, in the end? And were we all Solomon Grundys? These were questions that bothered me at the time. Another puzzling rhyme was the one that went:

> *Hark, hark,*
> *The dogs do bark,*
> *The beggars are coming to town;*
> *Some in rags,*
> *Some in bags,*
> *And some in velvet gowns.*

This rhyme puzzled me for a long time. There were beggars aplenty in the bazaar, and sometimes they came to the house, and some of them did wear rags and bags (and some nothing at all) and the dogs did bark at them, but the beggar in the velvet gown never came our way.

'Who's this beggar in a velvet gown?' I asked my father.

'Not a beggar at all,' he said.

'Then why call him one?'

And I went to Ayah and asked her the same question, 'Who is the beggar in the velvet gown?'

'Jesus Christ,' said Ayah.

Ayah was a fervent Christian and made me say my prayers at night, even when I was very sleepy. She had, I think, Arab and Negro blood in addition to the blood of the Koli fishing community to which her mother had belonged. Her father, a sailor on an Arab dhow, had been a convert to Christianity. Ayah was a large, buxom woman, with heavy hands and feet and a slow, swaying gait that had all the grace and majesty of a royal elephant. Elephants for all their size are nimble creatures; and Ayah, too, was nimble, sensitive and gentle with her big hands. Her face was always sweet and childlike.

Although a Christian, she clung to many of the beliefs of her parents and loved to tell me stories about mischievous spirits and evil spirits, humans who changed into animals, and snakes who had been princes in their former lives.

There was the story of the snake who married a princess. At first the princess did not wish to marry the snake, whom she had met in a forest, but the snake insisted saying, 'I'll kill you if you won't marry me,' and of course that settled the question. The snake led his bride away and took her to a great treasure. 'I was a prince in my former life,' he explained. 'This treasure is yours.' And then the snake very gallantly disappeared.

'Snakes,' declared Ayah, 'were very lucky omens if seen early in the morning.'

'But, what if the snake bites the lucky person?' I asked.

'He will be lucky all the same,' said Ayah with a logic that was all her own.

Snakes! There were a number of them living in the big garden, and my father had advised me to avoid the long grass. But I had seen snakes crossing the road (a lucky omen, according to Ayah) and they were never aggressive.

'A snake won't attack you,' said Father, 'provided you leave it alone. Of course, if you step on one it will probably bite.'

'Are all snakes poisonous?'

'Yes, but only a few are poisonous enough to kill a man. Others use their poison on rats and frogs. A good thing, too, otherwise during the rains the house would be taken over by the frogs.'

One afternoon, while Father was at school, Ayah found a snake in the bathtub. It wasn't early morning and so the snake couldn't have been a lucky one. Ayah was frightened and ran into the garden calling for help. Dukhi came running. Ayah ordered me to stay outside while they went after the snake.

And it was while I was alone in the garden—an unusual circumstance, since Dukhi was nearly always there—that I remembered the rani's request. On an impulse, I went to the nearest rose bush and plucked the largest rose, pricking my thumb in the process.

And then, without waiting to see what had happened to the snake (it finally escaped), I started up the steps to the top of the old palace.

When I got to the top, I knocked on the door of the rani's room. Getting no reply, I walked along the balcony until I reached another doorway. There were wooden panels around the door, with elephants, camels and turbaned warriors carved into it. As the door was open, I walked boldly into the room then stood still in astonishment. The room was filled with a strange light.

There were windows going right round the room, and each small windowpane was made of a different coloured glass. The sun that came through one window flung red and green and purple colours on the figure of the little rani who stood there with her face pressed to the glass.

She spoke to me without turning from the window. 'This is my favourite room. I have all the colours here. I can see a different world through each pane of glass. Come, join me!' And she beckoned to me, her small hand fluttering like a delicate butterfly.

I went up to the rani. She was only a little taller than me, and we were able to share the same windowpane.

'See, it's a red world!' she said.

The garden below, the palace and the lake were all tinted red. I watched the rani's world for a little while and then touched her on the arm and said, 'I have brought you a rose!'

She started away from me, and her eyes looked frightened. She would not look at the rose.

'Oh, why did you bring it?' she cried, wringing her hands. 'He'll be arrested now!'

'Who'll be arrested?'

'The prince, of course!'

'But *I* took it,' I said. 'No one saw me. Ayah and Dukhi were inside the house, catching a snake.'

'Did they catch it?' she asked, forgetting about the rose.

'I don't know. I didn't wait to see!'

'They should follow the snake, instead of catching it. It may lead them to a treasure. All snakes have treasures to guard.'

This seemed to confirm what Ayah had been telling me, and I resolved that I would follow the next snake that I met.

'Don't you like the rose, then?' I asked.

'Did you steal it?'

'Yes.'

'Good. Flowers should always be stolen. They're more fragrant then.'

Because of a man called Hitler, war had been declared in Europe and Britain was fighting Germany.

In my comic papers, the Germans were usually shown as blundering idiots; so I didn't see how Britain could possibly lose the War, nor why it should concern India, nor why it should be necessary for my father to join up. But I remember him showing me a newspaper headline which said:

BOMBS FALL ON BUCKINGHAM PALACE—
KING AND QUEEN SAFE

I expect that had something to do with it.

He went to Delhi for an interview with the RAF and I was left in Ayah's charge.

It was a week I remember well, because it was the first time I had been left on my own. That first night I was afraid—afraid of the dark, afraid of the emptiness of the house, afraid of the howling of the jackals outside. The loud ticking of the clock was the only reassuring sound: clocks really made themselves heard in those days! I tried concentrating on the ticking, shutting out other sounds and the menace of the dark, but it wouldn't work. I thought I heard a faint hissing near the bed, and sat up, bathed in perspiration, certain that a snake was in the room. I shouted for Ayah and she came running, switching on all the lights.

'A snake!' I cried. 'There's a snake in the room!'

'Where, baba?'

'I don't know where, but I *heard* it.'

Ayah looked under the bed, and behind the chairs and tables, but there was no snake to be found. She persuaded me that I must have heard the breeze whispering in the mosquito curtains.

But I didn't want to be left alone.

'I'm coming to you,' I said and followed her into her small room near the kitchen.

Ayah slept on a low string cot. The mattress was thin, the blanket worn and patched up; but Ayah's warm and solid body made up for the discomfort of the bed. I snuggled up to her and was soon asleep.

I had almost forgotten the rani in the old palace and was about to pay her a visit when, to my surprise, I found her in the garden. I had risen early that morning, and had gone running barefoot over the dew-drenched grass. No one was about, but I startled a flock of parrots and the birds rose screeching from a banyan tree and wheeled away to some other corner of the palace grounds. I was just in time to see a mongoose scurrying across the grass with an egg in its mouth. The mongoose must have been raiding the poultry farm at the palace.

I was trying to locate the mongoose's hideout, and was on all fours in a jungle of tall cosmos plants when I heard the rustle of clothes, and turned to find the rani staring at me.

She didn't ask me what I was doing there, but simply said: 'I don't think he could have gone in there.'

'But I saw him go this way,' I said.

'Nonsense! He doesn't live in this part of the garden. He lives in the roots of the banyan tree.'

'But that's where the snake lives,' I said.

'You mean the snake who was a prince. Well, that's whom I'm looking for!'

'A snake who was a prince!' I gaped at the rani.

She made a gesture of impatience with her butterfly hands, and said, 'Tut, you're only a child, you can't understand. The prince lives in the roots of the banyan tree, but he comes out early every morning. Have you seen him?'

'No. But I saw a mongoose.'

The rani became frightened. 'Oh dear, is there a mongoose in the garden? He might kill the prince!'

'How can a mongoose kill a prince?' I asked.

'You don't understand, Master Bond. Princes, when they die, are born again as snakes.'

'*All* princes?'

'No, only those who die before they can marry.'

'Did your prince die before he could marry you?'

'Yes. And he returned to this garden in the form of a beautiful snake.'

'Well,' I said, 'I hope it wasn't the snake the water carrier killed last week.'

'He killed a snake!' The rani looked horrified. She was quivering all over. 'It might have been the prince!'

'It was a brown snake,' I said.

'Oh, then it wasn't him.' She looked very relieved. 'Brown snakes are only ministers and people like that. It has to be a green snake to be a prince.'

'I haven't seen any green snakes here.'

'There's one living in the roots of the banyan tree. You won't kill it, will you?'

'Not if it's really a prince.'

'And you won't let others kill it?'

'I'll tell Ayah.'

'Good. You're on my side. But be careful of the gardener. Keep him away from the banyan tree. He's always killing snakes. I don't trust him at all.'

She came nearer and, leaning forward a little, looked into my eyes.

'Blue eyes—I trust them. But don't trust green eyes. And yellow eyes are evil.'

'I've never seen yellow eyes.'

'That's because you're pure,' she said and turned away and hurried across the lawn as though she had just remembered a very urgent appointment.

The sun was up, slanting through the branches of the banyan tree, and Ayah's voice could be heard calling me for breakfast.

'Dukhi,' I said, when I found him in the garden later that day, 'don't kill the snake in the banyan tree.'

'A snake in the banyan tree!' he exclaimed, seizing his hose.

'No, no!' I said. 'I haven't seen it. But the rani says there's one. She says it was a prince in its former life, and that we shouldn't kill it.'

'Oh,' said Dukhi, smiling to himself. 'The rani says so. All right, you tell her we won't kill it.'

'Is it true that she was in love with a prince but that he died before she could marry him?'

'Something like that,' said Dukhi. 'It was a long time ago—before I came here.'

'My father says it wasn't a prince, but a commoner. Are you a commoner, Dukhi?'

'A commoner? What's that, Chota Sahib?'

'I'm not sure. Someone very poor, I suppose.'

'Then I must be a commoner,' said Dukhi.

'Were you in love with the rani?' I asked.

Dukhi was so startled that he dropped his hose and lost his balance; the first time I'd seen him lose his poise while squatting on his haunches.

'Don't say such things, Chota Sahib!'

'Why not?'

'You'll get me into trouble.'

'Then it must be true.'

Dukhi threw up his hands in mock despair and started collecting his implements.

'It's true, it's true!' I cried, dancing round him, and then I ran indoors to Ayah and said, 'Ayah, Dukhi was in love with the rani!'

Ayah gave a shriek of laughter, then looked very serious and put her finger against my lips.

'Don't say such things,' she said. 'Dukhi is of a very low caste. People won't like it if they hear what you say. And besides, the rani told you her prince died and turned into a snake. Well,

Dukhi hasn't become a snake as yet, has he?'

True, Dukhi didn't look as though he could be anything but a gardener; but I wasn't satisfied with his denials or with Ayah's attempts to still my tongue. Hadn't Dukhi sent the rani a nosegay?

When my father came home, he looked quite pleased with himself.

'What have you brought for me?' was the first question I asked.

He had brought me some new books, a dartboard and a train set; and in my excitement over examining these gifts, I forgot to ask about the result of his trip.

It was during tiffin that he told me what had happened—and what was going to happen.

'We'll be going away soon,' he said. 'I've joined the Royal Air Force. I'll have to work in Delhi.'

'Oh! Will you be in the War, Dad? Will you fly a plane?'

'No, I'm too old to be flying planes. I'll be forty years old in July. The RAF will be giving me what they call intelligence work—decoding secret messages and things like that and I don't suppose I'll be able to tell you much about it.'

This didn't sound as exciting as flying planes, but it sounded important and rather mysterious.

'Well, I hope it's interesting,' I said. 'Is Delhi a good place to live in?'

'I'm not sure. It will be very hot by the middle of April. And you won't be able to stay with me, Ruskin—not at first, anyway, not until I can get married quarters and then, only if your mother returns… Meanwhile, you'll stay with your grandmother in Dehra.' He must have seen the disappointment in my face, because he quickly added: 'Of course, I'll come to see you often. Dehra isn't far from Delhi—only a night's train journey.'

But I was dismayed. It wasn't that I didn't want to stay with my grandmother, but I had grown so used to sharing my father's life and even watching him at work, that the thought of being separated from him was unbearable.

'Not as bad as going to boarding school,' he said. 'And that's the only alternative.'

'Not boarding school,' I said quickly, 'I'll run away from boarding school.'

'Well, you won't want to run away from your grandmother. She's very fond of you. And if you come with me to Delhi, you'll be alone all day in a stuffy little hut while I'm away at work. Sometimes I may have to go on tour—then what happens?'

'I don't mind being on my own.' And this was true. I had already grown accustomed to having my own room and my own trunk and my own bookshelf and I felt as though I was about to lose these things.

'Will Ayah come too?' I asked.

My father looked thoughtful. 'Would you like that?'

'Ayah must come,' I said firmly. 'Otherwise I'll run away.'

'I'll have to ask her,' said my father.

Ayah, it turned out, was quite ready to come with us. In fact, she was indignant that Father should have considered leaving her behind. She had brought me up since my mother went away, and she wasn't going to hand over charge to any upstart aunt or governess. She was pleased and excited at the prospect of the move, and this helped to raise my spirits.

'What is Dehra like?' I asked my father.

'It's a green place,' he said. 'It lies in a valley in the foothills of the Himalayas and it's surrounded by forests. There are lots of trees in Dehra.'

'Does Grandmother's house have trees?'

'Yes. There's a big jackfruit tree in the garden. Your

grandmother planted it when I was a boy. And there's an old banyan tree, which is good to climb. And there are fruit trees, litchis, mangoes, papayas.'

'Are there any books?'

'Grandmother's books won't interest you. But I'll be bringing you books from Delhi whenever I come to see you.'

I was beginning to look forward to the move. Changing houses had always been fun. Changing towns ought to be fun, too.

A few days before we left, I went to say goodbye to the rani.

'I'm going away,' I said.

'How lovely!' said the rani. 'I wish I could go away!'

'Why don't you?'

'They won't let me. They're afraid to let me out of the palace.'

'What are they afraid of, Your Highness?'

'That I might run away. Run away, far, far away, to the land where the leopards are learning to pray.'

Gosh, I thought, she's really quite crazy... But then she was silent, and started smoking a small hookah.

She drew on the hookah, looked at me, and asked, 'Where is your mother?'

'I haven't one.'

'Everyone has a mother. Did yours die?'

'No. She went away.'

She drew on her hookah again and then said, very sweetly, 'Don't go away...'

'I must,' I said. 'It's because of the War.'

'What war? Is there a war on? You see, no one tells me anything.'

'It's between us and Hitler,' I said.

'And who is Hitler?'

'He's a German.'

'I knew a German once, Dr Schreinherr, he had beautiful hands.'

'Was he an artist?'

'He was a dentist.'

The rani got up from her couch and accompanied me out on to the balcony. When we looked down at the garden, we could see Dukhi weeding a flower bed. Both of us gazed down at him in silence, and I wondered what the rani would say if I asked her if she had ever been in love with the palace gardener. Ayah had told me it would be an insulting question, so I held my peace. But as I walked slowly down the spiral staircase, the rani's voice came after me.

'Thank him,' she said. 'Thank him for the beautiful rose.'

MOST BEAUTIFUL

I don't quite know why I found that particular town so heartless. Perhaps because of its crowded, claustrophobic atmosphere, its congested and insanitary lanes, its weary people... One day I found the children of the bazaar tormenting a deformed, retarded boy.

About a dozen boys, between the ages of eight and fourteen, were jeering at the retard, who was making things worse for himself by confronting the gang and shouting abuses at them. The boy was twelve or thirteen, judging by his face, but had the height of an eight- or nine-year-old. His legs were thick, short and bowed. He had a small chest but his arms were long, making him rather ape-like in his attitude. His forehead and cheeks were pitted with the scars of smallpox. He was ugly by normal standards, and the gibberish he spoke did nothing to discourage his tormentors. They threw mud and stones at him, while keeping well out of his reach. Few can be more cruel than a gang of schoolboys in high spirits.

I was an uneasy observer of the scene. I felt that I ought to do something to put a stop to it, but lacked the courage to interfere. It was only when a stone struck the boy on the face, cutting open his cheek, that I lost my normal discretion and ran in among the boys, shouting at them and clouting those I could reach. They scattered like defeated soldiery.

I was surprised at my own daring, and rather relieved when the boys did not return. I took the frightened, angry boy by the hand, and asked him where he lived. He drew away from me, but I held on to his fat little fingers and told him I would take him home. He mumbled something incoherent and pointed down a narrow lane. I led him away from the bazaar.

I said very little to the boy because it was obvious that he had some defect of speech. When he stopped outside a door set in a high wall, I presumed that we had come to his house.

The door was opened by a young woman. The boy immediately threw his arms around her and burst into tears. I had not been prepared for the boy's mother. Not only did she look perfectly normal physically, but she was also strikingly handsome. She must have been about thirty-five.

She thanked me for bringing her son home, and asked me into the house. The boy withdrew into a corner of the sitting room, and sat on his haunches in gloomy silence, his bow legs looking even more grotesque in this posture. His mother offered me tea, but I asked for a glass of water. She asked the boy to fetch it, and he did so, thrusting the glass into my hands without looking me in the face.

'Suresh is my only son,' she said. 'My husband is disappointed in him, but I love my son. Do you think he is very ugly?'

'Ugly is just a word,' I said. 'Like beauty. They mean different things to different people. What did the poet say?—"Beauty is truth, truth is beauty." But if beauty and truth are the same thing, why have different words? There are no absolutes except birth and death.'

The boy squatted down at her feet, cradling his head in her lap. With the end of her sari, she began wiping his face.

'Have you tried teaching him to talk properly?' I asked.

'He has been like this since childhood. The doctors can do nothing.'

While we were talking the father came in, and the boy

slunk away to the kitchen. The man thanked me curtly for bringing the boy home, and seemed at once to dismiss the whole matter from his mind. He seemed preoccupied with business matters. I got the impression that he had long since resigned himself to having a deformed son, and his early disappointment had changed to indifference. When I got up to leave, his wife accompanied me to the front door.

'Please do not mind if my husband is a little rude,' she said. 'His business is not going too well. If you would like to come again, please do. Suresh does not meet many people who treat him like a normal person.'

I knew that I wanted to visit them again—more out of sympathy for the mother than out of pity for the boy. But I realized that she was not interested in me personally, except as a possible mentor for her son.

After about a week I went to the house again.

Suresh's father was away on a business trip, and I stayed for lunch. The boy's mother made some delicious *paratha*s stuffed with ground radish, and served it with pickle and curd. If Suresh ate like an animal, gobbling his food, I was not far behind him. His mother encouraged him to overeat. He was morose and uncommunicative when he ate, but when I suggested that he come with me for a walk, he looked up eagerly. At the same time a look of fear passed across his mother's face.

'Will it be all right?' she asked. 'You have seen how other children treat him. That day he slipped out of the house without telling anyone.'

'We won't go towards the bazaar,' I said. 'I was thinking of a walk in the fields.'

Suresh made encouraging noises and thumped the table with his fists to show that he wanted to go. Finally his mother consented, and the boy and I set off down the road.

He could not walk very fast because of his awkward legs, but this gave me a chance to point out to him anything that I thought might arouse his interest—parrots squabbling in a banyan tree, buffaloes wallowing in a muddy pond, a group of hermaphrodite musicians strolling down the road. Suresh took a keen interest in the hermaphrodites, perhaps because they were grotesque in their own way: tall, masculine-looking people dressed in women's garments, ankle bells jingling on their heavy feet, and their long, gaunt faces made up with rouge and mascara. For the first time, I heard Suresh laugh. Apparently he had discovered that there were human beings even odder than he. And like any human being, he lost no time in deriding them.

'Don't laugh,' I said. 'They were born that way, just as you were born the way you are.'

But he did not take me seriously and grinned, his wide mouth revealing surprisingly strong teeth.

We reached the dry riverbed on the outskirts of the town and crossing it entered a field of yellow mustard flowers. The mustard stretched away towards the edge of a subtropical forest. Seeing trees in the distance, Suresh began to run towards them, shouting and clapping his hands. He had never been out of town before. The courtyard of his house and, occasionally, the road to the bazaar, were all that he had seen of the world. Now the trees beckoned him.

We found a small stream running through the forest and I took off my clothes and leapt into the cool water, inviting Suresh to join me. He hesitated about taking off his clothes, but after watching me for a while, his eagerness to join me overcame his self-consciousness, and he exposed his misshapen little body to the soft spring sunshine.

He waded clumsily towards me. The water which came only to my knees reached up to his chest.

'Come, I'll teach you to swim,' I said. And lifting him up from the waist, I held him afloat. He spluttered and thrashed around, but stopped struggling when he found that he could stay afloat.

Later, sitting on the banks of the stream, he discovered a small turtle sitting over a hole in the ground in which it had laid its eggs. He had never watched a turtle before, and watched it in fascination, while it drew its head into its shell and then thrust it out again with extreme circumspection. He must have felt that the turtle resembled him in some respects, with its squat legs, rounded back and tendency to hide its head from the world.

After that I went to the boy's house about twice a week, and we nearly always visited the stream. Before long Suresh was able to swim a short distance. Knowing how to swim—this was something the bazaar boys never learnt—gave him a certain confidence, made his life something more than a one-dimensional existence.

The more I saw Suresh, the less conscious was I of his deformities. For me, he was fast becoming the norm; while the children of the bazaar seemed abnormal in their very similarity to each other. That he was still conscious of his ugliness—and how could he ever cease to be—was made clear to me about two months after our first meeting.

We were coming home through the mustard fields, which had turned from yellow to green, when I noticed that we were being followed by a small goat. It appeared to have been separated from its mother, and now attached itself to us. Though I tried driving the kid away, it continued tripping along at out heels, and when Suresh found that it persisted in accompanying us, he picked it up and took it home.

The kid became his main obsession during the next few days. He fed it with his own hands and allowed it to sleep at the foot of his bed. It was a pretty little kid, with fairy horns and an engaging habit of doing a hop, skip and jump when moving about the house. Everyone admired the pet, and the boy's mother and I both remarked on how pretty it was.

His resentment against the animal began to show when others started admiring it. He suspected that they found it better-looking than its owner. I remember finding him squatting in front of a low mirror, holding the kid in his arms, and studying their reflections in the glass. After a few minutes of this, Suresh thrust the goat away. When he noticed that I was watching him, he got up and left the room without looking at me.

Two days later, when I called at the house, I found his mother looking very upset. I could see that she had been crying. But she seemed relieved to see me, and took me into the sitting room. When Suresh saw me, he got up from the floor and ran to the verandah.

'What's wrong?' I asked.

'It was the little goat,' she said. 'Suresh killed it.'

She told me how Suresh, in a sudden and uncontrollable rage, had thrown a brick at the kid, breaking its skull. What had upset her more than the animal's death was the fact that Suresh had shown no regret for what he had done.

'I'll talk to him,' I said, and went out to the verandah, but the boy had disappeared.

'He must have gone to the bazaar,' said his mother anxiously. 'He does that when he's upset. Sometimes I think he likes to be teased and beaten.'

He was not in the bazaar. I found him near the stream, lying flat on his belly in the soft mud, chasing tadpoles with a stick.

'Why did you kill the goat?' I asked.

He shrugged his shoulders.

'Did you enjoy killing it?'

He looked at me and smiled and nodded his head vigorously.

'How very cruel,' I said. But I did not mean it. I knew that his cruelty was no different from mine or anyone else's; only his was an untrammelled cruelty, primitive, as yet undisguised by civilizing restraints.

He took a penknife from his shirt pocket, opened it, and held it out to me by the blade. He pointed to his bare stomach and motioned me to thrust the blade into his belly. He had such a mournful look on his face (the result of having offended me and not in remorse for the goat sacrifice) that I had to burst out laughing.

'You are a funny fellow,' I said, taking the knife from him and throwing it into the stream. 'Come, let's have a swim.'

We swam all afternoon, and Suresh went home smiling. His mother and I conspired to keep the whole affair a secret from his father—who had not in any case been aware of the goat's presence.

Suresh seemed quite contented during the following weeks. And then I received a letter offering me a job in Delhi and I knew that I would have to take it, as I was earning very little by my writing at the time.

The boy's mother was disappointed, even depressed, when I told her I would be going away. I think she had grown quite fond of me. But the boy, always unpredictable, displayed no feeling at all. I felt a little hurt by his apparent indifference. Did our weeks of companionship mean nothing to him? I told myself that he probably did not realize that he might never see me again.

On the evening my train was to leave, I went to the house to say goodbye. The boy's mother made me promise to write to them, but Suresh seemed cold and distant, and refused to sit near me or take my hand. He made me feel that I was an outsider again—one of the mob throwing stones at odd and frightening people.

At eight o'clock that evening I entered a third-class compartment and, after a brief scuffle with several other travellers, succeeded in securing a seat near a window. It enabled me to look down the length of the platform.

The guard had blown his whistle and the train was about to leave when I saw Suresh standing near the station turnstile, looking up and down the platform.

'Suresh!' I shouted and he heard me and came hobbling along the platform. He had run the gauntlet of the bazaar during the busiest hour of the evening.

'I'll be back next year,' I called.

The train had begun moving out of the station, and as I waved to Suresh, he broke into a stumbling run, waving his arms in frantic, restraining gestures.

I saw him stumble against someone's bedding roll and fall sprawling on the ground. The engine picked up speed and the platform receded.

And that was the last I saw of Suresh, lying alone on the crowded platform, alone in the great grey darkness of the world, crooked and bent and twisted—the most beautiful boy in the world.

SITA AND THE RIVER

The Island in the River

In the middle of the river, the river that began in the mountains of the Himalayas and ended in the Bay of Bengal, there was a small island. The river swept round the island, sometimes clawing at its banks but never going right over it. The river was still deep and swift at this point because the foothills were only forty miles distant. More than twenty years had passed since the river had flooded the island, and at that time no one had lived there. But ten years ago a small family had came to live on the island, and now a small hut stood on it, mud-walled hut with a sloping thatched roof. The hut had been built into a huge rock. Only three of its walls were mud, the fourth was rock.

A few goats grazed on the short grass and the prickly leaves of the thistle. Some hens followed them about. There was a melon patch and a vegetable patch and a small field of marigolds. The marigolds were sometimes made into garlands, and the garlands were sold during weddings or festivals in the nearby town.

In the middle of the islands stood a peepul tree. It was the only tree on this tongue of land. But peepul trees will grow anywhere—through the walls of old temples, through gravestones, even from rooftops. It is usually the buildings, and not the trees, that give way!

Even during the great flood, which had occurred twenty years back, the peepul tree had stood firm.

It was an old tree, much older than the old man on the island, who was only seventy. The peepul was about three hundred. It also provided shelter for the birds who sometimes visited it from the mainland.

Three hundred years ago, the land on which the peepul tree stood had been part of the mainland; but the river had changed its course, and that bit of land with the tree on it had become an island. The tree had lived alone for many years. Now it gave shade and shelter to a small family, who were grateful for its presence.

The people of India love peepul trees, especially during the hot summer months when the heart-shaped leaves catch the least breath of air and flutter eagerly, fanning those who sit beneath.

A sacred tree, the peepul, the abode of spirits, good and bad.

'Do not yawn when you are sitting beneath the tree,' Grandmother would warn Sita, her ten-year-old granddaughter. 'And if you must yawn always snap your fingers in front of your mouth. If you forget to do that, a demon might jump down your throat!'

'And then what will happen?' asked Sita.

'He will probably ruin your digestion,' said Grandfather, who didn't take demons very seriously.

The peepul had beautiful leaves, and Grandmother likened it to the body of the mighty Lord Krishna—broad at the shoulders, then tapering down to a very slim waist.

The tree attracted birds and insects from across the river. On some nights it was full of fireflies.

Whenever Grandmother saw the fireflies, she told her favourite story.

'When we first came here,' she said, 'we were greatly troubled by mosquitoes. One night your grandfather rolled himself up in his sheet so that they couldn't get at him. After a while he peeped out of his bedsheet to make sure they were gone. He saw a firefly and said, "You clever mosquito! You could not see in the dark, so you got a lantern!"

Grandfather was mending a fishing-net. He had fished in the river for ten years, and he was a good fisherman. He knew where to find the slim silver *chilwa* and the big, beautiful *mahseer* and the *singhara* with its long whiskers; he knew where the river was deep and where it was shallow; he knew which baits to use—when to use worms and when to use gram. He had taught his son to fish, but his son had gone to work in a factory in a city, nearly a hundred miles away. He had no grandson; but he had a granddaughter, Sita, and she could do all the things a boy could do, and sometimes she could do them better. She had lost her mother when she was two or three. Grandmother had taught her all that a girl should know—cooking, sewing, grinding spices, cleaning the house, feeding the birds—and Grandfather had taught her other things like taking a small boat across the river, cleaning a fish, repairing a net or catching a snake by the tail! And some things she had learnt by herself—like climbing the peepul tree, or leaping from rock to rock in shallow water, or swimming in an inlet where the water was calm.

Neither grandparent could read or write, and as a result Sita couldn't read or write. There was a school in one of the villages across the river, but Sita had never seen it. She had never been further than Shahganj, the small market town near the river. She had never seen a city. She had never been on a train. The river cut her off from many things; but she could not miss what she had never known, and besides, she was much too busy.

While Grandfather mended his net, Sita was inside the hut, pressing her grandmother's forehead which was hot with fever. Grandmother had been ill for three days and could not eat. She had been ill before, but she had never been so bad.

Grandfather had brought her some sweet oranges from Shahganj, and she could suck the juice from the oranges, but she couldn't take anything else.

She was younger than Grandfather, but, because she was sick, she looked much older. She had never been very strong. She coughed a lot, and sometimes she had difficulty in breathing.

When Sita noticed that Grandmother was sleeping, she left the bedside and tiptoed out of the room on her bare feet.

Outside, she found the sky dark with monsoon clouds. It had rained all night, and, in a few hours, it would rain again. The monsoon rains had come early, at the end of June. Now it was the end of July, and already the river was swollen. Its rushing sound seemed nearer and more menacing than usual.

Sita went to her grandfather and sat down beside him.

'When you are hungry, tell me,' she said, 'and I will make the bread.'

'Is your Grandmother asleep?'

'Yes. But she will wake soon. The pain is deep.'

The old man stared out across the river, at the dark green of the forest, at the leaden sky, and said, 'If she is not better by morning, I will take her to the hospital in Shahganj. They will know how to make her well. You may be on your own for two or three days. You have been on your own before.'

Sita nodded gravely—she had been alone before; but not in the middle of the rains, with the river so high. But she knew that someone must stay behind. She wanted Grandmother to get well, and she knew that only Grandfather could take the small boat across the river when the current was so strong.

Sita was not afraid of being left alone, but she did not like the look of the river. That morning, when she had been fetching water, she had noticed that the lever suddenly disappeared.

'Grandfather, if the river rises higher, what will I do?'

'You must keep to the high ground.'
'And if the water reaches the high ground?'
'Then go into the hut, and take the hens with you.'
'And if the water comes into the hut?'
'Then climb into the peepul tree. It is a strong tree. It will not fall. And the water cannot rise higher than the tree.'
'And the goats, Grandfather?'
'I will be taking them with me. I may have to sell them, to pay for good food and medicines for your Grandmother. As for the hens, you can put them on the roof if the water enters the hut. But do not worry too much'—and he patted Sita's head—'the water will not rise so high. Has it ever done so? I will be back soon, remember that.'
'And won't Grandmother come back?'
'Yes—but they may keep her in the hospital for some time.'

The Sound of the River

That evening it began to rain again. Big pellets of rain, scarring the surface of the river. But it was warm rain, and Sita could move about in it. She was not afraid of getting wet, she rather liked it. In the previous month, when the first monsoon shower had arrived, washing the dusty leaves of the tree and bringing up the good smell of the earth, she had exulted in it, had run about shouting for joy. She was used to it now, even a little tired of the rain, but she did not mind getting wet. It was steamy indoors, and her thin dress would soon dry in the heat from the kitchen fire.

She walked about barefooted, barelegged. She was very sure on her feet; her toes had grown accustomed to gripping all kinds of rocks, slippery or sharp. And though thin, she was surprisingly strong.

Black hair, streaming across her face. Black eyes. Slim

brown arms. A scar on her thigh: when she was small, visiting her mother's village, a hyaena had entered the house where she was sleeping, fastened on to her leg and tried to drag her away; but her screams had roused the villagers, and the hyaena had run off.

She moved about in the pouring rain, chasing the hens into a shelter behind the hut. A harmless brown snake, flooded out of its hole, was moving across the open ground. Sita took a stick, picked the snake up with it, and dropped it behind a cluster of rocks. She had no quarrel with snakes. They kept down the rats and the frogs. She wondered how the rats had first come to the island—probably in someone's boat or in a sack of grain.

She disliked the huge black scorpions who left their waterlogged dwellings and tried to take shelter in the hut. It was so easy to step on one, and the sting could be very painful. She had been bitten by a scorpion the previous monsoon, and for a day and a night she had known fever and great pain. Sita had never killed living creatures, but now, whenever she found a scorpion, she crushed it with a rock!

When, finally, she went indoors, she was hungry. She ate some parched gram and warmed up some goat's milk.

Grandmother woke once, and asked for water, and Grandfather held the brass tumbler to her lips.

It rained all night.

The roof was leaking, and a small puddle formed on the floor. Grandfather kept the kerosene lamps alight. They did not need the light but somehow it made them feel safer.

The sound of the river had always been with them, although they seldom noticed it; but that night they noticed a change in its sound. There was something like a moan, like a wind in the tops of tall trees, and a swift hiss as the water swept round the rocks and carried away pebbles. And sometimes there was a rumble, as loose earth fell into the water. Sita could not sleep.

She had a rag doll, made with Grandmother's help out of bits of old clothing. She kept it by her side every night. The doll was someone to talk to, when the nights were long and sleep elusive. Her grandparents were often ready to talk; but sometimes Sita wanted to have secrets, and, though there were no special secrets in her life, she made up a few because it was fun to have them. And if you have secrets, you must have a friend to share them with. Since there were no other children on the island, Sita shared her secrets with the rag doll, whose name was Mumta.

Grandfather and Grandmother were asleep, though the sound of Grandmother's laboured breathing was almost as persistent as the sound of the river.

'Mumta,' whispered Sita in the dark, starting one of her private conversations.

'Do you think Grandmother will get well again?'

Mumta always answered Sita's questions, even though the answers were really Sita's answers.

'She is very old,' said Mumta.

'Do you think the river will reach the hut?' asked Sita.

'If it keeps raining like this, and the river keeps rising, it will reach the hut.'

'I am afraid of the river, Mumta. Aren't you afraid?'

'Don't be afraid. The river has always been good to us.'

'What will we do if it comes into the hut?'

'We will climb on the roof.'

'And if it reaches the roof?'

'We will climb the peepul tree. The river has never gone higher than the peepul tree.'

As soon as the first light showed through the little skylight,

Sita got up and went outside. It wasn't raining hard, it was drizzling, but it was the sort of drizzle that could continue for days, and it probably meant that heavy rain was falling in the hills where the river began.

Sita went down to the water's edge. She couldn't find her favourite rock, the one on which she often sat dangling her feet in the water, watching the little chilwa fish swim by. It was still there, no doubt, but the river had gone over it.

She stood on the sand, and she could feel the water oozing and bubbling beneath her feet.

The river was no longer green and blue and flecked with white; it was a muddy colour.

She went back to the hut. Grandfather was up now. He was getting his boat ready.

Sita milked the goat, thinking that perhaps it was the last time she would be milking it; but she did not care for the goat in the same way that she cared for Mumta.

The sun was just coming up when Grandfather pushed off in the boat. Grandmother lay in the prow. She was staring hard at Sita, trying to speak, but the words would not come. She raised her hand in a blessing.

Sita bent and touched her Grandmother's feet, and then Grandfather pushed off. The little boat—with its two old people and three goats—rode swiftly on the river, edging its way towards the opposite bank. The current was very swift, and the boat would be carried about half a mile downstream before Grandfather would be able to get it to dry land.

It bobbed about on the water, getting smaller and smaller, until it was just a speck on the broad river.

And suddenly Sita was alone.

There was a wind, whipping the raindrops against her face; and there was the water, rushing past the island; and there was the distant shore, blurred by rain; and there was the small hut; and there was the tree.

Sita got busy. The hens had to be fed. They weren't concerned about anything except food. Sita threw them handfuls of coarse grain, potato peels and peanut shells.

Then she took the broom and swept out the hut; lit the charcoal-burner, warmed some milk, and thought, 'Tomorrow there will be no milk...' She began peeling onions. Soon her eyes started smarting, and, pausing for a few moments and glancing round the quiet room, she became aware again that she was alone. Grandfather's hookah pipe stood by itself in one corner. It was a beautiful old hookah, which had belonged to Sita's great-grandfather. The bowl was made out of a coconut encased in silver. The long winding stem was at least four feet long. It was their most treasured possession. Grandmother's sturdy shisham-wood walking stick stood in another corner.

Sita looked around for Mumta, found the doll beneath the light wooden charpoy, and placed her within sight and hearing.

Thunder rolled down from the hills. Boom—boom—boom—

'The gods of the mountains are angry,' said Sita. 'Do you think they are angry with me?'

'Why should they be angry with you?' asked Mumta.

'They don't need a reason for being angry. They are angry with everything, and we are in the middle of everything. We are so small—do you think they know we are here?'

'Who knows what the gods think?'

'But I made you,' said Sita, 'and I know you are here.'

'And will you save me if the river rises?'

'Yes, of course. I won't go anywhere without you, Mumta.'

The Water Rises

Sita couldn't stay indoors for long. She went out, taking Mumta with her, and stared out across the river, to the safe land on the other side. But was it really safe there? The river looked much wider now. It had crept over its banks and spread far across the flat plain. Far away, people were driving their cattle through waterlogged, flooded fields, carrying their belongings in bundles on their heads or shoulders, leaving their homes, making for high land. It wasn't safe anywhere.

Sita wondered what had happened to Grandfather and Grandmother. If they had reached the shore safely, Grandfather would have to engage a bullock-cart or a pony-drawn carriage to get Grandmother to the district hospital, five or six miles away. Shahganj had a market, a court, a jail, a cinema and a hospital.

She wondered if she would ever see Grandmother again. She had done her best to look after the old lady, remembering the times when Grandmother had looked after her, had gently touched her fevered brow, and had told her stories—stories about the gods—about the young Krishna, friend of birds and animals, so full of mischief, always causing confusion among the other gods. He made Lord Indra angry by shifting a mountain without permission. Indra was the God of the clouds, who made the thunder and lightning, and when he was angry he sent down a deluge such as this one.

The island looked much smaller now. Some of its mud banks had dissolved quickly, sinking into the river. But in the middle of the island there was rocky ground, and the rocks would never crumble, they could only be submerged.

Sita climbed into the tree to get a better view of the flood. She had climbed the tree many times, and it took her only a few seconds to reach the higher branches. She put her hand to her eyes as a shield from the rain, and gazed upstream.

There was water everywhere. The world had become one vast river. Even the trees on the forested side of the river looked as though they had grown from the water, like mangroves. The sky was banked with massive, moisture-laden clouds. Thunder rolled down from the hills, and the river seemed to take it up with a hollow booming sound.

Something was floating down the river, something big and bloated. It was closer now, and Sita could make out its bulk—a drowned bullock, being carried downstream.

So the water had already flooded the villages further upstream. Or perhaps the bullock had strayed too close to the rising river.

Sita's worst fears were confirmed when, a little later, she saw planks of wood, small trees and bushes, and then a wooden bedstead, floating past the island.

As she climbed down from the tree, it began to rain more heavily. She ran indoors, shooing the hens before her. They flew into the hut and huddled under Grandmother's cot. Sita thought it would be best to keep them together now.

There were three hens and a cockbird. The river did not bother them. They were interested only in food, and Sita kept them content by throwing them a handful of onion-skins.

She would have liked to close the door and shut out the swish of the rain and the boom of the river; but then she would have no way of knowing how fast the water rose.

She took Mumta in her arms and began praying for the rain to stop and the river to fall. She prayed to Lord Indra, and, just in case he was busy elsewhere, she prayed to other gods too. She prayed for the safety of her grandparents and for her own safety. She put herself last—but only after an effort!

Finally, Sita decided to make herself a meal. So she chopped up some onions, fried them, then added turmeric and red chilli powder, salt and water, and stirred until she had everything sizzling; and then she added a cup of lentils and covered the pot.

Doing this took her about ten minutes. It would take about half an hour for the dish to cook.

When she looked outside, she saw pools of water among the rocks. She couldn't tell if it was rainwater or overflow from the river.

She had an idea.

A big tin trunk stood in a corner of the room. In it Grandmother kept an old single-thread sewing-machine. It had belonged once to an English lady, had found its way to a Shahganj junkyard, and had been rescued by Grandfather who had paid fifteen rupees for it. It was just over a hundred years old, but it could still be used.

The trunk also contained an old sword. This had originally belonged to Sita's great-grandfather, who had used it to help defend his village against marauding Rohilla soldiers more than a century ago. Sita could tell that it had been used to fight with because there were several small dents in the steel blade.

But there was no time for Sita to start admiring family heirlooms. She decided to stuff the trunk with everything useful or valuable. There was a chance that it wouldn't be carried away by the water.

Grandfather's hookah went into the trunk. Grandmother's walking stick went in too. So did a number of small tins containing the spices used in cooking—nutmeg, caraway seeds, cinnamon, coriander, pepper—also a big tin of flour and another of molasses. Even if she had to spend several hours in the tree, there would be something to eat when she came down again.

A clean white cotton dhoti of Grandfather's, and Grandmother's only spare sari also went into the trunk. Never mind if they got stained with curry powder! Never mind if they got the smell of salted fish—some of that went in too.

Sita was so busy packing the trunk that she paid no attention to the lick of cold water at her heels. She locked the trunk, dropped the key into a crack in the rock wall, and turned to give her attention to the food. It was only then that she discovered that she was walking about on a watery floor.

She stood still, horrified by what she saw. The water was oozing over the doorsill, pushing its way into the room.

In her fright, Sita forgot about her meal and everything else. Darting out of the hut, she ran splashing through ankle-deep water toward the safety of the peepul tree. If the tree hadn't been there, such a well-known landmark, she might have floundered into deep water, into the river.

She climbed swiftly into the strong arms of the tree, made herself comfortable on a familiar branch, and pushed the wet hair away from her eyes.

The Tree

She was glad she had hurried. The hut was now surrounded by water. Only the higher parts of the island could still be seen—a few rocks, the big rock into which the hut was built, a hillock on which some brambles and thorn-apples grew.

The hens hadn't bothered to leave the hut. Instead, they were perched on the wooden bedstead.

'Will the river rise still higher?' wondered Sita. She had never seen it like this before. With a deep, muffled roar it swirled around her, stretching away in all directions.

The most unusual things went by on the water—an aluminium kettle, a cane chair, a tin of tooth powder, an empty cigarette packet, a wooden slipper, a plastic doll...

A doll!

With a sinking feeling, Sita remembered Mumta.

Poor Mumta, she had been left behind in the hut. Sita, in her hurry, had forgotten her only companion.

She climbed down from the tree and ran splashing through the water towards the hut. Already the current was pulling at her legs. When she reached the hut, she found it full of water. The hens had gone—and so had Mumta.

Sita struggled back to the tree. She was only just in time, for the waters were higher now, the island fast disappearing.

She crouched miserably in the fork of the tree, watching her world disappear. She had always loved the river. Why was it threatening her now? She remembered the doll, and she thought, *If I can be so careless with someone I have made, how can I expect the gods to notice me?*

Something went floating past the tree. Sita caught a glimpse of a stiff, upraised arm and long hair streaming behind on the water. The body of a drowned woman. It was soon gone, but it made Sita feel very small and lonely, at the mercy of great and cruel forces. She began to shiver and then to cry.

She stopped crying when she saw an empty kerosene tin, with one of the hens perched on top. The tin came bobbing along on the water and sailed slowly past the tree. The hen looked a bit ruffled but seemed secure on its perch.

A little later Sita saw the remaining hens fly up to the rock ledge to huddle there in a small recess.

The water was still rising. All that remained of the island was the big rock behind the hut, and the top of the hut, and the peepul tree.

She climbed a little higher, into the crook of a branch. A jungle crow settled in the branches above her. Sita saw the nest, the crow's nest, an untidy platform of twigs wedged in the fork of a branch.

In the nest were four speckled eggs. The crow sat on them and cawed disconsolately. But though the bird sounded miserable its presence brought some cheer to Sita. At least she was not alone. Better to have a crow for company than no one at all.

Other things came floating out of the hut—a large pumpkin; a red turban belonging to Grandfather, unwinding in the water like a long snake; and then, Mumta!

The doll, being filled with straw and wood shavings moved quite swiftly on the water, too swiftly for Sita to do anything about rescuing it. Sita wanted to call out, to urge her friend to make for the tree; but she knew that Mumta could not swim— the doll could only float, travel with the river, and perhaps be washed ashore many miles downstream.

The trees shook in the wind and the rain. The crow cawed and flew up, circled the tree a few times, then returned to the nest. Sita clung to the branch.

The tree trembled throughout its tall frame. To Sita it felt like an earthquake tremor; she felt the shudder of the tree in her own bones.

The river swirled all around her now. It was almost up to the roof of the hut. Soon the mud walls would crumble and vanish. Except for the big rock and some trees very far away, there was only water to be seen. Water, and grey weeping sky.

In the distance, a boat with several people in it moved sluggishly away from the ruins of a flooded village. Someone looked out across the flooded river and said, 'See, there is a tree right in the middle of the river! How could it have got there? Isn't someone moving the tree?'

But the others thought he was imagining things; it was only a tree carried down by the flood, they said. In worrying about their own distress, they had forgotten about the island in the middle of the river.

The river was very angry now, rampaging down from the hills and thundering across the plain, bringing with it dead animals, uprooted trees, household goods and huge fishes choked to death by the swirling mud.

The peepul tree groaned. Its long, winding roots still clung tenaciously to the earth from which it had sprung many, many years ago. But the earth was softening, the stones were being washed away. The roots of the tree were rapidly losing their hold.

The crow must have known that something was wrong because it kept flying up and circling the tree, reluctant to settle in it, yet unwilling to fly away. As long as the nest was there, the crow would remain too.

Sita's wet cotton dress clung to her thin body. The rain streamed down from her long black hair. It poured from every leaf of the tree. The crow, too, was drenched and groggy.

The tree groaned and moved again.

There was a flurry of leaves, then a surge of mud from below. To Sita it seemed as though the river was rising to meet the sky. The tree tilted swinging Sita from side to side. Her feet were in the water but she clung tenaciously to her branch.

And then, she found the tree moving, moving with the river, rocking her about, dragging its roots along the ground as it set out on the first and last journey of its life.

And as the tree moved out on the river and the little island was lost in the swirling waters, Sita forgot her fear and her loneliness. The tree was taking her with it. She was not alone. It was as though one of the gods had remembered her after all.

Taken with the Flood

The branches swung Sita about, but she did not lose her grip. The tree was her friend. It had known her all these years, and now it held her in its old and dying arms as though it were determined to keep her from the river.

The crow kept flying around the moving tree. The bird was in a great rage. Its nest was still up there—but not for long! The tree lurched and twisted, and the nest fell into the water. Sita saw the eggs sink.

The crow swooped low over the water but there was nothing it could do. In a few moments the nest had disappeared.

The bird followed the tree for some time; then, flapping its wings, it rose high into the air and flew across the river until it was out of sight.

Sita was alone once more. But there was no time for feeling lonely. Everything was in motion—up and down and sideways and forwards.

She saw a turtle swimming past—a great big river turtle, the kind that feeds on decaying flesh. Sita turned her face away. In the distance she saw a flooded village and people in flat-bottomed boats; but they were very far.

Because of its great size, the tree did not move very swiftly on the river. Sometimes, when it reached shallow water, it stopped, its roots catching in the rocks; but not for long: the river's momentum soon swept it on.

At one place, where there was a bend in the river, the tree struck a sandbank and was still. It would not move again.

Sita felt very tired. Her arms were aching and she had to cling tightly to her branch to avoid slipping into the water. The rain blurred her vision. She wondered if she should brave the current and try swimming to safety. But she did not want to leave the tree. It was all that was left to her now, and she felt safe in its branches.

Then, above the sound of the river, she heard someone calling. The voice was faint and seemed very far but, looking upriver through the curtain of rain, Sita was able to make out a small boat coming towards her.

There was a boy in the boat. He seemed quite at home in the turbulent river, and he was smiling at Sita as he guided his boat towards the tree. He held on to one of the branches to steady himself, and gave his free hand to Sita.

She grasped the outstretched hand and slipped into the boat beside the boy. He placed his bare foot against the trunk of the tree and pushed away.

The little boat moved swiftly down the river. Sita looked back and saw the big tree lying on its side on the sandbank, while the river swirled round it and pulled at its branches, carrying away its beautiful slender leaves.

And then the tree grew smaller and was left far behind. A new journey had begun.

The Boy in the Boat

She lay stretched out in the boat, too tired to talk, too tired to move. The boy looked at her but he did not say anything, he just kept smiling. He leaned on his two small oars, stroking smoothly, rhythmically, trying to keep from going into the middle of the river. He wasn't strong enough to get the boat right out of the swift current; but he kept trying.

A small boat on a big river—a river that had broken its bounds and reached across the plains in every direction. The boat moved swiftly on the wild brown water, and the girl's home and the boy's home were both left far behind.

The boy wore only a loincloth. He was a slim, wiry boy, with a hard flat belly. He had high cheekbones, strong white teeth. He was a little darker than Sita.

He did not speak until they reached a broader, smoother

stretch of river, and then, resting on his oars and allowing the boat to drift a little, he said, 'You live on the island. I have seen you sometimes, from my boat. But where are the others?'

'My grandmother was sick,' said Sita. 'Grandfather took her to the hospital in Shahganj.'

'When did they leave?'

'Early this morning.'

Early that morning—and already Sita felt as though it had been many mornings ago!

'Where are you from?' she asked.

'I am from a village near the foothills. About six miles from your home. I was in my boat, trying to get across the river with the news that our village was badly flooded. The current was too strong. I was swept down and past your island. We cannot fight the river when it is like this, we must go where it takes us.'

'You must be tired,' said Sita. 'Give me the oars.'

'No. There is not much to do now. The river has gone wherever it wanted to go—it will not drive us before it any more.'

He brought in one oar, and with his free hand felt under the seat, where there was a small basket. He produced two mangoes, and gave one to Sita.

'I was supposed to sell these in Shahganj,' he said. 'My father is very strict. Even if I return home safely, he will ask me what I got for the mangoes!'

'And what will you tell him?'

'I will say they are at the bottom of the river!'

They bit deep into the ripe fleshy mangoes, using their teeth to tear the skin away. The sweet juice trickled down their skins. The good smell—like the smell of the leaves of the cosmos flower when crushed between the palms—helped to revive Sita. The flavour of the fruit was heavenly—truly the nectar of the gods!

Sita hadn't tasted a mango for over a year. For a few moments she forgot about everything else. All that mattered was the sweet, dizzy flavour of the mango.

The boat drifted, but slowly now, for as they went further downstream, the river gradually lost its power and fury. It was late afternoon when the rain stopped; but the clouds did not break up.

'My father has many buffaloes,' said the boy, 'but several have been lost in the flood.'

'Do you go to school?' asked Sita.

'Yes, I am supposed to go to school. I don't always go, at least, not when the weather is fine! There is a school near our village. I don't think you go to school?'

'No. There is too much work at home.'

'Can you read and write?'

'Only a little...'

'Then you should go to a school.'

'It is too far away.'

'True. But you should know how to read and write. Otherwise you will be stuck on your island for the rest of your life—that is, if your island is still there!'

'But I like the island,' protested Sita.

'Because you are with people you love,' said the boy. 'But your grandparents, they are old, they will die some day—and then you will be alone, and will you like the island then?'

Sita did not answer. She was trying to think of what life would be like without her grandparents. It would be an empty island, that was true. She would be imprisoned by the river.

'I can help you,' said the boy. 'When we get back—if we get back—I will come to see you sometimes, and I will teach you to read and write. All right?'

'Yes,' said Sita, nodding thoughtfully. 'When we get back...'

The boy smiled.

'My name is Krishan,' he said.

Towards evening the river changed colour. The sun, low in the sky, broke through a rift in the clouds, and the river changed slowly from grey to gold, from gold to a deep orange, and then, as the sun went down, all these colours were drowned in the river, and the river took the colour of the night.

The moon was almost at the full, and they could see a belt of forest along the line of the river.

'I will try to reach the trees,' said Krishan.

He pulled for the trees, and after ten minutes of strenuous rowing reached a bend in the river and was able to escape the pull of the main current.

Soon they were in a forest, rowing between tall trees, sal and shisham.

The boat moved slowly as Krishan took it in and out of the trees, while the moonlight made a crooked silver path over the water.

'We will tie the boat to a tree,' he said. 'Then we can rest. Tomorrow, we will have to find out a way out of the forest.'

He produced a length of rope from the bottom of the boat, tied one end to the boat's stern, and threw the other end over a stout branch which hung only a few feet above the water. The boat came to rest against the trunk of the tree.

It was a tall, sturdy tree, the Indian mahogany. It was a safe place, for there was no rush of water in the forest; and the trees grew close together, making the earth firm and unyielding.

But those who lived in the forest were on the move. The animals had been flooded out of their holes, caves and lairs, and were looking for shelter and high ground.

Sita and Krishan had just finished tying the boat to the tree when they saw a huge python gliding over the water towards them.

'Do you think it will try to get into the boat?' asked Sita.

'I don't think so,' said Krishan, although he took the precaution of holding an oar ready to fend off the snake.

But the python went past them, its head above water, its great length trailing behind, until it was lost in the shadows.

Krishan had more mangoes in the basket, and he and Sita sucked hungrily at them while they sat in the boat.

A big sambhur-stag came threshing through the water. He did not have to swim: he was so tall that his head and shoulders remained well above the water. His antlers were big and beautiful.

'There will be other animals,' said Sita. 'Should we climb onto the tree?'

'We are quite safe in the boat,' said Krishan. 'The animals will not be dangerous tonight. They will not even hunt each other, they are only interested in reaching dry land. For once, the deer are safe from the tiger and the leopard. You lie down and sleep, I will keep watch.'

Sita stretched herself out in the boat and closed her eyes. She was very tired, and the sound of the water lapping against the sides of the boat soon lulled her to sleep.

She woke once, when a strange bird called overhead. She raised herself on one elbow; but Krishan was awake, sitting beside her, his legs drawn up and his chin resting on his knees. He was gazing out across the water. He looked blue in the moonlight, the colour of the young Lord Krishna, and for a few moments Sita was confused and wondered if the boy was actually Krishna; but when she thought about it, she decided that it wasn't possible, he was just a village boy and she had seen hundreds like him—well, not exactly like him; he was a little different...

And when she slept again, she dreamt that the boy and Krishna were one, and that she was sitting beside him on a great white bird which flew over the mountains, over the snow peaks of the Himalayas, into the cloud-land of the gods. And there was a great rumbling sound, as though the gods were angry about the whole thing, and she woke up to this terrible sound and looked about her, and there in the moonlit glade, up to his belly in water, stood a young elephant, his trunk raised as he trumpeted his predicament to the forest—for he was a young elephant, and he was lost, and was looking for his mother.

He trumpeted again, then lowered his head and listened. And presently, from far away, came the shrill trumpeting of another elephant. It must have been the young one's mother because he gave several excited trumpet calls, and then went stamping and churning through the floodwater towards a gap in the trees. The boat rocked in the waves made by his passing.

'It is all right,' said Krishan. 'You can go to sleep again.'

'I don't think I will sleep now,' said Sita.

'Then I will play my flute for you and the time will pass quickly.'

He produced a flute from under the seat, and putting it to his lips he began to play. And the sweetest music that Sita had ever heard came pouring from the little flute, and it seemed to fill the forest with its beautiful sound. And the music carried her away again, into the land of dreams, and they were riding on the bird once more, Sita and the blue God, and they were passing through cloud and mist, until suddenly the sun shot through the clouds. And at that moment Sita opened her eyes and saw the sky through the branches of the mahogany tree, the shiny green leaves making a bold pattern against the blinding blue of an open sky.

The forest was drenched with sunshine. Clouds were gathering again, but for an hour or two there would be hot sun on a steamy river.

Krishan was fast asleep in the bottom of the boat. His flute lay in the palm of his half-open hand. The sun came slating across his bare brown legs. A leaf had fallen on his face, but it had not woken him, it lay on his cheek as though it had grown there.

Sita did not move about, as she did not want to wake the boy. Instead she looked around her, and she thought the water level had fallen in the night, but she couldn't be sure.

Krishan woke at last. He yawned, stretched his limbs, and sat up beside Sita.

'I am hungry,' he said.

'So am I,' said Sita.

'The last mangoes,' he said, emptying the basket of its last two mangoes.

After they had finished the fruit, they sucked the big seeds until they were quite dry. The discarded seeds floated well on the water. Sita had always preferred them to paper boats.

'We had better move on,' said Krishan.

He rowed the boat through the trees, and then for about an hour they were passing through the flooded forest, under the dripping branches of rain-washed trees. Sometimes they had to use the oars to push away vines and creepers. Sometimes submerged bushes hampered them. But they were out of the forest before ten o' clock.

The water was no longer very deep, and they were soon gliding over flooded fields. In the distance they saw a village standing on high ground. In the old days, people had built their villages on hilltops as a better defence against bandits and the soldiers of invading armies. This was an old village; and, though its inhabitants had long ago exchanged their swords for pruning forks, the hill on which it stood gave it protection from the floodwaters.

A Bullock-Cart Ride

The people of the village were at first reluctant to help Sita and Krishan.

'They are strangers,' said an old woman. 'They are not our people.'

'They are of low caste,' said another. 'They cannot remain with us.'

'Nonsense!' said a tall, turbaned farmer, twirling his long white moustache. 'They are children, not robbers. They will come into my house.'

The people of the village—long-limbed, sturdy men and women of the Jat caste—were generous by nature, and once the elderly farmer had given them the lead they were friendly and helpful.

Sita was anxious to get to her grandparents; and the farmer, who had business to transact at a village fair some twenty miles distant, offered to take Sita and Krishan with him.

The fair was being held at a place called Karauli, and at Karauli there was a railway station, and a train went to Shahganj.

It was a journey that Sita would always remember. The bullock-cart was so slow on the waterlogged roads that there was plenty of time in which to see things, to notice one another, to talk, to think, to dream.

Krishan couldn't sit still in the cart. He was used to the swift, gliding movements of his boat (which he had had to leave behind in the village), and every now and then he would jump off the cart and walk beside it, often ankle-deep in water.

There were four of them in the cart. Sita and Krishan, Hukam Singh, the Jat farmer; and his son, Phambiri, a mountain of a man who was going to take part in the wrestling matches at the fair.

Hukam Singh, who drove the bullocks, liked to talk. He had been a soldier in the British Indian Army during the First World War, and had been with his regiment to Italy and Mesopotamia.

'There is nothing to compare with soldiering,' he said, 'except, of course, farming. If you can't be a farmer, be a soldier. Are you listening, boy? Which will you be—farmer or soldier?'

'Neither,' said Krishan. 'I shall be an engineer!'

Hukam Singh's long moustaches seemed to almost bristle with indignation.

'An engineer! What next! What does your father do, boy?'

'He keeps buffaloes.'

'Ah! And his son would be an engineer… Well, well, the world isn't what it used to be! No one knows his rightful place any more. Men sent their children to schools, and what is the result? Engineers! And who will look after the buffaloes, while you are engineering?'

'I will sell the buffaloes,' said Krishan, adding rather cheekily: 'Perhaps you will buy one of them, Subedar Sahib!'

He took the cheek out of his remark by adding 'Subedar Sahib', the rank of a non-commissioned officer in the old Army. Hukam Singh, who had never reached this rank, was naturally flattered.

'Fortunately, Phambiri hasn't been to school! He'll be a farmer, and a fine one too.'

Phambiri simply grunted, which could have meant anything. He hadn't studied further than Class 6, which was just as well, as he was a man of muscle, not brain.

Phambiri loved putting his strength to some practical and useful purpose. Whenever the cartwheels got stuck in the mud, he would get off, remove his shirt, and put his shoulder to the side of the cart, while his muscles bulged and the sweat glistened on his broad back.

'Phambiri is the strongest man in our district,' said Hukam Singh proudly. 'And clever, too! It takes quick thinking to win a wrestling match.'

'I have never seen one,' said Sita.

'Then stay with us tomorrow morning, and you will see Phambiri wrestle. He has been challenged by the Karauli champion. It will be a great fight!'

'We must see Phambiri win,' said Krishan.

'Will there be time?' asked Sita.

'Why not? The train for Shahganj won't come in till evening. The fair goes on all day, and the wrestling bouts will take place in the morning.'

'Yes, you must see me win!' exclaimed Phambiri, thumping himself on the chest as he climbed back on to the cart after freeing the wheels. 'No one can defeat me!'

'How can you be so certain?' asked Krishan.

'He *has* to be certain,' said Hukam Singh. 'I have taught him to be certain! You can't win anything if you are uncertain… Isn't that right, Phambiri? You *know* you are going to win!'

'I know,' said Phambiri, with a grunt of confidence.

'Well, someone has to lose,' said Krishan.

'Very true,' said Hukam Singh smugly. 'After all, what would we do without losers? But for Phambiri, it is win, win, all the time!'

'And *if* he loses?' persisted Krishan.

'Then he will just forget that it happened, and will go on to win his next fight!'

Krishan found Hukam Singh's logic almost unanswerable, but Sita, who had been puzzled by the argument, now saw everything very clearly and said, 'Perhaps he hasn't won any fights as yet. Did he lose the last one?'

'Hush!' said Hukam Singh, looking alarmed. 'You must

not let him remember. You do not remember losing a fight, do you, my son?'

'I have never lost a fight,' said Phambiri with great simplicity and confidence.

'How strange,' said Sita. 'If you lose, how can you win?'

'Only a soldier can explain that,' said Hukam Singh. 'For a man who fights, there is no such thing as defeat. You fought against the river, did you not?'

'I went with the river,' said Sita. 'I went where it took me.'

'Yes, and you would have gone to the bottom if the boy had not come along to help you. He fought the river, didn't he?'

'Yes, he fought the river,' said Sita.

'You helped me to fight it,' said Krishan.

'So you both fought,' said the old man with a nod of satisfaction. 'You did not go with the river. You did not leave everything to the gods.'

'The gods were with us,' said Sita.

And so they talked, while the bullock-cart trundled along the muddy village roads. Both bullocks were white, and were decked out for the fair with coloured beaded necklaces and bells hanging from their necks. They were patient, docile beasts. But the cartwheels; which were badly in need of oiling, protested loudly, creaking and groaning as though all the demons in the world had been trapped within them.

Sita noticed a number of birds in the paddy fields. There were black and white curlews, and cranes with pink coat-tails. A good monsoon means plenty of birds. But Hukam Singh was not happy about the cranes.

'They do great damage in the wheat fields,' he said. Lighting up a small hand-held hookah pipe, he puffed at it and became philosophical again: 'Life is one long struggle for the farmer. When he has overcome the drought, survived the flood, hunted off the pig, killed the crane, and reaped the crop, then comes that bloodsucking ghoul, the moneylender. There is no escaping him! Is your father in debt to a moneylender, boy?'

'No,' said Krishan.

'That is because he doesn't have daughters who must be married! I have two. As they resemble Phambiri, they will need generous dowries.'

In spite of his grumbling, Hukam Singh seemed fairly content with his lot. He'd had a good maize crop, and the front of his cart was piled high with corn. He would sell the crop at the fair, along with some cucumbers, eggplants and melons.

The bad road had slowed them down so much that when darkness came they were still far from Karauli. In India there is hardly any twilight. Within a short time of the sun's going down, the stars were out.

'Six miles to go,' said Hukam Singh. 'In the dark our wheels may get stuck again. Let us spend the night here. If it rains, we can pull an old tarpaulin over the cart.'

Krishan made a fire in the charcoal burner which Hukam Singh had brought along, and they had a simple meal, roasting the corn over the fire and flavouring it with salt and spices and a squeeze of lemon. There was some milk, but not enough for everyone because Phambiri drank three tumblers by himself.

'If I win tomorrow,' he said, 'I will give all of you a feast!'

They settled down to sleep in the bullock-cart, and Phambiri and his father were soon snoring. Krishan lay awake, his arms crossed behind his head, staring up at the stars. Sita was very tired but she couldn't sleep. She was worrying about her grandparents, and wondering when she would see them again.

The night was full of sounds. The loud snoring that came from Phambiri and his father seemed to be taken up by invisible sleepers all around them, and Sita, becoming alarmed, turned to Krishan and asked, 'What is that strange noise?'

He smiled in the darkness, and she could see his white teeth and the glint of laughter in his eyes.

'Only the spirits of lost demons,' he said, and then laughed. 'Can't you recognize the music of the frogs?'

And that was what they heard; a sound more hideous than the wail of demons, a rising crescendo of noise—*wurrk, wurrk, wurrk*—coming from the flooded ditches on either side of the road. All the frogs in the jungle seemed to have gathered at that one spot, and each one appeared to have something to say for himself. The speeches continued for about an hour. Then the meeting broke up, and silence returned to the forest.

A jackal slunk across the road. A puff of wind brushed through the trees. The bullocks, freed from the cart, were asleep beside it. The men's snores were softer now. Krishan slept, a half smile on his face. Only Sita lay awake, worried and waiting for the dawn.

At the Fair

Already, at nine o' clock, the fairground was crowded. Cattle were being sold or auctioned. Stalls had opened, selling everything from pins to ploughs. Foodstuffs were on sale—hot food, spicy food, sweets and ices. A merry-go-round, badly oiled, was squeaking and groaning, while a loudspeaker blared popular film music across the grounds.

While Phambiri was preparing for his wrestling match, Hukam Singh was busy haggling over the price of pumpkins. Sita and Krishan wandered on their own among the stalls, gazing at toys and kites and bangles and clothing, at brightly coloured, syrupy sweets. Some of the rural people had transistor-radios dangling by straps from their shoulders, the radio music competing with the loudspeaker. Occasionally a buffalo bellowed, drowning all other sounds.

Various people were engaged in roadside professions. There was the fortune-teller. He had slips of paper, each of them covered with writing, which he kept in little trays along with some grain. He had a tame sparrow. When you gave the fortune-teller your money, he allowed the little bird to hop in and out among the trays until it stopped at one and started pecking at the grain. From this tray the fortune-teller took the slip of paper and presented it to his client. The writing told you what to expect over the next few months or years.

A harassed, middle aged man, who was surrounded by six noisy sons and daughters, was looking a little concerned because his slip of paper said: 'Do not lose hope. You will have a child soon.'

Some distance away sat a barber, and near him a professional ear-cleaner. Several children clustered around a peepshow, which was built into an old gramophone cabinet. While one man wound up the gramophone and placed a well-worn record on the turntable, his partner pushed coloured pictures through a slide-viewer.

A young man walked energetically up and down the fairground, beating a drum and announcing the day's attractions. The wrestling bouts were about to start. The main attraction was going to be the fight between Phambiri, described as a man 'whose thighs had the thickness of an elephant's trunk', and the local champion, Sher Dil ('Tiger's Heart')—a wild-looking man, with hairy chest and beetling brow. He was heavier than Phambiri but not so tall. Sita and Krishan joined Hukam Singh at one corner of the *akhara*, the wrestling-pit. Hukam Singh was massaging his son's famous thighs.

A gong sounded and Sher Dil entered the ring, slapping

himself on the chest and grunting like a wild boar. Phambiri advanced slowly to meet him.

They came to grips immediately, and stood swaying from side to side, two giants pitting their strength against each other. The sweat glistened on their well-oiled bodies.

Sher Dil got his arms round Phambiri's waist and tried to lift him off his feet; but Phambiri had twined one powerful leg around his opponent's thigh, and they both came down together with a loud squelch, churning up the soft mud of the wrestling-pit. But neither wrestler had been pinned down.

Soon they were so covered with mud that it was difficult to distinguish one from the other. There was a flurry of arms and legs. The crowd was cheering, and Sita and Krishan were cheering too, but the wrestlers were too absorbed in their struggle to be aware of their supporters. Each sought to turn the other on to his back. That was all that mattered. There was no count.

For a few moments Sher Dil had Phambiri almost helpless, but Phambiri wriggled out of a crushing grip and, using his legs once again, sent Sher Dil rocketing across the akhara. But Sher Dil landed on his belly, and even with Phambiri on top of him, it wasn't victory.

Nothing happened for several minutes, and the crowd became restless and shouted for more action. Phambiri thought of twisting his opponent's ear; but he realized that he might get disqualified for doing that, so he restrained himself. He relaxed his grip slightly, and this gave Sher Dil a chance to heave himself up and sent Phambiri spinning across the akhara. Phambiri was still in a sitting position when the other took a flying leap at him. But Phambiri dived forward, taking his opponent between the legs, and then rising, flung him backwards with a resounding thud. Sher Dil was helpless, and Phambiri sat on his opponent's chest to remove all doubts as to who was the winner. Only when the applause of the spectators told him that he had won did he rise and leave the ring.

Accompanied by his proud father, Phambiri accepted the prize money, thirty rupees, and then went in search of a tap. After he had washed the oil and mud from his body, he put on fresh clothes. Then, putting his arms around Krishan and Sita, he said, 'You have brought me luck, both of you. Now let us celebrate!' And he led the way to the sweet shops.

They ate syrupy *rasgulla*s (made from milk and sugar) and almond-filled fudge, and little pies filled with minced meat, and washed everything down with a fizzy orange drink.

'Now I will buy each of you a small present,' said Phambiri.

He bought a bright blue sports shirt for Krishan. He bought a new hookah bowl for his father. And he took Sita to a stall where dolls were sold, and asked her to choose one.

There were all kinds of dolls—cheap plastic dolls, and beautiful dolls made by hand, dressed in the traditional costumes of different regions of the country. Sita was immediately reminded of Mumta, her own rag doll, who had been made at home with Grandmother's help. And she remembered Grandmother, and Grandmother's sewing machine, and the home that had been swept away, and the tears started to roll down her eyes.

The dolls seemed to smile at Sita. The shopkeeper held them up one by one, and they appeared to dance, to twirl their wide skirts, to stamp their jingling feet on the counter. Each doll had its own special appeal to Sita. Each one wanted her love.

'Which one will you have?' asked Phambiri. 'Choose the prettiest, never mind the price!'

But Sita could say nothing, she could only shake her head. No doll, no matter how beautiful, could replace Mumta. She would never keep a doll again. That part of her life was over.

So instead of a doll Phambiri bought her coloured glass

bangles which slipped easily over Sita's thin wrists. And then he took them into a temporary cinema, a large shed made of corrugated tin sheets.

Krishan had been in a cinema before—the towns were full of cinemas—but for Sita it was another new experience. Many things that were common enough for other boys and girls were strange and new for a girl who had spent nearly all her life on a small island in the middle of a big river.

As they found seats, a curtain rolled up and a white sheet came into view. A babble of talk dwindled into silence. Sita became aware of a whirring noise somewhere not far behind her; but, before she could turn her head to see what it was, the sheet became a rectangle of light and colour. It came to life. People moved and spoke. A story unfolded.

But, long afterwards, all that Sita could remember of her first film was a jumble of images and incidents. A train in danger; the audience murmuring with anxiety; a bridge over a river (but a smaller river than hers); the bridge being blown to pieces; the engine plunging into the river; people struggling in the water; a woman rescued by a man who immediately embraced her; the lights coming on again, and the audience rising slowly and drifting out of the theatre, looking quite unconcerned and even satisfied. All those people struggling in the water were now quite safe, back in the little black box in the projection room.

Catching the Train

And now a real engine, a steam engine belching smoke and fire, was on its way to Sita.

She stood with Krishan on the station platform along with over a hundred other people waiting for the Shahganj train.

The platform was littered with the familiar bedrolls (or holdalls) without which few people in India ever travel. On these rolls sat women, children, great-aunts and great-uncles, grandfathers, grandmothers and grandchildren, while the more active adults hovered at the edge of the platform, ready to leap onto the train as soon as it arrived and reserve a space for the family. In India, people do not travel alone if they can help it. The whole family must be taken along—especially if the reason for the journey is a marriage, a pilgrimage, or simply a visit to friends or relations.

Moving among the piles of bedding and luggage were coolies, vendors of magazines, sweetmeats, tea and betel-leaf preparations. The cries of the vendors mingled with the general clamour of the station and the shunting of a steam engine in the yards.

But there came the train!

The signal was down. The crowd surged forward, swamping an assistant stationmaster. Krishan took Sita by the hand and led her forward. If they were too slow, they would not get a place on the crowded train. In front of them was a tall, burly, bearded Sikh from Punjab. Krishan decided it would be a wise move to stand behind him and move forward at the same time.

Krishan stayed closed to the Sikh who forged a way through the throng. The Sikh reached an open doorway and was through. Krishan and Sita were through! They found somewhere to sit, and were then able to look down at the platform, into the whirlpool, and enjoy themselves a little. The vendors had abandoned the people on the platform and had started selling their wares at the windows. Hukam Singh, after buying their tickets, had given Krishan and Sita a rupee to spend on the way. Krishan bought a freshly split coconut, and Sita bought a comb for her disarranged hair. She had never bothered with her hair before.

They saw a worried man rushing along the platform searching for his family; but they were already in the compartment, having beaten him to it, and eagerly helped him in at the door. A whistle shrilled, and they were off! A couple of vendors made last-minute transactions, then jumped from the slow-moving train. One man did this expertly with a tray of teacups balanced on one hand. The train gathered speed.

'What will happen to all those people still on the platform?' asked Sita anxiously. 'Will they all be left behind?'

She put her head out of the window and looked back at the receding platform. It was strangely empty. Only the vendors and the coolies and the stray dogs and the dishevelled railway staff were in evidence. A miracle had happened. No one—absolutely no one—had been left behind!

Then the train was rushing through the night, the engine throwing out bright sparks that danced away like fireflies. Sometimes the train had to slow down, as floodwater had weakened the embankments. Sometimes it stopped at brightly lit stations.

When the train started again and moved on into the dark countryside, Sita would stare through the glass of the window, at the bright lights of a town or the quiet glow of village lamps. She thought of Phambiri and Hukam Singh, and wondered if she would ever see them again. Already they were like people in a fairy tale, met briefly on the road and never seen again.

There was no room in the compartment in which to lie down; but Sita soon fell asleep, her head resting against Krishan's shoulder.

A Meeting and a Parting

Sita did not know where to look for Grandfather. For an hour, she and Krishan wandered through the Shahganj bazaar, growing hungrier all the time. They had no money left, and they were hot and thirsty.

Outside the bazaar, near a small temple, they saw a tree in which several small boys were helping themselves to the sour, purple fruit.

It did not take Krishan long to join the boys in the tree. They did not object to his joining them. It wasn't their tree, anyway.

Sita stood beneath the tree, while Krishan threw the jamuns down to her. They soon had a small pile of the fruit. They were on the road again, their faces stained with purple juice.

They were asking the way to the Shahganj hospital when Sita caught a glimpse of her grandfather on the road.

At first the old man did not recognize her. He was walking stiffly down the road, looking straight ahead, and would have walked right past the dusty, dishevelled girl, had she not charged straight at his thin, shaky legs and clasped him round the waist.

'Sita!' he cried, when he had recovered his wind and his balance. 'Why are you here? How did you get off the island? I have been very worried—it has been bad, these last two days...'

'Is Grandmother all right?' asked Sita.

But even as she spoke, she knew that Grandmother was no longer with them. The dazed look in the old man's eyes told her as much. She wanted to cry—not for Grandmother, who could suffer no more, but for Grandfather, who looked so helpless and bewildered; she did not want him to be unhappy. She forced back her tears, and took his gnarled and trembling hand and, with Krishan walking beside her, led the old man down the crowded street.

She knew, then, that it would be on her shoulder that Grandfather would lean on in the years to come.

They decided to remain in Shahganj for a couple of days, staying at a *dharamshala*—a wayside rest house—until the floodwaters subsided. Grandfather still had two of the goats—it had not been necessary to sell more than one—but he did not want to take the risk of rowing a crowded boat across to the island. The river was still fast and dangerous.

But Krishan could not stay with Sita any longer.

'I must go now,' he said. 'My father and mother will be very worried, and they will not know where to look for me. In a day or two the water will go down, and you will be able to go back to your home.'

'Perhaps the island has gone forever,' said Sita.

'It will be there,' said Krishan. 'It is a rocky island. Bad for crops, but good for a house!'

'Will you come?' asked Sita.

What she really wanted to say was, 'Will you come to see me?' but she was too shy to say it; and besides, she wasn't sure if Krishan would want to see her again.

'I will come,' said Krishan. 'That is, if my father gets me another boat!'

As he turned to go, he gave her his flute.

'Keep it for me,' he said. 'I will come for it one day.'

When he saw her hesitate, he smiled and said, 'It is a good flute!'

The Return

There was more rain, but the worst was over, and when Grandfather and Sita returned to the island, the river was no longer in spate.

Grandfather could hardly believe his eyes when he saw that the tree had disappeared—the tree that had seemed as permanent as the island, as much a part of his life as the river itself had been. He marvelled at Sita's escape.

'It was the tree that saved you,' he said.
'And the boy,' said Sita.
'Yes, and the boy.'

She thought about Krishan and wondered if she would ever see him again. Would he, like Phambiri and Hukam Singh, be one of those people who arrived as though out of a fairy tale and then disappeared silently and mysteriously? She did not know it then, but some of the moving forces of our lives are meant to touch us briefly and go their way...

And because Grandmother was no longer with them, life on the island was quite different. The evenings were sad and lonely.

But there was a lot of work to be done, and Sita did not have much time to think of Grandmother or Krishan or the world she had glimpsed during her journey.

For three nights they slept under a crude shelter made out of gunny-bags. During the day Sita helped Grandfather rebuild the mud hut. Once again, they used the big rock for support.

The trunk which Sita had packed so carefully had not been swept off the island, but the water had got into it, and the food and clothing had been spoilt. But Grandfather's hookah had been saved, and, in the evenings after work was done and they had eaten their light meal which Sita prepared, he would smoke with a little of his old contentment, and tell Sita about other floods which he had experienced as a boy. And he would tell her about the wrestling matches he had won, and the kites he had flown, for he remembered a time when grown men flew kites, and great battles were fought, the kites swooping and swerving in the sky, tangling with each other until the string of one was cut.

Kite-flying was then the sport of kings, Grandfather remembered how the Raja himself would come down to the riverbank and join in this noble pastime. There was time in those days to spend an hour with a gay, dancing strip of paper.

Now everyone hurried, in a heat of hope, and delicate things like kites and daydreams were trampled underfoot.

Grandfather remembered the 'Dragon Kite' that he had built—a great kite with a face painted on it, the eyes made of small mirrors, the tail like a long crawling serpent. A large crowd assembled to watch its launching. At the first attempt it refused to leave the ground. And then the wind came from the right direction, and the Dragon Kite soared into the sky, wriggling its way higher and higher, with the sun still glinting in its eyes. And it went very high, it pulled fiercely on the twine determined to be free, to break loose, to live a life of its own. And eventually it did.

The twine snapped, the kite leapt away toward the sun, sailed on heavenward until it was lost to view. It was never found again, and Grandfather wondered if he had made too vivid, too living a thing of the great kite. He did not make another like it.

It was like her doll, thought Sita.

Mumta had been a real person, not a doll, and now Sita could not make another like her.

Sita planted a mango seed in the same spot where the peepul tree had stood. It would be many years before it grew into a big tree, but Sita liked to imagine sitting in the branches one day, picking the mangoes straight from the tree and feasting on them all day.

Grandfather was more particular about making a vegetable garden, putting down peas, carrots, gram and mustard.

One day, when most of the hard work had been done and the new hut was ready, Sita took the flute which had been given to her by Krishan, and walked down to the water's edge and tried to play it. But all she could produce was a few broken notes, and even the goats paid no attention to her music.

Sometimes Sita thought she saw a boat coming down the river, and she would run to meet it; but usually there was no boat, or, if there was, it belonged to a stranger or to another fisherman. And so she stopped looking out for boats.

Slowly, the rains came to an end. The floodwaters had receded, and in the villages people were beginning to till the land again and sow crops for the winter months. There were more cattle fairs and wrestling matches. The days were warm and sultry. The water in the river was no longer muddy, and one evening Grandfather brought home a huge mahseer fish, and Sita made it into a delicious curry.

Deep River

Grandfather sat outside the hut, smoking his hookah. Sita was at the far end of the island, spreading clothes on the rocks to dry. One of the goats had followed her. It was the friendlier of the two and often followed Sita about the island. She had made it a necklace of coloured beads.

She sat down on a smooth rock, and, as she did so, she noticed a small bright object in the sand near her feet. She picked it up. It was a little wooden toy—a coloured peacock, Lord Krishna's favourite bird—it must have come down on the river and been swept ashore on the island. Some of the paint had been rubbed off; but for Sita, who had no toys, it was a great find.

There was a soft footfall behind her. She looked round, and there was Krishan, barefooted, standing over her and smiling.

'I thought you wouldn't come,' said Sita.

'There was much work in my village. Did you keep my flute?'

'Yes, but I cannot play it properly.'

'I will teach you,' said Krishan.

He sat down beside her, and they cooled their feet in the water, which was clear now, taking in the blue of the sky. You could see the sand and the pebbles of the river-bed.

'Sometimes the river is angry and sometimes it is kind,' said Sita.

'We are part of the river,' said Krishan.

◆

It was a good river, deep and strong, beginning in the mountains and ending in the sea.

Along its banks, for hundreds of miles, lived millions of people, and Sita was only one small girl among them, and no one had ever heard of her, no one knew her—except for the old man, and the boy, and the water that was blue and white and wonderful.

THE LAST TRUCK RIDE

[Twice a day Pritam Singh takes his battered old truck on the narrow, mountainous roads to the limestone quarry. He is in the habit of driving fast. The brakes of his truck are in good condition. What happens when a stray mule suddenly appears on the road?]

A horn blared, shattering the silence of the mountains, and a truck came round the bend in the road. A herd of goats scattered left and right.

The goatherds cursed as a cloud of dust enveloped them, and then the truck had left them behind and was rattling along the stony, unpaved hill road.

At the wheel of the truck, stroking his grey moustache, sat Pritam Singh, a turbaned Sikh. It was his own truck. He did not allow anyone else to drive it. Every day he made two trips to the limestone quarries, carrying truckloads of limestone back to the depot at the bottom of the hill. He was paid by the trip and he was always anxious to get in two trips every day.

Sitting beside him was Nathu, his cleaner-boy. Nathu was a sturdy boy, with a round cheerful face. It was difficult to guess his age. He might have been twelve or he might have been fifteen—he did not know himself, since no one in his village had troubled to record his birthday—but the hard life he led probably made him look older than his years. He belonged to the hills, but his village was far away, on the next range.

Last year the potato crop had failed. As a result there was no money for salt, sugar, soap and flour, and Nathu's parents and small brothers and sisters couldn't live entirely on the onions and artichokes, which were about the only crops that had survived the drought. There had been no rain that summer. So Nathu waved goodbye to his people and came down to the town in the valley to look for work. Someone directed him to the limestone depot. He was too young to work at the quarries, breaking stones and loading them on the trucks; but Pritam Singh, one of the older drivers, was looking for someone to clean and look after his truck. Nathu looked like a bright, strong boy, and he was brought on board at ten rupees a day.

That had been six months ago, and now Nathu was an experienced hand at looking after trucks, riding in them and even sleeping in them. He got on well with Pritam Singh, the grizzled, fifty-year-old Sikh, who had well-to-do sons in Punjab, but whose sturdy independence kept him on the road in his battered old truck.

Pritam Singh pressed hard on his horn. Now there was no one on the road—no animals, no humans—but Pritam was fond of his horn and liked blowing it. It was music to his ears.

'One more year on this road,' said Pritam. 'Then I'll sell my truck and retire.'

'Who will buy this truck?' said Nathu. 'It will retire before you do.'

'Don't be cheeky, boy. She's only twenty years old. There are still a few years left in her!' And as though to prove it, he blew his horn again. Its strident sound echoed and re-echoed down the mountain gorge. A pair of wild fowl, disturbed by the noise, flew out from the bushes and glided across the road in front of the truck.

Pritam Singh's thoughts went to his dinner. 'Haven't had a good meal for days,' he grumbled.

'Haven't had a good meal for weeks,' said Nathu, although he looked quite well fed.

'Tomorrow I'll give you dinner,' said Pritam. 'Tandoori chicken and pulao.'

'I'll believe it when I see it,' said Nathu.

Pritam Singh sounded his horn again before slowing down. The road had become narrow and precipitous, and trotting ahead of them was a train of mules. As the horn blared, one mule ran forward, one ran backwards. One went uphill, one went downhill. Soon there were mules all over the place.

'You can never tell with mules,' said Pritam, after he had left them behind.

The hills were bare and dry. Much of the forest had long since disappeared. Just a few scraggy old oaks still grew on the steep hillside. This particular range was rich in limestone, and the hills were scarred by quarrying.

'Are your hills as bare as these?' asked Pritam.

'No, they have not started blasting there as yet,' said Nathu. 'We still have a few trees. And there is a walnut tree in front of our house, which gives us two baskets of walnuts every year.'

'And do you have water?'

'There is a stream at the bottom of the hill. But for the fields, we have to depend on the rainfall. And there was no rain last year.'

'It will rain soon,' said Pritam. 'I can smell rain. It is coming from the north.'

'It will settle the dust.'

The dust was everywhere. The truck was full of it. The leaves of the shrubs and the few trees were thick with it. Nathu could feel the dust near his eyelids and on his lips. As they approached the quarries, the dust increased, but it was a different kind of dust now—whiter, stinging the eyes, irritating the nostrils—limestone dust, hanging in the air.

The blasting was in progress.

Pritam Singh brought the truck to a halt. 'Let's wait a bit,' he said.

They sat in silence, staring through the windscreen at the scarred cliffs about a hundred yards down the road. There was no sign of life around them.

Suddenly, the hillside blossomed outwards, followed by a sharp crack of explosives. Earth and rock hurtled down the hillside.

Nathu watched in awe as shrubs and small trees were flung into the air. It always frightened him—not so much the sight of the rocks bursting asunder, but the trees being flung aside and destroyed. He thought of his own trees at home—the walnut, the pines—and wondered if one day they would suffer the same fate, and whether the mountains would all become a desert like this particular range. No trees, no grass, no water—only the choking dust of the limestone quarries.

Pritam Singh pressed hard on his horn again to let the people at the site know he was coming. Soon, they were parked outside a small shed, where the contractor and the overseer were sipping cups of tea. A short distance away some labourers were hammering at chunks of rock, breaking them up into manageable blocks. A pile of stones stood ready for loading, while the rock that had just been blasted lay scattered about the hillside.

'Come and have a cup of tea,' called out the contractor.

'Get on with the loading,' said Pritam. 'I can't hang about all afternoon. There's another trip to make and it gets dark early these days.'

But he sat down on a bench and ordered two cups of tea from the stall owner. The overseer strolled over to the group of labourers and told them to start loading. Nathu let down the grid at the back of the truck.

Nathu stood back while the men loaded the truck with limestone rocks. He was glad that he was chubby: thin people seemed to feel the cold much more—like the contractor, a skinny fellow who was shivering in his expensive overcoat.

To keep himself warm, Nathu began helping the labourers with the loading.

'Don't expect to be paid for that,' said the contractor, for whom every extra paise spent was a paisa off his profits.

'Don't worry,' said Nathu, 'I don't work for contractors. I work for Pritam Singh.'

'That's right,' called out Pritam. 'And mind what you say to Nathu—he's nobody's servant!'

It took them almost an hour to fill the truck with stones. The contractor wasn't happy until there was no space left for a single stone. Then four of the six labourers climbed on the pile of stones. They would ride back to the depot on the truck. The contractor, his overseer and the others would follow by jeep.

'Let's go!' said Pritam, getting behind the steering wheel. 'I want to be back here and then home by eight o'clock. I'm going to a marriage party tonight!'

Nathu jumped in beside him, banging his door shut. It never opened at a touch. Pritam always joked that his truck was held together with Sellotape.

He was in good spirits. He started his engine, blew his horn and burst into a song as the truck started out on the return journey.

The labourers were singing too as the truck swung round the sharp bends of the winding mountain road. Nathu was feeling quite dizzy. The door beside him rattled on its hinges.

'Not so fast,' he said.

'Oh,' said Pritam, 'and since when did you become nervous about fast driving?'

'Since today,' said Nathu.

'And what's wrong with today?'

'I don't know. It's just that kind of day, I suppose.'

'You are getting old,' said Pritam. 'That's your trouble.'

'Just wait till you get to be my age,' said Nathu.

'No more cheek,' said Pritam, and stepped on the accelerator and drove faster. As they swung round a bend, Nathu looked out of his window. All he saw was the sky above and the valley below. They were very near the edge. But it was always like that on this narrow road. After a few more hairpin bends, the road started descending steeply to the valley.

'I'll just test the brakes,' said Pritam and jammed down on there so suddenly that one of the labourers almost fell off at the back.

They called out in protest.

'Hang on!' shouted Pritam.

'You're nearly home!'

'Don't try any shortcuts,' said Nathu.

Just then a stray mule appeared in the middle of the road. Pritam swung the steering wheel over to his right; but the road turned left, and the truck went straight over the edge.

As it tipped over, hanging for a few seconds on the edge of the cliff, the labourers leapt from the back of the truck.

The truck pitched forward, bouncing over the rocks, turning over on its side and rolling over twice before coming to rest against the trunk of a scraggy old oak tree. Had it missed the tree, the truck would have plunged a few hundred feet down to the bottom of the gorge.

Two labourers sat on the hillside, stunned and badly shaken.

The other two had picked themselves up and were running back to the quarry for help.

Nathu had landed in a bed of nettles. He was smarting all over, but he wasn't really hurt.

His first impulse was to get up and run back with the labourers. Then he realized that Pritam was still in the truck. If he wasn't dead, he would certainly be badly injured.

Nathu skidded down the steep slope, calling out, 'Pritam, Pritam, are you all right?'

There was no answer.

Then he saw Pritam's arm and half his body jutting out of the open door of the truck. It was a strange position to be in, half in and half out. When Nathu came nearer, he saw Pritam was jammed in the driver's seat, held there by the steering wheel which was pressed hard against his chest. Nathu thought he was dead. But as he was about to turn away and clamber back up the hill, he saw Pritam open one blackened swollen eye. It looked straight up at Nathu.

'Are you alive?' whispered Nathu, terrified.

'What do you think?' muttered Pritam. He closed his eye again.

When the contractor and his men arrived, it took them almost an hour to get him to a hospital in the town. He had a broken collarbone, a dislocated shoulder and several fractured ribs. But the doctors said he was repairable—which was more than what could be said for his truck.

'The truck's finished,' said Pritam, when Nathu came to see him a few days later. 'Now 'I'll have to go home and live with my sons. But you can get work on another truck.'

'No,' said Nathu. 'I'm going home too.'

'And what will you do there?'

'I'll work on the land. It's better to grow things on the land than to blast things out of it.'

They were silent for some time.

'Do you know something?' said Pritam finally. 'But for that tree, the truck would have ended up at the bottom of the hill and I wouldn't be here, all bandaged up and talking to you. It was the tree that saved me. Remember that, boy.'

'I'll remember,' said Nathu.

RUNNING AWAY

Once, during my schooldays, my friend Daljit and I decided to run away. The main reason for running away was not to get back to the bazaars of Dehra, which we both missed, but to reach my uncle's ship in Jamnagar, Gujarat.

Uncle Jim was one of my father's cousins. He used to write to me off and on throughout the years. His letters came in envelopes that bore colourful stamps of different countries. They came from Valparaiso, San Diego, San Francisco, Buenos Aires, Dar-es-Salaam, Mombasa, Freetown, Singapore, Bombay, Marseilles, London…these were some of the places where Uncle Jim's ship called. He was seldom on the same route, and seemed to move leisurely across the oceans of the earth, calling at ports which had only the most romantic associations for me, for I had already read Stevenson, Captain Marryat, some Conrad and W.W. Jacobs.

In his letters, Uncle Jim often spoke of my joining him at sea—'When you are a little older, Ruskin.'

But I felt I was old enough then. I was sick of school and sick of my guardian. But that was not all. I was in love with the world. I wanted to see the world, every corner of it, the places I had read about in books—the junks and sampans of Hong Kong, the palm-fringed lagoons of the Indies, the streets of London, the beautiful ebony-skinned people of Africa, the bright birds and exotic plants of the Amazon…

When Uncle Jim's last letter had arrived, telling me that his ship would call at Jamnagar towards the end of the month, I felt a deep thrill of anticipation. Here was my chance at last! True, Uncle Jim had said nothing about my joining him, but he was not to know that I was seriously considering it.

It was not simply a question of walking out of school and taking a quick ride down to the docks. Jamnagar, on the west coast, was at least eight hundred miles from my school. I doubt if I would have made the attempt if Daljit had not agreed to come too. It isn't much fun running away on your own. It is even worse if you have a companion who is full of enthusiasm at the beginning and then backs out at the last moment. This leaves one feeling defeated and crushed. Daljit was not that kind of companion. He meant the things he said. About a month earlier, when I had told him of my uncle's ship and my wish to get to it, he had said, without a moment's hesitation: 'I'm coming too!' Daljit lived impulsively. Sometimes, he made mistakes. But he never went halfway and stopped. Someone had to stop him; otherwise he did whatever it was he set out to do.

Running away from school! It is not to be recommended to everyone. Parents and teachers would disapprove. Or would they, deep down in their hearts? Everyone has wanted to run away at some time in his life: if not from a bad school or an unhappy home then from something equally unpleasant. Running away seems to be in the best of traditions. Huck Finn did it. So did Master Copperfield and Oliver Twist. So did Kim. Various enterprising young men have run away to sea. Most great men have run away from school at some stage in their lives; and if they haven't, then perhaps it is something they should have done.

Anyway, Daljit and I ran away from school, and we did it quite successfully too, up to a point. But then, all this happened in India, which, though it forms only two per cent of the world's land mass, has fifteen per cent of its population, and so it is an easy place to hide in, or be lost in, or disappear in, and never be seen or heard of again!

Not that we intended to disappear. We were headed for a particular place, and as soon as I took my first step into the unknown, that first step on the slippery pine needles below the school, I knew quite definitely that I wasn't running away from anything, but that I was running *towards* something. Call it a dream, if you like. I was running towards a dream.

A narrow path ran downhill from the school to the road to Dehra, and we followed it until it levelled out, running parallel with the small stream that rumbled down the mountainside. We followed the stream for a mile, walking swiftly and silently, until we met the bridle path which was little more than a mule track going steeply down the last hills to the valley.

The going was easy. We knew the road well. And by the time we reached the last foothills, it was beginning to rain, not heavily, but as a light, thin drizzle.

We took shelter in a small dhaba on the outskirts of a village. The *dhabawallah* was sleeping, and his dog, a mangy pariah with only one ear, sniffed at us in a friendly way instead of chasing us off the premises. We sat down on an old bench and watched the sun rising over the distant mountains.

This is something I have always remembered. Not because it was a more beautiful sunrise than on any other day, but because the special importance of that morning made me look at everything in a new way, hence the details still stand out in my memory.

As the sky grew lighter, the pines and deodars stood out clearly, and the birds came to life. A black bird started it all with a low, mellow call, and then the thrushes began chattering in the bushes. A barbet shrieked monotonously at the top of a spruce tree, and, as the sky grew lighter still, a flock of bright green parrots flew low over the trees.

The drizzle continued and there was a bright crimson glow in the east. And then, quite suddenly, the sun shot through a gap in the clouds, and the lush green monsoon grass sprang into relief. Both Daljit and I were wonderstruck. Never before had we been up so early. Hundreds of spiderwebs—which were spun in trees and bushes and on the grass, where they would not normally have been noticed—were now clearly visible, spangled with gold and silver raindrops. The strong silk threads of the webs held the light rain and the sun, making each drop of water look like a tiny jewel.

A great wild dahlia, its scarlet flowers drenched and heavy, sprawled over the hillside and an emerald-green grasshopper reclined on a petal, stretching its legs in the sunshine.

The dhabawallah was now up. His dog, emboldened by his master's presence, began to bark at us. The man lit a charcoal fire in a *choolah*, and put on it a kettle of water to boil.

'Would you like to eat something?' he asked conversationally in Hindi.

'No, just tea for us,' I said.

He placed two brass tumblers on a table.

'The milk hasn't yet been delivered,' he said. 'You're very early.'

'We'll take the tea without milk,' said Daljit. 'But give us lots of sugar.'

'Sugar is costly these days. But because you are schoolboys and need more, you can help yourselves.'

'Oh, we are not schoolboys,' I said hurriedly.

'Not at all,' added Daljit.

'We are just tourists,' I lied unconvincingly.

'We have to catch the early train at Dehra,' offered Daljit.

'But there's no train before ten o'clock,' said the puzzled dhabawallah.

'It is the ten o'clock train we are catching!' said Daljit smartly. 'Do you think we will be down in time?'

'Oh yes, there's plenty of time...'

The dhabawallah poured out steaming hot tea into the tumblers and placed the sugar bowl in front of us. 'At first I thought you were schoolboys,' he said with a laugh. 'I thought you were running away.'

Daljit almost gave us away by laughing nervously.

'What made you think that?' he asked.

'Oh, I've been here many years,' the dhabawallah replied, gesturing towards the small clearing in which his little wooden stall stood, almost like a trading outpost in a wild country. 'Schoolboys always pass this way when they're running away!'

'Do many run away?' I asked. I felt a little downcast at the thought that Daljit and I were not the first to embark on such an adventure.

'Not many. Just two or three every year. They get as far as the railway station in Dehra and there they're caught!'

'It is silly of them to get caught,' said Daljit disgustedly.

'Are they always caught?' I asked.

'Always! I give them a glass of tea on their way down, and I give them a glass of tea on their way up, when they are returning with their teachers.'

'Well, you won't be seeing *us* again,' said Daljit, ignoring the warning look that I gave him.

'Ah, but you aren't schoolboys!' said the shopkeeper, beaming at us. 'And you aren't running away!'

We paid for our tea and hurried on down the path. The parrots flew over again, screeching loudly, and settled in a litchi tree. The sun was warmer now, and, as the altitude decreased, the temperature and humidity rose and we could almost smell the heat of the plains rising to meet us.

The hills levelled out into the rolling countryside, patterned with fields. Rice had been planted out, and the sugarcane was waist-high.

The path had become quite slushy. Removing our shoes and wrapping them in newspaper, we walked barefoot in the soft mud. All these little out-of-routine acts simply added to our excitement and thrill, making everything quite unforgettable for life.

'It's about three miles into Dehra,' I said. 'We must go round the town. By now, everyone in school will be up and they'll have found out we've gone!'

'We must avoid the Dehra station then,' said Daljit.

'We'll walk to the next station, Raiwala. Then we'll hop onto the first train that comes along.'

'How far must we walk?'

'About ten miles.'

'Ten miles!' Daljit looked dismayed. 'It'll take us all day!'

'Well, we can't stop here nor can we wander about in Dehra, neither can we enter the station. We have to keep on walking.'

'Alright, we'll keep on walking. I suppose the beginning of an adventure is always the most difficult part.'

Soon, the fields were giving way to jungle. But there were still some fields of sugarcane stretching away from the railway lines.

'How much further do we have to walk?' asked Daljit impatiently. 'Is Raiwala in the middle of the jungle?'

'Yes, I think it is. We've covered about four miles I suppose. Six to go! It's funny how some miles seem longer than others. It depends on what one is thinking about, I suppose. If our thoughts are pleasant, the miles are not so long.'

'Then let's keep thinking pleasant thoughts. Isn't there a

short cut anywhere? You've been in these forests before.'

'We'll take the fire-path through the jungle. It'll save us three or four miles. But we'll have to swim or wade across a small river. The rains have only just started, so the water shouldn't be too swift or deep.'

Heavy forests have paths cut through them at various places to prevent forest fires from spreading easily. These paths are not used much by people, since they don't lead anywhere in particular, but they are frequently used by the larger animals.

We had gone about a mile along the path when we heard the sound of rushing water. The path emerged from the forest of sal trees and stopped on the banks of the small river I had mentioned earlier. The main bridge across the river stood on the main road, about three miles downstream.

'It isn't more than waist-deep anywhere,' I said. 'But the water is swift and the stones are slippery.'

We removed our clothes and tied everything into two bundles which we carried on our heads. Daljit was a well-built boy, strong in the arms and thighs. I was slimmer. But I had quick reflexes.

The stones were quite slippery underfoot, and we stumbled, hindering rather than helping each other. We stopped midstream, waist-deep, hesitating about going any further for fear of being swept off our feet.

'I can hardly stand,' said Daljit.

'It shouldn't get worse,' I said hopefully. But the current was strong, and I felt very wobbly at the knees.

Daljit tried to move forward, but slipped and went over backwards into the water, bringing me down too. He began kicking and thrashing about in fear, but eventually, using me as a support, he came up spouting water like a whale.

When we found we were not being swept away, we stopped

struggling and cautiously made our way to the opposite bank, but we had been thrust about twenty yards downstream.

We rested on warm sand while a hot sun beat down on us. Daljit sucked at a cut in his hand. But we were soon up and walking again, hungry now, and munching biscuits.

'We haven't far to go,' I said.

'I don't want to think about it,' said Daljit.

We shuffled along the forest path, tired but not discouraged.

Soon we were on the main road again, and there were fields and villages on either side. A cool breeze came in across the open plain, blowing down from the hills. In the fields, there was a gentle swaying movement as the wind stirred the sugarcane. Then, the breeze came down the road, and dust began to swirl and eddy around us. Out of the dust, behind us, came the rumble of cart wheels.

'Ho! Heeyah! Heeyah!' shouted the driver of the cart. The bullocks snorted and came lumbering through the dust. We moved to the side of the road.

'Are you going to Raiwala?' called Daljit. 'Can you take us with you?'

'Climb up!' said the man, and we ran through the dust and clambered on to the back of the moving cart.

The cart lurched forward and rattled and bumped so much that we had to cling to its sides to avoid falling off. It smelt of grass and mint and cow-dung cakes. The driver had a red cloth tied round his head, and wore a tight vest and a dhoti. He was smoking a *beedi* and yelling at his bullocks, and he seemed to have forgotten our presence. We were too busy clinging to the sides of the cart to bother about making conversation. Before long we were involved in the traffic of Raiwala—a small but busy market town. We jumped off the bullock cart and walked beside it.

'Should we offer him any money?' I asked.

'No. He will be offended. He is not a taxi driver.'

'Alright, we'll just say thank you.'

We called out our thanks to the cart driver, but he didn't look back. He appeared to be talking to his bullocks.

'I'm hungry,' declared Daljit. 'We haven't had a proper meal since last night.'

'Then let's eat,' I said. 'Come on, Daljit.'

We walked through the small Raiwala bazaar, looking in at the tea and sweet shops until we found the cheapest-looking dhaba. A servant-boy brought us rice and dal and Daljit ordered an ounce of ghee which he poured over the curry. The meal cost us two rupees but we could have as much dal as we wanted, and between us we finished four bowls of it.

'We'll rest at the station,' I said as we emerged from the dhaba. 'We'll buy second-class tickets, and rest in the first-class waiting room. No one will check on us. We look first class, don't we?'

'Not after that walk through the jungle,' replied Daljit.

But we did occupy the best waiting room and Daljit made himself comfortable in an armchair. A train eventually came chugging in, and we were soon on our way to Delhi.

It didn't take us long to find a hotel once we got off at the Old Delhi Railway Station. It was called the Great Oriental Hotel, and was just behind the police station in Chandni Chowk. It didn't pretend to be even a third-class hotel, and for five rupees we were given a small back room which had a window overlooking the godown of an Afghan spice merchant. The powerful smell of asafoetida came up from the courtyard below.

We were tired and hot, so we tossed our belongings down on the floor and took turns at the bathroom tap. Then we stretched out on the only cot in the room and slept through the afternoon, oblivious to the noises from the street, the attentions of the insect population in the hotel mattress, and the creaking of the old fan overhead.

It was late evening when we woke up, and we were hungry again. Daljit opened the door and shouted. Presently, a servant-boy appeared.

'Bring us tea, toast, two big omelettes and a bottle of tomato sauce,' ordered Daljit with a confidence that I wished I had.

The omelettes, when they arrived twenty minutes later, were tiny. Both had obviously been made from one egg. The sauce had been diluted with water, and the toasts were burnt. The salt was damp, and we had to prise open the salt-cellar to get to it. The pepper, however, came out in a generous rush and made up the major portion of the meal. As our hunger had not been satisfied by this poor fare, we ordered eggs again, boiled eggs this time. No matter how tiny, they would have to be whole.

'Let's go out,' said Daljit after we had eaten the eggs. 'It's stuffy in here.'

'I'm still sleepy,' I said.

'Then I'll go out for a little while. I may go to the gurdwara.'

'Alright, but don't get lost.'

Drowsy, I closed my eyes, but the sounds of the city's unceasing traffic came through the window. Ships and distant ports seemed very far away but so did hills and mountain streams.

I fell asleep and woke up only when Daljit returned.

'I've solved our problem!' he said, beaming. 'We won't bother with the train. I met a truck driver, and he has offered to take us as far as Jaipur. That's more than a hundred miles. It will be quite safe to take a train from Jaipur.'

'When can your friend take us?'

'The truck leaves at four o'clock in the morning.'

'There's no rest for the wicked,' I said. 'Still, the less time we lose the better. It's Wednesday, and my uncle's ship might sail on Saturday. What will we have to pay?'

'Nothing. It's a free ride. The driver is a Sikh, and I persuaded him that we are related to each other through the marriage of my brother-in-law to his sister-in-law's niece!'

◆

At four the next morning, we made our way towards the Red Fort, its ramparts dark against the starry sky. The streets which had been teeming with so much life the previous evening were now deserted. The street lamps shed lonely pools of light on the pavements. The occasional car glided silently past, but it belonged to another kind of world altogether.

Near the Fort, we found a couple of dhabas which were still open. They did business with the truck drivers who slept by day and drove by night.

Our driver, a tall, bearded Sikh, loomed over us out of the darkness. He had a companion with him, also a Sikh, who was still in his underwear.

'You can get in at the back,' said the driver in his thick Punjabi which I could follow sufficiently well. 'We'll be off in a few minutes.'

The truck was parked beneath a peepul tree. We pulled ourselves up into the back of the open truck, only to find our way barred by what seemed at first to be a prehistoric monster.

The monster snorted once, stamped heavily on the boards, and sent us tumbling backwards.

'Bhaiyyaji!' cried Daljit to the driver. 'There's some kind of animal in here!'

'Don't worry, it's only Mumta,' said our friend.

'But what is it doing in here?'

'She is going with us. I am taking her to the market in

Jaipur. So get in with her boys, and make yourselves comfortable.'

There was now enough light to enable us to take a closer look at our travelling companion. She was a full-grown buffalo from the Punjab.

'An excellent buffalo,' said Daljit, who appeared to be familiar with the finer points of these animals. 'Notice her blue eyes!'

'I didn't know buffaloes had blue eyes,' I said dryly.

'Only the best buffaloes have them,' said Daljit. 'Blue-eyed buffaloes give more milk than brown-eyed ones.'

Fortunately for us, the Sardarji started the truck and an early morning breeze, blowing across the river, swept away some of the stench so typical of buffaloes.

We were soon out of Delhi and bowling along at a fair speed on the road to Jaipur. The recent rain had waterlogged low-lying areas, and the herons, cranes and snipe were numerous. Fields and trees were alive with strange, beautiful birds: the long-tailed king crow, blue jays and weaver birds, and occasionally the great white-headed kite, which is said to be Garuda, Lord Vishnu's famous steed.

As we travelled further into Rajasthan, the peacocks became more numerous; so did the camels loping along the side of the road in straight, orderly lines. And, as the vegetation grew less and the desert took over, the people themselves grew more colourful, as though to make up for the absence of colour in the landscape. The women wore wide red skirts, and gold and silver ornaments. They were handsome, tall, fair and strong. The men were tall too and the older among them had flowing white beards.

As the day grew older, and the sun rose higher in the sky, the traffic on the road increased; but our truck driver, instead of slowing down, drove faster. Perhaps he was in a hurry to dispose of the buffalo. Soon he was trying to overtake another truck.

The truck in front was moving fast too, and its driver had

no intention of giving up the middle of the road. It was piled high with stacks of sugarcane.

'It's going to be a race!' cried Daljit excitedly, standing up against the buffalo, in order to get a better view.

The road was not wide enough to take two large vehicles at once, and as the other truck wouldn't make way, ours had to fall in behind it, almost suffocating us with the exhaust fumes. We were thrown to the floorboards as the truck lurched over the ruts in the rough road, and Mumta, getting nervous, almost trampled us. Then there was a tremendous bump, a grinding of brakes, and we came to a stop.

As the dust cleared, we made out our driver's bearded face gazing anxiously down at us.

'Are you alright?' he asked gruffly.

'I think so,' I said.

'Did you overtake the other truck?' asked Daljit.

'No,' grunted our friend. 'He would not give way. You had better come in front.'

We agreed without any hesitation and his assistant rather grudgingly joined the buffalo.

After a few miles, the driver became friendly and told us that his name was Gurnam Singh.

It was getting dark by the time we reached Jaipur, so we were not able to see much of the city. We spent the night in the truck, sleeping in the back with Gurnam Singh. Mumta had been disposed of on the way. Jaipur nights can be chilly, even in summer, so Gurnam Singh considerately shared his bedding with us. Because he was accustomed to sleeping in the body of the truck, he was soon asleep, snoring loudly and rhythmically. Daljit and I tossed and turned restlessly. He kicked me several times in the night. The floor of the truck was hard, and retained various buffalo smells.

We had hardly fallen asleep (or so it seemed), when Gurnam Singh woke us up, saying that it was almost four o'clock and that he had to start on his return journey, this time with a load of red sandstone.

'What a life!' exclaimed Daljit, sleepily rubbing his eyes with one hand. 'I'd hate to be a truck driver.'

'One has to live somehow,' philosophized Gurnam Singh. 'I like driving. I knew how to drive when I was merely six or seven. The money is not so bad either. Now, when I get back to Delhi, I will have two days off, which I will spend with my wife and children. Goodbye friends, and if you pass through Delhi again, you will find me near the walls of the Red Fort.'

We waved to him as he shot off in his truck, throwing up huge clouds of dust, making a great noise and probably waking the local inhabitants. Dogs barked, and a cock began to crow.

We were on the outskirts of the city, facing a large lake. On the other side was open country, bare hills and desert. We could also make out the ruins of a building—probably a palace or a hunting lodge—among some thorn bushes and babul trees.

'Let's go out there,' suggested Daljit. 'We can bathe in the lake and rest. Then later in the morning we can come into the city and find out about trains.'

We set out along the shores of the lake, and it was a good half-hour before we reached the opposite bank.

There was no one in the fields, but a camel was going round and round a well, drawing up water in small trays. Smoke rose from houses in a nearby village, and the notes of a flute floated over to us on the still morning air.

It took us about twenty minutes to reach the ruin, which seemed like an old hunting lodge put up by some Rajput prince when game must have been plentiful.

The gate of the lodge was blocked with rubble, but part of

the wall had crumbled apart and we climbed through the gap and found ourselves in a stone-paved courtyard in the centre of which stood a dry, disused stone fountain. A small peepul tree was growing from the crack in the floor of the fountain. Finding nothing to do there, we made our way to the railway tracks again.

Daljit and I snuck on to a goods train. It was a hard night's journey. The train was agonizingly slow and stopped at many places. At one small station, a number of sacks filled with what must have been cattle-fodder were tossed into the wagon, almost burying us in our fitful sleep. But we found they were comfortable to rest on and lay stretched out on top of them until the first light of morning.

As the sky cleared, we knew we were not far from our journey's end. The landscape had undergone a complete change. We had left the desert for the coastal plain.

The tall waving palms parted, and then I spotted the sea.

It was the sea as I had always dreamt of it ever since my days in Kathiawar with my father. It was vast, lonely and blue, blue as the sky was blue, and the first ship I saw was a sailing-ship, an Arab dhow, listing slightly in the mild breeze that blew onto the shore.

The train stopped at a small bridge spanning a stream which wound its way across the plain down to the sea. We got down there and trudged the rest of the way to our destination.

Two hours later, we were at Jamnagar.

We stopped near a small tea shop and watched other people eating laddoos and *bhelpuri*. We couldn't even afford a coconut.

'Where is the harbour?' I asked the shopkeeper.

'Two miles from here,' he replied.

'Are there any ships in the port?' I asked, relieved yet anxious.

'What do you want with a ship?'

'What does anyone want with a ship?'

'Well there's only one and it sails today, so you had better hurry if you want to go away on it.'

'Let's go,' said Daljit.

'Wait!' said a young man who was lounging against the counter. 'It will take you almost an hour to get there if you walk. I will take you in my cart.' He pointed to a shabby pony cart close by. The pony did not look as though it wanted to go anywhere.

'My pony is fast!' said the young man, following our glances. 'Never go by appearances. She may look tired but she runs like a champion! Get in friends, I will charge you only one rupee.'

'We don't have any money,' I said. 'We'll walk.'

'Fifty paisa, then,' he said. 'Fifty paisa and a glass of tea. Jump in my friends!'

'All right,' agreed Daljit. 'There's no time to lose. Fifty paisa and buy your own tea.'

We climbed into the cart, and the youth jumped up in front and cracked his whip. The pony lurched forward, the wheels rattled and shook, and we set off down the bazaar road at a tremendous trot.

'I didn't know you had fifty paisa left,' I said.

'I don't,' Daljit replied. 'But we'll worry about that later. Your uncle can pay!'

As soon as we were out of the town and on the open road to the sea, the pony went faster. She couldn't help doing so, as the road was downhill. The wind blew my hair across my eyes, and the salty tang of the sea was in the air.

Daljit shook me in his excitement.

'We will soon be at the harbour,' he yelled joyfully. 'And then away at last!'

The driver called out endearments to his pony, and, exhilarated by the sea breeze and the comparative speed of his carriage, he burst into song. As we turned a bend in the road, the sea-front came into view. There were several small dhows close to the shore, and fishing-boats were beached on the sand. The fishermen were drying their nets while their children ran naked in the surf. A steamer stood out on the sea and though I could not make out its name from that distance, I was sure it was the *Iris*.

The cart stopped at the beginning of the pier, and we tumbled out and began running along the pier. But even as we ran, it became clear to me that the ship was moving away from us, moving out to the sea. Its propeller sent small waves rippling back to the pier.

'Captain!' I shouted. 'Uncle Jim! Wait for us!'

A lascar standing in the stern waved to us; but that was all. I stood at the end of the pier, waving my hands and shouting into the wind.

'Captain! Uncle Jim! Wait for us!'

Nobody answered. The seagulls, wheeling in the wake of the steamer, seemed to take up the cry—'Captain, Captain...'

The ship drew further away, gaining speed. And still I called to it in a hoarse, pleading voice. Yokohama, San Diego, Valparaiso, London, all slipped away forever...

THE PROSPECT OF FLOWERS

Fern Hill, The Oaks, Hunter's Lodge, The Parsonage, The Pines, Dumbarnie, Mackinnon's Hall and Windermere. These are the names of some of the old houses that still stand on the outskirts of one of the smaller Indian hill stations. Most of them have fallen into decay and ruin. They are very old, of course—built over a hundred years ago by Britons who sought relief from the searing heat of the plains. Today's visitors to the hill stations prefer to live near the markets and cinemas and many of the old houses, set amid oak and maple and deodar, are inhabited by wild cats, bandicoots, owls, goats and the occasional charcoal burner or mule driver.

But among these neglected mansions stands a neat, whitewashed cottage called Mulberry Lodge. And in it, up to a short time ago, lived an elderly English spinster named Miss Mackenzie.

In years Miss Mackenzie was more than 'elderly', being well over eighty. But no one would have guessed it. She was clean, sprightly and wore old-fashioned but well-preserved dresses. Once a week, she walked the two miles to town to buy butter and jam and soap, and sometimes a small bottle of eau de cologne.

She had lived in the hill station since she had been a girl in her teens, and that had been before the First World War. Though she had never married, she had experienced a few love affairs and was far from being the typical frustrated spinster of fiction. Her parents had been dead thirty years; her brother and sister were also dead. She had no relatives in India and she lived on a small pension of forty rupees a month and the gift parcels that were sent out to her from New Zealand by a friend of her youth.

Like other lonely old people, she kept a pet—a large black cat with bright yellow eyes. In her small garden she grew dahlias, chrysanthemums, gladioli and a few rare orchids. She knew a great deal about plants and about wild flowers, trees, birds and insects. She had never made a serious study of these things, but having lived with them for so many years had developed an intimacy with all that grew and flourished around her.

She had few visitors. Occasionally, the padre from the local church called on her, and once a month the postman came with a letter from New Zealand or her pension papers. The milkman called every second day with a litre of milk for the lady and her cat. And sometimes she received a couple of eggs free, for the egg seller remembered a time when Miss Mackenzie, in her earlier prosperity, had bought eggs from him in large quantities. He was a sentimental man. He remembered her as a ravishing beauty in her twenties when he had gazed at her in round-eyed, nine-year-old wonder and consternation.

Now it was September and the rains were nearly over and Miss Mackenzie's chrysanthemums were coming into their own. She hoped the coming winter wouldn't be too severe because she found it increasingly difficult to bear the cold.

One day, as she was pottering about in her garden, she saw a schoolboy plucking wild flowers on the slope above the cottage.

'Who's that?' she called. 'What are you up to, young man?'

The boy was alarmed and tried to dash up the hillside, but he slipped on pine needles and came slithering down the slope on to Miss Mackenzie's nasturtium bed.

When he found there was no escape, he gave a bright disarming smile and said, 'Good morning, miss.'

He belonged to the local English-medium school and wore a bright red blazer, and a red and black striped tie. Like most polite Indian schoolboys, he called every woman 'miss'.

'Good morning,' said Miss Mackenzie severely. 'Would you mind moving out of my flower bed?'

The boy stepped gingerly over the nasturtiums and looked up at Miss Mackenzie with dimpled cheeks and appealing eyes. It was impossible to be angry with him.

'You're trespassing,' said Miss Mackenzie.

'Yes, miss.'

'And you ought to be in school at this hour.'

'Yes, miss.'

'Then what are you doing here?'

'Picking flowers, miss.' And he held up a bunch of ferns and wild flowers.

'Oh,' Miss Mackenzie was disarmed. It was a long time since she had seen a boy taking an interest in flowers and, what was more, playing truant from school in order to gather them.

'Do you like flowers?' she asked.

'Yes, miss. I'm going to be a botan—a botantist?'

'You mean a botanist.'

'Yes, miss.'

'Well, that's unusual. Most boys at your age want to be pilots or soldiers or perhaps engineers. But you want to be a botanist. Well, well. There's still hope for the world, I see. And do you know the names of these flowers?'

'This is a *bukhilo* flower,' he said, showing her a small golden flower. 'That's a Pahari name. It means puja or prayer. The flower is offered during prayers. But I don't know what this is…'

He held out a pale pink flower with a soft, heart-shaped leaf.

'It's a wild begonia,' said Miss Mackenzie. 'And that purple stuff is salvia, but it isn't wild. It's a plant that escaped from my garden. Don't you have any books on flowers?'

'No, miss.'

'All right, come in and I'll show you a book.'

She led the boy into a small front room, which was crowded with furniture and books and vases and jam jars, and offered him a chair. He sat awkwardly on its edge. The black cat immediately leapt on to his knees and settled down on them, purring loudly.

'What's your name?' asked Miss Mackenzie, as she rummaged through her books.

'Anil, miss.'

'And where do you live?'

'When school closes, I go to Delhi. My father has a business.'

'Oh, and what's that?'

'Bulbs, miss.'

'Flower bulbs?'

'No, electric bulbs.'

'Electric bulbs! You might send me a few, when you get home. Mine are always fusing and they're so expensive, like everything else these days. Ah, here we are!' She pulled a heavy volume down from the shelf and laid it on the table. '*Flora Himaliensis*, published in 1892, and probably the only copy in India. This is a very valuable book, Anil. No other naturalist has recorded so many wild Himalayan flowers. And let me tell you this, there are many flowers and plants which are still unknown to the fancy botanists who spend all their time with microscopes instead of in the mountains. But perhaps, *you'll* do something about that, one day.'

'Yes, miss.'

They went through the book together, and Miss Mackenzie

pointed out many flowers that grew in and around the hill station while the boy made notes of their names and seasons. She lit a stove and put the kettle on for tea. And then the old English lady and the small Indian boy sat side by side over cups of hot sweet tea, absorbed in a book on wild flowers.

'May I come again?' asked Anil, when finally he rose to go.

'If you like,' said Miss Mackenzie. 'But not during school hours. You mustn't miss your classes.'

After that, Anil visited Miss Mackenzie about once a week, and nearly always brought a wild flower for her to identify. She found herself looking forward to the boy's visits—and sometimes, when more than a week passed and he didn't come, she was disappointed and lonely and would grumble at the black cat.

Anil reminded her of her brother, when the latter had been a boy. There was no physical resemblance. Andrew had been fair-haired and blue-eyed. But it was Anil's eagerness, his alert, bright look and the way he stood—legs apart, hands on hips, a picture of confidence—that reminded her of the boy who had shared her own youth in these same hills.

And why did Anil come to see her so often? Partly because she knew about wild flowers and he really did want to become a botanist. And partly because she smelt of freshly baked bread and that was a smell his own grandmother had possessed. And partly because she was lonely and sometimes a boy of twelve can sense loneliness better than an adult. And partly because he was a little different from other children.

By the middle of October, when there was only a fortnight left for the school to close, the first snow had fallen on the distant mountains. One peak stood high above the rest, a white pinnacle against the azure blue sky. When the sun set, this peak turned from orange to gold to pink to red.

'How high is that mountain?' asked Anil.

'It must be over twelve thousand feet,' said Miss Mackenzie. 'About thirty miles from here, as the crow flies. I always wanted to go there, but there was no proper road. At that height, there'll be flowers that you don't get here—the blue gentian and the purple columbine, the anemone and the edelweiss.'

'I'll go there one day,' said Anil.

'I'm sure you will, if you really want to.'

The day before his school closed, Anil came to say goodbye to Miss Mackenzie.

'I don't suppose you'll be able to find many wild flowers in Delhi,' she said. 'But have a good holiday.'

'Thank you, miss.'

As he was about to leave, Miss Mackenzie, on an impulse, thrust the *Flora Himaliensis* into his hands.

'You keep it,' she said. 'It's a present for you.'

'But I'll be back next year, and I'll be able to look at it then. It's so valuable.'

'I know it's valuable and that's why I've given it to you. Otherwise it will only fall into the hands of the junk dealers.'

'But, miss…'

'Don't argue. Besides, I may not be here next year.'

'Are you going away?'

'I'm not sure. I may go to England.'

She had no intention of going to England; she had not seen the country since she was a child, and she knew she would not fit in with the life of post-war Britain. Her home was in these hills, among the oaks and maples and deodars. It was lonely, but at her age it would be lonely anywhere.

The boy tucked the book under his arm, straightened his tie, stood stiffly to attention and said, 'Goodbye, Miss Mackenzie.' It was the first time he had spoken her name.

Winter set in early and strong winds brought rain and sleet and soon there were no flowers in the garden or on the hillside. The cat stayed indoors, curled up at the foot of Miss Mackenzie's bed. Miss Mackenzie wrapped herself up in all her old shawls and mufflers but still she felt the cold. Her fingers grew so stiff that she took almost an hour to open a can of baked beans. And then it snowed and for several days the milkman did not come. The postman arrived with her pension papers but she felt too tired to take them up to town to the bank.

She spent most of the time in bed. It was the warmest place. She kept a hot-water bottle at her back and the cat kept her feet warm. She lay in bed, dreaming of the spring and summer months. In three months' time the primroses would be out and with the coming of spring the boy would return.

One night the hot-water bottle burst and the bedding was soaked through. As there was no sun for several days, the blanket remained damp. Miss Mackenzie caught a chill and had to keep to her cold, uncomfortable bed. She knew she had a fever but there was no thermometer with which to take her temperature. She had difficulty breathing.

A strong wind sprang up one night and the window flew open and kept banging all night. Miss Mackenzie was too weak to get up and close it, and the wind swept the rain and sleet into the room. The cat crept into the bed and snuggled close to its mistress's warm body. But towards morning that body had lost its warmth and the cat left the bed and started scratching about on the floor.

As a shaft of sunlight streamed through the open window, the milkman arrived. He poured some milk into the cat's saucer on the doorstep and the cat leapt down from the windowsill and made for the milk.

The milkman called a greeting to Miss Mackenzie, but received no answer. Her window was open and he had always known her to be up before sunrise. So he put his head in at the window and called again. But Miss Mackenzie did not answer. She had gone away to the mountain where the blue gentian and purple columbine grew.